VITA

VITA

A NOVEL

Melania G. Mazzucco

Translated from the Italian by Virginia Jewiss

FARRAR, STRAUS AND GIROUX

NEW YORK

Farrar, Straus and Giroux
19 Union Square West, New York 10003

Copyright © 2003 by Melania G. Mazzucco
Translation copyright © 2005 by Virginia Jewiss
All rights reserved
Printed in the United States of America
Originally published in 2003 by RCS Libri S.p.A., Italy
Published in the United States by Farrar, Straus and Giroux
First American edition, 2005

The images appearing on pages 18, 93, and 238 are reproduced with the kind permission of the Capranica and Trulli families. The images on pages 44, 203, 296, 355, and 392 are reproduced with the kind permission of the Ciapparoni-Mazzucco family. The image on page 353 is reproduced courtesy of the Archivio Centrale dello Stato di Roma, Fondo Ministero dell'Interno, Direzione Generale della Pubblica Sicurezza, Divisione Polizia, Giudiziaria, fascicoli 10900-12900.

Library of Congress Cataloging-in-Publication Data
Mazzucco, Melania G., 1966–
   [Vita. English]
   Vita / by Melania G. Mazzucco ; translated by Virginia Jewiss.
   p.   cm.
   ISBN-13: 978-0-374-28495-4
   ISBN-10: 0-374-28495-4 (alk. paper)
   I. Jewiss, Virginia.   II. Title.

PQ4873.A98V57913 2005
853'.914—dc22

                                                        2005042044

Designed by Cassandra J. Pappas

www.fsgbooks.com

1   3   5   7   9   10   8   6   4   2

To Roberto, my father

America does not exist. I know because I've been there.

—Alain Resnais, *Mon oncle d'Amérique*

Contents

My Desert Places

This place is no longer a place, this landscape no longer a landscape. Not a blade of grass remains, no stalk of wheat, no bush, no hedge of prickly pear. The captain looks around for the lemon and orange trees Vita used to talk to him about, but he doesn't see a single tree. Everything is burned. He stumbles in grenade holes, gets entangled in shrubs of barbed wire. This is where the well should be—but the wells are all poisoned now, rotting with the bodies of the Scottish fusiliers killed in the first assault on the hill. Or maybe they were Germans. Or civilians. There is a smell of ash, of petrol, of death. He must be careful because the path is strewn with unexploded bombs, lying right in the middle of the road like big-bellied carcasses. Dozens of empty cartridges, useless rifles. Rusted bazookas, 88-mm stovepipes, long since abandoned and already over-grown with weeds. Dead donkeys blown up like balloons. Clusters of bullets like goat droppings. Bones stripped of flesh stick out of the dirt. The captain covers his mouth with his handkerchief. No, it can't be. My God, it wasn't supposed to be this way.

The road to Tufo is cluttered with burned-out vehicles. Motor-bikes trucks cars. Bullets have opened dozens of eyes in the doors, the wheels are reduced to scrap iron. Heaps of wreckage appear in front of him. As he gets closer, he realizes they're tanks. He passes them warily, as if they were a monument to defeat. He's not sure if they are the Churchills they lost in January or the Tigers the Germans lost the first time they abandoned the village. He climbs over the wing of a plane—intact, severed clean, the Luftwaffe symbol still visible. Its cabin lies exploded in the valley below. Finally he sees a tree: the first—or last. He quickens his step, his soldiers trudging along behind. It's hot and the sun is already high. What's gotten into you, Captain? Take it easy. It's an olive tree—completely incinerated, black as ink. It crumbles in his fingers. The cloud of dust makes his eyes water despite his Ray-Bans. Or maybe it's the smoke rising off the stones. Those smoking stones strike him more than anything else he has seen so far. His thoughts flow uncontrollably. Suddenly he has the feeling of having reached the place that was destined for him.

On the slope an emaciated old man approaches him. His hair is crusted with dust, his gaze glassy. He passes the captain as if he were a phantom. As if he weren't there. The captain is sweating in his uniform, and wipes his forehead with his palm. His men slow down, start joking around. They're young, recent arrivals sent to fill in the gaps on the southern front. But he knows why he's here, and he knows he is late. He should have come earlier, he really should have. But every now and then he was assailed by fragmented and involuntary images of memories not his own, vexing somehow, like the residue of a dream. They harked back to a lost and incomprehensible land populated by individuals with alien, remote faces, and the fear of having his estrangement confirmed had kept him far away. In the end, though, he'd come. They had entered other towns on top of their tanks—and to the sound of applause. But here the road is blocked, and they arrive on foot. His pockets are full of gifts, even though he's ashamed of bringing them, for his arrival also brings dust, destruction, and noise. The smoke clears; a stone wall emerges. So this was the spot. This, the first house of the village. But it is no longer a house—behind the wall the ground falls away. "That one came down in January," the old man mumbles. Or at least that's what the captain thinks he said because he can't really understand him. The old man studies the captain's uniform, the stripes on his epaulettes. Only twenty-four and already a captain. But the old man is not impressed. When the captain holds out a pack of Lucky Strikes, the old man shrinks away and disappears behind a heap of ruins. Could he be his grandfather?

He has come too late. The village no longer exists. His village? Vita's? Whose village? This place that is not a place means nothing to him. He was born far away—on another planet—and feels as if he's stepping back in time. The only road through Tufo is cut across by narrow alleys that drop into the valley on one side and climb up the hill on the other; now it is nothing more than a canyon between two walls of rubble, filled with the atrocious stench of dead bodies. Is this the odor of the past? Or of the lemon trees she still remembers? "The bombs, the bombs," repeats a feeble-minded old woman hunched on a straw chair in front of what might have been her house. She is knitting furiously. Her house is now a door hung on nothing. Dusty shadows wander among the ruins; they don't know who the soldiers are, and don't want to know. They're afraid it won't last this time either, and aren't sure if these soldiers have come to liberate them or to bury them for good. Everyone is old here. Where have the children gone who used to play in the streets? "Where is Via San Leonardo?" he asks the old woman, forcing himself to dig up a bit of the language they have in common. "My son," she responds with a toothless smile, "this is it."

This? But this isn't a street. This is a hole full of dust. They have destroyed everything. We have destroyed everything. Only one building is still standing. The roof has fallen in and there's no door. But standing nevertheless. The church. Its yellow facade is riddled with bullets, pieces of plaster have curled up like paper. There's no statue in the niche. And the three steps where Dionisia used to write . . . splintered, the second one completely eradicated. Her house is right here, opposite . . . Where?

The captain clambers up onto a mound of debris. His heavy boots kick up whirls of dust that burn his lungs and eyes. He scrambles over window frames, shredded curtains, a closet door, a mirror shard stuck in a slipper. His dust-covered face stares up at him. He sinks down onto a rafter resting atop the headboard of a bed. Only the brass pommel rises out of the rubble. The soldiers turn away so as not to look at the captain as he weeps. The old woman continues to knit, and the soldiers offer her a bar of chocolate. The old woman refuses; she doesn't have any teeth. They insist that she take it for her children. "I don't have children anymore, there's no one left," the old woman stammers. The soldiers don't understand her. All of a sudden the captain asks her, "Do you know Antonio? The one they called Mantu?" The old woman's eyes are clouded by cataracts. She looks at him a moment, then places her knitting needles in her lap, and points to a spot on the hill. "He went away," she says. The tone of her voice makes it clear he won't be coming back. "Do you know Angela, Mantu's wife?" Again, the same place on the hill. "She went away, too." Only now does he realize that the old woman's gnarled hand is pointing to the cemetery. But not even that exists any longer. The walls have crumbled, and in its place is a crater, an ulcer in the hill. The earth around here is red—as if it were wounded. But it isn't. There is no water in these hills. Whoever knew how to find the water underground would have been the lord of this village. "Do you know Ciappitto?" he murmurs, now fearful of her answer. "The Americans took him," the old woman mumbles. "They took him to Naples, to prison." "Prison?" he asks, surprised. An eighty-seven-year-old cripple? "He was a fascist," the old woman explains patiently. "But even he went away. He was ashamed because the people threw rocks at him, so he had a stroke on the way to Naples. Or so they said."

The dust has settled. The hill is a mound of gray ashes. Below him, the Garigliano River is a sparkling green ribbon on the charred plain. The sea is as blue as it has always been. "Where is Dionisia?" he finally asks. Vita wants him to ask this question. It's the reason he's here, after all. The old woman doesn't say anything this time. She pulls at the ball of wool, picks up her needles, crosses the tips, knots the threads, and then loosens them again. She nods and points to where he is sitting. To the mountain of rubble. And so the captain realizes there is no coming back. He is sitting on the body of his mother's mother.

All this took place many years before I was born. At that time the man who would bring me into the world was in high school and the woman in grammar school. They didn't know each other and could just as easily not have met in 1952 when they both enrolled in an English language class, convinced that knowing that language would improve their lives—and the fact that they preferred to fall in love and bring two children into the world to earning diplomas in English would not have changed anything or altered the substance of things. So what about the captain who came to Italy to fight with the Fifth Army on the southern front? I never met him, and I don't know what thoughts were running through his head on that day in May 1944 when he took possession of the ruins of a village called Tufo, like the stone from which it had been built. Until a few years ago, I didn't even know who he was, and in truth I don't think I know now. Yet this man is not irrelevant to me—in fact, his story and mine are so interwoven they could be one and the same. Now I know he could have been my father, and could have recounted his return to Tufo a thousand times as we barbecued steaks on a Sunday afternoon or did yard work at our house in New Jersey. But he never told me the story. Instead, the man who was my father told me another story. He spoke willingly because he loved telling stories and knew that only what gets told is true. He took his time, but when he was ready, he would clear his throat and begin.

We have always had something to do with water, he would say. We know how to find it where it can't be seen. In the beginning—our beginning—a long time ago, there was a dowser: his name was Federico. He would travel about the countryside with his divining rod, listening to the vibrations of air and earth. Wherever the rod pointed, that's where he would dig until he found the spring. Federico was a visionary, very thin and very tall, but a war of liberation buried him in the same earth he had chosen to live on. He was from the North, and settled in the South because of his idealism, his foolishness, and an obstinate vocation for defeat, all qualities or defects he would pass on to his descendants. "And then? Go on." Then there was a very poor stone breaker, an orphan and a vulnerable soul, who loved the land and would have liked to own it, but hated water. Even the sea. Dreaming to get back the land he'd lost, the man of stones twice crossed the ocean, but stones always sink to the bottom, and so twice he was condemned and sent back home with a cross marked in chalk on his back.

"And then what happened?" One day, in the spring of 1903, the fourth son of the man of stones, a twelve-year-old boy, small, clever, and curious, arrived at the port of Naples and boarded a ship of the White Star Line—it flew a red flag with a white star. His father had set him the task of living the life he'd been unable to live. It was a heavy burden, but the boy didn't know it, so he climbed the planks, all slippery with salt, that led to the passenger decks. He was happy, and had forgotten to remember to be afraid. The boy's name was Diamante, Diamond.

He didn't go alone. With him was a nine-year-old girl with a great mass of dark hair and deep dark eyes. Her name was Vita.

PART I

The Line of Fire

Good for Father

The first thing they make him do in America is drop his pants. Just to make things clear. He has to show his hanging jewels and his crotch, still smooth as a baby's bottom, to tens of judges stationed behind a desk. He stands naked, offended, and all alone, while they sit waiting, dressed, and arrogant. His eyes brim with tears as they smirk and cough with embarrassment. His shame is multiplied a hundredfold by the fact that he's wearing a pair of his father's drawers, enormous threadbare old things so ugly not even a priest would wear them. The problem is that his mother sewed the ten dollars he needs to disembark right into them so the money wouldn't be stolen at night in the steamship dormitory. Everybody knows that during those interminable twelve nights, all sorts of things disappear— life savings, cheese, heads of garlic, virginity—never to be found again. Diamante's money hasn't actually been stolen, but he's too ashamed to tell the island officials it's in his underwear, so he gets the brilliant idea to tell them he doesn't have any. The result of this extreme modesty is a cross drawn on his back and an order to move to the rear of the line so he can be repatriated as soon as the ship is ready to leave again. His whole voyage was pointless, his father and the mysterious Uncle

Agnello wasted a lot of money, and Vita—who has already gone ahead—will find herself alone in New York and God only knows what'll happen to her.

From behind the window the city shimmers on the water—towers touch the clouds and thousands of windows sparkle in the sun. The image of that city rising from the water and aiming straight for the sky will stay with him for the rest of his life—so near and yet so unreachable. Faced with catastrophe, with such an undignified failure, Diamante shamelessly bursts into tears and reveals to the interpreter his money's disgraceful hiding place. In the blink of an eye he's back in front, red-faced, his trousers around his ankles, his underwear torn open to get at the contents of the hidden pocket, and his most secret possession in his hand because he doesn't know where else to put it. This is how Diamante sets foot in America: naked, with his chilly pecker starting to proudly raise its head as he hops forward, trying not to trip. He waves the faded ten-dollar bill, ripe with the odor of his agonizing nights, under the noses of the commission members, but no one takes it, and the judges behind the table signal for him to pass. He has made it. By now he has already forgotten the shame and humiliation. So they made him strip? They made him drop his pants? So much the better. For even before setting foot on land, he has already learned that here he possesses only two riches, the existence and utility of which he didn't know of until today—his sex and the hand that holds it.

A far-off sound—perhaps the wheels of a cart echoing on the pavement—suddenly sends him into a fetid darkness. Instinctively he places his hand on the pillow and feels for his brother's hair. Strange, there is no pillow: his head is resting on a coarse and lumpy mattress. Diamante sits up. He looks out the window but doesn't see the shadow of the moon. He doesn't see anything because the window is no longer where it used to be. He finds himself in a windowless room, a closet really, crammed full of stuff like a junk shop. A room he doesn't recognize. On the floor under the bed next to his is a sinister-looking row of men's hobnail boots. But to whom they belong, and where the owners are, he couldn't say. He realizes he's famished, and it slowly sinks in that he's not at home. The rumbling, drunken voice of a man on the other side of the curtain is not his father's. Nor is the stench that assails his nostrils. His father smells of stone, lime, and sweat. But this is the stink of shoes, wine, and stale piss. Doors slam, footsteps, an extraordinary belch makes the walls shake, and then the curtain that divides his closet from another space opens. He is hit by a foul-smelling fart, a roar of laughter, and a beam of light. Diamante closes his eyes and falls back onto the mattress. It's all clear now. Once again he has dreamed of stripping in front of the commissioners, an incident that took place only two days ago but keeps replaying in his mind, and he will dream it until he dies. This is his second night in America. He has been brought to Prince Street, to a house so blackened, run-down, and decrepit it looks like it might collapse at any moment. The apartment, one of many on the top floor, belongs to Uncle Agnello. This is America.

A man enters the room, then another, another, and still another, until Diamante loses count. Someone stumbles onto the cot in front of his, someone else onto a creaky bed. He hears the thudding of furniture being moved about, sighs. People are getting undressed and the room reeks of armpits. One, two, ten agitated male voices echo around him. They belong to a gang of cutthroats devoid of any scruples and thirsty for blood. They are talking—in different dialects and at times incomprehensibly—about things that piss them off, low blows, and the two thousand bucks Agnello has to give somebody or else they'll cut off his nose and stick it up his ass, that way he'll really know what it means to be stuck up, that stingy, snobby upstart. They talk about the policemen who found a nine-year-old girl. Diamante is too scared to breathe. Someone swears and tells the rest of them to calm down, but no one pays him any attention. The voices turn nasty as they talk about Agnello's little baby doll—Vita, that is—who is only nine, but you can already see how pretty she'll be when she starts to blossom. They rip the blanket out of Diamante's hands. He can't see them because he is squeezing his eyes shut and stubbornly pretending to be asleep, but he knows they are looking at him. And so who have we got here?

Clearly he has sparked their curiosity; several hands run up and down his body, but after feeling around in vain for valuables, they withdraw. Diamante sleeps in his underwear, the same filthy pair from the other day because he doesn't have anything else—it's all been stolen. The voices go back to discussing the two thousand dollars, assassins, and blackmailers. Diamante trembles like a leaf in the wind. The blanket tickles his nose and makes him want to sneeze. The curtain moves again. Someone comes in and sits right on his mattress. *"Buonanotte,"* says a sleepy voice. "Get yourselves to bed and don't be making no noise, I gotta get up early tomorrow."

All of a sudden something hot brushes against Diamante's face. A foot. The newcomer has climbed into his bed. The foot smells. A toenail, hard and sharp like a horse's hoof, scratches his cheek. He doesn't move, afraid that if he does, the mysterious man will cut off his nose and stick it up his ass. The man with the foot stretches out on the mattress and stops short when he hits the unexpected obstacle of Diamante's body. "What the fuck is this?" he asks, jumping up. "A little present for you, at least you get to sleep with somebody, since the last time you were so lucky you were still in your mother's jug." The man with the foot swears under his breath, and pushes and kicks to make Diamante move. He banishes Diamante to the edge of the bed, and if it weren't for the wall, Diamante would fall right off. Satisfied, the man with the foot calms down. But the others have no intention of sleeping. They are too excited. Someone has lit a cigarette, and whiffs of tobacco float past him. He lacks air. He lacks everything. The dark hovers over him like a threat, and the voices without bodies grow even more desperate. A whole unknown world presses in on him in the heart of the night; whispers, shadows, and darkness crowd around him as he lies there defenseless. Flattened like a pancake against the wall, he is overcome with terror when the bandits start discussing the piece of a boy found in an underground construction site. They say *piece* not in the sense of a real fine specimen of a boy. Turns out he was just a twelve-year-old kid. No, a piece because that's all that was left of him. His head and trunk. No tongue. And no pecker.

"For Chrissake, go to sleep, won't you!" the man with the foot shouts. "Mind your own business. Shhh, enough already." But first, more blood, more murders and mutilations, until finally, little by little, the conversation begins to break off, the corpse in the construction yard mingles with heartfelt praise of the tits of a certain Lena and the correct spelling of the word *die*—as in PAY OR DYE, as it was written in the letter—and then gets mixed up with the talk about hundred-dollar bills—how many do you need to make two thousand?—and an argument over the best technique for sharpening a knife blade on a nose stuck up your ass. Between one sentence and the next the silences become longer. In the space of half an hour, the quarrelsome phantoms of the room drift into a deep sleep. Someone starts snoring and gets a kick in the face that makes him shut up once and for all. Even the noises from the street seem muted and more distant now. But Diamante can't fall asleep. He is shaking, thinking about a head without a tongue abandoned in a construction yard. About the foot pressing against his cheek. About faceless bandits who want to kill Uncle Agnello. Or who want to kill Diamante, even though he's just a little pipsqueak who doesn't scare anybody. Alas, it's true, he is a pipsqueak; even though he'll be twelve in November, he still looks like a little boy. Although in truth he isn't really a child and never has been—in fact, in front of the commission he already knew he was a real man.

He remains awake, motionless on the lumpy mattress in the humid, fetid air. When the first light of day filters through the curtain, he leaps over the man with the foot and onto the floor. He lands on an open can of sardines and cuts himself on the ragged metal edge. Stifling a cry, he kneels to examine the sleeping men. They have troubling faces, hairy black mustaches, skin burned by the sun, rings of wrinkles around their eyes, filthy hair, bulky hands. They would scare him if he met them on the street in the light of day—not to speak of the night. Except for the man with the foot. He has a scraggly mustache and a tall, spindly body like an asparagus. Diamante doesn't recognize him sleeping there, but this must be his cousin Geremia. He left last year.

The house on Prince Street is crammed full of pans, bowls, tubs, sacks of flour, barrels, and trunks. Diamante feels his way around wooden cages with plump clucking chickens and a pot of half-dead basil. He nearly breaks his nose when he bumps up against a plaster statue of the Madonna delle Grazie, patron saint of Minturno. The statue is damaged; evidently others had bumped into it as well, and were even less fortunate than he. He zigzags among damp undershirts, sheets, and socks dangling precariously from wires that slice up the room and slap against his face. Finally he trips over a double bed behind a screen in what seems to be the kitchen. Diamante gawks when he sees on the pillow next to Agnello's greasy head the pale neck of a woman, her arm, and—an unprecedented sight that takes his breath away—a naked leg, which has mischievously slid out from under the sheets in hopes of a bit of cool air. Diamante has no idea who the woman is. But that greasy head belongs to Uncle Agnello, and Uncle Agnello is married to Dionisia the letter writer. And Dionisia is still in Italy—she was at the station with his mother when he left. Both of them were crying. But not him. Curious, Diamante draws closer to the mysterious woman while munching on a cracker. He tries not to make a sound, but his foot inadvertently finds the chicken cage and the hens start squawking. The mysterious woman has hair the color of honey and eyes the color of vinegar. When Diamante realizes that if he can make out the color of her eyes, she must be awake and looking at him, he recoils with a start, knocks over the cage, and falls flat on the floor.

Agnello had rented the house on Prince Street from the neighborhood boss; given his insatiable desire to make money, he turned it into a sort of boardinghouse in the hope of recovering his expenses from purchasing the fruit and vegetable shop. Those men with the mustaches, even if they look like criminals, and probably are, are also his boarders. They pay for a bed, cleaning, and meals. Even Diamante is supposed to pay. Uncle Agnello doesn't give discounts. He has always been tightfisted because he's rich. Or he's rich because he's tightfisted. Out of stinginess he piles as many men as possible into these narrow rooms. There are cots everywhere, in front of the stove, behind every curtain, corner, and trunk. Diamante counts fourteen men and the woman with the naked leg. But he is looking for another woman, or a little girl, rather: Vita.

Vita's hand—damp, sticky with sugar, held tight in his—will turn out to be the only thing that Diamante remembers about the moment when the ferry drew close to the piers at Battery Park. All the others talk about how moved they were when they saw the immense buildings of Manhattan, blackened with soot, and the thousands of glass windows refracting the light as if sending some mysterious signal. Puffs of smoke crown the towers and blur their outlines, transforming them into an immaterial vision, a dream. Others tell of the smokestacks on the ships anchored along the quays, the flags, the signs announcing offices, banks, and businesses, the huge crowds thronging the port. But Diamante is too short to see anything of the promised land except a bunch of ragged rear ends and emaciated spines. He straightens his hat, a cap with a stiff visor, but it is too big for him, and it falls over his ears. With a hop he hoists his sack over his shoulder. The sack is nothing more than the casing from a striped pillow—*his* pillow—which now contains all his belongings. The laces on his tiny boots are so tight his feet hurt. He grips Vita's hand harder, fearful that any bump or shove or even just the inertia of the crowd might separate them. "Don't leave me," he orders her, "not for any reason, do not leave me." Vita is his passport to America, even if she doesn't know it. A rumpled and feverish passport, with snarled hair and a flowered dress. She should have the yellow receipt between her lips, but for some reason it isn't there. A receipt like the one they give you to claim your baggage. And, in fact, they were supposed to be claimed. On the yellow receipt was written GOOD FOR FATHER, but neither Vita nor Diamante had the slightest idea what those words meant. Vita nods and, to show him she understands, sinks her nails into his palm.

Everyone is searching for someone, calling out in dozens of unknown languages, harsh and guttural. Everyone has someone who has come to get them, or they are waiting for someone on the dock, a name and address scrawled on a scrap of paper—a relative, a fellow countryman, a boss. And most people also have work contracts, even though they all deny it. You had to. In truth the second thing Diamante did in America was make up a story, something else he had never done before. In a certain sense you could say he lied. It works this way: At Ellis Island the Americans throw a bunch of questions at you—an interrogation of sorts. The interpreter, a really evil bastard who clearly has made a career out of exercising his zeal against his

countrymen, explains that you must tell the truth and nothing but the truth because in America lying is the greatest of sins, worse than stealing. Except that the truth doesn't help them and it certainly doesn't help you. So you ignore the interpreter and tell them the story you've prepared. If you believe it, so will they. Look them in the eye and swear. I swear I do not have a work contract (but of course he has one, Uncle Agnello is sending him to Cleveland to work on the railroad). I swear my uncle will provide for me for the entire time I will stay in Nevorco (that's a good one, because Agnello is tighter than a sheep's ass). But the commission didn't waste time in verifying. They were in a hurry, for on the same day that he suddenly turned up, the commission had to examine another forty-five hundred of them, descended on America like the locusts in the Bible. The officials were exhausted and had been given orders to loosen the nets. They weren't paying much attention to his answers. So Diamante pulled up his pants—and screwed them over.

"You're hurting me, Diamà," Vita moans. He is squeezing her wrist so hard that the skin is white. "Stay close to me," Diamante responds. He looks like a soldier in that cap. She obeys. They disembark hand in hand and are immediately swallowed up by the restless crowd. Amid the deafening roar of vehicles, the creaking of winches and chains, the whistle of ships' sirens, and the shouts of passengers, somebody is selling rides to the train station, someone else a bed for the night, or fresh water, or directions, while others are here to relieve you of your wallet. A group of boys is perched on a coal heap, smoking cigarette butts and ready to knife the first wretched fellow who rounds the corner.

Diamante holds his passport between his teeth; his father's consent to expatriate is stamped there next to his personal characteristics. He is so busy elbowing his way that it doesn't occur to him to wonder why Vita isn't still chewing on the yellow receipt. When the rascals lurking around the wharf realize that those two kids holding hands are not being met by anybody, they descend on them, haggling over who gets first dibs. They try jumping them, but Diamante doesn't let himself be hoodwinked. He digs in his heels and pulls Vita close. She is smiling at all the well-dressed men who are smiling at her. About each one of them she thinks, This is my father.

· *Don't speak to strangers,* his father had reminded him over and over, and he had promised to remember. *Don't listen to anyone, stay on the island, and wait till Uncle Agnello comes to get you. He'll recognize you.* The problem was that Agnello hadn't come. Or that Vita was tired of waiting. It was bedlam in the reception hall. Yesterday, April 12, 1903, 12,668 people had landed on the island. Ships from Bremen, Rotterdam, Liverpool, Copenhagen, and Hamburg continued to dock. Three had arrived from Naples alone. And from their ship, the *Republic*, 2,201 had disembarked. No one had ever seen an invasion like this before, and the officials lost their heads. Groups flocked together like sheep between the gangways, first one, then another, then another. In the confusion, Vita fell in with a Gypsy woman with ten children in tow. Diamante followed behind her. If she's not going to wait for Agnello, who is *her* father, after all, then why should he? On the ferryboat the Gypsy woman realized she had twelve children instead of ten, but didn't say anything.

The crowd pushed them inexorably forward. They've already passed the barrier, now they're in front of the White Star Line warehouses where porters are unloading suitcases and stacking them in piles four or five yards high. Not just suitcases. Baskets of all shapes and sizes, bundles of cloth, sacks that have been torn and mended a thousand times. Some passengers, fearful of losing their baggage, have written their names in block letters. ESPOSITO, HABIL, MADONIA, ZIPARO, TSUREKAS, PAPAGIONIS—now these names seem to be begging their owners to come claim them, to save them from people's glances, from the shame of poverty. Diamante elbows and pushes, afraid the crowd will trample them. He turns around. The water is the color of granite, but he can't see the island anymore. With the umpteenth push, Vita's braids come loose and tumble down over her ears. Diamante tries to pin them up again, but she isn't paying any attention to her hair. Diamante may have screwed over the commissioners, but she has screwed over Diamante.

The first thing Vita did in America was a magic trick. She had come down with a fever during the night in the lifeboat and wasn't feeling too well sitting there in the waiting room on the island. Bewildered, she studied the faces of the strangers who fluttered by, coming to collect relatives. Severe muzzles topped by coppolas, mugs chiseled in stone, handlebar mustaches and rat's whiskers, hook noses, eyes pitch-black or aquamarine, leather or alabaster skin, pimples and freckles, husbands, grandparents, in-laws, sorrowful mothers, thirty-year-olds looking for the wives they've seen only in photographs, a sad old man howling his son's name. But her father wasn't there. "Is that him?" Diamante tugged at her and pointed to a man with a venerable beard who corresponded to the idea he had formed of Uncle Agnello, the richest man in Tufo, the first to go to America, armed only with a harmonica—and who now, little by little, was calling everybody to come over. He had already sent for fifty people. But Vita shook her head. That man could not be her father. Her father was a real gentleman who would travel to the island on his yacht. When he sees her he will raise his top hat, bow, and take her by the hand. *Princess*, he will say, *you must be my most adored Vita.*

In the reception hall was a man with a jutting chin. Vita noticed him because he was the worst dressed of all, with a horrendous green moleskin jacket and filthy checked pants. Prodigious tufts of hair sprouted from his hands, ears, nose, from the open triangle of his shirt. He stared at her alarmingly as he fanned his sweaty face with a newspaper. A dollar bill was stuck in the ribbon of his hat. He was ugly and the sight of him frightened her. Afraid, she clung more fiercely to Diamante's hand and hid behind his pillowcase. But the man with the chin kept staring at her. His greasy jacket collar was covered with dandruff. *Your father has a jutting chin and a dark face dented like a coffee bean. You remember him, don't you? You were already walking when he came to get*

*Nicola. But if you don't remember him, then remember this: he will have a dol-
lar bill stuck in the ribbon of his hat.* It was at that moment that the yellow receipt disappeared. Vita was holding it in her hand, staring at it in
despair—and all of a sudden it wasn't there anymore. Gone. Vanished
into thin air. Right after that she slipped in behind the Gypsy woman
and her ten children. And the man with the dollar bill in his hat will
be frothing in the Ellis Island reception hall because he has lost his
daughter. So much the worse for him because he is not her father.

But now that she has made the yellow ticket disappear and no one
can come and claim her anymore, she starts to cry. Hanging on to Diamante's hand, she bursts into tears on the Battery Park pier because she
knows full well that the man with the jutting chin really was her father. Or maybe she's crying because he had looked at her for so long,
studying the lineaments of her face, her little bare legs sticking out
from her short flowered dress; he had contemplated her with tender-
ness, he had smiled at her, but her father did not recognize her.

"Vita, quit whining!" Diamante exclaims, annoyed because he
doesn't know how to deal with the little girl's tears. He can't stand
girls. Vita hangs on his suspenders and starts dragging him down the
street. "I'm not whining," she protests, sniffing stubbornly. She dries
her snot with her fingers and wipes them on her flowered dress; fear-
less of being trampled or crushed, she pulls him through the crowds
and confusion toward the iron pillars with trains screeching overhead.
When the crowd finally thins out to only a man with a horse and a
street vendor selling sweets, Diamante turns around. But he can't see
the port anymore. Warehouses, wharves, ships, winches, and flying
trains have all disappeared. Around them are only houses. Low, ram-
bling, decrepit buildings with faded facades and laundry hanging in the
windows. They're lost.

When Agnello's landlord—who is also a moneylender, mediator, labor
boss, steamship- and train-ticket salesman, and trafficker in medicines
and foodstuffs—communicates that the work team Diamante was supposed to hook up with left for Cleveland, Ohio, yesterday on the
7:20 p.m. train, Agnello slaps the boy good upside the head till his ears
ring. He swears and curses his bad luck, *dio madonna cristo* and all the

saints of the calendar. The boss merely shrugs his shoulders, indifferent. Intimidated, Diamante moves off to one side, his right hand in his pants pocket while the left fiddles with his suspenders. He is ashamed to be barefoot and wearing somebody else's shirt, a shirt too big for him at that. Not even the suspenders are his. Rocco lent them to him, even though Diamante hasn't yet figured out whether Rocco is related to him or not. But Rocco was the only one of the fourteen inhabitants of Prince Street who said "Welcome" to him this morning.

A notice board covered with messages and announcements catches Diamante's eye. This basement is clearly a sort of employment agency, because those notices are offers for work. Wanted: 50 miners for Lackawanna County. 500 men for track work for the Erie Company, Buffalo and Youngstown. 200 men for leveling roads. Pay 2 dollars fifty cents. Cook for railroad crew in West Virginia. 30 excavators for the Lehigh Valley Railroad. Artificial flowers: Wanted 20 women as branch workers, Meehan 687 Broadway. 4 leaf workers 2 stem workers, 26 Waverly Place. Drapers finishers binders, Mack Kanner & Milius. 20 masons, 3 cartwrights, 7 stokers, 10 granite cutters, 2 steam boiler operators. The names of the destinations are liquid, mysterious, allusive: Nesquehoning, Olyphant, Punxsutawney, Shenandoah, Freeland.

As for what the two men are saying, Diamante doesn't understand a word because Agnello and the boss—an effusive, authoritative figure who is spasmodically searching for something in the cavity of his ear with the sharp nail of his little finger—speak in a language that sounds familiar but really is foreign. The only thing he understands is that the crew has already left for Clivilland. And that this Clivilland is far away. The railroad pays the trip—one way—for the workers and the foreman, but not for latecomers. Since the ticket costs at least sixty dollars and Diamante doesn't have even a single dollar to his name, well, Uncle Agnello, generous Uncle Agnello, who already paid this ungrateful tramp's passage to America, who had imposed on the boss's goodness and gotten him a place on a crew despite his age, who lied for him, guaranteeing that he was fourteen and strong and robust, when in fact he isn't even twelve and looks eight and is nothing but a skinny runt and a pest . . . Uncle Agnello really lets loose now. "And so I end up with this ragtag beggar, another mouth to feed in Nevorco, when I work like a dog to provide for my family—but I'm telling you, you lice-infested no-good bum, you listen up, I ain't working my ass off to make a little money just for your enjoyment, so if you don't go get yourself a job, I'll throw you outta the house, you hear? I'll rip your guts out, I'll leave you to die of hunger"—another blow that makes his ears ring—"you little beggar, you can go to hell . . ."

Dazed, Diamante follows Agnello outside. He trots along behind him, quickening his step and almost running so as not to lose sight of Agnello on the street, where there's so much confusion he still hasn't figured out how you can cross it without getting trampled. The street is packed with carts of all sizes and every type of goods, from rags to odds and ends for the kitchen, from oysters to knives. The sides of the street are lined with all sorts of shops; the signs are all in Italian, so for a minute Diamante wonders if he has crossed the ocean and is back home again. Beggars, lupine-seed vendors, knife sharpeners, naked children wandering amid heaps of garbage, surly men hanging around in front of greasy spoons and taverns, knots of men playing cards and who knows what else, women dressed in black with scarves on their heads just like in Italy. Then there are also the rather disturbing exotic fauna: curly-head types with cone-shaped hats, the kind wizards wear, or skullcaps like the Pope, and even Chinese with their wax-colored skin. Among all these strange and sinister people, Uncle Agnello advances at a ferocious pace as if pursued by the devil. Lots of people know him and everyone greets him, raising their hands to their hats because Agnello is an important man. Many revere him and call him "Uncle" as a sign of respect, and not because they are his nephews. Now that Diamante thinks of it, not even he is Agnello's nephew, and this is not an insignificant detail. Something tells him his not-uncle Agnello would have no problem leaving him to die of hunger.

Agnello never turns around to see if the boy is following him. He can go to hell, go back where he came from, for all he cares. That boy's a jinx. Sent by the devil to let him know the time for reckoning has come. But ever since Agnello stopped talking to God, he's not too tight with the devil, either. Still, it can't be a mere coincidence that yesterday, when he got back from his pointless trip to Ellis Island, the mailman delivered the fateful letter sealed with an open black hand: worse than a curse, this was a most powerful evil eye. Sooner or later everybody in the neighborhood who manages to set themselves up receives one. And Agnello is managing quite well. His fruit and vegetable store is really just a hole in the wall, only slightly more comfortable than a tomb, and it's on Elizabeth Street, a shady part of the neighborhood infested with brawling Sicilians. Nevertheless, it's beginning to acquire a steady clientele of housewives who pay their bills if not every month then at least every three, and is just starting to turn a profit. His boardinghouse is always full, never an empty bed because his woman—his American woman, Lena, that is—is a hard worker, and slaves away for eighteen hours a day without complaining. Even though she isn't really American. By now Agnello has a decent account with the boss on Mulberry and has managed to bring his whole family to New York. Except his wife, who was rejected by the Americans because of her eye ailment. It's not like the Americans go all soft if you're married and fond of your wife, who has always done her duty. It's not as if they think about the fact that you've been waiting for her for ten years, that you broke your back to bring her over, and finally you go to the island to collect her, all happy. No. They look her in the eye and if they see a rheum or a cataract they make a cross on her back and it's *Addio, Dionisia.* And the only thing left for you to do now is hope that your good wife with the bad eye will die as soon as possible so at least you can finally get married again and put an end to all the talk about your American woman because it could ruin your reputation. But there's no hiding prosperity, and word gets around soon enough that Agnello is well set up. First two shady-looking figures came by the fruit store and nosed insolently among his tomatoes, all shriveled from the frost, and told him to cough up two hundred dollars or they'd burn down the shop. Agnello told them to go to hell and bought himself a rifle and ammunition. For an entire month he never left his hole, sleeping sitting up in a corner between the cases of oranges and onions, the loaded rifle between his legs and his finger on the trigger. Ready to welcome visitors, he was. But now there's the letter. And that letter—he knows because it's happened to lots of others

—means serious trouble. Either you pay or you die. Agnello doesn't want to do either.

On Prince Street, the table is already set. Sunday is the only day of the week when everyone eats together. Fourteen containers—glass jars, milk tins, and the like—that serve as bowls are piled one on top of the other. Diamante really starts to worry now because he knows how to count and there isn't any bowl for him. Agnello sits down. He'll think about the letter with the black hand on a full stomach. Only then does Diamante see her. Hobbling along next to the woman with the bare leg, Vita is holding one of the handles of a pot, engulfed in a cloud of steam. The woman hoists the pot onto the table and serves Agnello, Agnello's son Nicola, and then Cousin Geremia and Cousin Rocco or whoever that is with the tattoos on his arm and the sweet smile that contrasts curiously with his incredible height. There aren't enough chairs for everyone, so the boarders take their bowls overflowing with macaroni and go sit on cots, basins, barrels, wherever they can find a place. Vita seems unhappy. Her hair is finally combed, revealing a pale and concentrated face. She's wearing an apron that's too big for her, and like Diamante, she's barefoot. When she sees him, she offers him a smile that makes up for all the slaps and threats and the useless journey to the Mulberry Street basement, and makes him proud to have missed that train for Cleveland.

Nicola takes a bite of macaroni and instantly spits it out. The oldest boarder, who suffers from aches and pains, stabs his fork in the pasta, which, to tell the truth, looks disgusting and is all stuck together, and says to Agnello that he pays ten dollars a month and if they want to serve him this rubbish that not even a dog would eat, then he'll find himself another boardinghouse. "Little Vita cooked today," Agnello explains as he grabs his daughter by her apron strings. "Give her time to learn and she'll get better at it." But the boarders disagree. This is not a cooking school. "You eat it then, it's revolting." But no, not even Agnello intends to eat it. He, too, spits out a piece of half-chewed whitish pasta and puts down his fork, disgusted. This is his day of suffering. He can't find peace anywhere, not even at home. He looks threateningly at Vita. "So what's this? So you're not even no good at

making the macaruni?" Vita is offended and bites her lip. She is so tiny
her chin doesn't even reach the rim of the pot. Everyone is looking at
her, and she scratches her head uncertainly. She feels trapped. Because
the house on Prince Street is full of strangers, her father first of all. Because her father lives with a stranger, a woman who reveres him as if
she were a servant and speaks to him formally with the *voi* and calls
him Uncle Agnello, but then sleeps in his bed and acts as if this were
her house, too. Because her brother doesn't go by the name Nicola
anymore, but Coca-Cola, and he talks strange and didn't recognize her
when the policeman with the red skin asked him, "Da ya no tis little
gherla?" Because Agnello wants to send Diamante to Cleveland and
she doesn't want to live here without him. The boy with the blue eyes
is her only friend amid all these wicked-faced strangers. When she
thinks about all these things, her eyes brim with tears.

"I put all that salt in the water on purpose," she declares brazenly.
"I don't want to cook. I don't want to stay here. I want to go home."
Delighted, Coca-Cola bursts out laughing. Agnello grabs Vita by the
wrist, and Diamante begins to wish that whoever sent the letter with
the black hand really would kill him. The boarders are enjoying the
scene and laugh up their sleeves. None of them had ever dared contra-
dict Agnello. At night they hope he'll be ruined and go back to being
scum like them, but during the day they lift their hats to his good fortune. Vita is silent, satisfied. There, she said it. She would never dis-
obey her father, but this guy with the chin isn't her father and she
wants to go home to Dionisia. Agnello removes a bill rolled up like a
cigarette from behind his ear and magnanimously offers that his boarders go to the tavern and drink his health. Then he orders his woman to
make me something to eat 'cause I'm dyin' of hunger, and pushes her
rudely toward the stove. "And you," he says to his son, who is fiddling
with a toothpick, "you look like a priest sprawled in that chair. Go to
the fruttostando, I don't want it to be left unwatched today." "B-b-but
it's Sunday," Coca-Cola stammers. Agnello puts a fist to his head and
Coca-Cola wobbles to his feet. He wonders if Agnello will use the belt
or the flyswatter or his hand on his sister. With him his father uses
everything—rolling pins, monkey wrenches, even a pickax. The Mazzuccos have always been bad-tempered. More stubborn than a jackass.

Harder to move than a mountain when they get something in their heads. Luckily for him, Coca-Cola doesn't have anything in his head. The boarders scramble out. Only Diamante sits still, perched on a barrel. But Agnello's gaze passes over him; he doesn't want to bother with him now. He'll deal with the problem of Diamante some other time. The kid already owes him two hundred and seventy dollars. If he had that money, half his troubles would be over. But the kid doesn't have a cent. Agnello turns to look at Vita and makes her sit down. Then he sticks a fork in her hand. Very softly because he doesn't feel like yelling just now, he says, "Eat."

Well, what did she think? That she came here for a vacation? Lena is exhausted. Since March she's been anemic, weak, and nauseous, with the sweats at night. Which could mean one of two things: either she's got tuberculosis, which would be a catastrophe because if the boarders found out they'd leave immediately for fear of catching it, or she's pregnant, and this too would be a catastrophe, in the first place because you can't trust a woman who isn't your wife, and second because you have to take care of a new baby until he's at least ten years old. But since he'd never take Lena to Bellevue, the city's free hospital, for a checkup or let those witches from the Tuberculosis Prevention Committee, who go around door to door collecting statistics on the impact of the disease in the Mulberry district, set foot in his house— and if Lena opened the door for strangers he'd beat the living daylights out of her so she wouldn't get out of bed for three days—for some time Agnello wasn't sure if he was living with a consumptive or a pregnant woman. In either case, he kept his hands off her for a while. But now he knows. Lena behaves just fine. She continues to do the shopping and the laundry, the cooking and the washing up, all the things she's supposed to do. But every once in a while she can't manage to keep on her feet and faints. She's gone all pale, her face as white as the scarf she used to wear on her head when he took her to mass on Sundays. That was a long time ago because Lena doesn't go to mass anymore. The priest says she's living in sin and he doesn't want to hear her confession. The only way she and her man can redeem themselves is by contributing to the construction of the church. At which point Agnello and Lena resigned themselves to living without the sacra-

ments. At any rate, Lena needs help. And that help is Vita. Why else
would he have had her come? He'd only seen her twice since she was
born. But she's a disappointment, this daughter of his. At nine years
old, she should already be a woman. Besides, that's what that liar of a
wife had written to him so as to induce him to take her. "As for how
Vita is growing, I can't complain. She's vivacious, happy as the sun,
and growing up all pretty and strong." Instead she tricked him: this
Vita is a feverish, hostile shrimp of a child. She'll never be able to carry
the sack of coal up to the fifth floor. Not to mention the washtub full
of laundry. He's already regretting having called for her and almost
feels like throwing her back in the ocean.

Agnello places the pot in front of Vita. *"Mangia,"* he repeats, sticking a forkful into his daughter's mouth. "We don't throw anything
away here. Not even a crumb goes to waste. This here is all hard-
earned. You're not getting up till you've eaten it all." Vita casts him a
challenging look. She is too stubborn to say she's sorry and too proud
to ask forgiveness. "Eat, for God's sake!" For three hours Diamante remains perched on the barrel, munching on stale biscuits. Over and
over Vita sticks her fork in the nauseating mix of salt, cheese, and broken pasta, by now all cold and sticky. She puts the fork in her mouth,
chews, and swallows, and chews and swallows, until her teeth hurt and
her stomach is so swollen and heavy she'll explode. She keeps chewing
and swallowing because she started, and Vita still believes that in life
you have to finish what you start, especially when your honor is at
stake. A solid mass is blocking her throat and she is so full there is no
room left and she can't possibly make it go down—but she drinks a
glass of water and chews and swallows some more, keeping her eyes
fixed on the pasta as she plunges her fork in. When the serving bowl is
finally empty, she feels as if she has a cow in her stomach. She'll never
be able to get up, she's too stuffed. But she holds her head high and
her neck straight and places two hands on the table. She feels like
throwing up. Diamante raises an eyebrow, worried, but Vita manages
to stand. Agnello, deep in his thoughts about the PAY OR DIE dilemma,
asks himself which would be the greater disgrace, death or poverty. He
traces the answer in the smoke rings that rise along the wall. As Vita
passes in front of him, she yells in his face, "You're still not my father!"

Precisely because that guy with the jutting chin isn't her father, it never crossed her mind to show up at Prince Street yesterday. Holding on to Diamante's hand, she wandered about unhurriedly, aimlessly, guided only by curiosity and joy. Everything was new, magical, wonderful. She had taken off her shoes—she wasn't used to wearing them and they hurt her feet—and strolled around barefoot, looking up in admiration and confusion at buildings so high they seemed to tickle the clouds. Her tears had dried up by now, and she was smiling. A mischievous smile, pleased and satisfied. She was sure they would come upon a piazza soon—every decent city, town, or village has a piazza. Naples has one, as does Caserta, Gaeta, Minturno, and even Tufo, a tiny hamlet of a thousand souls without even a carriage. Here there were parks, intersections, junctions, wild spaces. But no piazzas. And no churches, either—neither old nor new. When they finally found one, it was nearly three o'clock.

Set between a church—or what seemed like a church, even though it didn't have a cross on the roof—and a row of buildings so new that they made it seem like an intruder was a public garden. The church was called Saint Paul's Chapel and it was closed. But the iron gate onto the garden wasn't locked, only swung shut. The garden was really a cemetery, and eating lunch in a graveyard never brings good luck. The dead should be left in peace. But Diamante dropped his pillowcase and sat on what was surely a tomb, though it looked like a curbstone to him. The sun was high in the April sky and heating up the streets, but here in the shade of the leafy old trees it was like Paradise. Diamante rummaged around in his bag and then dumped everything out on the grass. All sorts of things came tumbling out: a shirt, three Tuscan cigars, a can of tomatoes, a comb, a piece of soap, a handful of walnuts, a bunch of dried figs, a small can of oil, three red peppers, two handkerchiefs, a string of dried sausages, a letter for Agnello from Antonio, a piece of cheese, and a package of crusty bread. His mother had given it to him before he left, but he hadn't needed it; he had eaten his fill on the steamer—it was an English steamer, of course, only fools take the Italian tubs. Now, thirteen days later, the bread was hard as a rock. But they hadn't eaten since the evening before, since Diamante had categorically refused to buy a sweet or a roll because he didn't know how much anything should cost here and, being rather tentative, he was sure they would trick him. There wasn't much to choose from. Vita bit into a petrified sausage and Diamante concentrated on opening the walnuts. There was an unearthly silence in Saint Paul's cemetery. It seemed so strange to be there with Vita. Alone in an unknown city, on the other side of the world. Alone with Vita, who was smiling, triumphant in her discovery that even in America there are ants. A tidy, compact line of them were greedily munching on the sausage crumbs. She let one climb onto the palm of her hand, but then killed it, disappointed. "Just the same as our ants," she said.

Diamante scrutinized Vita's flushed face. "We have to go," he said, but without conviction. He only said it because Vita had a high fever from the night in the lifeboat, and if she died they would blame him. "You're so moody, Diamante," she laughed, and bit his nose in revenge. Of all the boys in the village, Diamante was the only one who never laughed. He was a dreamer. Quick as a cat, he would climb high up in a carob tree where no one else could reach him, and shoot at the crows in the fields with his slingshot. He never missed a shot. Or he'd breathe air into toads with a reed, pumping them up until they burst. He fished for frogs in the backwaters of the Garigliano and killed them by biting their heads. He caught eels with his hands and never even deigned to notice little girls like Vita. Diamante kept to himself and did things his own way. Dionisia used to say that he was the smartest of them all, the only one who would do something with his life. Vita was in awe of him, in part because his blue eyes were so evasive you could never tell what he was thinking.

"Look," she said in a more soothing voice, and pointed to the giant face of a woman on a poster on the building across the way. The woman seemed to be looking at them and flaunted a red smile and perfect white teeth. "What is it? What does it say?" Vita insisted, she who never had time to waste learning to read. "It says LET'S SMILE, WOMEN, BUY LIPSTICK KISSPROOF 1.99." "And what does that mean?" Diamante, who didn't want to admit that he understood not a word, made up the umpteenth lie of the day. "There's a quack dentist behind that poster. He's good and doesn't hurt you with his pliers. That's why the woman is smiling." Vita shrugged her shoulders, disappointed. But the poster was beautiful nevertheless, with that smiling, happy-looking woman. Now that she thought about it, Vita had never seen a smile like that before. The women in Tufo didn't have all those teeth; they were usually missing one or two or sometimes all of them. Maybe that's why they never smiled. Diamante laid his head on his pillowcase. The sky was a dreamy blue. All of a sudden he felt empty and light, as if an unbearable weight had been lifted off him. He wasn't worried or preoccupied or guilty. Everything was so very surprising that anything seemed possible. It was an impossible and confused dream, but he didn't want to wake up. The woman was smiling. And he smiled at the sky. He knew he had to ask someone where Prince Street was, that fabulous name that had obsessed him for months, luring him on. But he put it off. He knew that, later, a moment like this would never come again. Later he wouldn't be able to sit on the grass with Vita's wavy black hair tousled in his hands. Later he would not comb her hair with his fingers, patiently untangling the snarls and braiding it again. Nor would he be able to doze off on the grass with her head on his lap. In that later time was his future—a man's job on a railway crew in some forest somewhere in this country. Vita threw him such an impertinent, wise smile that Diamante suddenly realized he would miss her when tonight or tomorrow at the latest, they would be separated, and after so many days of living with a little girl he would find himself with a bunch of brawny males in an American work camp. He was surprised he had thought of it only now.

They didn't have the slightest idea where they were. It was like being on the moon. The city—so grimy and colorful around the port—was more beautiful here. Gone were the dilapidated wooden houses, the ragged crowds and street vendors. Gone all the disheveled people who spoke in vaguely familiar dialects, the myriad boys playing in the gutters. Buildings with marble facades lined both sides of the street, and the pedestrians wore bowler hats and carried cane or bamboo walking sticks. Vita and Diamante walked close to the walls so as not to be noticed. But on Broadway and Thirty-fourth, a boy with threadbare cotton clothes, a hat, and a striped pillowcase on his shoulder together with a little barefoot girl with black hair and a flowered dress filthier than the sidewalk did not pass unnoticed. They dragged themselves along, their feet burning. The city never ended. Now and then it was interrupted; for a while they walked alongside a park, or yet another abyss where workmen were laying the foundations of a building, but then the city would start up again, even more imposing, beautiful, and luxurious than before. It was already five in the afternoon. Vita pressed her nose against a shop window. Only it wasn't exactly a shop. Six stories high, three hundred yards long, the immense building took up the whole block. In the window a slender, athletic woman revealed a naked arm. She was holding a strange utensil that looked like a snow-shoe. The woman was smiling. She wasn't a real woman, but then again, all the women here—even the real ones—seemed fake. They didn't dress all in black. They didn't cover their heads with a scarf. Or wear an embroidered bodice and skirts. They were very tall, very thin, very blond. They had radiant smiles, like the woman on the poster at the cemetery—white teeth, thin hips, big feet. Vita was fascinated; she had never seen women like this before. Maybe in the sun of this city she, too, would grow up to be like them.

"We've got to get out of here," Diamante said, tugging on Vita's dress. "Everybody's looking at us strange." Vita stuck out her tongue at a woman who had just gotten out of a carriage and was pointing them out to a man in blue standing at the intersection with his arms crossed. "So what?" Vita answered, in ecstasy before the mannequin. "If they don't want to see us they can poke their eyes out." All the same, everyone was looking at them as if they had just stolen a chicken. And a policeman was already coming over to them. His nightstick banged against his thigh. "Hey, kids!" His hair was yellow and his skin as white as a flounder. "Hey, come here!" Diamante and Vita were not very fond of guards, for they never brought good news. Whenever the authorities—it didn't matter if they were guards, policemen, mayors, or politicians from Minturno—dared come near Tufo, the village kids would throw rocks at them. Just to show how much they liked them. Vita pushed open the door and hurried in. They passed under an arch with the word MACY'S written on it and entered the realm of light.

Vita had never seen a place like this before. Nor would she see one again in the years to come, for she would not cross the border of Houston Street again soon. But that afternoon remained fixed in her memory with the vivid immediacy of a dream. It was all so quick—the whole visit didn't last more than three minutes—and she didn't have time to stop at all, Diamante was dragging her this way and that, and then they started to run because the policeman, with his whistle in his mouth, had come into the department store and was chasing them while huge blond salesmen were bearing down on them from all directions. The space was bigger than a cathedral, but even running Vita couldn't take her eyes off the pyramids of hats and gloves, mountains of colored scarves, heaps of hairpins and tortoiseshell combs, piles of silk and white cotton stockings—and it was all beautiful, marvelously, enchantingly beautiful, and Diamante was running and Vita tripped and the policeman was yelling "Stop those kids!" and everyone was turning to look at them until finally they ran into a room with transparent walls. It was a trap. A man in uniform guarding a brass panel pushed a button and the doors closed, locking them in. But he wasn't a policeman: just a bony Negro, shiny with sweat, with a hint of a smile on his lips.

Diamante had never seen a man with such dark skin except in *The Capture of Africa of 1896*, which was put on every year in Portanuova. But the soldiers in Menelik's army were covered in tar to make them black because they really were just like him, white schoolboys from Minturno. He had seen a few real black men in the popular almanacs, but they had bones in their hair and disks in their lips, not uniforms with gold buttons. They were savage cannibals, while this elegant and impeccable man seemed very important. All of a sudden the room with the transparent walls started to move, shooting upward. Diamante leaned against the wall, terrified. The room was flying! Unperturbed, the cannibal eyed Diamante's tiny dust-covered boots and the pillowcase on his shoulder. Then his dark eyes rested on Vita's little dirt-lined nose. She was clinging to Diamante because in the stories her mother used to tell her the black man was a deadly scourge, worse than the living dead and the wicked witches who steal children in the night. The black man steals curious little girls. But Diamante was no help; he was trembling himself as the room soared, vibrated, and rattled. When the doors of the box opened, they were on top of the world, and the policeman, salesmen, and department store manager were minuscule figures five floors below them. The elevator man shoved them out and pushed a button. As the doors closed on his mysterious face, he indicated the way out—right in front of them. The fire escape.

Night was falling when they were drawn to some woods in a park that looked like the countryside. They stretched out on the grass near a lake. The park was nearly deserted. Arrogant white swans paddled around as Vita washed her blackened feet. They ate the last sausage and the last handful of dried figs from the pillowcase. They were immensely happy and wished this day would never end. It was then that the Italian noticed them.

He was an organ-grinder. He came toward them pulling his barrel organ, which every now and then exhaled a note as it bumped along. "You can't stay here, my little ones," he said with a friendly smile. "The park is closed after sunset and if the cops find you, they'll put you in jail. You just arrive?" he asked, sitting down next to them. "*Sì,*" Vita answered proudly. "This morning, with the ferry from the island. We've seen the whole city." "Are you alone?" "*Sì,*" said Vita, throwing a complicit glance at Diamante. "Are you siblings?" "*Sì,*" said Diamante. "No," said Vita, "I hardly even know my brother. But Diamante lives on my street." The organ-grinder rolled some tobacco in a strip of newspaper and took a few puffs. They weren't suspicious of him, because he was Italian and played such beautiful songs. After walking on the moon all day, it was good to hear your own language spoken. It was good to have found a guide. "If you come with me, I'll show you a place where you can sleep." "Is it far?" asked Diamante. He would never be able to get his feet back in his boots again. "No, just around the corner. See the Dakota?" He pointed to a magnificent castle with towers, pinnacles, pinions, and turrets on the other side of the lake. "Right behind there."

It was the skeleton of an unfinished house. A missing plank in the fencing around the construction site led to a sort of basement. A piece of stained cardboard served as a mattress, and a board across two empty barrels made a table. The man pushed his organ against the wall amid heaps of garbage and rusted cans and invited them to lie down on the cardboard, while he wrapped himself up in a faded old blanket so full of lice it practically walked by itself. Excited, they told him about Tufo and Minturno, about Dionisia, who had been rejected by the Americans because of her eye ailment and who now was a letter writer; the stone breaker Antonio, whom everyone called Mantu and who was the most unlucky man of the whole village because he had crossed the ocean to America twice and twice was sent back; Vita's brother, whom Agnello had come to get in 1897; and Diamante's two sisters and three brothers, who died of hunger. Vita even showed him her treasures. A silver knife, fork, and spoon they had given her on the steamship, from the restaurant in first class. But that was not her real treasure.

Before leaving, Vita had filled her pockets with all sorts of magic objects—to get back home, she explained with a certain condescension. A rusty leaf from an olive tree, the crusty shell of a shrimp, a little ball of goat dung, the bones of a frog, a sharp needle from a prickly pear, a flake of plaster from the church (which was crumbling into a fine dust like talcum powder), a clam, the dried seed of a lemon as well as a whole lemon, now covered in a fuzzy white mold. The organ-grinder ignored the silverware but held each of those disgusting objects in his hand, showing that he understood their worth. He weighed them as if they were diamonds and then helped her wrap them in a handkerchief. He was kind and interested in their talk in a way adults never are. He offered them a glass of his wine, the only thing he had here from Italy. He had to insist because they didn't want to drink it. The wine tasted vaguely like medicine. Then he got all sad and said in a melancholy voice that they never should have come. This was a dreadful place, it wasn't true at all what they say about it over there. The only difference between America and Italy was the money: there was money here, but it wasn't for them. No, here, all you did was make money for somebody else. They should go back to Italy right away. If he could, he'd leave this minute. Only he couldn't. Sometimes it's difficult to go back home. On the other side, everyone believed he had become rich. Instead, the only thing he had left after ten years was his organ. Diamante was so disillusioned by the man's talk that he didn't say another word to him. This city was a beautiful wonder, he

already liked it better than any other place, and good luck was waiting
for him. He took off his jacket, covered Vita, and said that if he didn't
mind, they wanted to sleep now. It had been a very long day. *"Buona-
notte, bambini."*

When Diamante opened his eyes, the sun was already setting. The
organ-grinder was gone. So was his organ. But so were Diamante's
boots, Vita's shoes, her silverware, his jacket, shirt, suspenders, and hat.
Even his striped pillowcase with all his belongings was gone. And the
repugnant little bundle with the moldy lemon, olive leaf, and shrimp
shell was missing from the pocket of Vita's dress. Not one of her magic
items was here. The only thing left behind was his underwear, thrown
in a corner. Too threadbare even to be sold to a ragman. The inner
pocket, the one that had caused him so much embarrassment in front
of the commission on Ellis Island, was empty. Diamante lay still on
the cardboard for almost an hour, biting his lip so as not to cry. He
couldn't believe the man had robbed them. Them of all people, who
had offered him friendship and company, who had even trusted him
with their secrets. He felt Vita's breath on his cheek. He watched her
sleep, her face turned toward him, an expression of beatitude on her
lips. He didn't want to wake her. Didn't want to drop her in this building basement, amid garbage and man's injustice to men.

The policeman who intercepted them had rust-colored hair, fine as
corn silk. He spotted them as they roamed the park barefoot and half-
naked. He didn't say a word. Besides, they couldn't understand him,
nor he them. He barked in that incomprehensible language of his, and
when he grabbed Diamante by the ear, he pulled so hard he almost
yanked it off. It didn't do any good. Before him stood two filthy, disappointed, impenetrable little faces. Four eyes brimming with rage and
sadness. He pushed and shoved them toward the police cart at the entrance to Central Park and consulted with his colleague about what
to do with these two vagabonds. The other shrugged his shoulders.
There were hundreds of kids like them on the streets of New York.
When they caught them, they would take them to the charity shelters.
And if the children could not demonstrate they were able to maintain

themselves in America, if it turned out they were living at the expense of the city government—a weight, a threat, and a danger to society— they were deported. Repatriated on the first steamship. Uninvited strangers. Undesirable aliens. The policeman made Diamante climb up on the cart. He hid his face in his hands, ashamed that the passersby would think him a thief. Instead, he was the one who had been robbed, even though he didn't know how to say so, or how to make them believe he and Vita could have possessed anything worth stealing. "Come on, little one," the red-faced policeman said to Vita. But Vita didn't move. She kept feeling in her pocket as if the parcel could reappear somehow; it was impossible that the organ-grinder had taken even that, full as it was of objects that meant nothing to him but that were intended to transport her back home. But the bundle didn't materialize. "Come on!" the policeman repeated. Vita's dark eyes rested on Diamante's curved back. Naked, for he no longer had a shirt. The bones sticking out on his thin shoulders reminded her of wings. And so she bent down and picked up a stick out of a puddle. With a shaking hand, while the two policemen stared at her in astonishment, she wrote in the dirt: 18 Prince Street.

A Trip to New York

In the spring of 1997 I was invited to the United States. I was to be part of a group of writers, journalists, and professors speaking at the Library of Congress in Washington, D.C., in celebration of the opening of a section dedicated to Italian literature. I had no desire to go to the United States. Furthermore, I knew that I did not possess the qualifications to represent Italian literature in that I had published only one novel, the year before, and the experience had taken so much out of me that I was dreading the day I would yield to the temptation to publish another one. Many people praised my "youth," but I didn't know what it meant to be young. Nevertheless, the trip seemed a sort of gift, and as gifts are fortuitous and often revealing, they should not be refused. So I went.

I was thirty years old. For some time I had developed various obsessions, among them a pernicious rejection of light, the consequences of which were comic in a sense: it became an insurmountable difficulty to cross a sunny street or walk along a sidewalk not shaded by a balcony, canopy, or row of trees. I hadn't gone to the beach in years, and had even stopped traveling in the mountains, deserts, and high places where I had always loved to roam. I was unable to answer the telephone, the mere sound of which was enough to hurl me into depression, and the very idea of meeting someone new terrified me. Speaking in public was absolutely out of the question. The publication of my novel had in some ways forced me to confront all this. By the spring of 1997 my difficulties had even become the source of merriment between Luigi and me, the only two people other than the doctors and pharmacists who knew about them. Obviously, I did not want my illustrious travel companions to notice anything. I wanted them to like me as much as I liked them. The terrible strangers revealed themselves to be affable, courteous, and entirely pleasant. The distinguished philosopher of language who was the principal attraction of the group shared with me a transgressive addiction to nicotine, a serious crime in a country like the United States, which is engaged in a battle without quarter against smoking. More than once we ran into each other inhaling our forbidden cigarettes in basements or on sidewalks, like conspirators or criminals. The young writers, actors, public relations people, significant others, and spouses helped transform the trip into a sort of disorderly school outing. We spoke at the Library of Congress. The room was packed. Every one of us had agreed to speak in English. Even me.

I have always had trouble with English. I don't know why. When I was eleven, I insisted on signing up for French, a class no one wanted to take. "English is the language of the future," my father used to say (even though he gave up studying in 1952 when he met my mother). "I'm not interested in the future," I answered, convinced I would never see it. I learned French instead. Languages had an irresistible hold on me; I developed a passion for Greek and Latin and, armed with a dictionary and grammar book, studied Russian and Spanish on my own. When I was eighteen I decided the future was already here and left for England. Of my winter in Oxford I remember only the cabdriver's pesky children I looked after in exchange for lodging—a room wrapped in psychedelic flowered wallpaper in a row house in the city's foggy working-class outskirts. They were days of impenetrable solitude in a foreign city among inaccessible people I did not understand and who did not understand me. The students of the famous university gathered in pubs in the evening, but I was unable to talk

with them and stayed with the taxi driver's children. I was speechless—
which, for me, was equivalent to the most mortifying deprivation, absolute poverty. I shared my solitude with a gloomy Saudi Arabian
student who eventually asked me to marry him. It was the first and last
marriage proposal I have ever received. He proposed in English and
was refused in English. The goal of my stay had been achieved: I had
learned to survive.

Following the presentation at the Library of Congress, we had
three days free before our next engagement, which was to be held in
New York. We took the Metroliner and arrived at Penn Station one
April morning. At the time I was working on a novel about and for
Annemarie Schwarzenbach. A Swiss writer of dazzling, androgynous
beauty who died mysteriously in 1942 when she was only thirty-four.
During her intense and restless life, she lost and found several home-
lands: Switzerland, Germany, Persia, Congo, the United States. Various families: her own, composed of very wealthy silk manufacturers in
Zurich, nationalists, and patrons of music; that of Thomas Mann,
whose children, Erika and Klaus, had been her intimate friends since
her twenties; and the one she tried to make for herself through an improbable marriage to a French diplomat. Many women: the list of her
conquests reads like a catalog of nations, races, ages, and professions,
united only by their gender and social status—aristocratic or upper
middle class. Annemarie knew privilege and poverty, political commitment and Nazism, drugs and exile, nomadism and the loss of self. She
was a journalist, photographer, and voyager—always in search of the
absolute. She skirted the edges of schizophrenia, and experienced in
her own body the horrors of psychiatric treatment. Only in writing
did she find herself. After her death, she was quickly forgotten, however.

I spent those three days on pilgrimage to the places she had lived
before being expelled from the United States as an "unwelcome
guest." I went about the city seeking out hotels and mental hospitals,
psychiatric clinics and nightclubs. The Hotel Pierre, where she lived in
the fall of 1940 with her German woman-friend Baroness Margot von
Opel, turned out to be so ostentatiously luxurious as to seem vulgar.
The liveried doorman gave me his fixed smile, as he did to everyone—

an obligatory smile devoid of warmth. Cold checkered tiles led to elevators paneled in precious wood. Margot's room was in a tower. A powerful, neogothic, phallic tower. The walls were perfumed. And yet it was in these very rooms, muted with wall-to-wall carpeting, that the catastrophe had unfolded. Here was where Annemarie began her descent into hell. She ended up at Bellevue, and following her footsteps, I, too, soon found myself at the hospital on First Avenue in lower Manhattan.

I wandered through the halls of the renowned psychiatric ward. I spoke with Hispanic doctors who treat the Hispanic patients. Bellevue is still one of New York's public hospitals, and today's poor speak Spanish. A young doctor explained that in the 1940s most of the inmates were Italian. The Italians were the most pitiful ethnic minority in the city. Worse off than the Jews, Poles, Romanians, even the blacks. "The Italians were like blacks who couldn't even speak English," the doctor said. I nodded, stunned by this scathing connection. I had never thought of it in that way. I recalled the elderly people with farmers' faces who had stopped us the day before on Coney Island and tried to strike up a conversation. We couldn't understand each other. What they thought was Italian was really another language. Dialects spoken in the South long ago. They had called us *paisà*, compatriots.

And this is how, wandering around for hours in the interminable downtown streets that seem to lead nowhere, we ended up in Little Italy. Not a particularly populated or lively neighborhood—more like a museum or theater. It was depressing. Everything had been redone for the tourists: Italian flags, windows decorated in white, red, and green, restaurants with bogus Italian menus (the Neapolitan restaurant was serving Milanese-style cutlets and saffron rice). Our French guide cautioned us against using the word *Mafia* in Little Italy. A touch of racism, and pointless besides, for this was not really Little Italy. There were no more Italians here—they had all gone away, disappeared, blended into and canceled out by the America around them. None of the Mulberry Street bartenders, waiters, or restaurant owners felt the least nostalgia for the past. Like the guards at the war cemeteries or the trenches in the Dolomites, they were preserving the memory of a lost battle. On display was the postcard of a world that had never really existed, and that was now tidied up, purified, cleansed of all suffering, blood, and shame. We wanted to escape, go back to the Hotel Bedford on Fortieth Street (Annemarie had lived there, together with the Manns and other German artists in exile from Nazism), but it was almost two o'clock and we realized we were hungry. We bought a slice of pizza—very good—in a grocery store on Mulberry Street. There was only one bench, set against the opposite wall. It was in the sun. Luigi looked at me with alarm, but I crossed the street and sat down. The sun beat fiercely on our heads, but I didn't notice. And so my phobia ended that day, just like that, just as suddenly as it had begun.

Heading back to Fortieth Street, we got lost. In SoHo, a very trendy neighborhood. *Cool* was the irritating adjective most often used to describe it. Pastel-colored buildings two or three stories high and protected by massive cast-iron fire escapes housed pretentious boutiques (the jeans and clothes fashioned from synthetic materials were displayed like postmodern sculptures, set amid minimalist furnishings and blinding white walls), unapproachable cafés, and lofts where listless gallery owners exhibited African idols, natural fabrics, and aborigine masks. This neighborhood set the trends and decreed what was now passé, fatally out of style. A neighborhood for actors, young managers, directors, artists. A neighborhood for successful people. We stopped in front of a real estate agency. The announcements were accompanied by glossy photographs:

SOHO 1 br by Prince Street & West Broadway.
Very large one bedroom just off Prince Street in SoHo. Large private garden, available for long-term rental. Fully furnished all amenities (tv, vcr, telephone, full kitchen, full bath).
$2395

PRINCE STREET TWO BED
Great clean, safe building. Newly renovated.
Great for a share situation, especially nyu students. Lots of fun.
Cats are ok Dogs are ok
$2025

Ideal for students. At two thousand dollars for a one-bedroom apartment? Maybe that was the yearly rent. We looked at each other, amazed. Not a chance: the rents were monthly. Prince Street was the trendiest street in the neighborhood.

Prince Street.

A street with boutiques, art galleries, exotic clubs, restaurants where main courses cost twenty-five dollars.

Prince Street.

Why had I heard that name before?

Had I read it somewhere?

I looked at the three-story houses, the windows, the courtyards, the fire escapes.

"My father's father lived on Prince Street," I said absentmindedly to Luigi. "He came to America when he was a boy."

"When?"

I couldn't remember. It was an old story, and no one had told it to me for a long time. I hadn't ever been much interested in my family's history. All I wanted was to be rid of it. Who doesn't? We didn't visit our relatives often or see much of each other in my immediate family—a reciprocal attempt at independence. My father was friends with the revolutionary psychiatrist Franco Basaglia and was imbued with antipsychiatry. He maintained that families are poisonous and inflict incurable wounds, and that the most monstrous crimes are committed in families.

He had recounted some fragments of the story, though, as if it were a fable. He knew lots of them, and the Mazzucco fable was no less magical or mysterious. I remembered with a certain fondness the figure of Federico, the dowser from Piedmont, custodian of strange secrets of nature, and the boy Diamante, who went to America by himself when he was twelve years old, with ten dollars sewn in his underpants. I would have liked to leave home, too, when I was twelve, so despite everything I envied him. But I was embarrassed to recall the tragic figure of Antonio the stone breaker, whose children had died of hunger. I had been anorexic as a child, and every time I refused to eat, my father would ask severely, "How can you leave rice on your plate when your grandfather's brothers and sisters died of hunger?" The story of the Mazzuccos weighed on me like a wrong I had to expiate by gratefully accepting what was given me. To me, these people were remote, alien, distant. They were hard as rock, inflexible, cruel. I wasn't. I had nothing in common with them.

I was like Emma. I had her hair—wild, wiry, and willful. Her eyes. Her passion for poetry. Her emotional exuberance.

The Mazzuccos were males—laconic, controlled, authoritarian, tragically unable to communicate. People of stone.

Stone breakers.

Prince Street.

The sun was setting. The windows of the Prince Street art galleries shimmered with rosy reflections, and a warm glow spread over the street. Fleeing the stones of that village in southern Italy, Diamante had come here, to this very street.

But where, how, when?

I realized I didn't have any idea.

Panorama di Minturno

Welcome to America

UNDESIRABLE IMMIGRATION

It is gratifying to see a first-class paper like the *Times* sound a note of warning in regard to the dangerous influx of undesirable foreigners now being dumped upon us. This influx is not only undesirable but detrimental to the welfare of our country. You say most truly that it is our duty to open wide our doors to the oppressed of all the world over, and that if a person is poor and unhappy in the country of his birth he may claim our National hospitality as a matter of right. But our immigration laws are much too lax. In proof of this look into our prisons and penal institutions, and look at the daily record of murders and other crimes—all by these foreign criminals. And why is it that these savage and hot-blooded foreigners are almost always armed with stilettos or revolvers? Right here in our streets they are all armed. Not long ago I saw an Italian pushcart peddler draw a big knife on a small American boy who'd provoked him by some innocent prank. I tried for nearly half an hour to find a policeman. It was on Broadway, at noon. I found no policeman, and the would-be murderer escaped. Yes, by all means let the American people see that this foul stream of immigration is stopped, not merely restricted, the bars put up against this class of immigrant for forty or fifty years.

Samuel Conkey
(Brooklyn, April 28, 1903)

ITALIANS WARNED NOT TO EMIGRATE

While newly arrived Italians are crowding into New York by tens of thousands, some of the earlier immigrants are doing what they can to discourage further immigration. Their methods of discouragement are many. Some send home gloomy accounts of the country. Others write similar accounts for Neapolitan and Sicilian newspapers. There are poets in Mott and Mulberry Streets who sing of the hardships awaiting the newcomer in America. Even a crude form of verse has great attractions for the Italian. One of these broadsides tells: the new land is a humbug at best, where professors and laborers alike must dig, pick in hand. The poet closes his lament by urging his countrymen, especially the young, not to emigrate.

May 10, 1903

To the Editor of The New York Times
IMMIGRATION AND CRIME

Revere, Massachusetts, July 1, 1903

There can be not a particle of doubt in the mind of every intelligent American man and woman that unrestricted foreign immigration has had a great deal to do with the dangerous increase of crime in the United States. Our prisons, workhouses, and insane asylums are largely the outcome of the general trend and tendency of foreign immigration. The question affects the very foundation and existence of our republic. We are and for a great many years have been receiving into our midst the very dregs of European society, the scum of European cities, the pauper, the illiterate, the Nihilist, the Anarchist, by scores of thousands. A proportion of the industrious and only moderately ignorant find employment in our public enterprises. The residue settle down in our large cities, where the idle and shiftless add to the burden of the American tax-payer; the vicious and the criminal are welcomed by congenial comrades and the Anarchist finds fit audience for his blasphemous dribble. The results of this disposition of the foreign immigrant are most serious. The unemployed—and there are hundreds of thousands of such—soon succumb to their surroundings, and increase alarmingly the ranks of the lawbreakers. A great deal depends on immediate action. If the American people only knew more about the perils of unrestricted foreign immigration they would doubtless recognize the necessity for legislative restriction all the more clearly.

Eugene B. Willard

IMMIGRATION—A FASCINATING SUBJECT

Prescott F. Hall in his book (*Immigration*, Henry Holt & Co.) writes: "This current week a single immigrant ship debarked 2000 wretched creatures, broken in spirit, weak in body, and just able to pass the inspection admitting them to our shores as not certain to become public charges. There is nothing to equal it in history . . . We are assisting and witnessing a racial development rivaling Burbank's experiments in plant life. Never before and never again can there be such an opportunity for human stirpiculture. Yet immigration is thought dry and tedious even by those who marvel at Burbank's almost incredible results with mere plants, although we could if we would most powerfully mold and direct the sort of person a typical American should or will be . . . As travel became easier and cheaper, not love of liberty at any sacrifice, but mercenary motives animated later comers. We no longer get the people to whom we are kin, who understand us and whom we understand. We get people of alien bloods and tongues and habits. We are developing race and class and social distinctions and hatreds such as were unknown. We have un-American crimes and criminals of outlandish names."

Mr. Prescott F. Hall writes with conviction, but not with prejudice or passion. His argument is sober and reasonable.

Edward A. Bradford

Bad Boys

Vita has an infallible system for classifying the inhabitants of the boardinghouse. She separates them according to age. The old guys—all those over twenty—have mustaches, work, pay rent, address Lena with the formal *voi*, and have a wife and children in the old country far away, thoughts of which bring tears to their eyes: nostalgia will buy their return ticket. They're never home and Vita only sees them in the evening when they pick at their dinner, their plates balanced on their knees. The young tenants have either scraggly mustaches or none at all; they're often out of work because they're the first to be fired when the economy isn't thriving, and this year it's going from bad to worse. The boardinghouse is their only family. They'll see the old country again when their pockets are full of dollars—in other words, not anytime soon. The young boarders avoid the old ones and don't pay them the least attention; they keep to themselves and always hang around together. Lena is old even though she doesn't have a mustache or a family on the other side of the ocean. She's so thin she looks like an anemic adolescent, more like Agnello's daughter than his wife or servant. She has long, dull hair down to her hips and is a bit cross-eyed, but the green specks in her eyes shimmer when she laughs. And she laughs often, because Lena is not a serious woman and one day she will burn in hell with other sinners like herself. The males in the neighborhood turn their heads when she walks by because she has pointy tits and an ass shaped like a mandolin. They stick a finger in their mouth and snap it against their cheek, which means they want to stick something in her somewhere. Lena doesn't turn around. Looking straight ahead, she squeezes Vita's wrist as if to crush it and drags her around the corner. Males know more words than females, and lots more gestures. Before Lena can get her safely around the corner, Vita turns to look, and by the third time she's already learned how to make that sound. But as soon as she snaps her finger against her cheek, Lena reaches over and slaps her. When Vita complains to her father, Agnello grabs Lena by the arm and says, "So what's this all about? How dare you raise a hand against my daughter, don't you ever lay a hand on her again," and then he hits Lena twice, so hard her mouth bleeds. Lena can't tell Agnello about the finger snapping, so she doesn't defend herself—nor does she try to hit Vita again.

Lena's really not named Maddalena or even Lena, but her real name—Gwascheliyne something—is impossible to pronounce, and having a name no one can pronounce is like not having one at all. Not even she remembers exactly how to pronounce it, because she was just a little girl when her parents gave her to a family that took her to Lebanon to save her from the Russian czarists who were exterminating people of her race. But when she was twelve years old, the family sent her to America to marry a Circassian, who died straight off of consumption, and Lena found herself widowed and alone at thirteen. Lena comes from a mountain in the Caucasus that, at least according to her, rose out of the waters of the universal flood and opened up to let Noah's ark pass through. She, too, is a Circassian, a race that has brought forth poets, warriors, and slaves who live to love, drink, and defy death. The Circassian slave women's beauty is legendary; they are the most beautiful concubines of the pasha. And Lena is beautiful, too—tall, exotic, and strange. Now that she hangs around with Italians, she speaks Neapolitan with Lebanese words mixed in, and is greatly distressed to have forgotten her native tongue. Every time she hears a new language spoken, she brightens hopefully, but she's never been fortunate enough to find someone from her mountain: it seems that all the Circassians really were exterminated and she's the only one left in America. At night she dreams in her language, but during the day she can't speak it even by accident.

Lena is Agnello's servant and his wife—which, in a certain sense, is the same thing—but nobody is supposed to know about her on the other side of the ocean. That's why Agnello left Cleveland, where more people from Minturno live than in Minturno itself, and where he'd wanted to send Diamante. So Agnello came to New York. Not to Mulberry Street, though, with Desiderio Mazzucco living at number 91 and Antonio Mazzucco (not Diamante's father, however) at number 46, but to Prince Street, where the Sicilians live, and where everyone feels sorry for him because they think Dionisia died from her eye ailment and he was forced to remarry to give his orphaned children a mother. Shortly after her arrival, when the neighbors said to Vita how sad it is to grow up without a mother, and what a terrible misfortune it was that she lost hers, Vita thought they must have confused her with someone else. When she realized they really were talking about her, she said it wasn't true at all, Dionisia was plenty alive, only she was going blind in her right eye, and as soon as Agnello has his first million saved up, and he's pretty close because he's already really rich, they'll all pick up and go back to the old country. Lena will go off and become the concubine slave of some other married man, for such is the destiny of the Circassians. The neighbors stare at her wide-eyed. At first they think Vita is a brazen-faced liar. Then they think Lena is a brazen-faced whore. At any rate they take a disliking to both of them. But Diamante is not brazen-faced like Vita, and in order to be forgiven for having missed the train to Cleveland, he honors his agreement with Agnello when he writes letters home.

Dear beloved parents,

With this letter I communicate to you my perfect health and wish the same for you. I have found lodging in the house of an elderly woman who rents rooms and who was recommended to me by Uncle. It's fine, and cousin Geremia is here also. I have steady work and never miss a day. Yesterday we had a party for the landlady's seventieth birthday. We had fun and cried thinking about far away Italy.

I declare myself to be your son and I respectfully kiss your hands. Hug my little brothers for me. I think of them always and miss them very much.

Diamante had never lied to his parents before. He adores them and would risk his life for them. They are sacred, his father is Saint Joseph and his mother the Virgin Mary. But if Angela knew that Diamante was living with a woman who goes to bed with Agnello, she would make him leave and go to Cleveland—she's a good Christian and couldn't even begin to imagine certain foul things. Vita doesn't write letters home, but wonders what Dionisia would do. Maybe she would make her go back to Italy. Not a chance, Nicola warned her: Dionisia knows. She can't expect that a husband would remain faithful to a wife he hasn't seen in six years. A man is a man. Vita doesn't understand how her mother tolerates the situation, but since Dionisia wants only the best for her, if she sent her here, there must be a good reason.

At any rate, Lena's not seventy but twenty-four: they celebrated her birthday on June 15. They organized a party for her at the boarding-house and everyone got plastered for the occasion. Even Lena was tipsy, laughing and making the green in her eyes sparkle. Everyone was having fun in a way they never normally do on Prince Street. Geremia played the trombone and Lena taught Vita a Circassian dance, sacred steps to cast away evil spirits. But at a certain point Agnello, glass in hand, got shakily to his feet and told everyone to be quiet because he had an important announcement to make to his tenants. Silence. Lena stiffened and started saying, "No, no, Uncle Agnello, don't do it." But Agnello did it.

He said God was recompensing him for his many afflictions: in November an American child would be born. He said it just like that, but he actually seemed more confused and bewildered than happy, as if he'd been knocked upside the head. The old guys drank a toast with Agnello, envious of his young woman, and the boys stared at Lena, who had gone all red and then burst into tears. They were all drunk and tears are contagious. Soon everyone was crying, who knows why.

So this was the seventieth birthday party that Diamante wrote to his dear parents about. Seventy or twenty-four, it doesn't make much difference, though, because Lena is old no matter what and not as interesting as the boys. Unfortunately there are only three of them at the boardinghouse.

Rocco is seventeen and big as a tree. He likes to fight, but no one likes fighting with him. Rocco works in the subway as an excavator, but he's been out on strike for a while now. Work is stopped from Fifty-ninth Street up. Instead of working he marches, shouting to raise his pay and give him a new contract—why is it that American excavators work eight hours when we have to work ten? Agnello says Rocco has become a regular lazybones from hanging out with the wrong types in the neighborhood, and he feels bad just thinking about it because he had high hopes for that Rocco, he did. Agnello raised Rocco like a son after his father died when a one-ton steel I beam fell on his head in Ravenna, Ohio. But Vita likes it when Rocco is on strike because there are lots of cheerful young men coming and going, and Lena sings Circassian stories while she irons, songs that tell of the brave hero Lhepsch, who crosses the ocean, meets Lady Tree, makes love to her and then abandons her, just as a hero is supposed to do, walking across the wide earth in search of where the world ends. And even if Vita can't stand Lena because she's coquettish and her crooked eyes with green and vinegar-colored flecks monopolize the boys' attention, she has to admit that Lena's stories make you hold your breath—and he walks and he walks and after many adventures Lhepsch returns to the woman without ever having found the end of the world.

Coca-Cola looks like Vita, which proves he really is her brother, even if Vita doesn't remember him because Agnello came to Tufo to fetch him when she barely knew how to talk. He has pimples on his cheeks and rotten teeth; he always holds his hand in front of his mouth when he smiles so as not to unsheath his blackened cavities in your face. What's more, he stutters, and if you get too close, he'll shower you with spit. Because he's her brother they sleep in the same bed, in the little room with the window. Lena says it's not right, and wanted Vita to sleep with her, but Agnello prefers sleeping with Lena himself.

Life's already hard enough without being condemned to share your bed with your child. Besides, even if Nicola is thirteen, he has the brain of a five-year-old, a real imbecile, dumb as a doorknob. Her brother stutters, yes, but Vita doesn't think he's retarded. Under the sheets Coca-Cola tickles the soles of her feet and her knees and, in exchange for her tickling his bird, he'd like to tickle what he calls her bird's nest. He says it isn't a sin because she isn't really his sister— women console themselves when their husbands leave for America. Vita agrees with him because she'd prefer not to be Agnello's daughter. After much pondering about who the man who consoled Dionisia might be, she convinced herself it was none other than Prince Carafa, the owner of all the lands of Minturno and the richest and most powerful man in the whole province of Caserta. But Vita doesn't let Nicola tickle the spot he calls her nest, partly because Nicola's thing doesn't look at all like a bird. It's more like a carob pod, even though the pod is wrinkled and velvety while his bird is smooth, hard, and slimy. Frankly it's gross. Nicola works at the fruit store with Agnello, but sometimes he skips work and goes around demonstrating with Rocco instead. It's fun because it always ends in a brawl with the police. Their poster sticks make good clubs, and the policemen get the shits when they find themselves surrounded. Nicola is highly appreciated; Tufo kids learn how to throw rocks before they learn to talk, and with their slingshots they can hit a policeman's horse right in the eye from a hundred yards away. When Nicola gets home Agnello thrashes him with his belt, chases him with a rolling pin, and pounds him till his head is covered with lumps as big as cream puffs. Agnello says it's not like he can get any stupider than he already is. Nicola promises he will arrive punctually at work tomorrow, and has Lena put compresses on his wounds. Lena also gets the belt from Agnello because he goes crazy at the thought of the boarders dreaming of her and cuckolding him in their minds. But she puts the compresses on her wounds by herself. Lena knows a secret technique for not feeling pain, and if Vita behaves, she'll teach it to her one day.

The most serious of them all is Geremia, Diamante's cousin. He's on strike, too, just like Rocco. He also wanted those eight-hour workdays and a raise to two dollars an hour, and he even marched in the demonstrations, but they planted so many blows on him he repented. Now he's all long in the face because the contractor wants to hire blacks from the South instead of Italians. Geremia is angry with Rocco because the strike didn't go well. The American unions finked out, the Italian consulate sided with the contracting companies, and nobody defended the excavators. In the end they went back to work for ten hours a day with the same pay as before, but the ones who went on strike and called attention to themselves by shouting and protesting didn't get their contracts renewed. Rocco doesn't care, but Geremia says that a man without work is like a dog without an owner, and he has worn his feet off walking around looking for another construction job. According to Agnello, Geremia is a good boy and Diamante should be like him. Diamante tries. Geremia has grown a mustache to try and convince the team leaders he's older than his fourteen years and get more pay. He's timid and plays the trombone well. He'd like to become a musician and play in church or a band, but the only group that'll take him is the one that plays the marches at funerals.

Diamante is always tagging along behind the other boys; he's dying to be part of the group, but he's too proud to ask. Touchy and oversensitive as a monkey, he'd sooner cut his hand off than ask somebody for something. He can't find a job and has already fainted twice from hunger. The kids make fun of him, calling him Celestina because his light blue eyes make him look like a girl. But Vita doesn't think he looks like a girl. He looks like a boy, only cuter than the others. The boys don't want Vita hanging around with them, either. They say she is a female. Vita didn't realize that was a defect. True, being a female isn't a defect, only a disadvantage. The real problem is being little. Little girls aren't good for anything. Vita swears there's no difference. Things start to get interesting.

They're in the kitchen and are just about to leave, but then they stop. "Okay," Coca-Cola says, "show us, then." Vita shrieks. "No, it's not allowed! You'll shrivel up if you touch it and you go blind if you look at it." The boys laugh because it doesn't work like that in America. Vita becomes furious. Diamante looks at his bare toes. He doesn't interfere because he doesn't want to get caught in the middle. He knows how this game ends: everyone drops his pants and shows his pecker. Whoever's is smallest is a queer. And Diamante's is the smallest. But he isn't a queer, he's just younger; he'll turn twelve in November. The boys tease him anyway, saying that Celestina will soon be the cutest *gherla* on Mulberry. Well, so what if they shrivel up and go blind, so much the worse for them. Vita's certainly better than a Circassian concubine slave. She proudly lifts up her apron, revealing a pair of lacy underpants that go all the way down to her knees. Lena comes in the kitchen with a turban on her head—one of the rare occasions when she has washed her hair. "What are you doing, you miscreants?" She pulls down Vita's apron—"Look at you, you imp!"—and picks up the carpet beater and whacks Coca-Cola on the behind. He bursts out laughing, forgetting to cover his blackened teeth. Rocco grabs Lena by the shoulders, pins her arms down, and rips the towel off her head so that her hair falls over her eyes. Geremia nabs the carpet beater from her hands and they scuffle, looking like they are about to punch each other, but no one gets hurt. Vita doesn't understand anything. Diamante would like to throw himself into the fray, but he's new here and it doesn't seem proper to wrestle with the owner's woman, who is also pregnant even though she isn't showing yet. Diamante is very polite. The other kids aren't polite in the least.

The next morning, the voice of Enrico Caruso awakens her. How he managed to find the house on Prince Street is a mystery. Enrico Caruso is from Naples, but now he lives at La Scala or some other theater. Lately he's been making a name for himself in Buenos Aires and Montevideo, places near here, as well as in Rio de Janeiro, which is heaven knows where. Enrico Caruso is devastated because the stars were shining and he heard a footstep on the garden path. Vanished forever is his dream of love, the moment has fled. Enrico Caruso dies in desperation. But, glorious mystery, here he is again, alive and well and singing once more that the stars were shining and he heard a footstep on the garden path and on and on. Still half asleep, Vita drags herself down the hall. What a great honor he has paid Agnello in coming to his house. For Enrico Caruso used to be poor, just like us, his father was a mechanic and all his children died of hunger just like Antonio's. But now Enrico Caruso is famous, while Agnello has stopped playing his harmonica. "Music doesn't make money," he says, "and notes don't fill your belly." Enrico Caruso has a youthful masculine voice, velvety and full of passion. And so Vita starts hoping her real father might not be old Prince Carafa after all, but the young Enrico Caruso instead. Yes, it must be true. Enrico Caruso's singing career began at the Teatro Cimarosa in Caserta, where he certainly wouldn't have performed if he were already famous because everyone wants to flee Caserta. Dionisia went to hear him with Geremia's father, who was the cobbler in Tufo, but had he been more fortunate, had he been born in Naples or somewhere and studied at the music conservatory, he would have become a tenor as well. Enrico Caruso made a pact with the devil. He sold his soul in exchange for no one knows what exactly, but when the devil came onstage the country people jumped up and kicked the devil in the pants. So Enrico Caruso wasn't able to perform. But maybe he made love to the letter writer and nine months later Vita was born. So now he had come to Prince Street to collect his daughter. *L'ora è fuggita e muoio disperato.* Vita is moved. Halfway down the hall she stops and prepares to meet her fascinating father; she runs her fingers through her hair, curling the locks at the nape of her neck, bites her lips to make them red, and cleans her dirty face with spit. Only then does she enter the room, a smile ready on her face. The boys are seated around the table drinking coffee. But Enrico Caruso is not there.

A large horn towers over the table. Geremia turns a crank and Vita jumps when Enrico Caruso shouts in her ear. They all laugh at her shocked expression, but Diamante takes pity on her and explains that Enrico Caruso is hidden in the trumpet. Well, not exactly in the trumpet but on a black plate where an angel etches the disc with a feather from one of his wings. Under the trumpet is a wooden box— a phonograph—and from now on in this house there'll be music all day long. Lena runs her fingers over the records, looks admiringly at the trumpet, shines it with her breath, and is delighted to see her reflection in the metal. "But where did you find it?" she asks Rocco. "It must have cost a fortune." Rocco laughs and assures her it didn't cost a penny. Obviously, because they stole it last night from Raffaele Maggio's shop on Bleecker Street. They climbed through a small window in the back, lowering Coca-Cola by his feet, as he's the lightest. They made off with the box and a black disc with a speech by the King of England trapped in it, *Una furtiva lagrima, Ah, qual soave vision . . . bianca al par di neve, Questa o quella per me pari son, La donna è mobile qual piuma al vento, E lucevan le stelle* and *Ah! Vieni qui . . . no, non chiuder gli occhi vaghi,* and all the Gramophone G&T and Zonophone records. Unfortunately, Enrico Caruso only recorded enough arias for one afternoon, or else they'd have taken the whole of the previous season at La Scala as well.

"Stealing is a sin," Lena observes. "It says so on Moses' tablets, the seventh commandment." But Rocco argues that it's not a sin to steal from someone who has stolen from you. Vita can't imagine what the owner of a musical instruments store, a distinguished gentleman and the only customer who pays Agnello in cash, ever could have stolen from Rocco. Rocco explains that you only become rich by stealing from others. You don't necessarily have to steal money. You can steal all kinds of things. Somebody's time, health, youth, sentiments, dignity, his soul. Which proves that in any case ownership is a theft and work is the picklock thieves use to break into your life. Geremia was the one who wanted to steal Enrico Caruso—he's the only one of them who really understands anything about music—and swears that since Caruso is Neapolitan and sang in that stinking theater in Caserta, he really isn't very good but must have done some swindling in order to become famous. Still, Geremia doesn't care for this type of argument and tells Rocco he's becoming a delinquent. Rocco shrugs his shoulders and says if he wants to talk like that, their friendship is over. They stand up abruptly, knocking over their chairs, and scowl at each other. Both have knives in their hands. Who knows where they'd been hiding them. Everything goes all quiet, even Enrico Caruso has finally died in despair and is silent. Rocco and Geremia challenge each other with their knives, stabbing the air threateningly. One of them will certainly attack any second, but that's not how it goes. Instead they fall into each other's arms, kiss, and shake hands.

It's not true that Rocco is a delinquent. It's just that a while ago, when he was eleven, they surprised him stealing barrels of cod at the fish market. They took him to Juvenile Court, which is where they take bad boys. He ended up in school and learned to saw and plane wood. But he had no desire to become a carpenter. When he got out, Agnello took him to work with him on the railroad because he didn't want to give him the chance to ruin himself. There Rocco learned to use an ax. By the time he got fed up with trains, he was as big as an ox, and went to unload cargo at the port. There he learned how to use steel hooks. Then he went to work at the slaughterhouse, where he'd deliver the death blow, making the beasts collapse onto the automatic conveyor belts. There he learned how to use knives. And now he carries one on his belt. A knife with an inlaid wooden handle and a ten-inch-long blade. He says he uses it to shave, but Rocco doesn't even have a beard yet. His cheeks are as smooth as Diamante's.

Geremia puts his knife away, turns the crank, and Enrico Caruso starts suffering all over again. Who knows if he'll be less unhappy when he finds his daughter. Rocco leaves his knife in plain sight on the table, just to make clear who was right. Vita runs her finger along the blade; the edge is so sharp it draws blood. Rocco says it serves her right because little girls shouldn't play with knives. Vita sticks her finger in her mouth and stares at the blade with such rage that her head hurts. "I hope they cut your guts out," she snorts back, furious because Enrico Caruso isn't coming to New York after all, and even if he did, he wouldn't know where to find his lost daughter and could never make his way to Prince Street.

"Boys, I don't want to be seeing knives in this house," Lena says. Rocco grabs his knife to tuck it into his belt, but the blade breaks clean off at the handle and drops on the oilcloth. It's as soft and slippery as a dead fish. Vita is frightened and trembles for fear that Rocco will get angry. But Rocco hasn't understood: the knife's old, he thinks, he'll get himself another one. So he tells Lena not to worry because soon he won't be carrying a knife anymore. He'll carry a pistol instead. Everybody laughs. Everybody but Rocco, that is. He is serious. He points his index finger at Lena's temple and bends his thumb like a trigger. "I will have a pistol. There is nothing more beautiful, perfect, and deadly than a pistol. When you have a pistol, you're not scared of anyone." Vita is surprised because she can't imagine that Rocco, big Rocco, could possibly be afraid of anything. But no.

I am afraid of growing old.

I am afraid of becoming flaccid, resigned, vile, and obedient.

I am afraid of ending up knifed by someone like me.

Ever since he's been out of work, Rocco has taken to writing. After dinner he sits on his cot with a stack of papers on his knees. He puts the pencil in his mouth and thinks. He writes something and then, not convinced, crosses it out, balls up the paper, and starts again. Rocco attended school here, so he knows how to read and write American, but now he wants to write Italian. Only he gets confused and doesn't remember the names of things. "Celestina?" he asks one evening, grabbing him by his suspenders. Diamante's on his way out the door—he has to be at the factory exit by midnight to sell newspapers. "How do you spell *abbruscia*?" "What?" "Burn, *abbruciare*." "It's *bruciare*," Diamante says. "In Italian you say *bruciare*. B-r-u-c-i-a-r-e." "Only one *b*?" Rocco asks. He's rather surprised and is convinced Celestina is wrong. *Abbrusciare*.

"Trust him!" Vita yells. "Diamante's first in his class. The teacher wanted to send him to seminary to make him a priest!" "Not a chance," Diamante protests. "I wouldn't be caught dead being no priest. Priests wear dresses." "Were you the best in your class or not?" Rocco asks, pulling on his suspenders. "Yes," Diamante replies proudly. "The best of fifty students. I won the medal. But I quit after third grade. I'm the oldest in my family and have to take care of my brothers." Rocco doesn't have brothers, and even if he did, he certainly wouldn't work to take care of them. Everyone for himself, that's what he's learned in America. At school they explained to him that Italians are crucified on their families, just like Christ on the cross, which is what keeps them from progressing. He wants to progress, so he doesn't have a family. Rocco studies Diamante's face. What a strange kid. Sometimes he seems as wise as an adult, other times clever as an elf, and a fierce determination blazes in his childish blue eyes. Rocco recognizes that glow; he sees it in the mirror every morning when he washes his face. He likes Diamante but doesn't trust him. Ever since he and Vita arrived, everything in this house has gone topsy-turvy. One of them must have been sent by the devil, the other by an angel. But something tells him that it's not Diamante who is the devil's messenger.

"Are you good at writing letters in nice handwriting?" he decides to ask. "Sure," Diamante answers, flattered by the attention. Vita shouts that Diamante's handwriting is so perfect that back in Tufo he helped Dionisia write letters, sitting at her feet on the San Leonardo Church steps on Sundays. He'd scrape together a few pennies that way, but never spent them: he'd run and give them to his father instead. They go sit next to each other on the dark stairs: Rocco big and tall as a mountain, with a fist tattooed on his shoulder and rings in his ears like a pirate, and Diamante so tiny he looks like a kindergartner. Vita crouches behind them and peers over their shoulders. Rocco has ripped a piece of graph paper from Agnello's credit book.

The letter goes like this:

> If you don't give five hundred dollars to the Man with the Red Hand-
> kerchief you will meet between Fourteenth Street and Third Avenue
> next Monday at eleven o'clock at night your store will be burned.
>
> You think I'm fooling, but I am serious. You have three days, and
> then the end will come for you.
>
> Desperado

Diamante lowers his head over the page and writes. His eyebrows arch in perplexity, his face inquisitive. It seems a very poor joke, a stupid act of bravado. *You think I'm fooling, but I am serious.* But if it's not bravado, then it's a crime. His hand goes stiff, as if he had a cramp. He can barely speak. "Who is the Man with the Red Handkerchief? Who's Desperado?"

Rocco laughs and tucks the paper in his shirt. "An idiot. Or else a great criminal. I'll let you know on Monday." Diamante mumbles he has to go, he's late, he'll lose his job. Rocco holds him by the suspenders he had lent him. "Let me go," Diamante protests. "Let me go." Rocco's smile frightens him.

"Rocco," Vita asks him the next day, "are you with the Black Hand?" Rocco pretends not to hear her. He's kneeling between the chicken cages, his finger in a bottle of milk. He tries sticking his finger in the mouth of a black cat, a stray he found on Canal Street the night before. Someone had put it in a flask and tried setting it on fire. The cat looks as if it had been skinned alive. All its fur is falling out, and there are hairs everywhere. Only a patch under its tail is left. So much the better, because black cats bring bad luck. Vita kneels down, too. Rocco has managed to get his finger in its mouth, and the cat is sucking contentedly. "Rocco, are you with the Black Hand?" She yanks his finger away.

Rocco smiles as he tucks under his collar the red handkerchief he always wears around his neck. "What a little baby you are, Vita."

The Black Hand doesn't exist.

When Diamante fainted from hunger, Geremia sent him to look for work as a paperboy. If little Nino, who isn't even five years old, can do it, so can he. During his very first interview he showed he has all the right qualities: agility, self-assurance, intelligence. Not even his nationality turned out to be a disadvantage: when it comes to making money, the Italian combines the quickness of the Irish with the tenacity of the Jew. They put him in the same group as Nino, a homely, filthy little creature with a sickly air, sores on his feet, and the imploring eyes of a bastard. There are six of them in the group—the oldest isn't even thirteen. At five in the morning they're already stationed on Broadway with stacks of newspapers under their arms, and at midnight they're still peddling them outside the factory gates. They sell the *Araldo Italiano*—the Italian Herald—a colonial newspaper with offices at 243 Canal Street. It is unrewarding work. You walk a lot, make yourself hoarse yelling, and earn very little. Even though he gets up before dawn and returns home in the middle of the night, Diamante can't even scrape together five dollars a week. You have to molest passersby, follow them, tug at their sleeves, chase after them, beg them, exasperate them, practically threaten them. Nothing. It's like trying to foist off a dead dog.

The fact is that most passersby don't know how to read. Diamante's group is authorized to peddle between Broadway and Canal, but they're all uncouth illiterates down there, as Diamante has tried in vain to explain to the newsagent, a dapper northern Italian who complains that southern Italians are lazy. Not only do they not read the *Araldo Italiano*, they don't read anything. You try selling a painting to a blind man! You have to go above Houston to find somebody who knows the alphabet. And if you find one, he doesn't read Italian. And he already has a newspaper. *The New York Times*, the *Globe*, the *Call*, the *Post*, the *Journal*, the *Tribune*, the *Herald*, or the *New York World*, which even has funnies. Americans certainly don't need their little leaflet, barely eight pages, that only talks about Italians; as for American news, the *Araldo* doesn't say anything more than what's already in their papers, and is less interesting. Besides, it's not like the people above Houston jump for joy at the sight of them. Above Houston signs on doors say NO DOGS NIGGERS ITALIANS NEED APPLY. And on the bar windows NO DOGS NIGGERS ITALIANS. Diamante hears all sorts of insults and jabs, so he knows what that word that sounds like *guappo*, or bully, means now. They're saying *wop*, and it means Italian. And *Italian* is an insult—even though at school in Tufo they fooled him, telling him that Italy is the cradle of civilization and that Marco Polo Cristoforo Colombo Michelangelo Giuseppe Verdi and Giuseppe Garibaldi were Italians. The other insult he hears a lot is *dago*, which means the same thing. If you say *dago* to somebody, it's like you're saying he's lower than a horse with diarrhea. And if somebody says it to you, your blood boils, but if you don't have a knife—and Diamante doesn't—you just have to swallow the insult. If you insist on hanging out in front of their shop windows, the blond-haired people will sing a little ditty behind your back that sounds something like *guini guini goon*. *Goon* means gorilla. And the gorilla is the stupidest animal in the world. If somebody calls you *goon*, your mind clouds over and you really do feel like a gorilla set loose in a church. And then there's the most difficult word of all, *grinoni*, or greenhorn, which Diamante succeeds in deciphering only after weeks on the streets. It means rookie, means you can't say even one word in American. So it's really like saying stupid, fool, lout, uncouth. When they called him greenhorn, he had to swallow the insult because he didn't have a knife. After that, he stopped looking down on the uncouth idiots who don't know how to read the *Araldo Italiano*. Here, even he, the best in his class, is illiterate. Not even he knows how to read *The New York Times*. Such is the punishment for his arrogance. He was so proud when, among all the adults disembarking from the *Republic*, he was the only one who knew how to sign his name on his entry card to America. But pride is the worst of sins. So now he finds himself envying the blond-haired people who arrive at the elevated platform with a newspaper under their arm that they read while waiting for the train. They know things he'll never know, and when they look at him—bare feet, sagging suspenders, dark curly hair—they think greenhorn, and they are right. He envies them and wants to be like them. But envy, too, is a mortal sin.

They carry their unsold copies of the *Araldo Italiano* back to the base. The newsagent curses the ignorance of Italians who don't even read the Bible. So as not to throw the copies away, however, he resells them at half price to Diamante, who roams about in the middle of the night trying to get rid of them. Nino, a waif who has lived on the street since he was born, taught him a trick: hide the copies in a manhole or drain, keeping only one in your hand, and insist to the passersby that they buy the very last copy, please. And amazingly it works, especially when the passerby is in the company of a woman. Women have bigger hearts, of course, and even if it's only for an instant, they'll take pity on an unknown lout like you. In a city of women, nobody would be truly poor. But Diamante keeps the last copy for himself.

At night, he perches on the roof at Prince Street and devours those baffling words about the world he lives in, while Vita pesters him impatiently, hungry for news of his day, which is always more eventful than hers. Diamante hasn't figured out yet where the well-off people of Woptown or Dagoland are—that city within a city between Houston and Worth Streets, between Broadway and the Bowery, crammed full of 250,000 pieces of shit, that is to say, southern Italians. All those people who can afford to eat at the Gardens of Torino restaurant on Broome Street, buy themselves some Marsala, just arrived from Palermo, at Ahrens & Co., go to the Teatro Garibaldi or the Opera, have their horoscope read by Ida Alfieri on Navy Street, pay for an outing to Tompkins Park, or actually purchase a very expensive phonograph and Caruso records. In order to find out, he must forget that old saying in his village: "What you don't know doesn't exist." It does exist, you just have to learn to look for it.

The other kids taught him where to find the cadavers that fill the pages of the newspaper. They took him to see them because it's a frightening and horrendous spectacle that doesn't cost a cent. The bodies resurface in the Hudson and Harlem Rivers when the feet, to which the assassins attach the ballast, decompose and separate from the skeleton. They rise up in the backwaters of Jamaica Bay where Rocco and Coca-Cola go fishing, and in the canals where Geremia digs the channel for the new sewer. Or they're an oily clot of cinders in a shop devoured by flames. At night the district swarms with the lights of fires, as if there were a thousand Men with Red Handkerchiefs ready to lay waste to the world. The air tastes of wood and ash. The firemen arrive with carts, pumps, sirens, and ladders, but always too late. Diamante had only one explanation for all this. The Black Hand. A sophisticated and widespread organization, diabolical and ingenious, that terrorizes and tyrannizes Dagoland. Agnello didn't report them. But the *Araldo* derides the Black Hand men, who are neither sophisticated nor ingenious and don't even know how to spell, and praises the doctors and shopkeepers who report them to the police. Diamante still doesn't know who's telling the truth. But the newspaper never speaks of arrests.

At any rate, the *Araldo* only sells well on crime days. Luckily, they're abundant in America. In New York alone there's at least one a day. Every day in cities he's never heard of—places like Santa Fe, Wilmington, Scottsborough, Evansville—a Negro is whipped with barbed wire, hung from a tree, lynched by a festive crowd. Every day in far-off Wyoming the bandits assault and kill some poor traveler. Every day thousands of Jews are exterminated in Poland and Bessarabia. But there's no need to look so far abroad; here in the city, throngs of women are strangled, girls raped and killed by groups that abduct them while they wait for the omnibus after work; eleven-year-olds stab the boarder who deflowered them; men just off the boat are found dead at the port, their ten dollars for entering America missing, or killed while waiting to be repatriated, their savings vanished. Drunks roasted for a watch, men sliced up or shot to pieces in the middle of the street or in Mulberry Park while they enjoy the fresh air with their families on a Sunday evening. The Black Hand—which had so terrorized Diamante his first days in America—now means nothing more than a good day of sales and a Saturday afternoon with Vita at the puppet theater.

By dint of jumping on and off moving carts, and slipping into barbershops, brothels, and basements where tough guys bet on the horses, Celestina gradually grows rather insolent. Now he runs along the elevated train platforms with a bundle of newspapers under his arm. The forces of law and order cannot catch him there, where he's more annoying than a mosquito to his clients. He has learned to assault workers leaving their offices, and to enjoy the impotent hatred and terror his shameless insistence provokes in the bourgeois. To challenge the hoboes jumping freight trains at the depot, and to throw stones at the Irish Murphys, always aiming at the head where it hurts the most. Wearing a cotton beret, droopy suspenders, and a mischievous smile, he ducks into taverns and greasy spoons, crying, "Grisly American Crimes, Electric Chair for the Assassin, Secrets of the Executioner, The Black Hand's Latest Heinous Crime . . . !" He has learned to exaggerate the facts, to aggrandize the story in order to sell. Otherwise no one wants the paper. A dead woman is inevitably "Butchered" and "Mutilated." A train derailing becomes "A Railroad Disaster." A cold, and "The Queen of Italy Is Dying!" He yells, "Murder, Cadavers, Mutilations!" in a booming voice. They are magic words. Come here, boy, give me a copy. And since lots of people don't know how to read, on the way home he often sits in a tavern and recites the news to exhausted workers eager for distraction. Agnello makes him read the homicide news aloud. The more gruesome the better. Or maybe he's just glad it isn't him, that dead body with his balls stuffed in his mouth they found in an oil drum on the subway construction site. Agnello doesn't pay him for reading, but the workers offer him a beer. Or at least what the bartender calls beer—a sour yellow slop that tastes like rancid piss. Diamante can't bear to swallow it, and Nino begs him for his mug. Nino follows Diamante everywhere because he's the only newspaper boy who doesn't try to make dogs bite him during the dull moments when there's no work and the only way to kill time is to set the rabid strays on him. Nino hobbles behind Diamante into the taverns and sometimes even to his house. "Gimme your beer, gimme your beer." Diamante refuses because Nino is too small, but the workers pass him the last swig and bet a few cents on whether he can put his mouth to the tap and drain the whole keg. They roar with laughter when Nino falls down drunk on the floor. But Diamante doesn't think it's funny. His insides twist in knots.

In the summer, the temperatures soar so that walking on the sunbaked streets is like the ascent to Calvary and people drop like flies in the heat—in just one day there are twenty-one deaths. That's when their rivals start popping up. They sell the most important Italian-language newspaper in the city, *Il Progresso italo-americano*. The *Araldo* people hate that paper because it's reactionary, licks the ass of the powerful, and sided with the bosses against the striking subway excavators. It never mentions the Black Hand because admitting its existence would defame the good name of the Italian community. According to them, the Black Hand is an invention of the Americans—a publicity gimmick that appeals to bankers, artists, and people who want to think they've made it. But the two groups work the same area at the same time, trying to unload the same news on the same riotous public. On the first day, insults and threats fly. On the second day, bits of broken glass. On the third, pieces of track.

On the twentieth of July, Diamante finds one of the rivals waiting for him on the roof. It's Rusty's big brother, Nello, squat and slick as an olive. "Go dump your trash somewhere else," he threatens. "The *Araldo* isn't trash," Diamante snaps back. Even though he hasn't ever stepped foot in the office, he feels compelled to defend his newspaper. He likes reading it because it's clearly written and helps him understand things, so when he passes in front of 243 Canal Street, he is overwhelmed with respect and gratitude. The *Araldo* journalists say they write for the workers. Diamante hadn't thought someone could write for workers before. "I'm warning you," Nello insists, flashing the tip of a screwdriver. "You go somewhere else," Diamante responds. He doesn't want to challenge Nello and hasn't the slightest intention of doing so. But he doesn't want to lose his job. The news of the world, his new city, the Italian language, all the words and ideas he's discovering and knew nothing about, the dollars he sends to his father, Saturdays with Vita—these are the first satisfactions he has managed to snatch from America. He's not about to give all this up for fear of a screwdriver. "I'm not afraid," he says to Nello, arching his eyebrows to show he's tough. The truth is, he can't allow himself to be afraid.

All the tenants on the roof witness the scene. Some are from Basilicata, others from Campania, and most are from Sicily, so they all understand what's happening, and nobody raises a finger when Nello's screwdriver traces a cross on Diamante's forehead. The men sitting on the side of the roof facing the street keep on playing cards. The toddlers keep running around, stumbling and drooling—there are so many of them that everyone's hoping a cholera epidemic will eliminate at least a few. The women, gathered on the courtyard side, where there's a revolting, rotting stench, continue to prepare vegetables and squabble, accusing each other of the most trivial crimes, such as stinking up the building. They are specious arguments, sparked by the heat, and the fact there's not enough water for everyone. The only one who seems to have realized Diamante's ugly predicament is Lena, who invites him to come and sit next to her. No one fights with Lena because no one speaks to her. She and Vita keep to the filthiest corner of the roof, where not even a furtive puff of wind reaches. They sit facing each other, all sweaty, their dresses rolled up to their thighs. Lena's legs are long, white, and thin. Vita's are rounded and tanned. Lena is a woman—and desirable. Vita is a child. Ever since the men on the roof learned that Lena is a concubine slave, they all look at her hungrily. Only Diamante looks at Vita, asking himself how long it'll take for her to grow up, and if he'll still be in America when it happens. Because Antonio sent him here to grow up, to get to know the world, earn some money, and become strong, but certainly not to stay. It's only a question of time. Some grab their fortune in three years, others in ten. Vita hasn't noticed anything; she's spying on the baker's daughters playing hopscotch, tossing the chalk in the squares and hopping until they collapse from exhaustion, heat, and boredom. They never invite her to play, and the burning disappointment on Vita's face tells Diamante that many years must pass—and on the day she scorns those games, he'll be long gone.

Diamante's forehead burns where the screwdriver scratched him, but he won't go sit with the females. The boys are throwing dice and talking of whores and cunts. The cunts are hairy and the dice are loaded. Diamante doesn't throw because he doesn't want to lose his earnings. Nino—nobody knows where he really lives, but he always manages to sneak onto the roof—warns him to be careful, next time Nello'll cut up his gut. "Why doesn't he cut you up?" Diamante asks, suspicious. Nino sadly rolls his snot into a ball. He thinks a bit before responding. "Cuz I give him half of what I earn." Coca-Cola, conciliatory, suggests Diamante give him half, too. "No, I earn that money and it's mine." Rocco nods, pleased. Celestina is showing promise. He doesn't want to bow his head. So Rocco explains he'll have to cut Nello's gut and defend his job. "I don't cut up nobody," Diamante bristles. Geremia sighs. "You'll see then, they won't let you sell newspapers anymore. You'll have to find another job."

Which is exactly what happens. During the rainiest days of September, when the sky is black as soot and the runoff mixed with rainwater transforms courtyards into swimming pools, Diamante finds himself walking the muddy streets without his bundle of newspapers under his arm.

But this takes place only after the baby's funeral. For a while longer Diamante spends his nights on the roof reading the paper. When everyone else is asleep, Rocco comes and sits next to him, commandeers the *Araldo*, and sticks a pad of paper and pen in his hand. A real fountain pen with a silver nib. Stolen, naturally. Rocco smokes cigarette after cigarette while Diamante, sleepy and dead tired, takes a dictation exam.

Dictation Number One
I beg you to send the money we need. I am sorry to bother you, but I too have the right to live. Do not force me to dirty my hands. But if you do force me, I will drink your blood and that of your children.

Desperado

Dictation Number Two

My patience has run out. This is the last warning. Bring the money to the Man with the Red Handkerchief you will meet on the Brooklyn Bridge at midnight tomorrow, or else your house will be burned down. Your money or your life.

Desperado

Dictation Number Three

Bring $1,500 to the Man with the Red Handkerchief. If you miss the appointment your store will burn along with everything in it. We will burn everything.

Desperado

Conjugations of the verb *to burn.*

You burn, he burns, they burn.

The store will burn. We will burn in hell.

Rocco doesn't believe in God, but he believes in the devil.

Rocco says that we've already been through hell.

We will not burn. But you will burn.

The rich will knock at the gates of Paradise and will find them closed. They will burn. Their dollars will burn. They all will burn.

So why do you want to become rich?

Because I am afraid of growing old.

We will burn everything. Your cities, your banks, your streets, your schools, your offices, your wagons, your boats, your families, your tombs, your names.

The flames will rise up to the heavens and the smoke will blind you. You will flee and we will follow you, we'll pursue you wherever you go, until there's nothing left for you to leave behind.

Tremble, for we will take your place.

Can I ask you a question?

If you don't ask questions, nobody will ask them of you, Celestina.

Has anyone ever brought you the money, Man with the Red Handkerchief?

No. Nobody has ever showed at the appointment with the Man

with the Red Handkerchief. They sent the police once. They're not afraid of Desperado.

They're afraid of the Black Hand.

The Black Hand doesn't exist.

Have you ever really set anything on fire? Are you the one who sets the fires?

No. Not even the Man with the Red Handkerchief can make a bonfire by himself.

Why did they try to stick a knife in your back?

Because I wear the red handkerchief.

What do they want?

Desperado dead.

Why?

Because he brings the police into the neighborhood.

Does Desperado die?

He's already dead, Diamante.

Who killed him?

The Black Hand.

But if the Black Hand doesn't exist . . . ?

Dictation Number Thirteen

Dear Sir,

You have declared to the police that you are not afraid of us, and you do well as not a hair on your head will be harmed. Naturally, only if you bring us that money to the place we told you. If you do not, we will be forced to kill your wife. It's a real shame because we thought you loved her. We believed you were a man of honor, that for you family came before everything else, after God. Family is very important. But if money is more important to you, then act according to your conscience. We have nothing more to say to you.

                                                    The Black Hand

The American Brother

The American brother is born dead or dies being born prematurely. On the evening of August 23, the boarders are up on the roof gasping for air and the kids are down in the street. Lena is alone in the apartment. After the umpteenth "Get outta here before I grab you by the hair on your head, you foulmouthed thing, you're nothing but a rotten whore," Lena, who's not the type to pick a fight with a bunch of sweaty old crones, stopped going up to the roof. She passes the time at home now, thinking about her mountains and playing music loudly so that those who don't have a phonograph and never will—in other words, just about everyone—turn green with envy. Vita doesn't take advantage of her absence to make friends with the baker's daughters, though. She has withdrawn from the puerile games of children her age, who never invited her to play anyway, and has invented her own, more exciting ones. All alone, crouched among the rabbit cages, she strikes matches stolen from the kitchen against the rough soles of her boots and throws them in a pail coated with pure alcohol. The flames that flare up are not ordinary yellow or red or orange but an ineffable blue, deep and dense like the sky just before sunrise. The tenement's few windows give onto the courtyard. All of them are wide open, and from them rise kitchen fumes, husbands' curses, children's shrieks, the phonograph music, and the piercing cries of a woman.

Since the creature should be born more than three months from now and is only a bit bigger than a ball of wool, since the baker is beating his son, there's a brawl down in the street, and the neighborhood kids are hanging like baboons on the fire escape and egging both sides on, nobody realizes what's happening in Agnello's apartment. Mammoth Rocco is heroically defending himself against four hit men, dishing out more than he's taking. His resistance is impressive; he punches and kicks, and just when he seems on the point of capitulating, he hoists a heavy beam. It must weigh a ton, but he wields it as if it were a fountain pen, and the four men, already all bruised and beaten, disappear into the alley. Everybody will talk about it for weeks, especially as the hit men were the Bongiorno brothers, and nobody had ever seen a beam landed on the heads of the Bongiorno brothers before. In a sense this street belongs to them as much as if they'd purchased it.

When Rocco enters the house at midnight and goes to rinse his bloody nose in the washbasin, he doesn't notice right away that something is floating on the surface of the water. At first he thinks his nose has fallen off and landed in the basin, so he fingers it a bit before he's convinced that it's still where it should be, albeit bruised and throbbing. He lights the gas lamp but looks away too late. Rocco will never be able to forget the unnameable red thing floating in the dark water. He vomits right there on the floor and then pulls the curtain aside; Lena is naked, curled up in a ball on the big bed. Her hands, mouth, hair—and all the rest—are smeared with blood. She is moaning weakly, almost like a cat. Rocco cups his hand over his bloody nose and runs down the stairs to call Agnello, the inopportunely admiring neighborhood kids at his heels. But by now it's too late for the American brother.

A whole bevy of women crowd around Lena and her prematurely rent womb—the same heartless fat women who were spitting pumpkin seeds at her this morning—and apply a frenzy of bandages, gauze, and towels, one after the other, in a vain attempt to stop the hemorrhaging. Rocco, who worked at the slaughterhouse on Forty-second Street, a place of ferocious butchering and the most nauseating mess, cannot help but think that tonight the boardinghouse kitchen resembles the storeroom where he and his co-workers used to extract the innards and empty out the carcasses. Who knows if the body of a woman is filled with the same disgusting organs as a cow, the same intestines and sacs of bitterest bile. Who knows if he'll ever be able to look at Lena again. The boarders have already withdrawn to the roof, for this is no concern of theirs, while the kids gather on the stairs—this concerns them all too much. Coca-Cola has advised Vita to stay behind the curtain with the others and not interfere, but of course she doesn't pay any attention and elbows her way in among the women. So she sees.

Lena's nightgown is rolled up over her belly, her legs wide apart. A neighbor woman has stuck a rubber tube in her, the same one Lena uses to water the basil. She blows into the tube, inhales, and then places the end in a pail. The tube turns red and the pail starts to fill. Lena's face is expressionless, her gaze fixed on the ceiling, as if all this had nothing to do with her. "Work with me, pretty, push it out," the fat woman says, exasperated. "If it stays inside, you'll get infected and die." Vita doesn't move; she clings to the curtain and swallows hard. The pail spills over with a dense, sticky liquid that attracts petulant August flies. But what else does Lena have to push out if the American brother's already dead? Vita stares at the pail, the tube, Lena's stained legs, the blood on the mattress, the open wound. Okay, the American brother is dead, and now Lena has to die, too. If Lena dies, Agnello will go back to Dionisia, who can't come to America because of her eye ailment. Vita thinks of her mother every evening and morning, every minute. So much so that it seems as if she is living two lives, dwelling in two worlds at the same time—here with Lena, Diamante, and the kids in the upside-down world of Prince Street, a place as strange as the moon, and also with Dionisia in the familiar streets of Tufo. Lena bites her lip, moans, trembles, writhes, she's taking an eternity to die. Vita closes her eyes. God has heard her, God is infinitely good.

In the stifling shadows on the stairs, the kids silently pass around a butt. Diamante doesn't understand why they seem so dismayed all of a sudden. He's always had the impression that none of them cared a thing about Lena, and the rare times they talked about her, the conversation would inevitably lead to some obscene joke. He would never allow himself to offend Uncle Agnello's woman, the mistress of the house who washes his underwear and cooks him macaroni. Not to mention the olives and slices of bread he finds under his pillow. Even though Lena is a lost soul, he has nothing against her. He continues to write home that he gets on well with his seventy-year-old landlady, and now he's bogged down in a quagmire of lies. He's sorry to lie to his dear, beloved parents, but he doesn't want to end up in Cleveland because of Lena, either. It bothers him that the kids talk about her that way, but maybe those obscenities are really compliments, and their rough, almost brutal indifference is the only way they know to fall in love with a woman. Just when it seems as if they'll have to stay there all night without moving, Rocco rouses himself from his torpor and becomes all serious. "Agnello, what are we gonna do with the thing?"

Baptism is expensive and a funeral costs even more. The thing never breathed, so you can't really even say it was born. When the midwives perform abortions, they don't bury them, but simply throw them away. Agnello's in no mind to think about it. He's just received his second blackmail letter. He merely begs the neighbors to sew up his woman again. "Don't let her die," he pleads over and over again, wiping the sweat that's dripping in his eyes. He stays next to Lena all night long. Sometimes she seems conscious, at other times far away, but always alien, indifferent to the tragedy that has befallen her. He tries to console her, telling her they'll have another baby, another child, she's young and he feels as strong as a bull, he's barely forty, after all. Words, little crumbs, sweet as a lullaby. In truth he has no intention of having a child, just as he didn't before, and he'll be more careful next time. But he was careful this time as well, and can't understand how it happened. It'll have to disappear, and in the most Christian way possible. God will understand. Coca-Cola maintains the task is his, and he would like to take care of it in secret. But the kids on Prince Street don't have secrets. Like knights of old, they're united, together against the world. Geremia gets the shovel, Coca-Cola the torch, and Rocco will choose the place; he'll go first and lead the way, just as it should be. Diamante's new, so he's not really involved, but there's a task for him as well. He will carry the Gospel and read the right words for times like this, with the same diligence he applies to reading the crime news in the taverns. Even Vita has something to do. She has to sew the thing up in one of the good embroidered napkins.

The four boys hover contritely around the table while she sucks on the thread and then pokes it through the invisible eye of the needle. Now that the thing is all clean and smooth, it looks like a doll in the gaslight. Except that it's smaller than a hand. Rocco still sees it red and floating, and feels like vomiting again. Diamante notes that Rocco's handsome nose has swollen up like a cucumber; maybe those bastards broke it. But Rocco'll get his revenge; he's not one to let an insult go unanswered. Did the Black Hand hit men come to punish him because he pretends he's one of them? Vita is slow and unsure, her hand trembles, and the stitching runs irregularly along the hem of the napkin. "I want to come with you," she informs them as Rocco places the napkin in a box and ties it closed with string. The answer is cut and dried: absolutely not.

No one says a word along the way. Rocco holds the box to his chest as if bearing a gift. They head down toward the Bowery in single file, as if in procession. First comes Rocco, big, monumental Rocco with his nose still bleeding, then Geremia, sucking on his scraggly mustache, and Coca-Cola, chomping so intently on his chewing gum that his jaw hurts. Diamante brings up the rear; small, nimble, and anxious, he's convinced some catastrophe will occur tonight. Everyone is outside on this steamy August night. Someone greets them, but they don't respond. They are on a mission. They cross street after street after street, heading toward the tip of the island. The farther downtown they go, the more squalid, run-down, and chaotic the city becomes. It doesn't take much to realize that the abacus and not the alphabet is the key to this city—maybe the entire country. Streets don't have names here, but numbers. So do the public carriages, city blocks, buildings, and horse-drawn trolleys. It's easy: the bigger the street number, the more the neighborhood improves, and the people who live there are successful in life. The smaller the number, the less they count, and the people who live on streets with low numbers are worth nothing. We're on the very bottom rung: we live on the streets below zero.

Near the river the city becomes a labyrinth of factories and warehouses. The traffic thins out and the streetlamps are all dark, shattered by kids throwing rocks. Rocco has the East River in mind, so they head toward the docks near the dump. Rocco had brought along the kerosene bottle and matches, and snatched a bouquet of withered flowers from the first altar along the way. His idea was to set the flaming box on the surface of the water. Many years ago Rocco had discovered in a children's book that the Indians push their dead out onto the water, light them on fire with a torch, scatter flower petals, and sing. As the dead burn on this purifying pyre, the current carries them off and reunites them with the great spirit. It seemed a very poetic ceremony when he read it. But in New York the river is a stinking sewer, with bottles, dead rats, turds, and watermelon rinds bobbing on the current. The boys don't want to throw the American brother in there with all that trash.

"Why don't we bury him at the subway construction site?" Geremia suggests. He's been eager to return to the site where he was no longer wanted. He had excavated tons of earth along the line that would someday cross the entire city, gliding below the surface like a vein beneath the skin. Soon the trains will start running. They'll tile the station walls, and it'll be as white as a hospital. It'll never be a beautiful place and it's not outside, but lots of people will pass there; the baby will never be alone. "I ag-g-gree," stammers Coca-Cola. "Me, too," says Diamante. But Rocco wants to be cremated when he dies: he's too afraid of waking up in the dark. When the sheet clings to his face in the night, he wakes with a start, convinced he's dead. "No, let's head back toward the station. I've got a better idea."

Everything in this city seems as if it were being demolished—or built. As after a flood or an earthquake. Wherever you look you see scaffolding, iron skeletons thirty stories high, cranes, workbenches, catwalks, tunnels, holes, chasms a hundred feet deep that by day echo with thuds, pickaxes, and muffled voices, and by night with the shrill music of the wind playing against iron pipes and sheet metal. Everything is falling apart and everything is new. There are hundred-year-old houses and houses that sprang up yesterday, still uninhabited. Everything is being built in this city—railroads, hotels, banks, churches. On Seventh Avenue, between Forty-second and Forty-third, the New York Times skyscraper is going up. It will be the most amazing tall building in the city, 375 feet—the second tallest after the Park Row Building. Taller than the Manhattan Life Insurance Building, which is only 348 feet, taller than the Pulitzer, at 309, taller than the Flatiron, less than 300, and much taller than Trinity Church, which stops at 296 feet. "We'll take him up to the top floor. The American brother will look out over the city and spit on it." It's a grandiose idea and is immediately approved by all.

Enthusiasm puts wings on their feet. They run the whole length of Seventh Avenue. As fast as they can. Too bad they never find themselves in this part of town, or they'd know that the building is almost finished. The offices are scheduled to open in April of next year. The elevators have already been installed; only the glass for the windows is missing. The skyscraper has a square tower with a flagpole on top. But you have to really crane your neck to see it, and nearly lose your balance. Your head spins. The tower isn't finished yet, and scaffolding envelops it like an iron guardian. The stairs climb right up into the heavens; they look wobbly, unsteady, propped up in the air like a spider's web. "We'll kill ourselves," Geremia says. "Let's kill ourselves then," Rocco responds. The statement doesn't even cause a shiver. Only the old are afraid to die.

One after the other they climb over the construction-site fence. They've already trespassed at dozens of building sites to steal planks, coal, steaks, or boxes of fish, so they know how to avoid the barbed wire. Diamante, eager to shed once and for all his nickname Celestina, is the first to pull himself up onto the fence, the first to jump down into the dust. So much for *The New York Times*, which rebuffs him with pages carpeted in unknown words. The guards are playing cards in the porter's office, and even though they keep the door open for a little air, they don't notice a thing when four boys, light and inconsistent as shadows, bound up the stairs that connect the various layers of scaffolding, and climb the metal rungs. They've reached the third-floor level and Diamante is leaning out so he can peer into the window frames, imagining he sees the crime reporters at their desks in shirt sleeves with a pencil behind their ear, when a dog barks menacingly. Geremia catches Rocco's attention. "What can we do? We can't leave her there." Vita is perfectly visible astride the six-foot-high wire fence, illuminated by the construction-site lamps. Her long red skirt is caught on the barbed wire and she can't jump down or move. Christ. A hoarse order for that damn dog to be quiet issues from the porter's office. Vita shakes the fence. In vain. The barbed wire has coiled itself around her leg, ripped the cloth, and imprisoned her foot.

The boys don't move. They lean out into the void. What a mess. If they're found here, in the most expensive building in the city, at this hour, with the box and what's inside it, they'll be sent to Juvenile Court for sure. And it's all Vita's fault. Rocco's already been to the school where the Juvenile Court sends bad boys from the neighborhood, and has no desire to go back. He passes Diamante the box and climbs down. It's so light! As if it were empty. Maybe it really is, maybe there's nothing at all inside. How little a thing not born weighs. With his swinging stride and unhurried pace, Rocco crosses the open space. His arms dangle at his sides. He's so big he looks like a bear standing on his hind legs. When he sets her on the ground, Vita is in her underwear; what remains of her skirt is ensnared on the fence like a flag. Diamante thinks the guards will see it and they'll be nabbed. Deep down, he doesn't really care, though. He has never climbed a skyscraper before and wants to keep going. Even if it's only the scaffolding. The boys have never seen a female in underpants before because they've always taken women in a hurry, and always in the dark, so there wasn't much opportunity for studying undergarments. Now the lace glimmering in the shadows distracts them as they climb up the rungs. So much the better. Don't turn around. Don't look down. The city would seem unreal, painted on the bottom of a box, the distances would be deceiving, the sky would seem deceptively closer. They climb and climb and ask themselves what lies beneath that diaphanous screen of cloth.

Lena's New Testament is all torn, faded, and stained with sauce. Most of the pages are missing. There aren't any books in the house, and when the boarders have an urgent need to go, it's the best thing for wiping themselves. Lena has never noticed because she doesn't know how to read and is satisfied to keep the New Testament under her pillow. One page follows another, and by now all that remains is the prologue to the Gospel According to Saint John, which is not very appropriate for a baby's funeral. If you can call this a funeral, that is, and the red thing a baby rather than a mistake or a sin. "The same came for a witness, to bear witness of the Light," Diamante reads in a most solemn intonation, "that all might see—no, sorry, believe, it's hard to read—that all through him might believe. He was in the world, and the world knew him not." Chewing on his scraggly mustache, Geremia grasps the scaffolding and dangles out into the void for a second. He feels excited, as if he could fly away. The climb hasn't tired him and the height intoxicates him. He doesn't want to work underground anymore. He wants to work up here—close to God and the clouds. Now he knows that in America you can't suffer from vertigo, or else you'll remain under everyone else's heel. In hell. Coca-Cola's gaze lingers on his sister's frilly underpants. He's still not quite used to the fact she's his sister, and touches himself while he thinks of her. She's only nine years old, but so cute she already makes his head spin. Vita looks at the city vibrating below her and at the box Rocco holds in front of him, like an altar boy with the offering. Where do the dead go? Is it true that on moonless nights they move among the living, knock on doors, climb into beds, and attempt to avenge the wrongs they've suffered? And the American brother, did he suffer a wrong? Every day she had hoped he'd die because if an American child was born to Agnello, he'd never go back to Dionisia—and now he's dead. Will he come look for her? Will he be as minuscule as he is tonight, or huge like a ghost? How old are ghosts? "He came unto his own, and his own received him not. But as many as received him, to them gave he power to become the sons of God." Here Diamante stops, and is unable to read any further because the wind makes Nicola's torch flicker. "H-h-hurry, Diamà, we don't have t-t-time." The words blur into one another, the lines cross. It might not end like this, but Diamante chants, "No man hath seen God."

"Amen," Rocco says. "Amen," the others repeat, making the sign of the cross. The wind at the top of the tower is so fierce you'd fly away if you didn't hold on to something. The editorial offices will be up here one day, and the men who sit here will command the world. So will the American brother, but those men won't know it. From up here the city looks like the memory of a dream, the lights like drops of rain on a train window. In April 1904 the American flag will fly from the flagpole at the top of the tower, but on August 23, 1903, we are here on top of this tower and you will sense our presence. Eat your heart out, drop dead if you can't stand to see us. Shrivel up and die, all you who want to see us dead or in prison. The kids would like to sing, but the only songs that come to mind are Enrico Caruso's. Would it be a sacrilege? Of course not, there's a rumor that in the fall Enrico Caruso himself will come to America to seek his fortune, so you, too, will learn his songs. They sing all together at the top of their lungs, the stars were shining, she fell into my arms, oh sweet kisses, oh soft caresses—they can't quite remember the words, so everyone stitches the verses together in his own way. There are billions of stars up here, but they're not shining at all; they seem covered in dust. Rocco empties the bottle of kerosene into the box and closes it again. Everyone wants to be the one to light the fire, but in the end the privilege goes to Coca-Cola, as grieving brother and relative twice over. The wind blows out the matches one after another. It's a good thing Vita has brought hers. She pours her bottle of alcohol over the cardboard box. Their first bonfire will be blue. A flame flickers across the cover, embraces and engulfs it, but the fire doesn't catch right away. For one second the box is enveloped but remains untouched by the blue blaze. Then it begins to curl up. It blackens. Creaks. Collapses. Liquefies. Diamante covers his mouth with his hand. Ascension doesn't smell very good. The wind blows the flames in their faces, their hair, their shirts. Vita catches the sparks and watches them agonize in the palm of her hand. The fire flies. He flies. We all want to fly away. Four hundred feet above the earth. And the stars were shining. It looks as if he is touching them. Nothing falls back to earth. He simply vanishes, disappears. *Ciao.*

Geremia draws the tip of his shoe through the ashes, meticulously crushes and spreads them, as if he were caressing them. The others are still absorbed, staring at the sky where the never-born American brother has flown away. If Diamante thought they were capable of so much, he'd swear they were moved.

All of a sudden the voices of the guards arrive from inside the building like a gust of wind. Their torches throw cones of light on the steel beams, burst through the gaps in the planks, shine on the scaffolding and the dusty stars. Then the beams fall on them. The dogs are barking. "Who's there? Who's up there? Hey you, how the hell did you get up here?" The howling of the dogs is carried away on the wind. "Let's go, everybody down now—everyone for himself, we'll meet up at the house." "No, first we have to give him a name or else he won't go to heaven," Vita protests. Her teeth are chattering from the cold at four hundred feet, the evening's emotion, and guilt. She wanted the baby to die—but in its sleep, like so many other newborns who all of a sudden decide not to stay around and go back where they came from, and the doctors can't explain why. She wanted Lena to die—but not yet, because she still has lots of things to teach her—and certainly not like this. Vita desperately needs to pee. She's been crossing her legs and contracting her muscles for a while already, but now her legs are trembling and her lower belly hurts from holding it in. It would be ridiculous and humiliating to wet her pants right as the American brother is flying above the stars dimmed by the lights and spitting on the city, in front of the band of boys who let her participate in the secret ceremony. The dogs are getting closer and the name for the hurried baptism does not come to them. They hadn't thought of it before. They hadn't even noticed his presence, and if Agnello hadn't invited them to toast his future American child, they wouldn't have known anything about it. Lena is so thin that despite the pregnancy her vertebrae still show through her dress. "We'll call him Baby," Rocco says quickly. The name is approved with a collective nod of the head. *Buona-notte; ciao, Baby.*

The guards must have removed the leashes because the snarling of dogs is very close now. Coca-Cola puts out the torch. They slide down poles, pushing, banging into each other in the musty, shapeless darkness. The guards are presiding over the ladders, so there's no other way down. The metal burns their hands. Planks soar up at them. The poles are on fire. Go down where? Their feet rest on nothing. The skin of their hands catches fire and their pants spark from the friction. Hundreds of feet of darkness, light, wind, empty window holes, empty rooms, windows, windows, windows. The scaffolding leads nowhere. The facade has already been finished up to the thirty-fifth floor. All of a sudden the abyss opens up below Diamante. He must have gone the wrong way. He's too far to the right. Carriages pass by in the street below, the horses tinier than his pinky finger. He's on the verge of tears. So this is what happens if you write letters for the Man with the Red Handkerchief. He who walks with the lame learns to limp. He who goes to bed with the dogs wakes up with fleas. Now they'll arrest him, try him, and expel him from America—he had his chance and he wasted it. "This way," Nicola yells. In the darkness they clamber onto a narrow plank that extends toward the wastewater drainage pipe. The guards are yelling, they're on them again, evidently the elevators are already working, the dogs are pawing about, Baby came too soon, and the hasty cat gives birth to blind kittens. It smells of lime and stale heat. The waste pipe of the not-yet-born skyscraper is an ever-narrowing shaft, the walls get tighter and tighter, wetter, stickier, softer, and the red thing floats in the basin, Lena curls up in a ball on the bed with her womb torn open, and no one has ever seen God.

The shredded New Testament slips from Diamante's troubled heart. He doesn't know why, but he feels as if he's said goodbye tonight to his sixth sibling, who dies without ever having the chance to grow up, to become somebody. He wants to cry. The waste pipe is a cylinder just over a yard wide, with joints at regular intervals in the rubber. Like a worm. It must be a hundred yards long. He didn't see the other kids climb inside. Do you go feetfirst? Or headfirst? Hold on to the joints and try to drop slowly, or hurl yourself down like a deadweight, like on the slide at the fair? Diamante is the last one; the dog is biting his calf. Its teeth dig into flesh, like a trap closing on the careless mouse. He flails about, trying to shake the dog off, but it just bites harder. He grabs onto Rocco's pants so he isn't tempted to abandon him up here. "Help me, help me," he finds himself begging. Pleading in a baby voice that hardly seems his. The voice of Celestina. Panting, Rocco plants himself on the edge of the pipe, grabs him by the arm, and picks him up as easily as he'd pick a handkerchief off the ground. "Get in," he says, thrusting him into the hole. With Diamante still crying— "Don't leave me"—Rocco holds him by the heel with one hand and grabs the dog's head with the other. He sinks his fingers in the animal's eyeballs until it releases its hold and drops down in the darkness. Rocco, too, releases his hold, and Diamante slides down headfirst.

No one has ever seen God, but tonight Diamante has seen Rocco. How strong he is, and how brave. How Diamante would like to be his friend! He saved him from the dog, the guards, and Juvenile Court, even though Diamante had already told him he doesn't want to write letters for the Man with the Red Handkerchief anymore. And Rocco did all these things as he balanced himself in the dark, big and ungainly as he is, and hindered by the deadweight of a chubby nine-year-old girl. Because Rocco is holding Vita in his arms. In her underpants and unlaced boots and all upset, she wasn't climbing down fast enough. The pipe is narrowing. Diamante scrapes his hands against the joints, gets stuck, writhes about, works himself free, falls headlong again, bangs against the sides and bounces off the rubber walls. He never once worries he'll crash to the ground. Rocco wouldn't allow it. Somewhere down below there must be something inviting.

Rocco keeps seeing the red thing. And keeps trying to forget it. He buries his face in Vita's hair. Vita locks her ankles behind his back and her arms around his neck, trembling as if she were crying. But she's not. She would never show herself to be so weak, never ever ever. Rocco slides down, his jacket rips against the rubber, his feet brake against the joints, and the pipe sways. It's amazing how good such a tough guy like Rocco can be, Diamante thinks. He'd told her not to come with us, but she decided to just the same, even if nobody disobeys Rocco—and they sure are sorry when they do. Worse. And when Vita just can't hold it any longer and empties her bladder on his shirt, Rocco doesn't get angry, doesn't curse, doesn't even make fun of her as she deserves, as Diamante would do in his place. Rocco pretends not to notice that Vita's underpants are soaked, along with his only good shirt. He doesn't put her down even when they tumble into the lime pit, sinking in a soft pasty substance that feels like mud. Still holding her close to his neck, he gets up and weaves his big hands under her buttocks, those hands he never knows what to do with and that are always in the way. He carries her, wet as she is, across the potholes in the construction site, across the clearing illuminated by the lamps, up and over the fence, through the barbed wire, and then, with that unmistakable swaying stride of his, for dozens of blocks, through a city that gets increasingly less grand, increasingly less illuminated— Thirtieth Street, Twentieth, Tenth, zero—all the way home.

Vita is still clinging frantically to Rocco, her ankles behind his back and her arms around his neck. But her head is leaning on his shoulder; she's probably fallen asleep. Diamante, smarting from the dog bite as well as from the knocks and scrapes in the drainage pipe, limps along next to that giant Saint Christopher: he can't take his eyes off Vita's bare, lime-encrusted legs and that stain on Rocco's shirt. The dark spot seems like the coat of arms of a nobility he does not possess. Rocco sees the red thing and Vita's hair. Every once in a while he turns and casts a meditative glance at the boy trotting along beside him. Diamante intimidates him a little because he reads the newspaper, has such clear blue eyes, and knows a ton of stories Rocco doesn't. "Are you good at keeping a secret?" Rocco asks him when they reach the first blocks of Prince Street. "I've been keeping a secret," Diamante responds. "And you won't tell Uncle Agnello or the other kids?" "You know I won't, Desperado." "I just don't understand women," Rocco says, glancing doubtfully at Vita, her head resting on his big shoulder. She doesn't move. "It didn't come out by itself, that baby— she took it out." "Who?" Diamante whispers. He has completely lost his orientation this night, has hurled himself headlong into the dark in order to chase after the sense of things that are escaping him, things he doesn't understand. "Lena," Rocco responds, stopping to remove a long black hair from his mouth. "She's gone completely crazy. Stay away from her."

James Earl Jones's Twin

When I returned to Rome, I rummaged through my father's papers. They were in great disorder, stored in two metal cabinets in the family house I'd left years earlier. Piles of colored folders, shoe boxes stuffed with loose pages, tissue paper, newspaper clippings, typewritten manuscripts. I was hoping he had written about America. I was hoping that, with the passing of time, he had made his peace with his authoritarian father and had decided to write his story. Hoping he had accepted that the twelve-year-old boy was the same man who first instilled in him a passion for stories and then tried to keep him from believing—and living—them. Diamante had wanted my father to become a doctor, and my father had disappointed him. Roberto was only twenty-four years old when his father died. They didn't have time to really get to know each other. Neither did my father and I. On November 1, 1989—four days before his death—Roberto, manifesting a renewed interest in his family, organized a party: he called it the Mazzucco party. He reunited all the survivors. They weren't many: ten or so. I was the youngest. Contrary to his joyous intentions, that day has taken on the significance of a funeral, an open testament to the presence of ghosts. Afterward we understood that he had known. My father had a gift he didn't speak about willingly, and whose source was unknown. He saw what others didn't. He felt things happen, objects move, life quiver, sensing the tiniest shifts in the interstices of time.

But I didn't find anything among his papers. Just a few lines in an autobiographical story on his relationship with the authorities, published in 1979. The introduction recounts the misfortunes of his stone-breaking grandfather, Diamante's departure for America, and his uncles' and aunts' deaths from malnutrition:

> Devoured by a relentless hunger, dressed in rags and abandoned to their fate, as soon as they could escape the control of their doleful and dispirited parents, they would swallow flakes of plaster, clumps of dirt, tiny pieces of coal. The passage from that activity to ruined intestines and incurable disease was immediate. Yet all this did not occur in India, or in the Middle Ages, but in the 1890s, and not far from Rome. People were already building villas in the Castelli, going to Paris every year, talking about the imperial destiny of the nation.

There was nothing more, and much less, than what he had told me. Even though the project was never realized, maybe he had done some research in the Tufo archives. Perhaps he had collected precious documents, reconstructed the disordered fragments of memory. He was a historian. Many people called him Cato, but one of his favorite nicknames was the Professor. But I was mistaken.

All I found were some letters from his father's brother Leonardo, who had gone to live in Australia and had written a series of amusing anecdotes about his grandparents, his childhood, and Diamante's youth. My father was interested in the 1920s; he had preserved Leonardo's letters to Diamante because he hoped to publish a volume on the fierce repression of the Sanusi in Libya from the perspective of a proletarian military police officer who, forced to choose between hunger and the state, chose the state—and all the consequences. But he never wrote it.

I found a genealogical tree devoid of roots—and with the leaves dried up at the level of our generation. I also found all his vaguely tedious correspondence with an erudite figure from Turin who was also called Mazzucco, and who, in a lengthy and substantiated dissertation, proved the Piedmont origins of the surname. Which confirmed my father's opinion: he'd always felt out of place in Rome.

Another erudite man, this time from Padua, claimed that Mazzucco was a Venetian word. In the 1500s, Marin Sanudo speaks of the Mal di Mazzucco. It is a disease of the brain. A deadly disease.

My father suffered from the heat. In the summer he often wore shorts and canvas shoes with ankle socks. He was big, tall, with pale, rosy skin. Many people mistook him for a German, and this pleased him, I don't know why. Perhaps because of the characteristics of precision, rigor, and clarity he associated with the word *German*. We both loved to appear as something we were not. In my travels I had pretended to be Turkish, Jewish, Persian, French, Arab. Not necessarily a woman. The most amazing thing is that I was always believed. Sometimes I didn't even choose what to be: I seemed, and that was sufficient. At the Tegel airport in Berlin in January 2000, I was stopped by the border police, who suspected me of being a Palestinian terrorist. For an eternal half hour my Italian passport was considered false. In truth, both Roberto and I have decidedly Moorish characteristics. They say every one of us has a twin in some part of the world. We're not usually destined to meet or recognize him, or even know anything about him. But I found Roberto's twin: James Earl Jones, an extraordinary actor with a powerful voice and a good smile. He's an African-American.

In the foothills of the Alps, in the wool-working region near Biella, is a small ghost town. In 1960 it had 142 inhabitants, but later disappeared from the census of Italian towns. It had become irrelevant. A hamlet of Trivero, the town is called Mazzucco. My father's last voyage was to Mazzucco. It was October 1989. He would die suddenly twenty days later. The last images of him are taken with a trembling super-eight. The movie camera catches Roberto—tall, decidedly large, with frizzy graying hair and clear plastic glasses. He's wearing brown velvet pants, a red sweater, and an open windbreaker. He leans against the street sign indicating the town Mazzucco with a timid, vulnerable smile. It's foggy, but he is content. He has found what he'd been looking for. He thinks he has found the place where it all began.

The Black Hand

When Diamante would tell his children the story of his America, which they later told me, with variations and nuances according to each narrator's disposition (gullible and terrorized in Uncle Amedeo's case, ironic and entertained in my father's), the Black Hand made its sinister appearance on that very first night of adventure in Agnello's boardinghouse. Over the years, the pigsty stench of that night gradually disappeared; what remained was an anguished sense of bewilderment and the dreadful certainty of being at the mercy of superior and hostile forces. Diamante had awoken with a start in the heart of the night, in an unknown house and an unknown world, in a place where he felt completely defenseless. Yes, that was the precise moment when he heard the Black Hand mentioned for the first time. He was crushed against the wall and the bandits were talking about how a boy had been found hacked to pieces in the underground construction site. That boy's father had also received the letter with the black hand over a fist. Diamante hadn't understood what they were talking about.

One day was all he needed. On April 15, 1903, at 743 Elizabeth Street—just a few blocks from Agnello's boardinghouse—a man's body was found in a barrel, his throat cut through and his head almost severed as a result of eighteen stab wounds. *The New York Times* started calling Prince Street the "Black Hand Block." Between 1900 and 1910, every saloon or spaghetti joint on the street was probably a meeting place for blackmailers, baby snatchers, counterfeiters, thieves, swindlers, and rigged lottery ticket vendors: the unlucky winner was immediately robbed of his winnings and often killed. "Prince Street is full of Black Handers: they are found in practically every house," the father of a kidnapped child told the police years later. Not that the place where Diamante was headed, Ohio, was any more tranquil. A large colony of Minturno immigrants had sprung up between Cleveland, Ravenna, Akron, and Youngstown. In Ravenna alone there were dozens of homicides in those early years of the new century. The dead had Italian surnames. On July 4, 1903, in Mulberry Bend in New York, two hundred infuriated Italians attacked and practically lynched a doctor who wanted to take a fifteen-year-old boy who'd been wounded by a stray bullet to Bellevue Hospital. On the seventh of the same month, neighborhood youths assaulted some policemen who were attempting to arrest a kidnapper, and the battle, fought with daggers, razors, knives, and ice picks, left dozens wounded on the pavement.

A few weeks later four hit men broke Rocco's nose, and at the beginning of September Diamante had to give up his job as a newspaper boy. That job, which was so quickly stolen from him, nevertheless instilled in him an enduring veneration for newspapers. They were his high school education, teaching him much he hadn't known. They also gave him a gift that seemed pointless at the time: the Italian language. Reading the paper is a bad habit in our family. Only words have survived from those first confusing months so long ago. Stories that memory has transfigured, changed, or even invented. Only one thing is certain: some months after the arrival of his daughter and the boy with the blue eyes, Agnello, up to his neck in debt to his moneylender, sold the shop he had purchased less than eighteen months earlier.

Who was this Agnello? When on August 17, 1901, Antonio Mazzucco tried to land in America for the first time, he naively declared he was on his way to "nobody" and was rejected. His second attempt came to a conclusion on May 24, 1902, after a terrifying crossing last-

ing three weeks on the notorious steamship *Calabria* of the Anchor
Line; between one port authority fine and the next, the *Calabria* nevertheless stayed afloat for several more years. This time Antonio declared he was on his way to a certain Agnello Mazzucco, "relative,"
New York, 18 Prince Street. He was rejected just the same. I consulted
the "List of Alien Immigrants for the Commissioner of Immigration"
in the archives at Ellis Island. Antonio is passenger number 608. The
list records that he was in possession of twelve dollars and knew how to
read and write. In the box "deformed or crippled. Nature and causes"
is written "NO." Next to the box "condition of health mental and
physical" is written "good." So he was of sound constitution. And yet
a black mark appears next to his name. Since other black marks are
scattered randomly all over the page, I have the terrible suspicion they
are ink splatterings. Could this be the reason they sent him back?
There are no other papers pertaining to his case, and I will probably
never know the reason he was denied the chance to make a new life
for himself in the United States. Did Antonio really lose America because of an ink stain, or is the black spot by his name instead the sign
of an arbitrary, mysterious, definitive condemnation? In any event,
in 1902 Antonio was already fifty years old and didn't have another
chance. He was forced to remain in the village where five of his children had died, the village he hated with all his heart.

Agnello was much more fortunate. Looking back through the passenger lists in the Ellis Island archives, where the arrivals of other travelers from Tufo and Minturno are registered, I find that his name
appears often under "destination." Agnello was one of the first to
leave, along with Brigida Mazzucco, Costanzo Mazzucco, Desiderio
Mazzucco, Fiorentino Mazzucco, Ignazio Mazzucco, Placido Rasile,
Giuseppe and Pietro Ciufo. Before 1900 he is listed as a resident of
Cleveland. When he returned to the United States with his son,
Nicola, in 1897, he declared he already resided in the United States
and gave the address of the Erie Railways Company. But there is no
trace of his first landing at Ellis Island. Therefore, either he entered
America before the island was established or he came in clandestinely.
He is the point of arrival for an intricate network of travelers. Like the
Pied Piper, he beckoned them all from the other side. Curiously, when

he returns from Minturno with his son, he declares his profession as
"musician."

Those who went back to Minturno didn't know anything about his
musical talent—real or symbolic. They knew him only as a cantankerous railway foreman. Many feared and most hated him. He didn't leave
positive memories behind him. In Tufo, he was known as the one who
had abandoned his wife after a few weeks of marriage, who had given
her two children during two short winters when he had reappeared in
the village (newly rich and odious, and odious because he was newly
rich), and who had not returned to her when the Americans rejected
her. But in 1900 Agnello changed cities and jobs. Had he met someone? Was Gwascheliyne Hex'wpasch'e Meshbash—Lena—the person
who changed his life?

The only traces of Lena's fabulous yet banal existence are in the
New York City censuses. The Church of Latter-Day Saints—better
known as the Mormons—is compiling a sort of universal catalog of
families, maybe so each person, knowing where he is going, may also
discover where he came from. Or perhaps, in a more secular light, so
that at least some trace of our ephemeral passing remains. Millions of
birth, marriage, residence, and death certificates have been micro-
filmed. The Italians, with their congenital diffidence about remembering, eternity, and the universal, or maybe to ward off bad luck,
provided imprecise and contradictory information. But the Americans
were captured almost indiscriminately. The Family History Library of
the Church of Jesus Christ of Latter-Day Saints of Oakton, Virginia,
directs me right away to the Regional Archives of Manhattan, where
the complete microfilm collection of the New York City censuses is
preserved. The certificates show that Agnello declared Lena to be his
wife. They lived together until 1906, after which the traces get confused. Lena disappears and various homonyms start showing up. There
have always been too many of us. An expert on local history defined
the Mazzuccos as "an army," and added: "They were considered to belong to the lower classes." At any rate, in 1902 Agnello bought the fruit
and vegetable store on the corner of Elizabeth Street and received the
first letter in April 1903, as soon as business started to take off.

Probably after the summer (even hoodlums go on vacation),

Agnello received a second letter, which may have sounded something like this:

> Do you think we have forgotten you? Do you think we are far away from you? We have had other business to deal with till now, but your turn has come up again. You understand and know what we want from you. Send us the money right away to the place you know or else beware of our revenge. We will never take our eyes off you. Your days are numbered. Weep because your daughter is dead.

The letter was signed by a so-called Society of Death and adorned with skulls, daggers, swords, and pierced hearts, as well as a sinister array of insults, curses, and threats of torture. Similar letters started appearing in the newspapers after the first reports. It's also possible that Agnello was asked to help pay for a lawyer for the two gang bosses arrested on Prince Street in April 1903, and that he refused to pay, thus becoming a target for revenge when the two were released.

It's certain that Agnello did not report the blackmail to the police. Nor did he complain in the newspapers, as did Salvatore Spinella, owner of various buildings on Eleventh Street, who in 1908 told *The New York Times* that he had always been an honest man, but his house had been bombed five times since he had refused to pay the Black Hand. Now his tenants were leaving their apartments, his business was in ruins, his family in danger. How much longer could he resist before his own family was destroyed? Since Agnello did not have the money the blackmailers were asking for with growing—and ever-more-sinister—insistence, he paid them off with his shop. He sold out in November 1903. To his moneylender. Which may lead the malicious to suspect that the moneylender knew who was blackmailing him, or even that he'd sent the letters himself.

As Agnello was a man who would have preferred to die rather than to pay, one has to ask why he did so. Perhaps because he didn't want to see those who were close to him killed, and the presence of his daughter made him vulnerable. The blackmailers could easily have hurt Vita, as they did Francesco Scalisi, kidnapped when he was five years old and set free only after a payment of $250. Or the son of Peter

Lamanna, a rich undertaker, kidnapped when he was nine and bar-
barously murdered in 1907, or Michele, the son of Dr. Mariano
Scimeca, who was kidnapped on June 21, 1910, while playing on the
landing of his house at 2 Prince Street. Without knowing it, Vita may
have been the cause of her father's ruin.

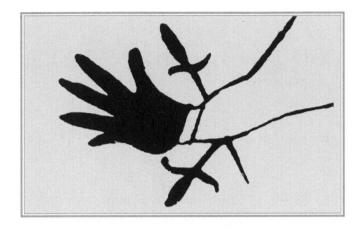

Cesare Cuzzopuoti's New Shoes

The difference between an American horse and an Italian boy is the following: If his owner leaves the horse out in the cold for too long, the Society for the Prevention of Cruelty to Animals can report him for abuse, slap him with a fine for up to five dollars, and remove the animal from his care. If he leaves the boy out in the cold, no one notices. The horse must be protected because he's worth more—there are only a few horses, but thousands of boys—but also because he's more fragile. The horse toils, submits, and obeys for as long as he can, but all of a sudden he stops in his tracks, snorts, arches his back, twitches his tail, kicks, sheds a tear from his big round eyes, and surrenders—he collapses in the dirty, mushy snow and dies. The boy survives. The horse belonging to the rag seller Tommaso Orecchio, known as Tom, collapses in the middle of Second Avenue one evening in February, and no whip or fist or caress is able to move him because all he wants to do is die. But when Diamante, petrified by the cold, falls, he picks himself up again, and at the end of his shift he goes home, just like yesterday, just like the day before, and all winter long.

It's past midnight when he closes the door behind him. Everyone's already asleep. Even Vita. He won't see her tonight, either. Now that he leaves at dawn and gets back so late, he only sees her on Sundays. Vita's laughter warms his ear when his frozen hands refuse to bend, when the cold is so intense his joints creak, when his wrists knuckles ankles bones grow so brittle they practically shatter like crystal. Diamante rummages among the tins over the stove and finds, amid the provisions marked D.M.—the only ones he has permission to touch— a can of beans. He rips it open and eats in the dark, crouched in his usual place on a barrel. In order to fool himself into thinking there are plenty more, he extracts one bean at a time, and chews slowly. His eyelids droop and he dozes off for a minute. He hasn't gotten enough sleep in months, and sometimes he falls asleep standing or sleepwalks his way home. There are times when he couldn't even say how he found the right street. All of a sudden he opens his eyes and finds himself in front of the building on Prince Street. He recognizes it by its rancid, stagnant smell. But now that smell means home to him, and breathing it in consoles him. With fingers slippery from the pickling juice, he fishes out another bean and places it on his tongue for a few seconds without chewing, savoring the slowly seeping flavor as the pulp gradually dissolves. He eats beans every night. A slice of bread and salami or a handful of olives and an onion at lunch. If the cart stops in front of a fruit and vegetable shop, he might manage to snatch an apple and slip it up his sleeve. It doesn't feel like stealing from Uncle Agnello anymore because Agnello no longer has his shop. He wept the day he turned the keys over to the boss—big tears that dripped down his wrinkled cheeks. Diamante looked the other way, ashamed to see a man as old as his father cry.

The can is already empty. By now Diamante knows it contains thirty-six beans. At five he'll be hungry again. But by then he'll be back on his feet and won't have time to notice. His head will spin, but he'll get used to it and will feel lightheaded all morning, as if he's walking through a foggy and insubstantial but not unpleasant dream. A disagreeable thought poisons his last bean, though. There's no more horse, so tomorrow it'll be up to him to push the cart to the scrap heaps at the pants factories and clothing workshops and over to the East River dump. It'll be his job to drag that broken-down heap of wobbly planks and railroad ties around the city and then to Baxter Street to weigh the rags on the scale, a dollar for every two hundred pounds. And then he'll be the one to push the empty cart to the courtyard on Pickers Row and say goodbye to Tom Orecchio as he heads off to the Old Brewery. If they collect two hundred pounds, he'll receive a quarter, a half-dollar if they collect four hundred, and— miracle of miracles—a whole dollar if they collect eight hundred. But miracles never happen here: at Loreto, Pompeii, and Lourdes, yes, but not one miracle has been verified in the United States, and that's certainly no coincidence. How many days can a boy outlive his horse? Ten? Twenty?

"Still awake?" a male voice suddenly asks him. "No," he answers and drinks down the brine; even though it tastes of salt and dirty water and stinks like a dead rat, it preserves a vague taste of bean. Rocco. He comes home later and later now, and sometimes doesn't come home at all. He's stopped loitering, and doesn't even hang out with the other strikers anymore. He has another job. When Vita asked him what type of job it was, seeing as how it doesn't have set hours or observe holidays, Rocco answered that he worked with his fists. He'd already gotten himself noticed during the strike; he'd picked off more policemen on his own than all the other excavators put together. Not even when four men ganged up on him, the way they did the night of Baby's death, were they able to flatten him. Everybody thinks he'll become a boxer. But the boxers who fight in beer-hall basements always have swollen faces, while Rocco's is fresh and smooth. He confessed to Diamante he never really thought about finding a job. Don't listen to the bosses and the priests—work degrades you. Do you know that ditty about tough guys? I'll live half the year by hook or by crook, and the other half by crook and by hook. Whatever it is he's doing, Rocco's earning more than he was before. He has just purchased himself a new wardrobe (three black suits with stripes and wide lapels), given a stack of 78s to Lena, a bone-handled razor to Coca-Cola, a collar with silver bells to his cat, and a talking doll to Vita, a real mechanical marvel that utters words like *Mommy, Daddy, I love you*, and so on, and he didn't steal the stuff this time because it was still wrapped in the paper from the store. A store on Fifth Avenue—the brightest, flashiest, most extraordinary avenue in the entire city—where Diamante has never set foot for fear of hearing them chant *guini guini goon* behind his back. Rocco has rented a room all for himself from Uncle Agnello, the only one with a window and a real bed, crowned with a massive iron headboard. From the junk shop he bought a real nightstand, a white ceramic chamber pot, a print with the face of a bearded prophet (not Garibaldi or Christ, though Diamante can't remember his name), and a wicker bed for the cat. His is the only room that's always neat. Vita sweeps it and makes the bed every morning, and washes his socks and undershirts, while Lena brushes his clothes and cooks meatballs just for him. Rocco has not become his friend, and Diamante is dying of envy.

"How's it going?" Rocco mumbles, aware that Diamante is looking longingly at the slice of bread on which he's slowly and meticulously spreading peanut butter. "Rondello's dead," Diamante whispers bitterly. "Who?" Rocco asks, curious now. "Was he killed?" "Yes." Whenever there's talk of crime, Rocco wakes from his habitual indifference to the world around him and inquires brightly if they used a knife or a pistol. "Rondello was a horse, Rocco, he died of exhaustion." Diamante had given him that high-sounding name. Rondello was the name of Buovo d'Antona's horse, a descendant of Emperor Gostantino. If a lame nag can be a noble steed, he figured, then one day he might become a knight. Disappointed, Rocco wedges the slice of bread into his mouth. Diamante slips off the barrel, and drags himself to his cot. He still shares it with Cousin Geremia, and by now he knows every inch of his feet, every hair on his toes. Diamante can tell what sort of work he did that day by the blisters on his soles; he knows if he was digging sewers by his smell, if he shoveled snow by his chilblains, or if he was excavating a building site by the mud—but he couldn't say if Geremia still has a mustache or has grown wide sideburns like Rocco because he never sees his face anymore. Geremia is always working. He's become as zealous as a Kraut. On Sundays he goes to sweep the church. Which church Diamante isn't sure, because he has no intention of going with him. Geremia slaves away sixteen, eighteen hours a day, and the rest of the time he sleeps. Coca-Cola says he's already old.

Rocco grabs him by the sleeve. "It's not polite to leave me to eat by myself." "You're the one who's eating, and I don't have time to waste sitting here watching you," Diamante replies. "Who do you think you are, you little shit?" Rocco bristles. "It's the truth," Diamante responds. "The truth's a nun who'd never let herself be touched by the likes of you. The point is, I'm bigger than you. You gotta show me respect." "Likewise." Diamante draws the curtain, pushes aside the blanket, and curls up on the cot, fully dressed. Now he's the one who pushes Geremia up against the wall because now he's the one who comes home last. He's making progress. A few seconds later, the curtain opens. The phosphorescent eyes of Rocco's cat glimmer in the darkness, and Rocco's cordial smile gleams white, just like in the ads. Despite his biceps, unusually large frame, and crooked nose, thanks to the hit men's punches, Rocco has a sweet face and a good-boy air. But he's not a good boy. Lucky him. "How brave are you?" Rocco asks as he hurls the cat in Diamante's face. "Really brave?"

Diamante's never been to Brooklyn. Sometimes, when he and Tom Orecchio dig around in the East River dump, he lifts his eyes from the twisted wreckage and disemboweled couches, and glances at the iron bridge that links the two shores. Everyone is in awe of that bridge. But not Diamante. On the Garigliano River a few miles from his house is an iron suspension bridge. True, it's smaller than this one, but just as magnificent. It's merely a matter of dimensions. Everything is bigger here—the river, port, houses, even the people. But if size is all that matters, he wouldn't be worth anything, and that's not possible. It can't be. Diamante has never taken the iron bridge to Brooklyn before, but now he's crossing it by bike. When he turns around to look, the city being sucked up by the dark glows like a magical nativity scene set in snow and water.

It's late. The cold has already carved pointy icicles on the cornices. Electric lamps form puddles of light in the darkness. Except for the odd carriage, the streets are deserted. The cold is so intense it hurts to breathe and cuts you like a saw. But Rocco doesn't seem to notice. He clenches a cigarette between his teeth and pedals. A wisp of steam rises from his coat, as if his back were smoking. If the temperature rises, it'll start snowing again. There's much celebration in Manhattan when it snows because it means there's work for the shovelers. It's hard work, the shovel is so heavy and the snow so compacted it takes Diamante more than three hours to clear one block. The shopkeepers complain when they find out he's the one sent to clean the sidewalk in front of their doors. They say he's the worst shoveler in New York. But the salt soon melts the snow; you need a real blizzard for three days of work in a row. Every now and then Rocco throws him a provocative look. Diamante, teeth chattering from the cold and clinging to the handlebars, smiles. He's not afraid of Rocco. He knows perfectly well Rocco stole the bicycle uptown. The neighborhood brats cheered when he came pedaling back to Prince Street because they want to grow up to be like him. Vita and Nino painted it black. Black is now Rocco's favorite color. He gave his red handkerchief to Diamante, but Diamante never wears it in case someone still remembers the Man from last summer. The people on the block have started to fear Rocco. But not Diamante. Afraid of a bear with earrings? Diamante? Who crossed the ocean by himself and slept in Central Park where not even the tough guys dare go after sundown? He's even stolen dogs right out from under people's noses. He'll show him what he's worth. Rocco's nothing but a braggart.

Rocco passes the cigarette and Diamante casually takes a drag. The taste of tobacco is nauseating, but all real men smoke. Rocco's patent-leather shoes shine in the dark. He hasn't deigned to look at Diamante for months. The last time was when they were taking a bath together. The tub is small and they were crammed in like a screw and a nut. Their bodies touched. "Celestina, you know your hair's starting to grow in?" Rocco commented as he passed his hand over Diamante's tiny pink shrimp, where a miserable, dark little curl was actually sprouting. He suggested he cut it to make it grow in thicker. As soon as he was alone, Diamante grabbed Agnello's razor and pruned the tuft of hair. For weeks, every time he closed himself in the bathroom, he'd study the situation, itching with impatience. But nothing was growing back. Rocco'd screwed him over. "Get down," Rocco says as he brakes. "We're here."

A high wall behind which wind-beaten cypresses rise encircles what seems to be a villa. There's a closed gate, nothing else. It's two in the morning. Not a soul in sight, not even a streetlamp. The ideal location for an ambush. Rocco thrusts a chisel in his hands. "What am I supposed to do with this?" Diamante asks, surprised. "If your name isn't really Celestina, if you're brave, you'll climb over the wall and look for Cesare Cuzzopuoti's tomb. There's an angel with a sword on it, his father had it made to show how rich he is. What an ass. Instead of giving the money to the poor, or enjoying it himself, he prefers to insult everybody." "Who is Cesare Cuzzopuoti?" Diamante is starting to regret having come with Rocco. What does he care about Rocco? He's got nothing to prove. Even if he never grows another hair, he's already a man, free to make decisions about his own life. Nobody tells him what to do. He works like a man, lives like a man, earns like a man—Celestina doesn't exist and if he ever did, he's dead now. "A good guy," Rocco sneers. "Why else would they have killed him?"

"Killed!" Diamante nearly shouts. The dead who've been murdered never rest in peace. They wander the earth taking revenge. If you go out at night, you risk running into them. Diamante doesn't like this business. He wants to get out of here, go back home. Even if tomorrow he'll have to go to the dump and break his nails digging in the frozen dirt just to scrape together a few rags, scraps so threadbare and thin they don't even move the needle on the scale. But Rocco is immobile in the cold, his cigarette between his lips and his hat shoved down to his nose so half his face is hidden. Rocco looks at him and laughs. "This Cesare liked to play cards. Didn't care about anything else in life. I put the ace of hearts in his casket myself. People usually put in a rosary, but Cesare never prayed. He only knew how to play cards, so before closing the lid I slid the ace of hearts between his fingers." "You knew him?" Diamante asks. "Never saw him alive. Only dead. At Cozza's."

That name doesn't mean anything to Diamante. He certainly didn't come all the way to America to meet people. The only reason he's here is to save money and help his parents. It doesn't seem like much, nothing really—but he hasn't managed to do even that. In ten months all he's sent is a miserable forty dollars. Forty dollars that cost him endless hunger and fatigue. Rocco laughs. He can't believe Diamante's never heard of Mr. Cozza, whose real name is Lazzaro Bongiorno, casket manufacturer, embalmer, and funeral director. In Tufo they would have called him a gravedigger. But here he's an undertaker, which sounds much more distinguished. He's thin as a skeleton and always dresses in black, which is why they call him Cozza, or mussel. "I work with him," Rocco says smugly. "At the funeral parlor, Cesare's friends asked me to put the ace in the casket." "But what the hell have I got to do with this Cesare?" Diamante wants to know, turning the spike in his hands, uncomprehending. "Find Cesare's tomb, go in, and open the casket—it's not welded. The stiff's got a gold watch in his pocket he won't be needing anymore. Take it and bring it to me." Diamante shudders. Rocco's asking him to steal. From a dead man. The murdered are the most dangerous and vindictive of the dead. Prayers don't soothe them. Never ever. "Oh, excuse me, they must have taught you stealing is a sin, and you, best in your class, of course you learned the lesson well." Diamante wavers. "Whose side are you on?" Rocco insists. "On the side of a shit who has himself buried with a gold watch? You'll never own a gold watch. You don't own a damn thing." Diamante is confused; it's true that stealing is a sin, but it's also true that he doesn't own anything. "So you're just another Uncle Tom," Rocco concludes, disappointed. "You're on the side of the rich with their golden watches and the cops. So much the worse for you. You can go on collecting rags."

"It's not about the stealing," Diamante stammers. "So much the worse then. You'll pee in your pants, you little shit," Rocco concludes, climbing back on his bike. "I knew it, you're not cut out for it, you'll never have the courage to look a dead man in the face." Diamante grits his teeth, his blood boiling. He hurls himself at Rocco, yelling. "I saw my brothers die! I was with Talarico and Amedeo. Their stomachs exploded because we ate the plaster off the church wall. They died, but I didn't—I'm hard as a diamond, I can digest rocks. I'm not afraid of the dead. I'm not afraid of anyone. And I don't give a fuck about stealing from some rich-ass shit." "Bravo," Rocco says as he shakes him off. "Show me." Diamante clutches the chisel. He'd like to stab Rocco with it, but instead he clenches it between his teeth and heads for the wall of the Green-Wood Cemetery. He wedges his foot in a crack between two bricks, feels around for a handhold, and climbs. When he pulls himself up to the top of the wall, the city is at his feet. Throbbing with light, bright and far away.

The Cuzzopuoti tomb rises up in the most monumental part of the cemetery, at the end of a gravel path punctuated by crosses, angels, and Madonnas. The angel with the sword looks like it's made of papier-mâché, even though it has to be marble. Diamante doesn't understand a thing about sculpture, but it doesn't seem worth a millionaire's fortune. At any rate, if he were the dead one, his father certainly wouldn't pay to have an angel sculpted for him. He'd bring him to the churchyard wrapped in a sheet, just like he did with his other children, and bury him in the earth because he wouldn't even have the money for a box. So Cuzzopuoti arouses neither fear nor pity in him. The dates of Cesare's brief life are carved on the stone: 1882–1904. *Requiescat in pace.*

Using the chisel as a lever, Diamante raises the slab and inserts a branch in the crack. He tries to slide it on the branch, but the slab is too heavy. He kneels over the hole and makes out a deep pit—black as hell. Rocco hasn't given him a lamp or taper, so when he slips into the opening and lets himself drop, for a few minutes all he sees is darkness. The light of the moon outside is far away, like the dim reflection of the sun when you dive to the bottom of the sea. The tomb smells of cold, dirt, and rotten flowers. The walls on both sides are lined with bunks, like a steamship dormitory—except that on these bunks are seven walnut boxes instead of sleeping bodies. All with metal handles. Most of them are ruined, the wood swollen from humidity. Only one looks new. CESARE on the label. "Dear Cesare," Diamante says out loud, to screw up his courage, "I have come to ask for a loan." His hands tremble and his teeth chatter. The immense silence, an absolute void in the night—not even the call of a bird or the beating of wings—makes him feel he's the only living thing in this kingdom of the dead. The underwater silence of the hereafter. So much for celestial songs. But this Cesare certainly didn't go to Paradise. Diamante tries to lift the lid, but can't. He climbs up into the bunk but has to straddle the casket, as there isn't much space. He ties his coat over his face and yanks on the lid with all his might.

Diamante screams. Half of Cesare's face is stuffed with cotton wool. Someone blew his head off. With time, the cotton wool has become soaked with liquid and has turned dark. Diamante is severely tempted to jump down and flee. But he doesn't move. He isn't leaving there without the watch. The rest of the face is sleeping. Cesare doesn't seem irritated by his presence, or excessively dead. They'd dressed him in a snazzy striped suit and tie, and a vest with mother-of-pearl buttons and gold cufflinks. He's got on a fabulous pair of brand-new shoes, never worn, the soles still smooth. And in his hands he's holding a rosary, not an ace of hearts. Even more strange, there's no gold watch in the vest pocket. Pressing his coat against his face so as not to breathe in the stench of putrefaction rising from the cadaver, Diamante, trembling and increasingly frightened, rummages feverishly in the jacket pockets. He finds a picture of the Madonna of Pompeii, a grain of rice, a horseshoe to ward off bad luck, even a cockroach—but no watch. "I'm not leaving here without that watch," he cries, on the verge of tears "Where did you hide the watch?" He empties the pants pockets, and even searches under the shirt. Cesare is as hard as marble. But the watch isn't there.

When he tries to close the casket, the lid doesn't want to slide along the box. It remains askew, and Diamante can make out the half face of Cesare through the open crack. But he doesn't have time, he can't stay one minute longer in this dormitory of the dead or he'll faint —asphyxiated by fear. He jumps down onto the tomb floor and tries to climb up the stone shelves toward the slice of moon filtering down from above. But either the slab has moved or he's grown smaller because now his hands can't reach the lip of the tomb even when he stretches on tiptoe. Nose in the air, he stares at the light of the moon and feels as if he's fallen into the bottom of a well. Half-faced Cesare could get angry. Not to speak of his relatives, who've been lying there undisturbed for a good ten years at least. He wants to scream. But who will come pull him out? Rocco's too far away. And if the custodian was to catch him, how could he possibly explain he isn't a real thief, just an apprentice? And in what language? No one had warned him that in this country he'd become small and powerless again, like a child before he learns the names of things, who cries and gesticulates but can't express himself, who weeps without being able to say why he's afraid or what's hurting him. But Diamante will learn the language of the blond-haired people one day. He'll read *The New York Times* and no one will call him "gorilla" ever again. He tries again, grasps the handles of a coffin, and pulls himself up to the dormitory's second level.

He turns around in the low cubicle on his hands and knees, but can't climb to the next level. He's stuck. He could pray to Jesus, the little Madonna delle Grazie, San Leonardo, or even God himself, but he doesn't trust them anymore—it's as if their powers had stayed on the other side of the ocean. He needs air, and the stench of death filtering from Cesare's open casket is making his head hurt. What a shameless destiny, to die at the bottom of a tomb. And on a Friday. When tomorrow he could go for a walk with Vita. Ever since he's been working with Tom Orecchio, the thought of Vita is the only bright spot in his day. When they unload rags, he always manages to squirrel away a strip of lace or a little bit of cloth. At night he goes down and washes them in the fountain and then makes her scarves, shawls, handkerchiefs. He rummages through the trash for her, to bring her a broken toy or an iron train that has lost its wheels. On hands and knees, he scours whole acres of mud, picks through wreckage, forages in the snow; he forgets he's there to look for rags, and gets distracted by a broken hoop that maybe could still roll on the sidewalk, or the pudgy leg of a doll. In total secret, he'd been making a doll, gluing the pieces together bit by bit. A real porcelain doll, not cloth. He'd planned on giving it to her as a gift. Vita had never had a doll, as there was always a neighbor's or relative's baby to cradle. Even on Prince Street she changed the diapers of Melchiorra Corpora's baby, a stunted little newborn who clearly wouldn't survive the winter. In fact, he died one December night, leaving Vita without her toy and bawling that she wanted to go home. That was the day he got the idea to make her a doll. And it was almost finished. Only the head was missing. Diamante grasps the handle of the coffin that sticks out on the next level. He grabs it with both hands and dangles in the void. When he jumps, his coat drops into the dark. He hangs there for a few seconds, uncertain whether he should follow his coat or the light. But he'd been too late, as usual. Rocco already gave her a doll. Vita had sat it on the kitchen table and made it listen to Enrico Caruso. A real doll, not one made out of rubbish. A porcelain doll with blond hair and a smile with thirty-two white teeth, a doll who speaks American.

Rocco laughs when Diamante jumps down from the cemetery wall, his hair standing on end and looking over his shoulder as if an army of the dead were chasing him. A diaphanous moon glows in the sky like a weak taper. Diamante's face is gray with cobwebs. He'd tossed something over the wall, and now bends to pick it up. He doesn't even look at Rocco. Sitting on the edge of the sidewalk, he takes off his broken old shoes. "Where's the watch?" Rocco asks. "I don't see the watch." "Liar," Diamante whispers. Rocco shakes his head. "I knew you weren't brave enough to go into the tomb." Diamante throws a ruined shoe at him. Then Rocco realizes that Diamante is putting on a magnificent pair of black patent-leather shoes over his socks, threadbare and full of holes. A few sizes too big and terribly odoriferous, but new. Never worn. The soles perfectly smooth. Rocco smiles. He's judged right yet again. It's not easy to pick out a swift kid in this neighborhood full of sheep. Most of them are scared shitless, and simply let themselves be devoured by the wolf. People who'd realize there's a moon in the sky only if it fell on their heads. He walks over to his bicycle leaning against the wall and gleaming in the yellow moonlight. "Hop on," he says, pleased. When Diamante settles himself on the handlebars, Rocco wraps his scarf around his neck and places his black hat on his head. It's too big and falls over his eyes. "I'm really happy for you, Diamante," Rocco says. What do you know, it's the first time he hasn't called him Celestina. "You're finished rummaging in the trash. You just got yourself a real job."

The Case of Vita M.

In 1909 *Rivista di Emigrazione* published an article entitled "Italian Women and Children in the North Atlantic Division." Reports on Teresa S., Carmela of Mott Street, twelve years old, and Carlo R., six years old with scabies, are followed by a scanty report on the "Vita case."

> Vita M., aged 10, in America 11 months. Has never gone to school. Lives with her family and 7 boarders in a house of 4 rooms. Father in America 16 years, former owner of a fruit store. The young mother, neuropathic, claims the child helps her run the boardinghouse, and due to grave economic problems they recently had to take on the job of making artificial flowers at home. Also living in the house are: 1 boarder aged 18 (employee in a funeral parlor, criminal record for theft, brawls and contempt), 2 street musicians, and 4 boarders, whose identity it was impossible to verify.

Is this Vita? Vita was not living with her mother, and there is no mention in the file of Nicola, Diamante, or Geremia. Could it be that, as minors without proper working papers, they were not reported?

Furthermore, in 1909 Vita was fifteen, not ten. She turned ten in 1904. Could the inspector have collected these cases in the preceding years? Or perhaps it's just a coincidence. After all, there must have been other young girls named Vita in the North Atlantic Division. At any rate, the "Vita case" contains a rigorous exam of the minor's dwelling place.

House in distressed conditions (rent 18 dollars), foul-smelling. Four rooms, poorly kept, only 1 (rented) ventilates onto the street, 1 onto back courtyard, 2 small rooms with no windows and kitchen with small opening. Low ceilings, infected air, wet laundry hanging inside. A blackbird walking on the stove. Cat. Chickens. Type of board: C (poor). Only one latrine, located on landing. Unauthorized work in the home by women and minors. 12–14 hours work a day, until 11 p.m. Verified case of failure to report to school: a juvenile girl not registered on the required school lists lives in the apartment. (Prince Street).

The representative from the Charity Organization Society presented herself at 18 Prince Street on March 4. No one opened the door, obviously. Resolute and impassioned, she wedged her way into the narrow alleyway and crossed the courtyard cluttered with barrels and wreckage and flooded with wastewater. The broken door flapped on its hinges, revealing a rickety wooden staircase. Clinging to a greasy rope, slippery as a snake, that was supposed to steady whoever dared go up or down, she climbed from floor to floor, knocking on doors. The women were at home making garters, ties, and corsets; hemming gloves; putting the finishing touches on trousers and coats; sewing on buttons; and constructing velvet flowers for a dollar a day. The children were gluing on stems and leaves and pulling out tacking threads. The whole building was a sweatshop echoing with voices, orders, and warnings—but no one opened the door. Americans had the annoying habit of showing up unexpectedly at people's houses, and for all sorts of reasons. To sell antiflea lotion or the Bible, verify lodging statistics, report the evils of child labor or illegal work in the home—in short, to stick their noses into the affairs of good, honest people.

The inspector was getting discouraged and climbed to the last floor only out of scruple. She knocked without conviction on a door with flaking paint and a coral horn to ward off the evil eye, from behind which echoed the bombastic voice of Enrico Caruso. *Questa o quella per me pari sono*—this woman or that, they're all the same to me. The representative stared in disgust at the coral horn. These Italians were unspeakably primitive. And filthy as animals. The landing was covered in trash and swarming with black flies. As she ascended those abominable stairs, risking her neck at every step, she had the sensation a dog was watching her. But now she realized with alarm that its tail was long and hairless; it was as big as a dog, but the cur was really a rat. She was surprised when the door opened. A little girl stared at her with big black shining eyes, and incredible as it seems, she was smiling. The representative didn't get many smiles in the Italian neighborhood. Around here they don't know how to distinguish between a charity organization and a criminal one. She and her organization wanted only to help: as it says in their by-laws, "individual improvement through social improvement." She looked at her watch. It was ten twenty in the morning. That child should have been in school.

"Where is your mother, little one?" Vita stared at her without understanding. The lady—blond, with tiny wire-rimmed glasses and an intruding stare—constituted a sensational novelty in her day. By this hour, she had finished her rounds at the market and shops, deposited her purchases in front of the stove, washed the boarders' underwear in the tub, scrubbing till her arms hurt and the yellow stains around the crotch had faded. All that remained was the endless boredom of attaching petals to artificial roses. Every time Lena finished a dozen roses, she'd toss them in a box. They earned eighteen cents for every twelve dozen—which meant that to earn one dollar, they had to make a good sixty dozen, or 720 roses. Their hands worked automatically now, selecting petals by touch. Lena's blossoms were the best on the whole block. Her roses looked real. But they were fake, devoid of scent, devoid of beauty.

The inspector glanced about the hovel. Laundry draped everywhere. Three hens with a grave form of alopecia scratched at the floor, a hoarse blackbird pranced about in an iron cage over the sink, a half-skinned cat picked its way among dirty dishes and mounds of cloth,

needles, thread, scissors, and glue. The humidity was almost at satura-
tion level in the poorly ventilated, poorly heated apartment. She crept
into the room that served as both workshop and kitchen. A young
woman with an emaciated face was bent over the table, her hands immersed in a rose garden. Lena went white when she saw the representative. "You shouldn't have opened the door, Vita!" she murmured.
But Vita flashed her a mocking smile and then, with exaggerated gestures, as if she were communicating to a deaf-mute, invited the
stranger to sit down. The woman shooed the cat away, fearful of fleas.
Vita offered her a coffee, steaming, black, and thick, but the American
did not want to drink it. Then she offered her a piece of the sublime
Neapolitan dessert from Sunday's meal, which the woman also refused.
Finally she presented a rose she'd made, which the representative accepted, if for no other reason than as proof. "Why isn't this child in
school?" she asked Lena severely. But Lena didn't even lift her head.
She'd been in America for twelve years, but had never realized it. She
had spoken Arabic with her Circassian-Lebanese husband, Armenian
with the traveling salesman who took her after her first husband died,
Swedish with the sailor she ran off from the second with, and Neapoli
tan with Pulltooth. All she knew how to say in American was the
prices of her specialties. The representative tried in vain to start a conversation, but, given the insurmountable linguistic barrier, eventually
she put away her pencil, closed her folder, and departed.

Two days later, she returned with the truant officers—Mr. Pugliese
and Miss Cavarata. Unfortunately, they were Italians, and subjected the
reluctant Lena to a fierce interrogation. While Lena mumbled confusedly, afraid of making a mistake or harming Agnello, Vita, or herself,
the woman filled out a report and marked it with crosses. At the end
of the interrogation, the society representative and the two inspectors
left with Vita in tow.

Vita danced through the neighborhood, gazing on the dilapidated
hovels and tattered crowds as if she'd never see them again. When
Nino, crouched in front of the post office picking at his lice, ran up to
ask her where she was going, she smiled gleefully. Anywhere the three
strangers took her would be better than the house on Prince Street.

Before she came to New York, she hadn't known what boredom was. In Tufo, she'd always been surrounded by relatives, neighbors, and friends. She'd help her mother in the fields, or bring water to the harvesters; she knew everyone and everyone knew her. The days passed quickly, without her noticing. But here, time had stopped. The winter had been interminable. Alone all day with Lena, scrubbing laundry and pots, ironing jackets and trousers, boiling potatoes, slicing onions, cleaning vegetables, and even sewing roses these past few months. Agnello didn't want her playing in the street—street children become delinquents and drunkards when they're six, like Nino, not to mention the stray bullets and shoot-outs—or taking care of the neighbors' children, envious, wicked people he considered responsible for his ruin. He wouldn't even allow her to go to the shop on Elizabeth Street. She liked that hole in the wall redolent of tomatoes and hot peppers, but Agnello didn't want her working in the fruit store—his women were supposed to stay at home, not go out and about dealing with strangers. She was allowed to make roses as long as Nino went to collect and deliver the boxes at the employer's. Besides, one day as she and Lena were doing the shopping, Vita had found another man behind the pyramids of tomatoes in the shop. The new owner. Agnello only wanted Vita to help run the boardinghouse. But the boardinghouse had become a revolving door. Ever since Uncle Agnello's reputation had been ruined beyond repair, what with losing the shop and Lena not being his wife, respectable tenants no longer came to stay with them. The mustached men had left. Now only the most restless, rootless types came, and departed as soon as possible. They stayed for such a brief period Vita didn't even have time to learn their names. All she remembered of them were the quarrels, provocations, and traps that awaited her as soon as she was alone.

So, with the boys out all day, her only company till Sunday consisted of roses, Enrico Caruso, and Lena. Vita continued to wish Lena would die, and she scrutinized her face every day for signs of omnipotent God's punishment. But Lena was not dying. She got up every morning at four. Still half asleep, she'd make coffee for the boarders, straighten the cots, drag herself like a sleepwalker to the market stalls, bargain stubbornly over a potato and a handful of peas, and then set off toward home, all curved over her shopping bags, without resting for a second. There she would do the laundry, iron, cook, and sew seven dozen roses, all the while singing and telling stories so as not to fall asleep or prick herself with the needle. Because after two hours your hands would get all tingly, and after four you stopped feeling them; you could jab your finger without realizing it, and if you stained a petal, even just one, you lost a whole day's earnings. Then she would wash, darn, sweep, and cook again until sunset, when the men came home to eat—some standing, others hunched over on barrels—and after dinner she would wash the pots and sew another hundred or so roses. At midnight she climbed into bed. Agnello, who'd already been sleeping for a while, would get undressed—in winter the house was so cold he slept with his clothes on—climb on top of her, and move about for a few minutes, imprisoned and swallowed up by her diaphanous flesh; their bodies would become unrecognizable, merging and disappearing like shadows on a wall. The creaking of bedsprings would make the entire house vibrate, and everyone else would hush and perk up their ears. Soon after, the creaking of other bedsprings would join in. Then all would become immobile again: the plates would stop clattering on the shelves, bodies would once more find consistency and form, and Agnello would turn to the wall and fall back asleep. And Lena would remain supine, staring at the squiggles of humidity on the ceiling. Sometimes she'd get up and go sit in front of the sink. Rocco's cat in her lap, she would sit there without moving, whispering meaningless words. And so it was all winter long, every day, without pause, without change. And Vita watched and kept silent, helped out by sewing roses or pressing gnocchi with her finger, and asked herself what was the point of suffering so if happiness is as fleeting as a continually interrupted dream.

One January morning while she was brushing Vita's hair, Lena started singing *La donna è mobile*, a cynical and lying song the kids really liked, in which woman is compared to a feather on the breeze, capricious in word and thought. Vita was so surprised by Lena's behavior and asked her so many questions that in the end Lena confessed she had dreamed of her child. All excited, Vita told her that she dreamed of him, too,

that Baby visited her every night—he was a good ghost and told her
not to worry because he'd flown directly to Paradise from the New
York Times tower, and the witch who was following him had fallen
off her broom because there was too much wind. Baby had become
their guardian angel. Lena's reaction was lukewarm, for she had been
speaking of another child, of whom Vita knew nothing. This other
child of Lena's should have been dead for a while now, but last night
the Virgin Mary sent her a vision and Lena learned he wasn't dead after all; the commander of a ship had saved him and taken him to his
villa on Long Island. He had raised him and now he wore nice clothes
and was at least five years old. "But when did this child die?" Vita insisted, tilting her head because Lena was so absorbed she'd forgotten
about the brush in her hair. When she lived in Cleveland under the
railroad tracks, and the racket of the passing trains would make him cry
all day long. The baby was called Senjeley Pshimaqua like her Circassian husband, who had died of tuberculosis a long time before, and
he wouldn't grow even though she held him at her breast for hours,
nursing him till her nipples hurt; but she didn't have any milk and he
wasn't able to drink a drop. Senjeley was covered in sores; the mice
would nibble at his skin when she left him to go work for Pulltooth,
and he would look at her as if to say, *Stop making me suffer, don't you
have a heart? Set me free, let me return to our people, what are you waiting
for?* And so she had set him free. She had wrapped him up in a black
shawl with a rock sewn into it and thrown him crying into Lake Erie.
The rock wasn't heavy enough, or she hadn't sewn it in well; at any
rate it had come loose and the shawl unfurled like a fan and was carried away by the current with Senjeley's head floating like an orange.
That was all she saw. Lena claimed she had never told anyone any of
this before, least of all Agnello; it wasn't his fault she had thrown her
child in the lake, even if he did have something to do with it because
he had just asked her to be his woman, but anyway, she was sorry and
had asked God forgiveness, God who could understand her because he
had crucified his son. And of course God had understood, and now
Lena doesn't want any more children. But last night the Virgin revealed the miracle: Senjeley had been saved from the waters, just as our
people had been saved from the universal flood, and now he's happy.

Lena recounted the death and salvation of Senjeley in the same tone of voice, as if she were speaking of equally true and equally credible facts. The smile on her lips was so desperate that Vita had to look away. Lena is fooling herself; Senjeley is a ghost just like Baby. And so Vita began to dream of Senjeley as well as Baby. But her dream was nothing like Lena's because Senjeley had been spirited away by the witch. He was all black and blue, and would cling to her and try to drag her down to the bottom of the lake. Vita was afraid of him, and of Lena. So she happily followed the inspectors.

They brought her to a white building next to Saint Patrick's Church. She realized immediately it was a school. Vita kicked and screamed because she had already gone to school in Italy and didn't want to go back. She had even invented a little song that went like this: "A-E-I-O-U, no more school for you know who." She didn't know how to sit still for four hours and listen to the teachers' litanies as they snootily revealed the secret of how to succeed in life when they hadn't done so well themselves. She would run away at the mere sight of the schoolhouse, which, like all the public buildings in Tufo, was squalid, neglected, and falling to pieces, looking more like a poorhouse or a prison. She would flee to the countryside, to breathe in the smell of the earth after rain, of fig trees baking in the sun, to savor the dusty silver of the olive trees, the leathery stalks of the agave plants, the sudden violence of a thunderstorm. Vita had always been this way, even though her mother was the village letter writer and would say that ignorant men are empty reeds who let themselves be played by the winds, and that the only way to raise yourself up and better your condition is to go to school. Vita knew that for a woman the only thing that counts is the kind of marriage you make, or that is made for you. For example, Angela Larocca didn't even know how to write her name, but she had married Mantu, who was good and kind, and they were still together, while Dionisia with all her letters had only earned herself an eye ailment and Agnello with his jutting chin and beatings, who made off to America two months after their wedding. In Italy, they'd left Vita in peace after two years of torment, and no one ever asked her why she didn't go to school. A-E-I-O-U, no more school for you know who.

But here it's impossible to buck the system. They made her sit in the back of the fifth-grade classroom and closed the door. The other children jeered at her. "What's your name?" a blond-haired teacher asked. Vita refused to look at him and stared at the wall in disgust, at a small picture of a bearded, solemn-faced man. The teacher gave up. Besides, he could read the newcomer's name—the umpteenth greenhorn from the Mulberry District—in the register. He started to trace words on the blackboard. American words. Vita didn't understand them. The teacher walked among the desks as the other children scratched in their notebooks and raised their hands. Chinese, Irish, Jewish, but they all spoke American. To pass the time Vita doodled in her notebook and thought about Nino, who was free as a bird. At that hour he would be on his way to Lena for the roses, and she would offer him a glass of milk, wash his face, and even put his filthy clothes in the washtub together with the boarders'—if Agnello found out he'd beat her—and then he'd go wandering about the city, nobody to drag him off to school because he was nobody's child and nobody gave him any grief. She thought about Diamante, who at that hour was at the Bongiorno Bros. funeral parlor nailing together boxes for the dead. It must be thrilling to see so many living people and so many dead bodies. But Diamante was a boy, like Nino. Nearly a man, in fact. His voice was changing and had acquired a husky timbre. And he no longer took her to the puppet theater on Saturdays. Her heart ached when Diamante, acting all cheeky in his fancy suit, would barrel down the stairs with Rocco and Coca-Cola and disappear into the night. The neighborhood was full of women, prostitutes living in basement rooms. The boarders talked about the whores on President Street who were only ten years old—just like her. Once when they were alone, Vita had asked Lena where the men went. Lena smiled faintly. "They go have fun." "Why can't they have fun with me?" "Because they love you," Lena had answered pensively. Vita was perplexed by this, for she'd never have fun with someone she didn't love.

She flipped through her desk mate's book. There were dozens of illustrations: a round white house with columns and a flag, a blond boy with a stupid face, happy blond-haired families who lived in clean little rooms with pink wallpaper set on green lawns without any trash.

On the wall in front of her, the bearded man in the picture smiled at her confidently, condescendingly. When Vita smiled back, he fell from the wall and shattered loudly on the floor.

"I go to school," she said to Diamante as he sat on the stairs smoking after dinner. "It's an American school." "Good for you" was his only comment. "Want to trade?" Vita proposed. "We can't." Diamante stubbed out his butt on the sole of his shoe. For a while now he had been wearing a magnificent pair of patent-leather shoes; their only defect was that they smelled awful, like carrion. At any rate, he didn't look so tattered now, and ever since he'd stopped rummaging in the dump with Tom Orecchio and started hanging out with the grave diggers from Bongiorno Bros., he'd taken on the aloof air of a prince— impoverished and poorly dressed, but a prince nevertheless. And yet Vita would have given anything to go back in time, to three months ago, when Diamante would come home dusted in snow or encrusted in mud, the broken toys he'd fished from the dump poking out of his ragged coat. He would present his finds to her with a proud yet hesitant smile. Or he'd take her up to the roof and show her the puppies, and they'd kneel and let them lick their hands. Diamante stole the dogs for Pino Fucile, who would sell them to the dog pound, where they'd be put down. Usually he'd steal strays, but if he couldn't find any, he'd snatch dogs with owners who were distracted one second too long. He'd grab them by the snout, hold the jaws closed so they couldn't bite him, and stuff them in a sack. But just like all his other jobs, that one didn't last long, either, because Diamante hid the puppies in cardboard boxes on the roof, and would only turn in old dogs. But if an old mutt looked at him when he was taking it to die, Diamante would let it go. He fed the puppies milk on the sly. Except for Vita, no one knew about it, and she felt important that Diamante trusted her. But Coca-Cola eventually found them and went and sold them as white meat to the people in the basement, who made a living showing a bear around Manhattan. The animal was kept in such a tiny cage and was so famished that he ripped the puppies apart with one swipe of his paw.

"If you learn American, will you teach me?" Diamante said all of a

sudden. "What will you give me?" Vita answered back, disappointed
he wasn't more sympathetic. "I'll tell you about the knights," he proposed. "I already know about them." He treated her like a child, but if
the knights weren't good enough for him anymore, then neither were
they for her. "I'll read you the adventures of Riccieri and Fegra Albana
of Barbary." "No, I don't like that one. She kills herself." "The story of
Fioravante and the beautiful Drusolina?" "No, that ends sadly, too;
she's all old and ugly when she sees Fioravante again." "How about
The Thousand and One Nights?" "What story's that?" Vita inquired diffidently. Diamante ran his fingers through his hair and smiled know-
ingly. "It's a story of love and sin." Vita shrugged her shoulders and
Diamante stared at her pouting, hostile lips. He clenched his fists nervously, determined not to lose this opportunity, but he didn't know
what would convince a stubborn little girl to pay attention to the
teacher and not abandon her studies. Money? He didn't have enough.
Presents? He'd already given her plenty. Attention? Between his new
job and new friends, he didn't have much time for her. He had nothing else to offer. Vita didn't realize the opportunity she was being
given. He would have given anything not to have to bang coffins together, to sit in a classroom and learn how to speak all over again, so
that when he went above Houston Street they wouldn't realize he was
a dago and wouldn't sing *guini guini goon* anymore. Then he could find
work as a messenger boy or assistant in one of those skyscraper offices
with flying elevators and red carpets in the lobbies. Then he could
walk into a department store and buy himself a tie without being
kicked out, or sit in the theaters with big signs on Broadway with
women in fur coats and men in top hats, instead of in the puppet tent
with the workers. Then he wouldn't be ashamed to open his mouth
the way he is now and let everyone know straight off he's from Italy. In
America when they look at him, he keeps his mouth shut and opens
wide his blue eyes, staring silently in hopes they just might think he's
one of them.

"A kiss," Vita burst out all of a sudden. "What's gotten into you?"
Diamante was flabbergasted. Vita straightened her apron with her
hands and explained: those kisses Agnello gives to Lena when he lies
on top of her. And even though Diamante shook his head, saying it

was impossible, wrong, and a mortal sin, Vita repeated with conviction, "I want a kiss for every word."

So Diamante stopped going out with Rocco and Coca-Cola on Sundays, even though Coca-Cola teased him, called him a little stinker, freckle face, you no-good coffin maker you, you're hopeless. Diamante swallowed the insults and waited fearfully until Agnello went down to the tavern and Lena started sifting the flour. Then he would close the curtain, sit on his cot, and make room for Vita. That little girl, flat as a board and undeniably still a child, had something no other woman in the neighborhood had: words. The first step is to give a name to things. That way you always know where they are. If you don't know their names, you can't look for them. *Job, train, bed, fire, water, earth, hearth, hurt, hope.* A kiss on her hair, on her cheek, another on her nose, hands, the curve of her elbow, neck, eyelids, eyelashes. Afterward her skin would burn as if it had been scorched. Is this what's meant by a *love story*? This sensation of fear, joy, and turmoil that makes you blush, your heart pound, your knees tremble? Diamante would stand up all shaken and feeling like a thief. Vita's kisses were bitter like wild lemons. And like wild lemons, they quenched his thirst.

On Sundays, to practice, they'd walk up the Bowery and cross Eighth Street reading the signs on the shops. The city revealed itself. The *butchery* was simply a meat market, the *elevated* nothing more than a train overhead. The city lost its glamour, power, and mystery. It even seemed less hostile. And they actually discovered a real piazza—with trees, sparrows, and a fountain. It was called Washington Square, and when Diamante went to work in the office in the skyscraper he would live there. In the night, when Agnello fell asleep after mounting Lena, Diamante would climb over Geremia's inert body, and Vita would wriggle her way through the barrels. They would squat on the dark stairway for hours, face to face, whispering, touching—*help, work, cry*—kissing—*kill, live, pray*—ears, fingers, nape, chin, knee, nails, palms, calves, shoulders, dimples. Mouth.

But then Nino betrayed her. Vita had known him for a while because he often hung around the shop begging in that feeble voice of his, sounding like a lost cat, and Agnello would always give him a few rotten bananas. Nino, thin and mangy as a stray dog, would sit on the ground outside the shop and devour them immediately, never saving any for later. When Vita asked him why, Nino replied wisely that in this country you can't put anything aside because somebody stronger than you will take it. So a full stomach right away and hunger tonight is better than hunger now as well as later. But Nino never complained, and Vita was struck by his endurance and his will to survive. Vita was rebuked, she rebelled and protested, was slapped and sent to bed without supper, while Nino slithered like a serpent through the beatings, hunger, and injustice everyone dumped on him. He was the bottom of the heap. He'd bow his head when they stole his newspapers or earnings, grin and bear it when they nicked his bananas, cry when they hit him. But his rebellion was limited to a few tears. Headstrong and unshakable, he'd gather up the newspapers the bigger kids had thrown in the sewer out of spite, and, limping on bare feet ruined by the cold, take up his rounds again. Vita compared him to the mosquito larvae that hide among the reeds in the backwaters of the Garigliano. They are fragile and invisible, but also stubborn, intelligent, patient, and able to survive in impossible environmental conditions. They die if they sink, and need to stay on the surface of the water in order to breathe. There they hover, making the water tremble for something to eat— and there they remain until they've grown and can fly away. They eat water! Nothing. They live on air and water, the minimum they need to survive, because that they can always find.

Nino would knock at Prince Street after sunset. Rubbing his eyes, bleary and glued shut by a cold, he'd run to fill the coal pail for Lena and then drag it up the stairs with precisely the attitude of those backwater larvae who wait patiently to fly away and in the meantime make do with the swamp. Vita, on the other hand, would complain and protest, and Agnello's slaps often left the trace of five fingers on her cheek. Nino's gaunt face as he quickly licked out the bowl—he had to be gone before the others came back—troubled her, for it called her back to reality, to a world where arrogance and injustice touch everything and everyone. No one is innocent. His big eyes full of devotion and his servile passivity disturbed her. Yet she was patient with the larva Nino, who not only was precociously wise but also had blond curly hair like Baby Jesus in the manger scene. She understood why Lena would make him warm his hands over the burner and lend him a blanket so he wouldn't die of cold sleeping in a barrel when the temperature dropped to ten below zero. Vita would tell him stories while she cooked, especially her favorite: that her father was a famous tenor named Enrico Caruso who had come to America especially to find his daughter who had been taken away from him.

If Nino didn't believe her, all he had to do was go to the Metropolitan, where Caruso's name and black mustache were on all the posters. Her father was incredibly handsome, his voice was like velvet, and he owned a turreted castle on Central Park, but was forced to entrust Vita to some poor fellow from the numberless streets. He had to sacrifice everything dear to him in the name of success, but soon he'd be coming to get her and take her away. Vita stirred the soup. Nino scratched his scalp—the lice were biting—and listened to her describe Enrico Caruso's castle on Central Park, with all those towers and pinnacles and thousands of windows. She went on in such detail that Nino quieted down and convinced himself it was all true. "Don't tell anyone, it's a secret between me and my father." Nino would swear, scratching so hard with his dirty fingernails that his skin was red and sore, crusted over with pus and scabs. And he coughed, shaking from a violent attack that rose from the depths of his soul. Analytic by nature, Nino was very taken by Vita's stories, and one morning he asked why, if her father was so rich, he let her prick her fingers with a needle making artificial roses that didn't even smell. Vita didn't know what to say and reflected at length before responding. "Because he is good, and he thinks that everyone is like him." "Ah," Nino exclaimed, "I never thought of that." Perhaps his father was good, too, just like Enrico Caruso, and that explains why he left him at the Five Points orphanage, because he thought everyone was good like him. Later Vita was sorry she'd told Nino that fib, and she didn't like Enrico Caruso anymore, even though she wasn't sure why, and wasn't convinced she still wanted him as a father. Even if he had a jutting chin and dark, wrinkled skin like a coffee bean, even if he had left Dionisia and didn't want to go home, she couldn't change the fact that Agnello was her father.

Then she started going to school. Her days were different, and she
forgot about Nino. Now she only thought about ways to escape
Agnello's surveillance and hole up with Diamante in the water closet,
on the stairs, or in the coal bin, and repeat *street, railroad, mouth, love,*
and make him kiss her hair, hands, eyelids. Her heart pounded, she felt
desolate, impoverished, and lost until he arrived; when he touched her
shoulder a tingle would spread from the roots of her hair to the tips of
her toes, and a sharp pain pierced her chest when she had to leave
him—as if they had torn away a piece of her flesh. She began to keep
close watch on her father's eye movements, smell his breath, and guess
how many glasses of wine he'd drunk. He slept better when he
drank—not even Lena's being near would wake him. The tables had
turned; now it was the daughter who watched over the father. She
noted his fits of drowsiness, his idleness, his trips to the pawnbroker;
she tested his acoustic abilities by walking on tiptoe behind his back,
and even went so far as to defy his nightly panting in that house without walls. She moved curtains and glided about in the dark, all the
while thinking: I'm good at this, I've worked magic, I've become invisible.

Nino was getting worse. The most violent coughing fits brought
up blood. He told her not to worry because he coughed all the time,
but Vita didn't trust him and recoiled from his presence. Maybe it was
instinct, maybe she, too, was just a larva in the swamp—survival above
all—maybe it was just her tremendous unease, that insuppressible disgust caused by other people's illnesses. But whatever it was, she didn't
let him come in the house anymore, and would bring him his bowl on
the stairs, careful not to breathe near him. Nino wouldn't stay long;
now that the weather was milder, he didn't need to warm his hands
over the stove. Vita continued to kiss Diamante, discovering how complicated the human body is and how many of the parts that seem useless are actually made to be touched by another's lips. Ever more sure
of herself, she began to escape with him to the roof, where they could
see the entire city lit up and glittering in the dark and no one could
listen to their whispering.

Agnello realized his daughter was hiding something from him. He
ordered his son to keep watch over her, but Coca-Cola turned a blind

eye because for a while now he had had his own secret nocturnal movements. Suspicious and uneasy, Agnello would patrol for hours, monitoring the danger zones—water closet, coal bin—but his daughter would merely smile at him. He couldn't imagine that Vita, his own Vita, was capable of deceiving him. Then, one Sunday in June, he realized it was true. Vita was helping Lena prepare a fava bean and pea soup. She was frying onions, euphoric because Diamante had proposed she go with him and the others to the museum of wonders after lunch. The New York Museum was at 210 Bowery, the biggest museum of all, with a bearded woman, the Queen of the Amazons, Skeleton Man, Floyd the Flying Man, a unicyclist, the Tattooed Girl weighing 485 pounds, the giant Zulu twins with arms thirty-six inches around, an albino woman, the Kinetic Demon who climbs perpendicularly up walls, the skull of the pirate Tamany, and all the rarities and marvels of the planet. Lena was looking at Diamante as if he, too, were a marvel, and Vita was surprised to see his cheeks redden because that was how he blushed when he kissed her. Incapable of suspicion, however, she dropped fava beans, peas, five artichoke hearts, and two lettuce leaves in the water. She was helping Lena prepare the fish balls when her father screamed that they were just stupid shenanigans for suckers, that the albino woman made herself white with baking soda, the bearded woman was a man in a dress, the Zulus were Negroes from Virginia, and the skeleton man just a poor starving wretch in a tight shirt. "But I want to go anyway," Vita protested. Agnello scrutinized her with hatred.

He had fallen into a deep depression months ago. Ever since he sold the shop, he'd felt useless. He had looked for another job, but the boss told him he wasn't in good enough shape for factory work, the railway, or repair work on the electric lines out West. But since Agnello had provided him with so many good, docile, and obedient workers at very competitive prices all these years, for which he was grateful, in the end he offered him a post as foreman on the Canadian Pacific Railways for five dollars a day. It was a good job, even if it meant he'd have to go back to threatening his men with a shotgun, something Agnello had done for years and didn't look forward to repeating. Besides, the work camp was so far away—in the middle of the

Saskatchewan plains, at least a ten-day journey. And he didn't want to leave his children and Lena alone for six months. He didn't trust America or them. So he would stare at them and growl, their cheerfulness wounding him. The boys were joking around, talking about the Queen of the Amazon, and Coca-Cola was telling Lena she should come along to the museum of wonders as well, and Lena smiled, tempted. Vita was shaping the fish balls and sticking her fingers in Diamante's mouth so he could taste how good they were. Agnello had an overwhelming desire to kill them all. He'd been much calmer when he lived alone. His children did nothing but cause him problems. They didn't take care of him, and all they thought about was laughing and having fun. My God, they didn't even notice his presence. "Will you cut it out now? I'm dyin' of hunger, you fucking fools!" he growled.

"Oh, don't worry, Papà," Vita snapped back in English. "You'll eat like a god!" Agnello glared at her, outraged at her brazen-faced disrespect. So not only was Vita betraying him, but she also jeered at him. He could imagine Nicola abandoning him. He was vain, a good-for-nothing, and mesmerized by the dishonest life. Agnello had brought him to America too late, and he'd only grasped the worst things, the evil. And Agnello feared Lena would abandon him. If she weren't so unpredictable, she probably would have left him already. Only her folly kept her there with him. That, and the fear of ending up back where he had found her—in a rat's nest under a railroad bridge, where she scurried around half naked for that quack dentist Painless Pulltooth and serviced men for twenty-five cents. Less than it cost to eat lunch at the tavern. She was all rumpled and awkward—she danced well, but was worthless as a lover.

Agnello had just returned to Cleveland from the railway camps in a fairy-tale forest, dense, dark, and frightening, when he met her. He hadn't gone to bed with a woman in ages. He had a cavity and was looking for someone to pull his tooth. On Mayfield Road he met Painless Pulltooth and his Tantalizing Tweezers, five wretched females half dead with hunger who danced bare-legged even though it was freezing. Lots of castoffs from New York and Chicago whorehouses drifted into the countryside when their vaginas went slack and no one wanted them anymore. Writhing around this lurid dentist, they sang and danced in order to tempt spectators to get their teeth pulled. A dollar a molar, Painless Pulltooth promises, quick extraction and guaranteed pleasure. Pulltooth must be about fifty—a hearty face, dyed blond hair, bushy eyebrows. Agnello gathered instantly he was no dentist and would probably give him an abscess, but then his eyes met Lena's. The gaze of someone who lives on another planet—where pain and evil cannot reach. An ageless woman, wearing practically only her hair, a tight bustier squeezing her adolescent breasts, and torn fishnet stockings hugging her spindly legs.

He plucked up his courage and went forward. The crowd applauded. He sat still as the Tantalizing Tweezers fixed a white sheet around his neck. Painless Pulltooth carried on, claiming his hands were as light as dragonfly wings, and that he hypnotized his patients with beauty. The Tantalizing Tweezers took to twirling about him, shaking their hips, fannies, breasts—everything they had—all withered like a rotten fig, broken down, or overflowing. It wasn't a pretty sight. He looked at Lena's protruding bones. The narrow hips, pointed collarbone, shoulder blades like two parentheses. Or two wings. The Tweezers sang, "I'll heal you with no weeping, I'll make you dream without sleeping," and other ditties on the same artistic level. Agnello opened his mouth. Painless Pulltooth pressed his tongue with an iron blade and the Tweezers sang, completely out of tune. He tied a thread around the molar. Not exactly, more like an absurd-looking ribbon, a good ten yards long. The Tweezers danced with the ribbon, passing it between their legs, placing it in their mouths, sucking, licking, moaning. The crowd was going wild with excitement. Lena danced in front of Agnello, the ribbon in her fingers. She moved as in a daydream, absentminded and untouched. Then she put the ribbon in her mouth and started to spin, wrapping it around her hips. The ribbon went taut. The closer she came, the greater the pain; as the distance between them decreased, the tooth loosened. Then everything blurred. Agnello found himself with a mouth full of blood, a crater where his tooth had been, and his pants all wet. The crowd was clapping wildly. Painless Pulltooth collected dozens of volunteers, swarms of railroad workers willing to endure anything to be near the Tantalizing Tweezers. Lena's face was expressionless, like an angel on a candlestick. She was not of this world. Not there. Agnello could not convince himself he had felt pain—quite the opposite. Pleasure. The piercing pleasure of suffering. Lena pressed a rag soaked in chloroform to his mouth. "Sleep," she whispered, "dream of me."

So, despite the fact that Lena had shown her legs to entire crews of diggers wintering in Cleveland, Agnello took her just the same. He was tired of living like a guard dog, always barking at his men, of being feared, hated, and completely alone. If it hadn't been for Lena, he wouldn't have left the crew, wouldn't have come to New York, wouldn't have bought the shop, wouldn't have run a boardinghouse. He wouldn't have tried to live like a man instead of a beast in this god-forsaken city.

But he couldn't accept the fact that even Vita was thinking of abandoning him. And if Vita learned things he didn't know, she'd start to laugh at him. Start not giving a damn about his rules and teachings, lie to him. Behave like an American. But Agnello didn't want to forget the rules from that other world he'd been forced to leave behind and to which not even he wanted to return. To make light of those rules would be to make light of his sixteen years in America, of all the sufferings he had endured, and transform them into senseless sacrifice. Vita must not disown him. He'd opened this boardinghouse for her as well—Vita was the hope of the family.

Nino gnawed on a crust of bread, squatting on a pile of newspapers. "Wanna banana?" Agnello asked. "No," said Nino. "Good weather doesn't last, you know," Agnello said, studying the sky. "Opportunities come limping and leave running. Wanna plate of spaghetti?" "No," Nino replied, angelic. "What do you want for telling me what Vita's up to?" Agnello insisted, and since a larva makes do with very little, lives only to survive, becoming insensitive to temperature, light, and heat, since his life is reduced to a perpetual floating, a desperate struggle awaiting the right season, since the only thing that interests him is survival, and therefore he doesn't disdain a near-total hibernation of the other vital impulses, Nino answered.

Up on the roof, Nino was wrapped in a blanket, smoking a butt and coughing. He wanted to warn Vita not to meet Diamante that night, but lacked the courage because if he said something, Vita would know he had spied on her. He recognized her figure sliding in the shadows between the cages, her stealthy steps retreating toward the railing. *Boy*—he heard Vita's voice. The furtive smack of a kiss. *Girl*—a stifled moan. Agnello and Coca-Cola jumped on her just as Diamante's lips fumbled for her cheek. "Slut! Whore!" Agnello shrieked furiously, while Diamante, staggering from a blow, took advantage of Coca-Cola's feigned distraction to slip away in the darkness and make himself scarce. Screaming and whirling his belt, Agnello dragged her to the ground. Vita did not yell or complain because fortune is made of glass—it shimmers as it breaks—and what mattered was that Diamante hadn't been caught. Otherwise Agnello would have killed him, or Diamante would have killed Agnello. They were hot-blooded, both of them. The neighbors came up, drawn by the shouts; they were all there in the dark, disheveled and drowsy, irritated because the ruckus had ruined their sleep. "Whatsa matter? Whatsa matter?" they asked. "No-a you bisinis," Agnello responded. Even Lena came up, all sleepy, in a half-unbuttoned pajama top so you could see her pointy tits. Nino was squirreled away behind a barrel, his hands over his ears. Vita didn't ask for help, didn't beg forgiveness. She did not seek refuge in the treacherous arms of Lena, who, the more she pleaded, the more Agnello became irritated, convinced she had set a bad example for his daughter. Vita did not yell when Agnello slapped her around, or when he cracked his worn belt across her back. Not even when he started to whip her with the iron laundry line, thrashing till his arm grew numb. "Be good now, enough, my father, stop or you'll kill her," Nicola dared to utter under his breath, fearful of diverting the laundry line from his sister's back to his own. Agnello's fury abated, and he dragged Vita by the ear toward the rabbit cages.

Despite the landlords' prohibition, the neighbors raised rabbits for butchering in order to make a few bucks. The children tended them: they'd bring them lettuce leaves at dawn, and in the evening they'd clean out the cages. Nino would often help as well, in exchange for a tomato. He would have liked to have a rabbit, but had no place to keep one, and nothing to feed it besides. Sometimes in winter, he wouldn't even find an apple core for himself in the trash heap. The last cage was empty. Agnello opened it, flung Vita inside, and locked the door. "Now let's see if you manage to get out and go around disgracing yourself," he snarled. The cage was twenty-four inches high and thirty-six inches long. Vita couldn't stand or lie down; she had to crouch on her hands and knees, even though her joints hurt and started to swell after an hour. "Let me out, let me out, I didn't do anything wrong, I won't do it again," she cried, pressing her face against the metal grating. The rabbits in the next cage squeaked as they chomped their lettuce and carrots, chattering in the dark. "I won't do it anymore! Papà! Papà!" She was short of breath from yelling, her voice hoarse. She looked at the lock for a long time, stared at it as she had with the picture of President Lincoln, but she was too weak, or her eyes too wet with tears—the lock didn't budge. By dawn her wrists had given out, she was thirsty, and didn't even have the energy to cry. A creak, the door to the roof opened, the shuffle of feet, the neighbors, the hobbling gait of Nino. All she could see through the grating was the head of lettuce as it approached, a green blotch in the morning light diffusing across the roof. "Let me out, Nino!" she cried desperately. Nino put his face up to the cage, a gentle smile under his blond curls. "I can't, I can't, I'm sorry." "I'm hungry, I'm thirsty, water, water, please, it hurts." Her back was in flames, her arms felt broken. The neighbors' children shuffled off. Nino peered into the grating. "Let me out, Nino." She couldn't take it anymore, her ears were ringing and big, black, hairy spiders were darting across her field of vision—but then she caught his guilty look and understood. Vita didn't say anything more. Nino slipped away and didn't show his face again. For the entire day they forgot about her; it was pointless to call out and cry because no one was going to come. The sun inflamed the tar on the roof, melted the asphalt in the pails, burned her skin. Her saliva had dried up, her lips were splitting from thirst, she had cramps in her stomach and pins and needles in her arms, and she was all wet from having peed in her pants. The rabbits scuffled in their cages, teeth chattering, the odor of carrots and rotten lettuce. The buzzing in her ears was deafening and she saw black—she thought it was nighttime. She fainted, and came to crouched over like a brooding hen. It was the only position she could manage now that she could no longer feel her

arms and knees. The glaring lock loomed enormous in front of her.
Sun everywhere, stabbing pains, burning thirst, cramps, weakness,
buzzing. Black spiders in her eyes. The solid lock on the chain. Odor
of carrots and piss. The lock. The chain. She didn't even realize they'd
opened the cage. Diamante and Coca-Cola were pulling her out, laying her down on the burning tar. "Vita . . . ," Diamante murmured,
"Vita, can you hear me?"

The wound from the laundry line healed in three weeks, leaving a
lightning-shaped scar, rough to the touch and slightly porous, but Vita
never went back to school. At the beginning of the new academic
year, the Charity Organization Society representative came looking
for her. The first time, Lena tried to explain the child was sick and
couldn't leave the house. The representative threatened to initiate paperwork to fine the reluctant parent. The second time Coca-Cola said
Vita had left for Youngstown, had gone to stay with relatives. The representative reported Agnello to the court, and the paperwork got held
up in an office somewhere, along with thousands of other cases. The
third time, the inspector was overcome by a sense of discomfort standing in front of the horn of coral. In the end, if those inferior and brutal beings considered her their enemy rather than their ally, she who
only wanted to help, if they didn't want to educate their children, improve their lives, elevate their morale, help them to become true
Americans, what could she possibly do? She was just an idealistic
benefactress, a minuscule grain of sand in the workings of destiny.
Vita's name remained on the Saint Patrick School's register for the entire scholastic year 1904–05, even though she didn't attend one single
lesson and the teacher stopped reading her name when he called the
roll. In the following academic year, 1905–06, the list under the letter
M read as follows: MacDuffy, Mazzoni, Meyer. Her name had disappeared.

Vita never forgave Nino. She didn't see him for weeks. Then one day
she ran into him as he was pestering passersby, the usual newspapers
under his arm. She spat in his face. She ignored him, from then on and
forever. Nino had died in the rabbit cage—dead and buried—a lying
friend, a traitor. If she sensed he was around—in front of the post of-

fice, in an alley, on the decrepit stairway—she'd turn her head and climb past him whispering, "A spy is no child of Mary." She never said anything else to him. Inflexible, incapable of forgiving a cowardly spy even if he was nobody's child and had never been given anything in life, not even a happy memory. It might be necessary to lie or deceive, but never to betray a friend, not even for a rabbit, the only thing Nino had ever dared ask for in his wretched existence as a larva living on nothing his entire life. Because it was a rabbit Agnello had promised him in order to extort his daughter's secret. A rabbit to cuddle under the covers on the subway vents in the winter. "It's your fault, Vita, you shouldn't have been kissing Diamante," he would mumble as he ran after her. Vita refused to listen. "Let's make up, Vita." "No, so much the worse for you. If you hadn't spied on me, we'd still be friends and I'd still tell you stories."

Nino couldn't breathe anymore. At the start of winter he was spitting up so much blood that he collapsed on the street—they found him blue in the face, nearly frozen to death. Lena dragged him home and sent Nicola to look for the doctor despite Agnello swearing that you can't offer charity to just anybody, they were hardly the Catholic Church. She laid him on Diamante's cot. Vita didn't come near him. He disgusted her and she no longer hid the reason why. "Your blood is gross and I don't want to touch you." Nino was weeping. "Vita, Vita, I love you," he would cry, but Vita wouldn't respond. The doctor wanted to be paid before he crossed the threshold. He knew how clever this sort of people were. He wasn't about to risk leaving empty-handed. Agnello refused to waste a cent on that waif despite Lena's pleas, and in the end Diamante dug into his savings he kept in the baby-powder tin and wasted a month's salary to be told, "There is nothing that can be done, tuberculosis in its final stages, extremely contagious, you need to take him to the hospital."

While they discussed who should take him to Bellevue, which was on First Avenue, so not exactly around the corner, and below freezing outside, with the fog turned to ice and a wind that sliced your face, Nino curled up on the cot and stared intently at Vita. "Just tell me one thing, Vita," he asked in a tiny voice, pursuing his final, foolish desire. "Am I Enrico Caruso's child, too?" "You?" She laughed. "You, Nino?

No, you, no, you're nobody's child. Sleep now, they'll bring you to the hospital soon," she added, sorry not to have told him yes; after all, it wouldn't have cost her anything, and not even she was Enrico Caruso's child. Tomorrow I'll tell him yes, I'll even tell him his father will come collect him in an automobile when spring comes and take him to the tower in the castle, she was thinking as she drifted off to sleep, her face buried in the pillow.

The next day at dawn Nino was no longer there. Diamante and Geremia had taken him on the trash cart to the charity hospital. "When are we going to see Nino?" she tortured Lena, but Lena hesitated. That place was a sort of condemned city, a castle with iron gates and crenellated towers like a fortress, a workshop where they patched you up with no compassion in the name of a charity that was not dispensed in the city of others. It was the inferno of the worst-off, the last painful and humiliating wound the devastated bodies and souls of the most forsaken endured in their lives. Diamante promised to take her, but not before Sunday because during the week he had to work late at the funeral parlor. If he wanted to make his way up the ladder, he had to show he was always available. Vita counted the days. She put aside an artificial rose for Nino and waited. But on Sunday, as she was getting ready, tying a red ribbon in her hair, Agnello, eyes shining, told her it was pointless. Nino had already gone home. *Why are you crying?* Vita wanted to yell. *You who were only capable of turning him into a spy!* Her wrath erased her sorrow and she wasn't even able to weep for Nino, who had gone away on the sly, secretly, begging pardon for the disturbance.

Agnello paid for a real Bongiorno Bros. funeral, with white garlands and a cart pulled by white horses. The boys thought he had done it for Lena, who had taken that nobody's child to heart, perhaps because she'd thrown her own child in the lake. In truth Agnello did it for Vita. All the inhabitants of the neighborhood came to the procession because everybody knew Nino, and everybody had kicked him in the pants or bought his last copy at least once. The men stood with legs spread, hat in hand, the newsagent placed a newspaper on his coffin and Vita an artificial rose, the women made the sign of the cross and Lena blew her nose, repeating over and over, my baby, my poor

little baby. The priest spoke Latin well, there were lots of white flowers, even the coffin was white, with a raised gold cross on the lid. It
was a nice funeral. Nino would have been so happy, he never would
have expected such a grand procession, as if he were the king of the
neighborhood. But then Diamante placed Nino's beat-up old cap on
the coffin and climbed up next to the coachman. As they headed toward the Hart Island cemetery, on the island off the Bronx, where, far
from stares and embarrassment, the city of New York buried poor
souls, vagabonds, and nameless people in common graves, Agnello caressed Vita's hair. She burst into tears and wanted to cry out that she
wasn't the child of Enrico Caruso, either, no, neither was she. But
Nino had already gone home.

The Gift

Vita had discovered it by chance. Perhaps it had always been there—wherever she was, there was also that *something*. But she became aware of it all of a sudden, in that vast hall on Ellis Island. It wasn't inside her, but wasn't somewhere else, either—it was always near her, close by like her shadow. She didn't know if it was a gift, a punishment, or a congenital defect like a heart murmur or a walleye. Objects recognized her. They felt her presence. Other people called it distraction. Carelessness. Glasses would break, pans come unhooked from the wall and crash to the floor, doors would close, leaving her to roam around outside for hours. A young girl with her head in the clouds. Vita knew she had to remember not to stare at objects for too long when other people were around. She had to *seem* like them, to pretend. At all costs. Half close her eyes if she found her gaze lingering on a pail balancing awkwardly on the stairs, a birdcage perched on a windowsill, objects that looked out of place, uncomfortable somehow, precarious, ugly. But sometimes she would forget. And in that moment her eyes would speak, revealing her thoughts, desires, and hatreds—emotions not even she knew were there. The pail would tumble down the stairs, the cage would fall and set free the goldfinch. Plates, forks, brooms became animated, liquid; they repositioned themselves in space, harmoniously creating a secret order. All without her lifting a finger or uttering a word. Afterward she would turn around suddenly, fearful that someone might have seen her. But all they would have seen was a little girl with black hair and an incomprehensible smile shaking a tablecloth out the window or sweeping the stairs.

Diamante hadn't told anyone about the mysterious disappearance of the yellow ticket. He wasn't sure he had seen correctly, maybe he was mistaken: everything was so strange and unnatural on the day of his arrival. Besides, he didn't really believe it. He was suspicious of anything that couldn't be touched or explained rationally. Vita had probably managed to roll the ticket up in her hand and throw it away. Something like that. If at other times he had the feeling he'd surprised her as she was carrying on a dialogue with a silently resisting plate, he preferred to think she was playing a secret game to which only she knew the rules.

With time, however, the objects in the Prince Street house manifested a disturbing energy—they started to walk, to disappear. Nothing seemed to stay where it had been put. Everything moved, silently and furtively. Agnello's belt buckle was found all twisted and soft under the mattress. The lock on the rabbit cage she'd been imprisoned in had melted out of shape and dangled on its chain as if it had been baked in a furnace. The laundry line was cut in pieces. The bottles filled with gasoline that Coca-Cola kept hidden under his bed exploded, flooding the room and filling the air with an acrid stench. And Geremia saw with his own eyes—I swear to God—the water pitcher slide the whole length of the table and stop right in front of his glass, which is where it would have been if he'd had time to ask her to pass it.

But then Coca-Cola and Diamante surprised her, and nothing was ever the same again. It was nighttime. They were coming back from Second Street, where they'd done a little favor for some friends of Rocco's, setting fire to the barbershop of a man named Capuano, a greedy, stubborn Neapolitan who refused to make friends. It took less time than they'd thought. Thirty seconds and Rusty had forced open the shutters and broken the window. Coca-Cola sprinkled the barber-

shop walls with gasoline and lit the fuse in the bottle, while Diamante
strolled back and forth in the dark on the other side of the street, ready
to whistle if anybody not wanting to mind his own business happened
by. Everything had gone smoothly. No witnesses. The fire had caught
well, without doing too much damage. Nothing more than a little
demonstration. No wounded. Message delivered. If the greedy Capuano had not understood the boys' warning, then the big guys—
Nello, Elmer, and Rocco—would explain it better. Diamante and
Coca-Cola entered the house on tiptoe so as not to wake Agnello. Vita
didn't realize they were there. She was seated at the kitchen table, her
nightgown glowing in the shadows. In her outstretched arms she held
Diamante's knife, the tip pointing up to the ceiling. Which explains
why he hadn't been able to find it earlier. Vita was immobile, concen-
trating, not doing anything at all. Eyes wide open and empty, she
stared at the knife as if she were asleep. All of a sudden the blade
started to bend. Irresistibly. Folding over itself like a melted candle.

"Vita!" Diamante exclaimed. "What are you doing?"

She turned red. As if she were guilty of something. What remained
of the knife fell onto the table. She didn't respond.

It was a good knife.

Sturdy, as Rocco knew well. He had used it quite a bit before passing it on to his pupil as a token of their eternal friendship.

Blades don't melt in the sun.

The case was put before the great Rocco.

Coca-Cola swore that Vita had done it with her eyes and on purpose.

"I seen it with my own eyes, I swear, cross my heart and hope to
die."

"I don't believe it. It can't be true."

Blades don't melt in the sun.

Vita knew they could not understand. They would never understand what was there beside her. They weren't capable—they lacked
the imagination.

Contemplating Vita's dark hair silhouetted like a Chinese shadow puppet against the white sheets hung up to dry, Rocco finally understood

who had sent her here. This little girl would allow all of them to abandon Prince Street once and for all. She would *move* them, literally, as she did with the glasses and belt buckles. Belfiore the palm reader, who predicts the future at 179 Prince Street, claims that only great mediums possess the capacity to impart motion to objects—move, bend, or break them—without touching them, with the simple force of their thoughts. It's not a talent you can invent. You could study for a hundred years and never learn it. "Who are these mediums?" Rocco had asked her, anxious. "Those who move between this dimension and another." "What other?" "The other, that's all." Rocco thought about the holy men, fanatics who preach the end of the world, and fortune-tellers who pretend to speak with spirits and the souls of the dead. Hundreds of them in the city. People's credulity was equal only to their desperation. Every one of those charlatans, with nothing more than a rapacious ability to thrive on the pain and ignorance of others, collected ten dollars a visit. They didn't have Vita's gift, but it was enough to move a glass ball, a little table, or even nothing at all—the consultation only lasted a few minutes—to pocket what a gravedigger earns in a month. A talented girl like Vita represented a fabulous business, inestimable capital. Everything would be different from now on. No more fists, fires, knives, blood, sweat. To hell with Lazzaro Bongiorno, dead bodies, and shopkeepers who don't want to pay up. He'd never had anything against them and would much prefer to break a few of Cozza's ribs than the bones of some guy with a hill of potatoes. Thanks to Vita, all of this was finished. And soon to be forgotten. They would fix up a room for the holy girl. Scarlet curtains on the windows. Red lampshades. Vita in the shadows, a line of black coal around her eyes, her hair loose, crazy-looking. The child saint. Eleven years' worth of arcane wisdom. Diamante would copy out or invent some oracle that was incomprehensible and therefore suitable for every occasion. Whoever heard it would think those words had been uttered for him alone. Vita merely had to learn her lesson and recite it as if in a trance. The ineffable child saint seated on the edge of the couch who makes windows vibrate and grandfather clocks chime just by looking at them.

"Get dressed, princess, let's go for a spin. I'm taking you uptown."

Vita stared at him and bit her nails. She seemed frightened. Now that her secret had been torn from her and was no longer hers, it almost disgusted her, and she would have traded it for Nicola's stupid enthusiasm or Diamante's silent consternation. "It's not for that, is it?" she asked Rocco as he held out her raincoat. He avoided her gaze, suddenly terrified she would make him fly out the window or set him on fire for planning to market her to the desperation of others and the insatiable curiosity of the world. But Vita herself would have been grateful. For her, too, it would mean the end of sheets to launder, crass boarders who taught her things a young girl shouldn't know, artificial roses, sacrifice, and suffering. Soon the rumor would circulate and her fame would spread beyond the neighborhood. She would end up in society salons. Inconsolable widows, spinster aunts, men of science, and doctors would vie for her company. She would be invited to move silver platters at some noblewoman's table. Summoned to the White House to guess the number of wildcats Theodore Roosevelt would kill on his next hunt in Arizona. They would all become rich. Rich, famous liars.

Rocco explained that each one of us has a gift—just one. And that God has given it to us so that we may use it. To deny or refuse it would be like denying God. Vita responded that it happened to her sometimes, but didn't depend on her. It wasn't her will, but something much more powerful. Rocco replied that she was too young to be able to recognize her will, and therefore she attributed to some inscrutable power what in reality was her own self. "So what?" Diamante asked indifferently. That *something* belonged to Vita. It was hers. Rocco said everything's shared here. And Vita was the gift God had sent to Prince Street.

Vita and Rocco entered the jewelry store exuding dignity. He sporting a striped suit, she in a sailor dress and white shoes. Unfurling his most gracious eloquence, Rocco explained to the salesman that it was his sister's first communion and he wanted to give her a gold chain. Not something vulgar, but a delicate piece, finely worked. Something precious. Vita had never been to a jeweler's before. She placed her hands on the glass counter and gazed at the gold chains nestled on black velvet cushions; they were of every length, shape, weight, and consistency. Rocco chatted with the salesman, and every once in a while he would wink at her, as if to invite her to begin. But the necklaces didn't move. Nothing happened.

Rocco didn't say a word as he climbed onto the bicycle and waited for her to settle on the handlebars. He was furious. Vita gathered her skirt between her knees so it wouldn't get caught in the spokes and stared at the streetlamps as they sputtered to life. The wind smelled of lime trees and horse droppings. It was already springtime. And then it would be fall and then winter once again. Relentless repetitions. The seasons have no future. Rocco kept his hands on the handlebars so as to keep from slapping her. "Why didn't you do it?" "Because it's not for sale," Vita replied.

"When God gives someone a gift, he doesn't want that person to keep it for himself," Rocco cried. "He wants you to share it with others."

"You don't even believe in God, so why do you keep talking about him?" Vita demanded. She was pale and tired-looking. Rocco hunched over the handlebars and pedaled fiercely in order to release the disappointment mounting in him. He thought about how he would have to go on breaking noses, burning shops, and cutting up shopkeepers, how Diamante would have to go on washing dead bodies, and Geremia digging in the sewers. It wasn't fair. "You should have done it, Vita." She should have understood. He sped past the rows of carriages heading downtown. "You aren't like other people, Vita, and you can't do anything about it. It's already happened to you."

"You aren't like other people, either, and you can't do anything about that," Vita countered. Rocco didn't want to talk to her anymore. Her perspicacity and naive wisdom irritated him. This stupid little girl had something others search for in vain, but she didn't know what to do with it. This obstinate and irresponsible girl. She'd be fabulous in the scarlet shadows of the salon, pronouncing obscure prophecies about people's secrets. All she would have to do is sit there in the dark and let her gaze wander over their bodies and faces in order to know them better than they could ever know themselves.

Rocco pedaled faster and faster. The idea took shape all on its own.

At the end of the street was the factory wall. Rocco accelerated. He headed the bicycle right for it to see if she would be able to avoid the collision. But Vita didn't accept the challenge. She clung to the lapels of his jacket and stared fixedly at his ashen-colored face. In the end Rocco took his feet off the pedals and pulled on the brakes with all his might. But he was going too fast, the wall was too close. The bicycle hit the wall with a deafening, metallic crash.

People came running. Rocco was massaging his neck in a daze. Vita didn't move. Her body stretched out on the pavement, black hair fanned out like a crown, skirt thrown up above her skinned knees. "Vita?" Rocco started to yell. "Vita? Damn it! Answer me, Vita!" Rocco kneeled in a puddle but didn't dare touch her for fear she would crumble in his hands, or wilt like the blade of that blasted knife. Someone advised him not to move her because if she has hit her head . . . Someone else was moistening her forehead. Rocco was in a cold sweat. His eyes burned. He had hated her so fiercely he'd been ready to kill her. Without even thinking about it.

The woman who ran the bread cart said the little girl didn't seem hurt. No blood to be seen, and all her bones intact. As strange as it sounded, it looked as if she were sleeping. "Vita?" Rocco yelled, shaking her by the arm. "Vita!!!" Don't let her be dead. Don't let it be that I killed her. Not Vita, not her of all people.

When Vita opened her eyes, she didn't know where she was or what all those people around her were doing. The bicycle lay twisted on the pavement. Her eyes found Rocco's distraught face. He was smiling at her, looking all worried. Tender. He massaged her temples, brushed off her skirt. He'd gone back to being the Rocco she had always known. The most mysterious and sweetest of the boys. When the crowd dispersed, she told him she felt extremely tired. It was always like that, afterward. As if she had made a superhuman effort. "After what?" Rocco exclaimed. He was sitting on the sidewalk, trying to straighten out the front wheel because otherwise he'd have to lug the bike home. "After I've done it," Vita said. Rocco stared at her uncomprehending as she placed an object in his hand. In the dark it felt like a stone. The Eye of God. He could have sworn he saw it hanging on the wall in the jewelry shop, imbedded in a wooden triangle. It was there the whole time they were examining the gold necklaces. "I asked God to choose for me. If he didn't want to, it wouldn't have come down from the wall, right?" Her voice was little more than a whisper. "Right," Rocco assured her.

He never thought about bringing her along again. He thought that every gift is freely given and good for nothing. It identifies us, makes us who we are, growing with us and for us. But everyone is responsible for his own. His gift was his fist and his sangfroid with a knife and with people. People didn't exist for him; they had the same indifferent reality of a stone or a tree. It had taken him a while, but now he had come to understand and accept it—and himself. Vita would have to decide how to accept her gift. Had she wanted to, she could have made a lot of money performing for the crowds at the New York Museum or in some rich person's salon. If she had only asked him, he would have taken her to unlock villa gates and apartment doors, move trains at the depot and intercept tons of coal, ransack travelers' suitcases at the White Star Line warehouses, select her favorite combs and barrettes at the department stores on Thirty-fourth Street.

But Vita never asked him.

The Persistent Perfume of the
Lemon Tree

My father's brother, Amedeo, was a schoolteacher. In the 1940s, right after the war, he had worked as a theater critic. He was a competent critic, informed and impartial. But he gave it up. "I had to make a living," he told me. The Mazzuccos were of the belief that the theater, writing, poetry, and music were pleasures satisfied at hunger's expense. It was forbidden to complain or confess, to show weakness, ignorance, or fragility. Failure in school, love, or health was not allowed. If they did fall ill, they suffered in silence until hospitalization proved inevitable. Many of them died before being hospitalized, and the rest were desperately hypochondriacal. The Mazzuccos feared pleasure and were always denying themselves, I don't know why. Perhaps in the beginning, there was someone who yielded to every pleasure, and later regretted it for reasons incomprehensible to me. They all adhered to an obsessive cult of rectitude, loyalty, discipline, culture, conscience (the supreme Being that substituted for God in the nonreligious or atheist family), and self-sacrifice to the point of self-destruction. This strange web of irreconcilable expectations engendered neuroses, suffering, and madness. My grandfather, my father, and I have all lived with the certainty—or fear—of going insane, constantly spying on ourselves in order to identify the precise moment in which the insanity would take over.

My father's brother, tormented since his youth by a series of extremely painful illnesses, which he faced with the stoicism of an ancient sage, was now confined to an easy chair in the living room of his Monteverde Nuovo apartment in Rome. He never went out. When the weather was nice, his chair would be moved onto the balcony that jutted out over the busy street below. A lemon tree gave off a persistent perfume, and my uncle would breathe it in with eyes closed. If the lemon tree became diseased, he would realize it right away. His family situation had transformed him into a sort of Thomas Bernhard character without his knowing it. He was going blind and could no longer read. He had been a formidable reader. All the Mazzuccos were. Who knows what demon they exorcised by reading. Even Antonio, who had only completed the first grade, read furiously. My uncle was the firstborn, and had been given the name of Diamante's favorite brother, Amedeo. My uncle was very proud of this name, even though he knew it evoked a broken and incomplete life and cast its shadow on him as well. When I went to talk with him in 1998, he was seventy-eight years old. His thick, kinky hair was dazzling, a beautiful snow white of a purity I never found anywhere else. He had delicate features, large, full lips, clear, glassy blue eyes, and furrowed eyebrows that seemed to express a perennial dissent. Those eyebrows—that dissent—are the only physical characteristic passed on in the family, and they remain our most distinctive feature.

He told me right away that his memory was confused. Since he couldn't read and didn't receive enough stimuli, his brain was growing feeble, like a plant deprived of light. And yet his judgments remained sharp, both moving and unyielding, and his point of view was disenchanted and bitter. During our sporadic encounters over the years— me immobile, eyes fixed on that fascinating white hair, he immobile in his chair, eyes fixed on something I wouldn't know quite how to define—I realized that the present for him was a confused and unreal dream, a universe teeming with senseless plots and signs. But in the past he moved freely. When he talked, he wasn't there with me, a prisoner of paralysis and shadows. He was somewhere else—precisely in that place in time I wanted to go to. There, Amedeo was neither paralyzed nor blind; he could run and see clearly—Diamante, Antonio, the lemon tree, Tufo, the slingshots, the stones. The sea.

"He went to America in the spring," he told me.

"In what year?"

"1903."

"Are you sure? Papà wrote that he was fifteen."

"We always felt older than our years. And our bodies understood us. My hair turned white when I was twenty. No, it was 1903. It was the year the Pope died. He missed the train that was supposed to take him to Cleveland. I don't know why. He never told us. But he went to Cleveland later. Cleveland seemed like a horrible mistake to him."

"What did he say about New York?"

"I never asked him. When we were young, your father and I used to devour comic books and adventure stories. Many of them were set in America. They were teeming with Cheyennes, cowboys, prairies, buffalo. Matiru, the King of the Redskins. That's what we imagined America was like when he talked. We never realized he'd lived in a big city—a metropolis. We didn't even realize America was inhabited by Americans, not redskins and buffalo. He never talked about the Americans. He used to talk about the Italians, though, and with an unshakable pessimism. And yet, precisely for that reason, he attempted to die for them several times."

"Why?"

"He had chosen Italy. He loved Italy, even though his love was never reciprocated. He tried to convince me to go to New York at least once. He used to say that seeing lots of places allowed you to remain young in your old age."

"Did he ever tell you anything about the boardinghouse on Prince Street?"

"He said it was run by an elderly relative of his uncle. A seventy-

year-old Neapolitan woman. Ugly. Dirty. I think she was called Maddalena, or Lena. Something like that."

Amedeo remembered everything: the boardinghouse, the Black Hand,
Cousin Geremia, the railways, Diamante's duties as water boy. Someone was always missing from his stories, however. He never once mentioned Vita.

When I consulted the passenger lists in the Ellis Island archives, I discovered the names of the twenty-two hundred people who had made
the crossing with Diamante on the *Republic*. Now I can say I know
every one of them. The ship—after Naples it docked in Gibraltar—
carried Italians and Turks. But in 1903, at the time of the Ottoman
Empire, the word *Turk* meant many things: Jews, Greeks, Armenians,
Albanians, Syrians, Lebanese, Slavs, Berbers. The first to disembark at
Ellis Island was Athanapos Kapnistos, a sixteen-year-old from Crete,
followed by Marie Kepapas, a nineteen-year-old from Salonika. Then
in succession came groups from Beirut, Rhodes, Macedonia, Samos,
Vasto, Fano, followed by dozens of young people from Platì and
Gioiosa Ionica, Gerace, Polistena, Scilla, Agropoli, Nicastro, Nocera,
Teramo, Castellabbate. Most of them were about twenty years old.
The youthful passengers on that ship—and on all the other ships in
those years—did not fit the image I had created by looking at photographs in exhibitions and museums, images that impressed themselves
so profoundly on my memory that they shaped my imagination. Sorrowful and incomprehensible figures, distant and far away. In my mind
I see the sad faces of peasants, their sad wives all dressed in black, their
sad children; I see their sad bundles containing all of the nothing they
owned. Perhaps I see a stereotype. Could it be that all these young
people without baggage—with an *S* for *single* in the box indicating
marital status—did not intend to go back? I run down the interminable list of names—Saverio Ricci from Brodolone, seventeen years
old; Aniceto Ricco from Montefegato, seventeen years old; Annibale
Spasiani from Sgurgola, sixteen; Giuseppe Vecchio from San Coseno,
fourteen . . . and I begin to realize that for an entire generation of adolescents, America was neither a destination nor a dream. It was a fan-

tastic and familiar place, where, with the consent of adults, they completed a rite of passage, an initiation. Other generations had military service, the war in the trenches, partisan activity, protests. The youth born in the last decades of the 1800s had America. At fourteen, sixteen, eighteen (some earlier, some later), in groups, together with cousins, brothers, friends, they had to complete the crossing—die—if they wanted to grow up. If they wanted to survive, to rise again. They faced America in the same way that tribal youth from Australia, Papua, and New Guinea faced the mythical monster that would swallow them up and vomit them back out as men. They had to be abandoned, lost, given up for dead. And then they had to go back. But only some of them actually did: the protagonist of many an initiation fable travels, pushes beyond the limits of the known world, only to end up discovering a world he likes better than the one left behind—and there he stays to begin another life.

Some of the last to disembark from the *Republic* were twenty-two passengers from Minturno. Their names appear on pages 95 and 96. A heterogeneous group: ten men between the ages of twenty-four and thirty-eight, a woman age thirty-one, eight adolescents (Pietro Ciufo, age fourteen; Ferdinando Astane, fifteen; Angelo Ciufo and Giuseppe Tucciarone, sixteen; Antonio Rasile, Pasquale Tucciarone, and Alessandro Caruso, seventeen; Giuseppe Forte, nineteen), a child (Filippa Ciufo, five), and two young women (Elisabetta and Carmina Ciufo, seventeen and twenty-one years old). Of the adults, two were named Leonardo Mazzucco, at least one of whom must have been Diamante's uncle. They declared they were headed for Cleveland.

Diamante had never talked about having left with other people. Solitude was the epic element of his voyage, so I was surprised by this discovery. Even more surprising was the fact that Diamante did not disembark with Pasquale and Giuseppe, two slightly older cousins he would meet up with years later on the railroad. Both returned to Italy. From Diamante's correspondence I gathered that Giuseppe went missing at the front on the Piave River in 1917, and Diamante was devastated by his death. But in 1903 Diamante wanted to show he knew how to get along without them. After the twenty-two people from Minturno had disembarked, a Lebanese family got off: Sabart David with his wife and ten children, the youngest of whom, Habil, was six. The next passengers are Diamante and a nine-year-old girl: Vita Mazzucco.

In my father's tales, which I tried desperately to remember, but which surfaced as irremediably scattered and contradictory fragments, Vita popped up out of nowhere at Diamante's side. She was already in America, as if she had always been there. She was there and then she was gone. Censored, perhaps out of respect or from distraction. A persistent amnesia prevented her figure from emerging from the fog of legend and becoming something more than a forgotten name.

And yet that legendary name corresponded to a flesh-and-blood person whose real image differed drastically from that of the stories. She was an American lady who in the 1960s regularly sent gift packages laden with food and clothing to my mother, my sister Silvia, and later also to me. I never met her, but my mother had. Shortly after Silvia's birth she had come to our house "to meet Roberto's daughter." She had come a long way . . . "She spoke English and didn't understand Italian very well. She was generous, a simple soul, I'd say. Quite intelligent. Your father said she never went to school. She loved him very much." Why? "He was like a son to her."

My father's sister kept a signed photograph of her—the faded stamp from the Minturno print shop places the date as August 1950. A small, plump woman with a contagious, sunny smile. A shapely figure—soft and welcoming. So different from the scowling faces of the Mazzuccos and the lyrical confusion of Emma. And yet she, too, was a Mazzucco. Perhaps there was another way, another possibility: amid that harsh, masculine notion—narrators and stone breakers—was a woman. Who was neither poet nor saint nor puritan. And I longed to find her place, in her story and in mine.

I began to look for Diamante's twenty-two traveling companions. I was too late. They had all been dead for a long time. Their descendants were dispersed on another continent. Nowhere to be found. The Ciufos stayed in America. Some Tucciarones returned and bought the land where my father learned to hate the countryside as a child. I found no trace of Ferdinando Astane. As for Caruso, they told me that he, too, had returned, but only after the Second World War. He had lived in the United States for fifty years. Unfortunately, he died in the 1970s. If I was interested, a granddaughter of his was living in an old-persons' home in the Aurunci Mountains. I hesitated. If I told her I was looking for a little girl who had left for America almost a hundred years ago, she wouldn't even know whom I was talking about.

The nursing home resembled a nomad camp, made up of rusty containers probably left over from the time of the earthquake in the Ir-pinia Valley. It rose up on an uncultivated patch of land that didn't even try to resemble a garden on the edge of town. On the other side of the street someone had discarded an old refrigerator, a mattress, and two car seats. No one had bothered to remove them. Marianna Zini-cola was born in the United States, and the conversation proceeded by leaps and silences, in flashes of clarity and misunderstanding. In January 1999 she was ninety-three years old. She told me that the women from Tufo are known for their longevity—seventy out of a hundred live more than a century—and I noted that it was a shame I wasn't from Tufo. She laughed. A robust, suspicious woman with big dark eyes, protruding cheekbones and hands ruined by arthritis. Her companions sat crocheting in an enormous room, decorated with only a crucifix and a few colored prints. One was a reproduction of Van Gogh's sunflowers. It was late January. The grass was gray in the rain. At the next table, four elderly guests were playing cards. I tried in vain to explain who I was. She had met too many Mazzuccos. In America or here? In America. Where in America? New York.

Had she ever heard of a certain Vita Mazzucco? Marianna Zinicola looked at her hands and twisted the wedding band on her swollen finger. She had been widowed sixty years ago. Perhaps this container, this makeshift building in which she had found suitors and friends, was preferable to the solitude of a rest home in some American suburb. Or maybe in America they don't expect you to live to be one hundred. It's a young country, a country for the young. "Yes, I met Mrs. Mazzucco in New York." Vita had opened a restaurant in the 1930s. It was during the Depression and everyone was out of work. Marianna Zinicola hadn't known which way to turn and wanted to ask the well-off *paisà* for help, though the old women advised against it. "Vita didn't associate with our people and had a bad reputation; she'd run away with a gangster and gotten married scandalously late." But Marianna went to see her anyway. Vita—may God bless her—took her in to work in the kitchen. "Ah," I said, "and did you stay long?" "Until I came back to Italy. Seventeen years." She sighed. Perhaps speaking of the past disturbed her. Perhaps I was being too brusque with her. "Perhaps I shouldn't ask you all these questions." She looked at me, surprised. "People think memories make us sad. But it's the opposite. We become sad when we forget."

No, unfortunately she hadn't saved anything from that period in her life. What was she supposed to keep? She was illiterate and so didn't have any letters or postcards. It was all in her head. But she still had her wedding pictures. Did I want to see them? Of course.

She shuffled down the hall in her slippers. The neon lights sputtered. The other guests shot me severe looks: they probably thought I was an ungrateful granddaughter who had abandoned the elderly relative to the public health services. The room was silent—like in an aquarium. One nurse was reading *Confidenze*, a romance magazine. Another, seated near the entrance, was attempting a crossword puzzle. Marianna Zinicola returned with a rusted old cookie tin full of buttons, pictures of saints, greeting cards, ribbons, petrified sugared almonds, and a page torn out of a tourist guide, perhaps the New York *Baedeker*. Page 234, year unknown.

**VITA—52*nd* Street, corner of Broadway*

Yesterday's cuisine for today's tastes. Run by the owner, a small, loquacious Italian woman who offers her interpretation of traditional recipes using seasonal ingredients; dishes are elegantly presented. Don't miss the turtle with peas, cod alla marinara, sour cherry tart, zeppole, mostaccioli, and the best stuffed goose I've ever eaten. Pleasant, airy dining room. Service slow. Prices are a bit high. Reservations required. *Highly recommended.*

Marianna Zinicola beamed with satisfaction. "She was famous, no? Important people came. Even Charles Lindbergh, the airplane man.

Vita did everything herself. She was used to giving orders. Did everything her own way. She was hardheaded. They'll break it one day, I used to say. And she'd laugh and tell me: then I'll bind it up. The gangsters put a bomb there, the Negroes set fire to the office, all sorts of things happened, but she never so much as complained."

The room was furnished with Formica tables that reminded me of school desks, and most likely that's what they were. Everything in the nursing home was third-, fourth-, even fifth-hand. The furniture, sweaters, nightgowns, the attention of the annoyed nurses, opaque windows, floors, and radiators. And yet, as the immortal Marianna Zinicola smiled and caressed that piece of paper, thinking on all the successes and sorrows of her boss and friend, I realized she knew everything about Vita.

Bongiorno Bros.

Bongiorno Bros. puts on the most spectacular funerals in the neighborhood. A majestic pair of white horses in crimson saddlecloths and black plumes somberly pulls a funeral cart with big, shiny windows and cushions covered in white roses and lily of the valley. The coachman dons a top hat and purple livery. The swaying of the carriage, the solemn pace of the procession, the colors of the trimmings, and the choreographed tears and weeping are personally attended to by the boss, who supervises his funerals like an orchestra conductor. The funeral parlor also rents women who cry and display great anguish, and for eminent personalities, unemployed men who join the procession and lend it a particularly impressive air. Like all Bongiorno Bros. employees, Diamante wears white gloves, a bowler, a black suit, and is forbidden to laugh while on duty. The funeral home, located on the Bowery, consists of three rooms: an entranceway with ornamental plants and chairs for callers, a mortuary chapel, and a large hall for the wake with purple and black drapery, candelabras, a crucifix, fresh flowers, and wreaths; there's even a fan in summer and a heater in winter. Out back and in the basement are the secret rooms where the bodies are washed—for some, this is their second full bath since birth—and dressed. Then Shimon Rosen makes up the dead faces and purses their lips in such a way as to make them look like they're smiling. Because in the end, nobody's happy to die, not even a suicide.

Out back a long, narrow courtyard is stacked with pine, cedar, mahogany, and chestnut planks. The carpenter saws and polishes the boards and nails together the coffins, while the engraver applies the finishing touches. There are always twenty or so ready for use, lined up along the wall as samples. Some are deep and solidly built, complete with velvet upholstery, wrought-silver handles, and a small window for the face. Others are made of zinc, flimsy, with hardly enough space for a pillow. Many are white and tiny. Coffins for children. Children die more than adults, the young more than the old. In fact, Diamante's been working at Bongiorno Bros. for a year, but he still hasn't seen the corpse of an old person. Having proved he's not afraid of the dead, Diamante goes to get them—in their homes, in the streets where they've been crushed by a cart or an automobile, on construction sites, in cradles, at public and private hospitals. Sometimes even in the taverns where their guts have been sliced open, their throats cut, or their hearts pierced with a knife. Lots of Mr. Cozza's dead die an unnatural death. But then again, is there such a thing as a natural death?

Diamante loads the dead onto the cart, accompanies them on their last trip through Manhattan, unloads them in the storeroom, and stretches them out on a table, forcing them into their definitive horizontal position. Then he measures them for the coffin—height, length, heaviness. Together with Shimon, who has just arrived from Lithuania and speaks only Ostrogothic, he washes them, wipes them with a sponge, disinfects them with an aseptic lotion that smells of hospital, greases their hair with brilliantine, curls it with rollers or straightens it with red-hot irons, cuts their nails, and shaves their cheeks. Then he leaves Shimon in charge of this secret space, which is cluttered with brushes, hand mirrors, face powders, and perfume bottles, and looks more like an actor's dressing room. Shimon Rosen is Jewish, but since he's a real makeup artist, Mr. Bongiorno hired him anyway. Shimon, whom everyone calls Moe, has the gift of making people happy. He makes men with sad, disfigured, or wicked faces seem serene and satisfied. He restores a smile to women who probably hadn't smiled in years; when they arrive at the funeral home, stabbed by betrayal, their mouths are twisted in such inconsolable expressions of surprise, pain, or disappointment that Diamante can't bear to look at them. Shimon even fixed a beatific smile on Nino's scrawny face, so that everyone said, "Look how happy he is!" As if he had anything to be happy about, a six-year-old child who dies alone in a charity hospital.

When a dead person is laid out in the hall, Diamante's task is to make sure the family members always have plenty of fresh drinks and coffee while they mourn and talk—none too discreetly—about the inheritance. It seems strange to him that the dead don't remain at home until the funeral instead of in the Bongiorno Bros. hall, dressed to the nines as if going to a party, and then locked up all alone when the party's over and the funeral home closes. Rocco explained that in America people are happy, smiling, and optimistic; they don't want to think about death, so they're glad to pay somebody else to take care of it for them. As a matter of fact, Diamante's job is financially rewarding and even instructive. It didn't take him long to discover how wonderful, perfect, and fragile a woman's beauty is. Their bodies no longer hold any secrets for him. Each one is different, each one a universe, an enigma, a blessing. He loves them madly—their hair, curly pubes, white legs, and pale feet. When he kisses them on the forehead, he imagines for an instant they'll awaken and smile at him. He has learned how precarious a woman's beauty is; it passes as quickly as a summer storm. After twenty, it's already just a memory. Which is why he must hurry to put aside some money so he can marry Vita. Diamante has also learned more useful notions at the funeral home: that death can do arithmetic, for example. A child's funeral costs twenty-five dollars, but Agnello had to cough up at least forty to rent the white cart and coffin for Nino. An adult can't die decorously for less than a hundred dollars. And if he wants to die in style, arriving at the cemetery in a car, for example, he'll need three hundred. Death is an irreparable injury—particularly for those who are still alive. It's better not to have any relatives to bury, and Diamante considers himself lucky he didn't call his brothers over.

In America it's best not to die at all. Maybe that's the reason nobody ever talks about death. Diamante intends to avoid it like the
plague. At any rate, he's in fine health, especially as he eats a lot more
now than when he sold newspapers or collected rags. He manages to
save half his pay, and Agnello's boss sends it to Italy for him. Even
though the boss pockets a heavy percentage for the inconvenience, at
least he doesn't steal it all, as do lots of others who profit from people's
naïveté. A month later, the dollars that survive the siftings of various
intermediaries arrive at the Minturno post office, where Antonio goes
to collect them, undoubtedly very proud of his son's progress. Diamante can almost see him standing there, hat in hand, timid, diffident,
and vulnerable as always, and feels quite proud of himself. He hasn't
told his father about the funeral home, however; Antonio's rather superstitious, given all the misfortune befallen him since his birth, so
Diamante wrote that he'd found work as an errand boy in an office.
After all, lying may be a sin worse than lust in America, but not in
Italy. Everybody tells lies there, starting with the landowners, teachers,
and priests. The funeral parlor pays him a dollar a day, which seems fair
enough. Consequently, Diamante now highly reveres Mr. Bongiorno,
who has risen rapidly in his eyes to the top of his list.

Finally, after all the poor souls who'd been crushed by work, here
was an Italian who'd made it. A man who worked hard and was successful. And success had washed away the stain of his origins, his
gnarled and calloused hands, the poverty of his language—a bastard
mix of a dialect nobody speaks anymore, not even in his native village,
and an American nobody understands. Lazzaro Bongiorno is described
respectfully in the newspapers as "the best undertaker, and extremely
popular," and his funerals are praised for their organization and pomp.
He belongs to influential patriotic associations recognized by the consul and is invited to greet emissaries of the Italian government when
they arrive on this side of the ocean. Friend to businessmen and merchants, Lazzaro Bongiorno has a nice house on St. Mark's Place with a
doorman at the entrance and curtains on the windows, a wife with a
fur coat, and a red-faced, big-nosed daughter whose fine clothing and
elegant hairstyle transform her into a fascinating young miss. He's so
thin his mustache seems pasted on a skull. He always dresses in black

and scoffs at the evil eye. "Black makes you look important," he told Diamante when he hired him, handing him the suit worn by the previous errand boy. "Better to be feared than mocked." "For sure," agreed Diamante, who up till now had been mocked by all and feared by none. Bongiorno treats his boys well because he, too, was once an errand boy; he, too, once collected rags and shined shoes. In addition to the Jew, he even has Negroes on his payroll. This is because, long before he discovered he could make a fortune sending the bodies of ill-fated souls who'd died in America back to the Italian relatives who pined for them as if they were holy relics, Mr. Bongiorno had worked on a plantation near New Orleans. As a southern Italian, he was considered the dregs of the dregs, the undesirable link between the black and white races. And closer to the first than to the second. Astonishing though it seems, as a result of that experience, Mr. Bongiorno actually likes Negroes, pays them almost as well as the others, and listens to them sing for hours. After a successful funeral, he hands out big tips all around. And wherever Mr. Bongiorno goes, Rocco follows him like a shadow. Rocco walks next to or behind him; Rocco precedes him when they enter a restaurant, and waits for him in front of the door while he eats or plays cards. In essence, Rocco is his bodyguard. But it took Diamante a good many months to figure out why the much-revered Mr. Bongiorno would have need of a bodyguard.

Diamante has been working at Bongiorno Bros. for a while when Rocco starts asking him to stay on after closing time. On certain evenings, the hall for the wake fills with people, despite the American embarrassment regarding death. After the family members, errand boys, and apprentices leave, new visitors arrive—all men and all with faces hidden by broad-brimmed hats. Diamante agrees instantly because ever since Agnello robbed him of Vita's kisses, the house on Prince Street has lost all its allure, and any place is better than that kitchen where he tries with melancholy to remember them. He doesn't have to do anything; he can read the newspaper or go to the makeup room and peek at the dirty postcards Coca-Cola gives him. But if some Irish policeman from the precinct arrives, he has to say a wake is going on. Diamante knows perfectly well the visitors don't even know the dead man, and he'd prefer not to tell more lies in

America, as he's told too many already. But one lie leads to the next, and pretty soon you're sunk. So he stays in the atrium or on the doorstep and keeps an eye on the visitors' bicycles. Some of the men tip him when they leave. In Italy he would have been mortified. But here the only thing that bothers him is when they call him Spilapippe, Pipe Cleaner.

Rocco explained that all tough guys have a nickname. They never use their real names with each other. Instead they use an adjective, like Fat, Slim, Dirty, or animals like Hog, Cricket, Beetle, Tick, or a reference to some episode—Dizzy, Match, Coal. Or an American version of their first name, like Rusty for Oreste, or Elmer for Adelmo. At Bongiorno's nobody knows who Rocco is. They all call him Merluzzo, which means cod. Maybe because of that old story about his stealing barrels of cod at the market, or maybe because when something's none of his business, or when he's supposed to pretend it's not, he knows to make dead-fish eyes. Or maybe they just like mispronouncing his name. Rocco doesn't mind because a cod is a big fish. Better to be a cod than an anchovy. Diamante got the name Spilapippe because he's as thin as a pipe cleaner. It's better than Celestina, but it still doesn't go down too well with him. Besides, Diamante is already a nickname; he earned it because he survived all his older siblings. He likes it—the diamond is the hardest of all minerals. You can't cut a diamond, not with a knife, not even with dynamite.

Spilapippe is sharp and ambitious, so it's only natural that Rocco starts waking him up in the night and bringing him along when they set fire to shops and warehouses. He doesn't have to carry the bottles filled with gasoline or even the matches; he's just a sentinel, what they call a "lighthouse," and has to whistle a song if he hears footsteps or sees someone coming. What song? The song Lena always sings when she wants to let you know Agnello's left for work and she's feeling lonely. *La donna è mobile qual piuma al vento.* A provocative song that gives him goose bumps and stays in his head all day. Lena's sensual voice and the ridge of her spine under her pajamas fill him with a burning desire. *È sempre misero chi a lei s'affida, chi le confida mal cauto il core! Pur mai non sentesi felice appieno chi su quel seno non liba amore!* (He who trusts her or gives her his heart is always wretched! But he who does not drink love from her breast can never be completely happy!) The night turns red, the flames reflected in the puddles light up the street, and the sparks carried on the breeze lick against the buildings and then melt like snowflakes in the rain, dying as they drop onto the cobblestones. The smell of burning wood and ash reminds him of Tufo in the winter, so sometimes, even though he's happy because America is a wonderful place and fortune has smiled on him, Diamante wants to cry.

Shortly before Diamante left for America, the bandit Musolino was arrested. After his daring prison break—right out of a novel—he became the most wanted man in all of Italy. The story of his escape was a blazing epic of murder and vengeance, followed passionately by everyone in Italy. Guilty of seven homicides and numerous other attempts, with the extraordinary price of fifty thousand lire on his head—though it failed to tempt anyone to betray him—hounded by the carabinieri, the army, and the police, Musolino won the people's sympathy and gradually came to be seen as a defender of the poor and oppressed, a symbol of rebellion against poorly interpreted and poorly applied laws. Children played "Musolino" in the streets, traveling musicians sang his exploits, puppet-theater managers included his figure among the Knights of France, newspapers exalted his legend, and women—imprisoned in the renunciations of an asphyxiating respectability, dreaming an impossible transgression—fell in love with him. The bandit became a new Edmond Dantès, persecuted by the powerful and in search of just revenge, roaming the mountains of Aspromonte as did the fugitive Jean Valjean the bowels of Paris. A hero. But in October 1901, by mere chance—a string of barbed wire snagged his heel—the carabinieri shackled him and locked him away. The news was sensational.

The scene of his capture was reproduced in hundreds of fliers, popular prints, almanacs, and newspapers. Diamante and his brothers saw them. He wasn't even ten at the time, Leonardo was seven, and Amedeo the Second barely four. The children studied the image of the bandit in chains: dressed in a dark hunter's jacket, brown trousers, and black boots, he was escorted by a group of carabinieri on horseback. The horses were big and white. And the bandit was thin, pale, *normal-*

looking. Eighty years later, on February 12, 1980, Leonardo wrote to my father from Sydney, Australia, where he had gone to join his son who worked for Alitalia; on that far-distant day of their youth, he recalled, he and Diamante had decided to change their fate.

One evening when Papà was more tired than usual from work and upset by the lack of basic necessities in the house, he pronounced these exact words: *My dear sons, if in your future you are destined to live the same life I am living, I would prefer that God take you as he has taken all your older brothers.* Diamante and I responded: *Dear Father, you can be sure that when we grow up, we'll find a way not to be farm laborers in Tufo like you. We'll go work somewhere else—if we can, we'll become office workers or join the military.* I explained that I would enlist as a carabiniere because I had just read a little booklet bought at the Minturno Saturday market; on the cover was the famous Calabrese bandit Musolino, in chains between two carabinieri on horseback. It made such an impression on me that I secretly dreamed of becoming one of them one day. Thus my brother and I both achieved our declared goal, deserting that primitive place which ignored every principle of civilized life, where the destitute languished from work and hunger under those infamous, egotistical tyrants, the landowners.

In 1980 Leonardo still remembered the magnificent plumes of the horses, the red and blue uniforms of the representatives of the forces of order, the irresistible fascination they had exercised on his imagination. The sense of security and implacable justice they conveyed. Leonardo realized his childhood dream: with only a fifth-grade education, he nevertheless pursued a military career. In 1918 he was among the first to enter liberated Gorizia, and in 1919 he chased after Roman criminals, his successes prominently reported in the pages of the newspaper *Il Messaggero.* In 1921 they sent him to chase the far more dangerous rebels in Libya. He pursued them across the Sahara Desert, in the saddle of a white horse. Only then did he realize he was riding in the wrong direction—and some time later, during the years that marked the apogee of fascism, he hung up his uniform.

But all Diamante saw in the print was Musolino. That thin, pale

normal young man who had kept in check the authorities of the Kingdom, had shamed and mocked them, and eluded all their traps, snares,
and ambushes for years. He had rebelled against his destiny as a starved
and exploited peasant. Not content merely to survive, he wanted to
live. Even when they captured him and unjustly condemned him to
twenty-one years in prison, he had not yielded. He opened up a passage in the prison walls and escaped. And even though in June 1902
they condemned him for life and sent him to the inhuman Portolon-
gone jail on the island of Elba, the chains that bound his wrists meant
nothing. Musolino was a free man.

Moe Rosen knew how to make up the faces of the dead because he
knew how to make up his own. He often came to work with a black
eye, bruises, or a broken nose, but he'd head to the dressing room and
skillfully apply greasepaint and powder. Unlike his clients, however,
Moe didn't need any special treatment to smile. He found a way to
laugh at everything—himself first of all. Diamante had trouble understanding what was so funny, but eventually he came to see the basic
philosophy that underlay Moe's black humor: there might be no end
to the bad, but there's no end to the good, either. And the good is always ahead of us. Never behind us.

Moe had arrived in 1904 with his father, mother, two brothers, and
three cousins. When the Russo-Japanese war broke out, the czar had
called up Moe's older brothers to fight. Of all the tribulations a Jew in
Russia had to face, one of the worst was to end up in the army, where
he ran the risk of being wounded, abused, or killed by his companions
long before the enemy could get near him. So the Rosens sold all their
worldly goods and fled. They were industrious people: Moe's father
had already opened a pawnshop on Grand Street, and the cousins
played in the Jewish theaters. Diamante began to think of them as Indian guides who could show strangers the way into enemy territory.
The Rosens spoke Yiddish, but from his job at Bongiorno Bros. and
his visits to Prince Street, Moe quickly adopted the most colorful Calabrese insults and Sicilian proverbs. He also learned some choice
Minturno expressions: *te puzzi cionga'* (hope your legs shrivel up), *va-
vattenne* (go to hell), *puzzi passa' 'nu uaio* (hope you get screwed), *puzzi*

fa 'na scura morte (hope you drop dead). Diamante and Moe Rosen spent countless hours together, and as they washed and shaved the dead bodies, they also scrutinized each other suspiciously.

Moe's spiky hair made him look like an artichoke, his ears flapped in the wind, and he always had a smile on his face. He was already sixteen, but his eyes had the limpid gaze of a child. He was skinny as a toothpick, his clothes hung off him like rags on a scarecrow. His entire wardrobe consisted of one pair of black trousers held up with string and a frayed shirt that ripped every time he moved. Between one dead body and another, Moe would make drawings. On anything—brown wrapping paper, cardboard, old newspapers, business cards stolen from the basket in the funeral parlor. Moe would draw the faces of the people laid out on the table. He looked at them in a way nobody else did, and saw into their most secret selves. The impertinent slant of a nose. An authoritative wart. A cleft chin or protruding jaw, a low, slanted forehead. Diamante thought he was a prodigy. Moe dedicated hours to those cadavers nobody else cared about. He was the only one at the funeral parlor, and the only one in all of America, who felt compassion for the dead.

He kept his pencils in a drawer and never took them or his drawings home after work. And he always stayed late. Like Diamante, he earned extra cash for being willing to lie to the Irish police about the wakes. So as the voices of the relatives faded into a sad and solemn dirge at the end of the day, if there were no other bodies to recompose, Moe would bring out his pencils and Diamante would pull Vita's primer from his pocket. He would read the same pages again and again—the pages where his lessons had been interrupted and the words stolen from him—repeating halfheartedly the idiotic yet insurmountable sentences. If someone came in, they were quick to make pencils and primer disappear into the makeup drawers.

As the months passed, Diamante began to find Moe Rosen's company more agreeable than that of the boys at Prince Street. Maybe it was because Moe lived on the other side of the Bowery and knew nothing about the fires, Rocco's pistol, and the hoodlums. Diamante avoided Vita now because he didn't want to lie or steal kisses from her or have Agnello flay her with the laundry line again. And he avoided

Rocco and his friends because he didn't want to give him all that remained of what was good in him.

And Geremia had left. He didn't like the atmosphere at Prince
Street anymore—the nighttime action, the bottles filled with gasoline
under Coca-Cola's bed, the bonfires, the brass knuckles Rocco hid in
his shoes, the loaded gun, and the new boarder, Elmer, who'd been accused of killing a pastry cook, but whose case was dismissed after the
witness was fished out of Jamaica Bay. Geremia would say that once a
guy like that claps eyes on you, he'll never lose sight of you. It might
seem like he's helping you, but there's no such thing as a free lunch,
and before you know it, you're caught in the middle, and then you're
done for. So he'd taken a job in the anthracite mines in Pennsylvania.
Wherever that was. He didn't want to leave, though. It's not like he'd
dreamed of becoming a miner. If someone had suggested it to him a
year ago, he would have laughed. "Are you crazy? I ain't no mole. I'm
a musician. I want to climb up and up, and look down at the past from
above." Geremia didn't say goodbye to anybody. He didn't know how
to tell Agnello, who was killing himself to buy back the store and had
nothing to do with these nighttime doings. He was afraid to tell
Rocco, who'd never forgive his betrayal—they'd shared lots of things,
and up on the New York Times tower they'd made a pact even though
they didn't actually swear or declare anything. But still. Everybody
united around the American brother, together forever, no matter what
happens. And whoever's not with us can shrivel up and die. Geremia
tried to convince Diamante to leave with him. The prospect of finding
himself underground, surrounded by the familiar faces of people
who'd left Italy before him and still hadn't managed to return must
have seemed intolerable to him. "Come with me, Diamante," he'd say.
"Cousins should stick together. Let's get out of New York while
there's still time. Trust me, a live dog is better than a dead lion. We'll
work two, three years in the mines, put away a few thousand dollars,
and then we'll go home. There's no place for us in America." "I already have a job, I don't need another one," Diamante would respond.
The truth dawned on him that day. His cousin was a loser.

The world is divided into two kinds of people: the *uàppi* and the
tòtari—the wise guys and the fools, the strong and the weak, the win-

ners and the losers. The losers exist to serve the winners and take the blame for them. That's how it's always been, in Italy and in America. But here there's no middle ground—it's all black and white, and gray hasn't been invented yet. Agnello is a loser. And so, unfortunately, is Geremia. The only time Rocco even mentions him now that he's off ruining his health in the mines is when he insults him. He calls him Uncle Tom, like that Negro in the history books he had to learn about in school in America. That good Negro who's always saying "Yessir" and does everything he can to make himself acceptable in the boss's eyes. But he'll never be acceptable because he'll always be a Negro. But not us—we're like the other Negroes who kick and scream: we won't go down like pigs. We'll shoot them if they try to put a rope around our necks and dangle us from a tree. Maybe Diamante's father, Antonio, is a loser, too. He is for sure, or else he wouldn't have let them throw him out of America twice, wouldn't have let five children die of hunger. But Diamante's not a loser. And if he has been, he doesn't plan on being one anymore.

Moe Rosen was different. He wasn't a winner, but he wasn't a loser, either. Moe somehow eluded the sorts of classification everyone else seemed condemned to. He didn't beat up or threaten shopkeepers. He read the Bible with the same pleasure with which Diamante read the newspaper or the illustrated almanacs. More important, he read books at the Lenox Library, a sober-looking building where, unlike the churches, anyone—even a boy dressed in rags like Moe—could enter. Sometimes Diamante would accompany him right up to the entrance and he would have liked to follow him into that building that looked like a palace or parliament house, but he never did; he didn't want them throwing him out as soon as he opened his mouth. Moe was going to night school to learn American. Diamante would have liked to accompany him there as well, but it was a school the rich Jews had opened for the poor Jews. Moe invited him to attend, but the rich Italians hadn't opened a school for poor Italians just off the boat. On the contrary, the rich Italians were ashamed of them and said that Italy wasn't really united, but was actually two different countries and races—those from the North are good and trustworthy Celts, while those from the South are foul-smelling Latin thugs. In short, there are two types of Italians: northerners and nothingers. But when Diamante tried to explain how uncomfortable and embarrassed he felt when they called him a dago, Moe didn't understand. He was used to it. Even in the country where he'd lived before, people spoke a different language and insulted him. You have to make your own way. Emerge. Rise above.

Moe wanted to become a famous painter. But since he wasn't so naive as to confuse desire with talent, first he wanted to see if he stood any chance of making it. He didn't want to be just another dabbler. Either a great artist or nothing. And if he wasn't great, then he'd abandon painting completely, do something else. In order to contend with true art—the real thing—Moe would go about the city looking at paintings in museums, and Diamante would go with him. He'd always thought paintings were only in churches, but in America the churches were white-walled and bare, while the museums were as sumptuous as cathedrals. For the price of a ticket, you could look at paintings all day long. The paintings didn't say anything to Diamante, and he was only interested in the Madonna-and-child images. He liked almost all the Madonnas—dreamy, sweet, and maternal, not like any woman he'd ever met. He dreamed of having a woman like that beside him, of being held in her arms forever. Bewitched and enamored, he would stare at those paintings until the guard grew suspicious and invited him to move along, fearful that at any moment that kid dressed like a punk from the suburbs would pull out a knife and slash the canvas.

But Moe even looked at the paintings of trees, flowers, and crows. His father, a very religious gnome with a prophet's beard and curls down to his shoulders, was hysterically opposed to the artistic aspirations of his son. His god had some grudge against images, and the old man would burn Moe's drawings if he found them. He was the one who bruised Moe's face and crushed his fingers with a hammer. If he got too carried away, he would send someone around to the funeral home to say his son had bronchitis. And so Moe Rosen preferred Dagoland, where nobody beat him if he drew chickens, rabbits, and children on the courtyard walls or the coal bin. The dagoes merely thought he was crazy and would laugh at the strange pictures he'd leave behind. But they didn't get rid of them. Moe would paint suffering animals, wide-eyed creatures with half-open beaks, the screaming anguish and desperation of wilting flowers. He was attracted to weak, wounded things—the plucked and killed chicken dripping over an iron pail, or the runt of the litter destined to be attacked, crushed, and devoured by the other dogs. Flies, chickens, dead mice, the boundless ranks of the wounded: he would have liked to save them all. Because he couldn't, he painted them.

Moe painted Nicola's rotten teeth. He drew Rocco with his flayed cat in his lap and an absent expression on his face, as if he'd hidden somewhere so no one would find him, and now couldn't find his way home. For Diamante he painted the ship *Republic* on the curtain that separated his cubbyhole from the rest of the house. He painted a tree on the only door in the Prince Street apartment, and when he realized that the kitchen, where Vita and Lena spent most of the day, was windowless, he painted a fake window on the wall. "What would you like to see when you look out?" he asked. "The New York Times skyscraper," Vita said. "The mountains," said Lena. So Moe painted two girls leaning on the windowsill, seen from behind. In the background he placed the skyscraper and behind that, a chain of purple mountains dusted with snow.

At the funeral parlor, photographers would immortalize the dead before the service. The Vigorito Company on Hester Street—specializing in portraits, groups, enlargements, processions, landscapes, interior shots, photographs on buttons, wedding pillows, porcelain, wood, and watches—always had a sign in the window:

Wanted: young men, 18 or younger, who would like to learn photography. In six months you'll be able to run your own photography studio.

The announcement had yellowed because it wasn't as if the Vigorito Company offered a salary to those young men for six months. When Vigorito (who ran the studio by himself and had written the word *Company* in the hopes of attracting clients) discovered Moe's familiarity with dead bodies, he proposed the boy take over the morbid task he had reluctantly performed. You need skill to photograph a dead person—much more than for a living one, to whom you can say, "Smile, look this way, tilt your forehead, raise your chin." The dead person is like a statue, even though he's not a work of art. The dead are as imperfect as the rest of us, and most definitely not perfectible. Vigorito's offer was a lucrative one because the American dead always had some relative on the other side of the ocean who wanted to see them one last time. So Moe Rosen, who'd never seen a camera before, accepted the new task right away—even without pay—and in the autumn of 1905 he quit his job at Bongiorno Bros.

He asked Diamante to go work with him at Vigorito's. "We'll learn the trade, in six months we'll buy a camera and go into business for ourselves. We'll make postcards. Have you ever considered how many foreigners there are in New York these days? Ten thousand arrive every day. If every one of them sends just one postcard to their relatives back home, we'll be millionaires." Diamante was tempted. Without Moe, the funeral parlor, caskets, and funerals would lose their sense of ritual and become once again simply what they were. The dead laid out on the bench would flaunt their absent expressions of supreme indifference; every trace of superficiality, pettiness, or malice would disappear from their faces, and only their most rudimentary characteristics would remain. They would regain the ephemeral dignity life had taken from them, but without Moe Rosen, they would no longer find peace or a smile. Diamante didn't want to keep working at Bongiorno Bros. without his oddball friend, and he knew that Moe, his Indian guide, was revealing the path to the heart of the enemy fort. He knew he should follow him. But he just couldn't let himself do it. He needed to make money—not a lot, but right away. "Come with me, for art's sake," Moe insisted. "Don't listen to your relatives. Don't end up like your cousin, who traded in his trombone for a train ticket to the mines. Art will always bring us something to eat. An artist is never poor."

To celebrate Moe's new job, they went to Cherry Street, where the cheapest whores are. They planned on picking up one to share, but Diamante didn't find any he fancied—they all seemed vulgar, worn-out, and repulsive—while Moe chose the ugliest one on the whole street, three teeth missing and wrinkles like parentheses around her lips. She took them to an attic room that reeked of piss and rotten fish. The whole thing was so venal and perfunctory Diamante didn't even get hard. But Moe lost his virginity in her arms. It took all of four minutes.

Moe liked old, ugly, lonely women. Syphilitic prostitutes with bandages hiding their sores, consumptives. Crazies. The ones other men ignore, use, mistreat, or humiliate. As they headed back toward Prince Street, where Moe was anxious to finish painting the kitchen window, he asked Diamante if he planned on marrying Lena. Diamante said that nobody—not even Uncle Agnello—thought of marrying Lena just because he enjoyed sleeping with her now and then. Lena had been Diamante's first woman. It was she who had lifted the weight of inexperience from him; at first, the procedure had taken less time than it takes to boil water for pasta, but later they needed more time than they had at their disposal. Back when he worked collecting rags with Tom Orecchio's horse, Lena would get up when she heard him come in, and, unbeknownst to Agnello, who would have smacked her if he'd found out, warm him a glass of milk even if he didn't have the money to pay for it. It was their first secret. One secret led to another, and before long they'd ended up in bed together.

Lena appealed to Diamante's rage, but her kisses didn't taste like the ones he'd bought from Vita. Lena tasted of solitude, and embracing her was like holding a wave—no one. Lena had no consistency, no memories. Sometimes Diamante feared he'd become like her one day—forget where he came from, who he was, who his people were. Maybe this was the reason Lena stayed with Uncle Agnello, who was violent and sullen as a fox, and ugly with that hooked chin that practically touched his nose: it was Agnello who'd decided she was called Lena. He was the only one who had ever said to her, "This is your house, where I am is your home." Since Lena belonged to Agnello, when Diamante first touched her he had a strange sensation of desire mingled with disgust, defiance tinged with revenge. But in the end, it's not like we have to marry the women we have fun with. Besides, even though Lena was fornicating merrily with a minor, she was already twenty-six. No, Diamante would marry Vita, even if Agnello wanted to find her a husband from outside the neighborhood—a doctor, a lawyer, a notary, a winner—like Mr. Bongiorno. Diamante intended to be that winner.

Moe responded that the desire to win is a thing for losers. He said he was happy Diamante hadn't set his mind on Lena because as soon as he'd developed a clientele as a photographer, he intended to ask her to marry him. Diamante advised him to forget about it because she was completely crazy. As he said it, he recalled that Rocco had told him the very same thing two years before, and realized that Lena had also slept with Rocco. It was a tough blow to his pride, and he ended up breaking things off completely with her—cured of the attraction she'd always held for him. But it was too late.

The Lamp

Vita always kept a lamp burning on the stool next to her bed because light keeps the *janara* away. The *janara* is the witch who comes to steal children, and since she's already been to this house once, she knows the way. Of course nobody else knows about her, and Vita would be ashamed to admit she still believes in such things at her age—after all, she's not a baby anymore. She started bleeding two months ago, but since she didn't tell anyone (whom could she have told? boys don't understand these things), and washed the rag out in secret, the witch probably hasn't realized it, either. At any rate, Vita knows witches exist, just as she knows the dead come back to look for you as ghosts, cats, lightning, and wasps, to hurt you and avenge themselves for all the wrongs they endured. So despite Coca-Cola's protests, Vita keeps the lamp lit during the night; now that they've both grown, he sleeps in a different bed and could face the other way if it really bothered him. But when she wakes up, the lamp is out. Behind the curtain someone murmurs quietly, laughs, and sighs. Of course Vita knows that someone is Diamante, having fun with Lena. She also knows she can't do anything about it, so she merely lights the lamp again and falls back to sleep.

That's not how things go in her dream, however. The alcohol in the lamp is all used up, and the wick goes out. So she gets up, takes the extinguished lamp, goes into the corridor, and looks for the bottle of alcohol. She can't find it because somebody has moved it, and she has to search all around. When she finally finds it, Diamante has gone back to his own bed. All is quiet. The curtain is still slightly open. Lena has already fallen asleep, breathing peacefully in the big bed, and in the dark it sounds like the wind rustling against the door. Vita is curious to see her expression after having been with Diamante, so she lights the lamp and holds it close to her face. Lena is smiling. Sleeping and smiling. In reality, Vita would never think of setting the alcohol lamp on the nightstand so she could get closer, so she could touch Lena's hair, her naked arm, her breast sticking out of her unbuttoned pajamas. She would never breathe in Lena's scent—vinegar mixed with sea—but that's exactly what happens. Now the lamp lights the pillow, lights Lena's honey-colored hair, her lips wet with saliva, her smile, while darkness is all around. Since Vita has had the same dream for weeks, she knows the lamp will soon fall on the bed, soon flames the intense, deep blue color of the sky before dawn will dart up from the alcohol-soaked blanket—so she forestalls that instant of bewildered enchantment by waking herself up. And since she always wakes up screaming, Agnello's already there, sitting on her bed, running his hand over her hair, and repeating, "Nothing happened, it was just a scary dream."

Vita is drenched in sweat, her heart pounding wildly. She doesn't want to fall back asleep because she doesn't want to see Lena's contented smile again—but Agnello assures her that nightmares don't return. "Sleep, my child." Vita closes her eyes and then opens them again suddenly to make sure her father hasn't put out the lamp. Agnello is still sitting there with a blanket over his shoulders. He seems to have aged all of a sudden, and all his hair has fallen out. He doesn't work nights anymore, and doesn't leave her bedside until sunrise. No one asked him to stay, but he knows he must. Vita would like her father to hold her hand, but Agnello would never do that, and she's afraid to ask him. Time stands still. Maybe Agnello has fallen asleep sitting there because he's dead tired. But she's not; she stares wide-eyed at the wick floating in alcohol. All around is darkness, except for a cold blue glimmer hovering around the flame. If she falls asleep again, even for an instant, Lena opens her eyes, blinks, and stiffens because Vita has surprised her, has been spying on her in her most intimate moments. "What do you want?" Lena asks in her soft voice, the same voice she uses to attract boys to her bed. "Go back to bed, go to sleep now." "I'm cold, can't I sleep with you?" Vita mumbles. Lena realizes she can no longer see her. "Vita," she says quietly, "what are you looking at? Stop it, Vita!" The lamp falls onto the blanket. Lena lights up like a torch.

The White Star

The *New York Times* reported inclement weather for April 15, 1906, Easter Sunday. It rained until noon, remained cloudy until three, and didn't clear until evening. The temperature was cool: it was fifty-three degrees at three in the morning and barely got up to sixty that afternoon. The arrival of Henri Comte de la Vaulx, the most successful balloonist of his day, who had already flown across the Channel and was here from France to promote the art of flying in America; the lynching of three Negroes (innocent) in Missouri; and the scandal caused by the writer Maksim Gorky, kicked out of a New York hotel for passing off his girlfriend as his wife, left little space in the newspaper for Italy (and Italians). In the Sunday insert, amid the photographs of famous men, all Americans, appears that of Enrico Caruso, verging on obesity but elevated to the status of champion of the Italian race, together with the Italian prime minister Sidney Sonnino, who had the advantage, however, of being the son of a Jew and an English Protestant. The only other Italians mentioned are two cadavers. One is the assassin Giuseppe Marmo, who was hanged in Newark for the murder of his brother-in-law Nunzio Marinano. The other is the editor Domenico Mollica of Lipari, who resided at

415 East Fourteenth Street and was killed by the Black Hand—shot in bed as he slept. On April 16, 1906, the name of Fernando Sarà, known as Prophet, was supposed to appear there as well. But Diamante decided otherwise.

On Easter morning of 1906, Diamante goes to whistle *La donna è mobile* in front of the house of a man called Prophet. He's one of the guys from the wakes. A stocky type, built like a bull, and a good friend of Cozza. Or so he thought. Inseparable, they were. Bongiorno and Prophet often went to eat cannoli together at the pastry shop on Elizabeth Street. And now, as the bells sound the alarm and the passersby rush to lunch without betraying the slightest joy that Christ is risen after so much suffering, Diamante, under a tremendous downpour, is leaning on a fire hydrant in front of Prophet's house—a house made of brick and with a cast-iron fire escape. A comfortable house where Agnello would like to live but can't because he doesn't earn enough money washing skyscraper windows. But he'll have to move soon anyway because there's starting to be talk of demolition orders. The Mulberry District housing scandal is raging in all the newspapers. The neighborhood has been defined as "a receptacle of crimes and vice," "a breeding-ground for infection and a disgrace for America." Builders smell a deal. Diamante hopes they really will knock down their decrepit tenement. That way they'll be forced to move and discover another slice of America. In Vita's primer it says that the United States is the second-largest country in the world in terms of size—Russia, which gave rise to Moe, being the largest—and the first in terms of natural resources, mineral riches, miles of railroad track, and fluvial water flow. But all he's seen of this immense country is one city—one neighborhood, to be precise.

Prophet had gone to mass and will be coming back at any moment. It'd be better if he weren't late, because if Diamante has to wait too long on this hydrant, somebody will notice him. What the heck is that boy doing sitting out there in this incredible downpour? Diamante pulls his hat down over his eyes. Lately he's taken to wearing a widebrimmed hat that hides his face. Lately the Syrian boys shine his shoes for free, and the newspaper boys give him a copy of *Il Progresso*. He has grown a thin mustache and wears his hair highly tapered, a wave at his forehead. The Prince Street boys are a grand success. Diamante more than the others. Even more than Rocco. The truth is, the girls are afraid of Rocco. And he reciprocates by avoiding them like the plague. In the world of tough guys, such behavior is synonymous with buggery, impotence, or distinction. In Rocco's case, it's certainly the third. But at number 18 the girls wait at the window for Diamante and smile at him when he comes home from work. Coca-Cola's girlfriends fleece him, but they never want Diamante to pay. A rare privilege because all they think about is money. Not that Diamante blames them; he, too, is always adding things up, calculating the savings he can send to Tufo. Coca-Cola's girlfriends are less demanding than Lena. She would move her hips and use her legs like pliers, looking at him the whole time, and afterward her crossed eyes would sparkle with such a green-flecked happiness he'd stand up feeling all proud. The chorus girls at the Villa Vittorio Emanuele café don't sing as well as Lena, but they sit better on his knee. Often he doesn't even know their names. They have made-up names, too—Sherry, Lola, Carmen. He prefers to ignore the fact that they're really Filippa, Carmina, Maddalena.

After a few minutes, Diamante spots the two men waiting for him to identify Prophet. They're standing next to a cart where a woman is selling bread. They're not from the neighborhood. They've come from the outside. Expressly for Prophet. Mr. Bongiorno hadn't told him that. All he said was, *When Prophet passes you, greet him—pronounce his name loudly and clearly—and then walk away whistling.* Strangely, Diamante is sweating, even though it's cold and the rain feels like ice. Everything is gray, dirty, and confused. He tries to calm down. He had planned on giving Vita a gold chain for her twelfth birthday. With a heart-shaped pendant, a pledge of sorts. He had purchased it on installments a few months ago from the jeweler—a Jewish relative of Moe's—and already had her name engraved. But after the incident with the lamp, he wasn't sure what to do with the chain. He didn't want to give it to Vita anymore, and ended up having it melted down and handing the money he got for it to Uncle Agnello. Diamante still owed him money. Rocco says it's stupid to pay back debts. Never pay off old debts, and let new ones grow old. It's just as well—he's too young to get engaged, only fourteen and five months. What's more, he's no longer so sure he still wants to marry Vita. A girl capable of doing something like that. Even though she did it for him. Or maybe she didn't mean to do it, or know what she was doing. The violence in her frightens him. Vita hasn't spoken to anyone since the night of the lamp. She goes out in the morning to do the shopping, but Diamante knows she wanders the streets of New York, as if she might run into Lena.

Vita takes the pot off the fire. The pasta water is already boiling. The sauce is thick and smells good. She tastes it, adds a basil leaf. A gloomy silence pervades the house. After the records melted, the phonograph horn merely collected dust, and now it's only good for hanging dish towels on. Agnello looks at his watch and swats flies with his newspaper. He's developed the American habit of buying the paper. But until Diamante gets home he won't know if Comte de la Vaulx managed to fly his balloon or the coal miners are still on strike. He doesn't want Vita to read him the news because he wants her to forget all the wicked things they taught her at the American school. And Nicola's a blockhead, nothing upstairs. Besides, he's never home. He won't even eat with his family on Easter, says he's working overtime. As if Agnello doesn't know Nicola doesn't even have a job; he spends his money smoking opium in the back room at the Li Poo laundry until the world looks like Paradise and the Chinese women with feet so tiny you could hold them in one hand blossom with youth. Though in reality they're old and deformed. Agnello's given up on this son of his. The big empty bed with the blanket tucked under the pillow makes him sad, and he thinks about the American baby. He'd be two and a half now, would know how to walk and say his father's name. If things had worked out, he would have married Lena. Who would have gone looking for the papers from his first marriage? And Lena would never have gone to Italy to tell anyone. Lots of people had two wives, and both were happy. Agnello would have given his son an American name. Not that there's anything wrong with Italian names. Pietro, for example, has a nice ring to it. But it would have been bet-

ter for the baby, would have spared him getting spit on, if his birth cer-
tificate said Nelson, Jack, or Theodore, like President Roosevelt. Or
Washington. An important name for an important man. But such was
not his destiny.

The two men are smoking under their umbrellas. The rain drips off
Diamante's hat and onto his nose. He wants to leave. He has never
whistled to identify somebody before. Only to warn of passersby or
danger, to avoid something, not provoke it. Why has Cozza gotten
him mixed up in this? Yesterday he'd called him into his office, and
Diamante thought he was going to offer him a raise because he's the
sharpest of all the boys. Diamante would like to become a regular employee, talk with the families of the deceased, explain discreetly that
everything will be taken care of, that their beloved is in good hands,
they can leave it all to him. Diamante knows how to be polite, discreet. He knows a ton of words. He respects the dead. And the living,
since he's lost so many loved ones himself. He would be a model employee. But Bongiorno has no intention of promoting him that way.
But why me? Because he trusts you, he tells himself. And he doesn't
trust Coca-Cola, who, despite his talent with matches, is careless, as
flighty as a butterfly. Coca-Cola opens his mouth too much, despite
his blackened smile. To feel important, he goes around boasting in
front of the girls and showing off the scar from the bullet he took in
the buttock one evening when a bar owner got furious and ran after
him, unloading his entire magazine. Rocco warned him: "If you
weren't my foster brother, I'd have somebody cut you up."
    And Diamante knows Rocco means it because he told him how to
do it when he gave him his knife. The most important thing is to twist
the blade in the guy's guts. Don't just sink it in. Shove it in all the way
up to the handle and then slice upward. That way the wound won't
heal. And look him in the eye, feel the power in your hand as he begs
and implores you to spare him. That's the best part. Rocco explained
it all in such a clear, calm manner, as if it had nothing to do with him.
Nothing matters to Merluzzo as long as no one tries to cut up Cozza.
Rocco is completely oblivious to everything else. With the exception
of his cat, Soot, for whom he never forgets to buy lungs and entrails,

and whom he feeds personally. He's always saying how intelligent cats are, not servile like dogs, and even if Soot were to grow tired of owing him something and picked up and found another owner one day, it would only demonstrate the feline's liberty, not his ingratitude. The other exception is Diamante; Rocco boasts he's the one who introduced Celestina to the business when no one else would have even bet a dime on him. But Diamante's no longer terribly proud of this. He'd started partly as a dare, partly to earn a bit of money—and because the smell of the fires reminded him of hearth and home. Because he thought he shared Rocco's beliefs, and was merely taking back what had been stolen from him. But the cracks in Rocco's arguments widened, the foundation crumbled, and now Diamante doesn't believe them anymore. Rocco might be the avenger of injustice, but he fights injustice with injustice and makes the wrong people pay. When Diamante tried telling him he didn't want to go out at night anymore because he wanted to become a regular employee, Rocco looked disappointed. "This is a world with no doors and no windows—nobody gets out," Rocco said without raising his voice, without stopping petting Soot's tail, erect and vibrating with pleasure. Without even looking at him. And Diamante understood: not only was Rocco no longer his friend, but he'd cut him up himself if he had to—with no emotion and no remorse.

Agnello sits smoking and brooding. Vita approaches him hesitantly. For a while she thought that now he was alone he'd quit his job, buy passage on the steamship, and take her back to her mother. But no. Agnello kept on climbing skyscrapers, brush in hand, kept on looking in at the people in their offices as he washed their windows. He never talked about going back to Italy, and never mentioned Lena's name again. But Vita knows he thinks about her. Sometimes she watches him as he sits at the table in the evening, cranking the phonograph handle. The records were ruined in the fire; curled and melted, they don't sing anymore, so no sound comes out of the wooden box. Agnello hears the music in his head, though, and he sits for hours, eyes closed, listening. Vita would like to tell him she didn't mean to, I didn't do it on purpose. But it wouldn't do any good. It happened.

And besides, Agnello would merely say, God sees everything, it was God's will. But Vita knows God had nothing to do with it. God wasn't watching the lamp.

After the accident no one ever mentioned Lena's name again. Not even Diamante. Only the lanky Jewish boy Moe came looking for her. He always used to stop by Prince Street on his way to night school. He'd invent some excuse—to touch up the color of the window, or add a bird and more snow on the mountains. He'd climb on the bench and paint while Lena bent over the kitchen sink below him preparing shrimp with oregano and oil. Moe never looked at her, never even spoke to her, but he'd stay in that uncomfortable position until she moved. Only then would he get down. Once he'd invited her to the cinema, where he had begun spending his afternoons when he was tired of being shut up at Vigorito's developing photographic plates, but Lena had declined. Moe didn't get discouraged; he came back just the same. He had begun painting the tub where everyone bathed—at least every now and then—to look like a meadow with reeds and frogs. But he didn't want to finish it. It was almost as if he were patiently waiting for something. Then, the last time he came, Lena was no longer there. Moe didn't say a word. He just looked about as if he'd lost something, and then turned around and left. He never finished the tub. Vita is the woman of the house now. She does everything. Cooks, washes, irons, sweeps, sews roses. In the evening her back aches and she's so dead tired, she couldn't care less about being the mistress of the house. Sometimes she thinks she'd rather not even make it to her thirteenth birthday. She's had enough already.

Someone's been knocking at the door for several minutes. Insistently, impatiently. Since the boarders have their own keys, it must be Doctor Lanza. Even though Agnello says he's a crook and a fraud who couldn't even cure the flu, he has him come by every Sunday to check on his daughter's health. She's been having trouble sleeping, and he's afraid she'll become ill. "Vita! Can't you hear the doctor knocking? Go open the door!" Agnello shouts. Vita can't stand doctors. The doctors from Bellevue had taken Lena away on a stretcher. She was delirious and they covered her with a sheet. Only her hand stuck out. She deserved it—that woman had the devil in her and made Agnello forget

Dionisia, and Diamante forget Vita. But her screams woke the entire house and the blue flames destroyed the mattress, the sacks of flour, and the flowered curtain. Even the chickens died. The doctors disappeared up to the third floor. When they came back, Vita plucked one of them by the sleeve. "Does it show?" she asked. "Of course it shows," he answered rudely. "Second-degree burns." The knocking starts again. "For Chrissake, Vita, answer the door! What you waiting for?" "Come in, please have a seat." The doctor is not alone. In fact, it's not the doctor after all, but an icy individual with a hooked mustache and horn-rimmed glasses, who is accompanied by two men in uniform. Policemen. The man speaks: "Is this the residence of a certain . . ."

Prophet approaches slowly, his flabby cheeks jiggling with every step. A real tough guy. Not a loser, and certainly not a good guy. Thickset and sporting a tattoo. Ten years ago, he was the one who'd go around beating up shopkeepers, collecting rents, breaking noses and ribs. He lives like a parasite on the blood of the workers. He's never worked a day in his life, has never earned his bread. Diamante doesn't feel the slightest sympathy for him. But he does still feel a shadow of sympathy for himself. His head is exploding. The words of the song are pounding in his brain, but not on his lips. *La donna è mobile qual piuma al vento muta d'accento e di pensiero.* All you have to do is whistle the theme. And say, Happy Easter, Prophet. Then go. Walk away. It's none of your business. It has to do with those two strangers, who've come on purpose from some other neighborhood. They're armed, pistols under their jackets. He can see the bulge from here. Professionals. They'll shoot him cold, two bullets. Cozza will put on an unforgettable funeral, complete with the black car with tinted windows and the driver in livery. And in a month or maybe a year, Diamante will be able to send his parents a money order. A real one. Angela will stop her complaining, stop making everyone miserable with her rancor. Stop tying strips of cork to her feet. He's always been ashamed of that; all the other women have a pair of clogs at least. Only his mother wears pieces of cork for soles and has to tread carefully, as if she were walking on glass; often the cork would get stuck in mud or manure, and if she tugged too hard it would come off. How many times had he seen her struggle to free her foot without losing that cork! Such a pathetic sight, it made his heart bleed. Angela will stop picking fights, stop accusing Antonio of being incompetent and a failure. And Antonio will no longer have to toil by the sweat of his brow on someone else's land. He'll finally be able to buy himself that piece of land the government and landowners had always denied him. Your father—your dear, vulnerable father—will stop begging you to climb into the cistern and fill the demijohns for him because when he sees that water, so black and smooth at night, he feels like drowning himself. Leonardo and Amedeo will not die, as did all your older siblings. They'll live. Your father's letter arrived yesterday. Amedeo's finishing up third grade and is even better at school than you were. He asks why you don't write more often, it's not as if distance and the years can loosen the ties of blood, and we all eagerly await your letters. Prophet's shadow is squat and ungainly. Diamante has never spoken to him, doesn't even know him. But this man has beaten, blackmailed, and killed with no remorse. A hoodlum. And this is how hoodlums die—when someone else takes their place. Musolino killed seven people—none of whom was responsible for the injustices he'd suffered—and they locked him away until the end of his days, until he went crazy and forgot he was even called Musolino.

Agnello decides to get up from his chair when he hears his daughter scream. The man with the horn-rimmed glasses is sweating in his undershirt. A piece of paper in his hand, he's stubbornly repeating, "Does this man live here?" "No, no, no!" Vita shrieks, and Agnello, uncertain, keeps mum as he scrutinizes the men planted like cypress trees among the crates and tubs. They're blond, clean-shaven, inflexible. Agnello relaxes. He'd feared they were the loan sharks' henchmen, come to claim the last hairs on his head, his few remaining teeth, and his final hopes of raising himself up again. But Rocco keeps them at bay: he's sworn that as long as he's around, no one will lift a finger against Agnello, who's like a father to him. Luckily, these men are only police. They're even carrying handcuffs and a pistol. Whadda these sweaty bastards want? Come to get Rocco? Or that wretched Elmer?

Or that good-for-nothing bum Coca-Cola? Or maybe Diamante, who knows what that boy's been up to. Agnello had never liked him. Always thought he was cleverer than everybody else. Always brought bad luck. Agnello's life had gone to the dogs ever since Diamante'd shown up at Prince Street. He'd lost his shop, his honor, and Lena. What did he have left? Whadda these cops want in my house? The neighbors must have seen them arrive. They'll talk about it for months. Agnello will be disgraced. "There's nobody here, just me and the girl," he says. "They're all out." White as a ghost, Vita peeps from behind the curtain, just as she did that night, and with that same haunted look. Standing behind the flaming bed, immobile—spectral. She's the reason he lost Lena. But a father has to stay with his daughter. Even though he'll never find another woman like Lena.

"I am under orders to read you the law," the man with the horn-rimmed glasses recites in perfect Italian. "Law Regarding Obligatory Instruction." "No!" Vita shouts. "Go away, go away, who told you to come here?"

> The State of New York. Penalties against parents who fail to send their children to school. Not more than 5 dollars for the first infraction. Not more than 50 for every subsequent infraction. In case of recidivism, fine plus 30 days in prison.

Agnello doesn't understand what he has to do with the law of the State of Nevorco. How can you violate a law you don't even know exists? Besides, he's already paid the fine, five dollars if he remembers correctly, isn't that enough? He tries to shake off Vita, who is still screaming, having realized long before Agnello that policemen don't come to people's houses just to collect a fine. "In conclusion, have I made myself clear?" the man with the horn-rimmed glasses spits out. "You are under arrest. Come with me without making a scene." "Whadda you talking about, arrest! Prison!" Agnello explodes, struggling to free himself. "Don't mess with me or I'll break you to pieces!" Vita screams that she's the one who should be put in jail, she was the one who looked at the lamp, who has the wickedness inside—sure, Agnello's a blockhead and has lots of faults, but hers are even greater, even though she didn't mean to burn Lena—she wasn't even angry with her—she didn't mean to! "Papà! Papà!" she yells, clinging to the policemen's blue uniforms while Agnello swears and curses. What the hell does the school want with him, he's never even gone to school, and why in the world does my daughter have to go, to do what? He'll send his next child, if he has another, he'll call him Washington, he'll be a good American. "Yes, I swear it, let me go, you sons of bitches, goddamn!" "Papà! Papà!"

"It's all a mistake, right, Vita?" Agnello despairs, suddenly suspicious. "Tell 'em how much your papà adores you." The men, who don't give a damn about this outburst of paternal love, twist his arm behind his back, handcuff him, and push him toward the door. "Papà! Papà! Papà!" The man with the horn-rimmed glasses shoves Vita aside, then mumbles something to the policemen about the people from the Children's Aid Society being late, and what're they supposed to do with the girl? Vita springs like a tarantula at the policemen. "Little Vita, my love," Agnello supplicates, "calm yourself, don't be causing no trouble." But Vita evades the policemen's grasp and clings to her father, holds him so tight his knees nearly buckle under this explosion of affection. Vita, who in three years, ever since she made him go all the way to Ellis Island for nothing, has never called him "my papà," not even once, who broke his heart by going around telling everyone that story about Enrico Caruso, now smothers him with kisses and caresses his hairy cheek. But Agnello doesn't respond. He lets himself be knocked about, endures it all because things always go wrong for him—even straw sinks when I put it in water—what an unfortunate poor old man I am, who travails for everyone else, and they don't even let me spend Easter Sunday with my daughter. Vita assails Agnello with kisses, as if she could remedy the fact that Lena slept with Diamante, that the lamp fell on Lena's bed, that Lena ended up in Bellevue bandaged like a silkworm in a cocoon, and Vita doesn't have anyone to talk to anymore because it's not the same with boys, that Lena will never return to Prince Street again.

Vita is in a state, slapping and cursing. Maybe she's trying to get herself arrested as well, but the policemen push her brusquely against the table and go out onto the landing, unsure whether they should wait for the Children's Aid Society, bring the girl with them, or merely cart off the bewildered and ashamed dago with the trembling chin. Doors open one after another, and the stairway fills: old women who love to gossip about criminals and delinquents, chewing on the words *Black Hand* as if they were clots of phlegm; the neighbors who don't let Vita play with their children; the men who whistled at Lena, put a finger in their mouth, and made disgusting gurgles when she walked by; the brats who made obscene gestures with their hands. And all these faces are saying the same thing: you deserve it, you're nothing but a bunch of sinners.

Prophet takes out his house key. He must be about forty, not even. Big, drooping shoulders, dull face. Here he is, just a few feet away. He brushes against Diamante. Diamante looks at him. And Prophet looks back. Maybe he's asking himself where he's already seen that boy with the arctic blue, implacable eyes. Hit man's eyes. Capable of shooting you in the face without giving it a second thought. Prophet passes him with a shudder of relief. "They want to kill you, you must leave right away," Diamante whispers. Prophet doesn't even turn. But Diamante knows he heard. Prophet enters his house. Diamante bites his lip. The two strangers with pistols turn and pretend to stare at a man coming back from church, his wife on his arm. Diamante signals with his head: No. He stays there in the rain, water dripping down his collar, pretending everything is normal, that it is perfectly natural that someone other than Prophet has entered his house, where now shutters are being closed. What should I do? Show them I'm calm, sure. Ignorant. Smile and wait.

At one o'clock, Diamante can't bear the tension any longer and hops off his fire hydrant. When he passes in front of the two strangers, he says, "He must've stopped in at some bar." Then he forces himself to walk very slowly toward Prince Street. In half an hour, Cozza will know the deal has been blown and that Diamante, Rocco's pupil, has betrayed him. In an hour, they'll come get him. Will they cut out his tongue? Slice off his bell clapper—castrate him like a capon? Butcher him, twisting the blade in his guts, cutting from bottom to top so the wound won't heal? Look him in the eyes while he begs them to spare

him? Hack him to pieces and stuff him in a barrel? Will Rocco be ordered to knife him so as to redeem himself? And will Rocco do it?
Diamante understands perfectly well the Bongiorno Bros. command-
ments. Honor your masters and companions. Do not name them in
vain. Obey your father. He doesn't have much time. As soon as he
rounds the corner, he starts to run.

He found Vita sitting on the stairs with the cat in her lap, the door to
the apartment wide open, and the courtyard, slippery stairs, and landings full of gossiping women. The boarders were eating bread with
sauce, disappointed that all this confusion had ruined their Easter dinner. To think that the girl had promised them lamb with thyme! Who
ever would have imagined that wild Vita would become the best cook
on all of Prince Street? They used as few words as possible. The police
took Uncle Agnello to prison. No one quite understands why. But if
we don't get him out, the landlord'll throw us all out on the street. We
have to go to the station and help him. Where? The police station. Are
you coming? Later, Diamante told them. The apartment was teeming
with strangers, but his only worry was running into sweet, mellifluous
Rocco. He grabbed the powder tin in which he kept his savings,
jammed his only spare pair of underwear in his pocket, and put on his
other shirt over the one he was wearing. He knew Vita was watching
him, but he didn't look at her. The cherry-colored bow in her hair
had come loose and she was smiling—yes, there was definitely a smile
on her lips.

　　"Don't worry about them taking Papà away," she whispered, tugging on his jacket. "I went myself to the inspectors to tell them I can't
go to school because he forces me to make paper roses and fettuccine.
I want to go back to school because I love you and I want our words
back. We're free now. No one will ever separate us again." Diamante
was so agitated he couldn't make sense of what Vita was saying, but realized there was something absurd, mistaken, tremendous about it. He
had no time to lose. "I've forgiven you, Diamà. I've even forgiven
Lena. I didn't make the lamp move, I won't do it again—never again."

　　Diamante still didn't turn around. He haphazardly stuffed all his belongings in his pockets: comb, razor, passport. Only then did Vita

realize Diamante was leaving. "Where are you going?" she asked, planting herself in front of the curtain to keep him from rushing out. "I can't tell you, Vita." He tried pushing her aside, but she clung to his jacket, put her arms around him, squeezed him so tightly her nails dug into his skin. Hot and sticky hands. How Vita had changed! Her figure had rounded out, and her body now concealed soft inlets he would have liked to slip into. I've gone mad! What the heck am I thinking? "Don't leave me." Vita's voice was so intense that for one quick second he thought of taking her with him. Isn't that what he'd always wanted? To take her away from all this? But how could he possibly manage with a twelve-year-old girl? He'd end up in jail and she in reform school. "Vita," he said, caressing her face with his hands, "I love you, too. You're my girl. I swear I'll come back." Her lips trembled, her eyes staring at the underpants sticking out of his pocket. He was leaving. With everything he owned. And without her. Diamante hurled himself out the door and her heart burst. One minute longer, and he'd never have left. As he stumbled down the stairs, he realized he'd forgotten Vita's primer—his only weapon, his only hope of making it without taking shortcuts. But there was no time to go back and get it.

The doors closed and the elevated train rattled past the third-floor windows of the buildings on Second Avenue. For one piercing instant he saw tables set for Easter dinner and families gathered around lamb and potatoes. He glimpsed lonely newspaper boys in deserted streets, prostitutes aimlessly leaning against walls, stray dogs, boarded-up shops, motionless winches, and then the metallic gray surface of the river bobbing with empty bottles, apple cores, tires. Only then did he realize that in his haste he had taken the wrong train. He was headed toward Brooklyn, not the big train station in the center of the city. It was a holiday, so the rest of the car was empty, except for the seat in front of him. There sat a girl in a blue dress and a cherry-colored ribbon. Vita.

Diamante had expected there to be a huge crowd at Coney Island, five hundred thousand people, a million even, a buzzing, shouting, laughing swarm—and in the midst of those hundreds of thousands of faces, bodies, and smiles, no one would have noticed his face, his body. He was a nobody and nobody would find him. But there weren't very many people at the amusement park: a few bewildered families wandering around gaping at deserted attractions, and a mere two hundred miserable creatures hovering on the Brighton Beach boardwalk. It had rained all morning, and no one had come. But Diamante didn't have the energy to leave and finally gave in to a sense of stunned amazement, as if today were a holiday just for him—whereas the others were expiating a wrong of which only he was innocent. At the feet of the Russian mountains, where empty little cars struggled and rattled their way to the peak, he felt his inside pocket to make sure he could buy Vita a Sunday of joy—in spite of, against everything. Vendors strolled among the booths, selling roasted corn, fritters, peanuts, and ice cream, and an ancient, toothless woman was winding cotton candy on a stick. The popcorn looked like an ocean of clouds, but when he put it in his mouth, it crunched against his teeth. It tasted like rubber and salt, and stuck to his tongue. He wondered if that was the taste of Vita's mouth.

Vita was dazed. By now she's stopped asking him, *Where are we going, why are you running away, what have you done?* They didn't speak, but glided, almost without seeing, past the rattlesnake charmer and the fake ship rolling on fake waves you could ride for a modest price if you wanted to experience the pleasures of seasickness. The only place Vita lingered was at the glass incubators, where premature babies lay breathing. The newborns were minuscule, like Baby, and they were alive. She was glad to see Baby again because he was her guardian angel, and she needed him today. She ignored the roaring tiger, but screamed delightedly when a gust of wind lifted her skirt, revealing for an instant the irregular hem of her stockings as they walked along a bridge. Hoping no one had noticed the distracting white of her shapely thighs, Diamante dragged her to safety amid a chorus of whistles. He had noticed, though, and the sight sent him floating above the sparse crowd, the smell of fried food, the merry-go-round, and the furious music of several orchestras, which seemed to be intent on drowning each other out. He felt as if he had lifted the anchor that had been holding him in port; finally, for the first time in his entire, suffocating existence of orders and obligations, he was free.

A line of couples were jostling in front of a darkened pavilion, hoping to conquer a secluded corner for kissing and caressing, but the man at the entrance was yelling like a hyena in labor to convince hesitant customers and Diamante was dissuaded. A clown swayed on stilts and a booth was selling lottery tickets: for ten cents, you could win a bicycle. Vita didn't want to try because she wouldn't have known what to do with a bicycle even though it was pretty, with radial wheels and a wooden seat. Diamante would have liked a bicycle, however. He would have pedaled across America, stopping only when he was too far away to return. They passed booths where people were practically coming to blows over the chance to feast their eyes on scantily clad exotic beauties. His money burned a hole in his pocket. I'll spend it all today, so when they come get me, there won't be anything left to steal. "What do you want me to buy you, Vita? Candy? A ticket for the knife thrower? A photograph with the automatic camera, African tribal dances?" "A picture, Diamà, we don't have one of us."

Diamante dropped a quarter in the machine and they posed in front of the accordion device. Stiff, with forced smiles on their lips. He dressed all in black like a bat with a leather bow tie and derby, she with a cherry ribbon in her hair and gold earrings. He with the tense expression of a gambler who's made too big a bet, she with the face of an urchin who's broken the rules but knows she'll get away with it somehow. They were handed a sepia-colored card. Their faces were a blurry glow—as if at the last minute they'd decided not to let themselves be captured, not to consign that unique moment of life to a dead memory. Diamante was a dark flash, Vita a light stain. Their features overlap and are indistinguishable, as if they belonged to one and the same person.

The orchestra had begun playing dance music and a wave of motion rippled through the beer hall rotunda. People eyed one another, chose partners, and held each other tight, abandoning themselves to the cheerful piano and violin music. "Can you dance, Diamante?" Vita asked as she sucked on a piece of popcorn, the last of the deflated cloud in the paper cone. "Yes." In truth he'd never danced with a girl before—he'd merely watched as couples threw themselves into the tarantella during the July festival. But this didn't sound like the tarantella—or the cancan Coca-Cola's girlfriends imitated in the cafés—and the notes didn't sound like anything to him. "Let's dance then, I'm dying to dance." Vita spit out the popcorn and tugged at his sleeve. Diamante hesitated, afraid of cutting a sorry figure, but Vita dragged him through the couples to the center of the rotunda, placed her hand on his hip, and suddenly the music entered his legs and they flew around the circle. With the illusion of leading, Diamante let himself be buffeted about by Vita. They danced well together; Vita was so relaxed and easy that everything else disappeared—the clumsy feet of the other dancers, the stink of fried food, Cesare's shoes, which still gave off a faint odor of death after all these months, and the fear of being found, taken, and done in.

By seven o'clock they were dying of thirst, so they collapsed at a table in the beer hall, and Diamante squandered a conspicuous portion of his fortune on hot dogs and Coca-Cola. No alcohol, because it's prohibited on Sundays. Americans felt an immediate and definite horror not only for death, misery, and disease, but also for alcohol—as if it were the cause of people's ugliness rather than the obvious consequence. As they sipped their soda, crushing slivers of ice between their teeth, Vita thought she glimpsed Agnello's jutting chin, and for an instant she wondered if it wasn't a crime to be dancing with Diamante while her father was suffering the irreparable shame of prison because of her. But the chin quickly disappeared and Agnello faded from her mind, along with Prince Street, the alcohol lamp, Lena's absent expression in the Bellevue hospital bed, the unforgivable yet forgiven betrayals, and all the rest. A diaphanous sliver of moon rose above the water, and the lamps put out a rosy glow. Diamante sipped his Coca-Cola and Vita tapped her feet under the table. She could still feel him in her arms, two bodies joined in one movement. "Diamante, are you running away because you killed somebody?" she started to say, but he interrupted her. "Shhh, let's talk American." "Why? What's got into you?" "Let's pretend we're Americans, Vita," Diamante whispered, fiddling with the brim of his hat. "Let's be like everybody else. Let's have fun tonight. *I feel so happy*," he began. She looked at him, not understanding. "You taught me that, remember? *I am happy. I'm happy, too. Happy*," Diamante insisted. "Whatever you say, Diamante, happy."

The vendor was calling out lottery numbers and a girl with a garter belt wrote them on a blackboard. "Did you win?" she asked, peeking at his ticket. Diamante got up and wedged his way through the crowd. Sitting in the Coney Island beer hall under a dramatic April sunset, Vita filed her dirty nails on the beveled edge of the table and was surprised to find herself thinking that things aren't flat and painted, but have numerous dimensions, just like the Green Lady on the island. Circle around her and she changes as you move. You see her shoulders, flame, crown, or backside encrusted with salt. Today the Statue of Liberty was showing her most noble aspect—the flame—because truth is only found in your own movement: things are neither good nor bad, they are what they are, they're what happens. She had wept when she left Tufo and boarded the train with Diamante and his father because she didn't want to leave and cross the ocean. She wanted to stay right where she'd always been, to see from her window a thousand times more the sun setting in the Tirreno, hear the caged canary sing when the first ray of dawn struck the lane, pick lemons on her grandfather's land; yet she probably won't ever see any of those things again. But who's to say it wasn't a good thing in the end? There's no sense crying over misfortune. Who's to say it's not good luck instead? And there's no point in rejoicing over happiness: who's to say it's not a misfortune? Destiny is what hasn't happened to you yet. Diamante came back and sat next to her; he hadn't won the bicycle. Just as well, what would I do with it? When they throw me in the East River with a stone in my mouth and my feet in a cement block, I won't be able to pedal anywhere.

The free dances were over. A bruiser in a spangling stars-and-stripes jacket and a towering top hat started yelling into his megaphone to clear the rotunda, folks, because the long-awaited dance marathon is about to begin. Sign right up, only costs a dime, magnificent prizes and a cotillion for everyone. Diamante headed for the registration booth. If I were American, if I'd been born in a house with columns on Central Park, I'd be called Diamond, and no one would come looking for me to rip my heart out. So he didn't hesitate to write: Diamond. But he couldn't think of an American surname, given as how he didn't know any real Americans, apart from the president of the United States of America, so then he added: Roosevelt. If my name were Diamond Roosevelt, I would conquer the world. He put the pencil down, and Vita picked it up as if it were incandescent—an enemy. She couldn't believe Diamante would sign his name that way. That "Roosevelt" was offensive and unforgivable to her. She was proud to have the same name as his and wouldn't allow him to renounce their name. So she canceled out Roosevelt, rubbing so hard she made a hole in the paper, and recorded instead an illegible scribble.

They were assigned the number 9. It'll bring us good luck, Vita thought. The dance marathon was an endurance competition; the couples, judged by a panel of "experts," would be eliminated one at a time. The prize was a metal trophy with CONEY ISLAND 1906 inscribed on it, thirty dollars, and a white, furry puppy, not even a month old, peeking out of a wicker basket. I hope we don't win, Diamante was thinking, otherwise I'll end up selling that puppy to be put down, just as I did with the others, which is murder if you think about it, and I'd rather put down a hoodlum like Prophet than a puppy.

All those who'd been left out—the cynical jokesters, the curious, the solitary types without a girlfriend, and those who couldn't even get themselves a hired dance partner—crowded around the edge of the rotunda, shouting, ready to cheer on now this couple, now that one. Everybody participated, and no one was ashamed or shy: the young and not so young, even the old geezers. A worker endowed with a sizable double chin danced with a homely, freckle-faced girl; a worn-out harlot paired up with an underage lad; couples in love gazed tenderly in each other's eyes, thinking of the darkness that awaited them on the beach; husbands and wives who no longer cared for each other moved with a tired, listless familiarity; two elderly string vendors from the Bowery, still in love, held each other tight; bricklayers danced with their lovers; train conductors with partners they'd met half an hour earlier and whose name they'd forgotten to ask; and gangsters from the city's worst neighborhoods attracted the eyes of all the women. In part for their garish suits—pea green, sunflower yellow, raspberry red—and in part for the pistols they tranquilly packed under their arm.

Vita kneeled in the dust in her pretty blue dress and painstakingly unlaced her boots. She entrusted them to a woman seated at a table plaintively waiting for an admirer, and begged her to hold on to them. Liberated, she took her place in front of Diamante and guided his hand to her waist. "You can't, all the other women are wearing shoes, they'll disqualify us," Diamante said. "Either I dance like this or not at all." So Vita danced barefoot, and it was a pleasure to stamp the wooden boards of the rotunda, cold now that the sun had gone down and the only light was an impossible, unreal blaze of electric bulbs. Artificial, just like everyone's joy. They'll eliminate us right away because we're too young, Vita was thinking as she held her Diamante tight, dressed in black like a shadow. They'll eliminate us right away. She wanted to cover her ears so as not to hear their number being called: NOVE. Or rather, NINE.

TWELVE, THIRTY-THREE, FORTY-FIVE, EIGHT. The number nine was not called. The disappointed couples stopped dancing and melted back into the whistling crowd, half of whom were cheering for the raspberry-colored gangster and the rest for the ancient lovers. NINETEEN, THIRTY-SIX, TWENTY-TWO, the pianist was drenched in sweat, his shirt stained dark under his arms; he traded off with a player who worked the ivories for twenty minutes, changing rhythm, running through the entire repertory of popular music, that's what they paid him for, paid him poorly, but at least he earned his bread, ELEVEN, THIRTY-FIVE, THIRTEEN, Diamante's eyes lightened, the shadows left him, and he was happy to be still in the running because as long as he was dancing no one would come looking for him, and he didn't have to think about tonight or tomorrow, about Prophet's face and big Rocco's disappointment, Rocco who'd taken a chance on him and been betrayed, because he was still holding Vita tight in his arms, so light she seemed not to touch the floor, not tired in the least, so deeply absorbed in the music that she didn't even realize he was looking at her differently now, no longer as the little Vita who sold him kisses to make him blush. TWENTY, the panel of experts eliminated the sunflower gangster amid a roar of disapproval, threats, and a demonstrative shot in the air, just to make noise, "Keep it up, kids," whispered the gangster's partner, whose sweat had an exciting aftertaste, pleased they'd been eliminated because now that Irish idiot would take her to one of the more shady hotels on the oceanfront and finally pay her for the nuisance of keeping him company. FIFTEEN, that's how old I am, Diamante thought as he caressed the silk rose he'd been wearing in his buttonhole for months and that today finally seemed to have bloomed, to be giving off a delicate perfume. What am I going to do with Vita? Where can I go with her? Pino Fucile was reported by Guglielmina's mother and ended up in prison for abduction and she in reform school as a "delinquent minor," which is how they label young girls who have sex. THIRTY-SEVEN, TWENTY-FOUR, the crowd marked the rhythm with their hands, some people were dancing outside the rotunda, not giving a damn about the registration fee, prize money, dog, and metal trophy, now he'll say NINE, and a chill ran down Vita's spine, FIVE, FORTY-TWO, THIRTY-EIGHT, Diamante was so handsome, everyone was looking at him, even the professional dancers drinking soda all alone, and so were the women with partners, tall women out of ads, but Diamante was dancing with her, with barefoot Vita, the tiniest one of all—Vita, who couldn't have danced with anyone else because her nose would have been right at her partner's belly button, and you know what people would think. FOURTEEN, TWENTY-SEVEN, ONE, heads were rolling swiftly now, the judges looked each other in the eye and indicated now this couple, now that, while the puppy, inexhaustible, whimpered in the basket, hoping for an owner who wouldn't sell him to the dogcatcher or gangs who bet on rats that ripped puppies to pieces. TWO, THIRTY-FOUR, TEN, Vita's bare feet left dark marks on the wood, THIRTY-ONE, SIX, and if I said she's my sister? We have the same name, after all. This is my sister, we're on our way to our relatives who will take care of us—but if you really loved her, you'd take her back home this very night— TWENTY-NINE, THIRTY, Diamante looked around, the dance floor was easier to navigate now, each couple had ample space for maneuvers, and he dragged Vita to the center, the sides, past the sweaty piano player, under the eyes of the judges because he was no longer afraid of hearing the number nine called, SEVENTEEN, in front of the spectators so they could see how well they danced together, barefoot Vita with her gold earrings and Diamante without anything, FORTY-THREE, he found malicious pleasure in the thought of Agnello rotting in prison because if he weren't locked up it wouldn't be just slaps and rabbit cages this time, but shotguns and bullets all the way to the South Street pier, back to where you came from, you lice-infested lout, I hope a tarantula burrows up your ass. Fuck you, Vita's mine, I'll take her west with me, we're leaving, you'll never see us again. SIXTEEN, THIRTY-TWO, FORTY-ONE, Vita was thinking about the Minturno fairs, but those memories were fading, she could barely hold on to them, even though the Minturno piazza was pretty, too, in the shadow of the castle, with women encased in lace and the smell of salt cod sandwiches. TWENTY-THREE, she no longer heard the numbers being called, the music barely entered her ears, EIGHTEEN, THREE, now the spectators embraced the impossible cause of the gravedigger dressed in black and the Gypsy with filthy bare feet, they cheered them on, in part as a joke, in part to spite the others, look at the kids go, go kids, but they didn't even hear them, every now and then they smiled at each other, repeating the word *happy* like a magic formula, encouraging each other to resist even as their legs started to go numb, the exhaustion of this eternal day crushed their backs, and Diamante's feet were swimming in the shoes of a dead man, rubbing painfully against the stiff uppers and aggravating his sores. TWENTY-SIX, FOUR, "Hey, dago, tell Bongiorno *buongiorno*," the pea green gangster said as he left the floor. Bongiorno, who's he? I never met those wicked people, I merely dreamed all those coffins, cadavers, the makeup room, disinfectants, bandits, but I never met him, I never stole Cesare's shoes—never. THIRTY-NINE, FORTY, Vita sees the two amorous string vendors collapse, they'd been dancing so closely but now her green varicose veins were about to explode, she was killing herself just to hold on to her shriveled husband—how strange, Agnello had stayed in America even though his wife had an eye ailment, and Angela bickered all day long with her husband who hadn't gone to America—how different this country was, maybe here it really was possible to grow old together without drowning in bitterness. TWENTY-FIVE, how much time had passed since that July Minturno fair? Three years? It felt like another life, I won't go back, and strangely, I don't want to anymore, SEVEN, Diamante's heel was one huge bloody blister, what was the most important word he'd bought from Vita? He'd traded the word *time* for her throat, *past* for the mole on her cheek, *future* for her lips, moist, red, and sealed. TWENTY-EIGHT, someone broke through the crowd, people were drifting off in dribs and drabs, it was getting late and the ferries for Manhattan were already full and the only way to get on was to elbow and shove, the celebration was ending, just as it began, on the notes of the violin, and the ground was littered with paper, broken bottles, torn newspaper, pumpkin seeds, cotton candy sticks, and corn cobs, the sad inheritance happy people leave to the day after. TWENTY-ONE, the two elderly lovers gave way to youth, but they'd taught them a fine lesson, and now the announcer in stars and stripes was yelling, inciting what remained of the crowd to participate in the final, agonizing selection. Diamante and Vita looked up to discover that they and another couple were the only ones left, a waiter from Ocean Avenue and his wife, a big-breasted Creole whose sagging dried figs had dropped to her waist, then the orchestra struck up the final waltz, Vita, sure now, looked him in the eyes and a second before the announcement, said to him, "We've won, Diamà"—FORTY-FOUR, yelled the man with stars and stripes, "and the winners are, the winners are" . . . he hesitated, perplexed, studied the registration list . . . "Mr. Diamond and Miss M. . . . ," weak applause, tired clapping, the music stopped suddenly, the remaining spectators shouted, "Bravo, kids," and the announcer, completely exhausted, yelled from the judges' booth to come collect your trophy and dog. Diamante hugged her tightly. "*Brava, Vita.*" She pushed him away with a laugh and eyed him. "*Bravo, Diamà.* This one's a present," she said, and then kissed him on the mouth. It took his breath away.

The puppy whimpered on Diamante's shoulder as he marched quickly behind Vita, following the light patch of her blue dress. The ocean lapped at an endless beach; only if they strained their eyes could they

make out the lights of some vessel far in the distance. They skirted the
edges of interminable bathing establishments, delineated by changing
cabins and fences, passed by closed-up stands, boathouses, warehouses.
The waves ebbing onto the sand made a sleepy rustling sound. Vita's
boots dangled around her neck as she walked determinedly on her
black, leathery, unfeeling feet. Diamante would have liked to do the
same, but he'd lost the habit and his errand boy's soles were no longer
tough enough. Until a few minutes ago they were still coming across
shadows and voices: other people from the amusement park, latecomers rushing to catch the last ferry scattered along the beach—but now
they were alone in the dark. "Let's stop a minute," Diamante said.

The night was cold and the sky bristled with stars. Diamante
dropped onto the wet sand. "Just for a few minutes." Vita looked at
him sympathetically, but she was worried because they absolutely had
to catch the last ferry. It was dangerous to spend the night on Coney
Island. Besides, the night was when lots of freight trains left the depot
on the Hudson. At night it was easier to elude the guards, sneak over
the fences, climb onto a train. Dawn would surprise them hidden away
in a freight car, headed who knows where   toward a better America,
without Agnello, Cozza, Rocco, without mistakes and temptations.
Diamante gallantly spread his black gravedigger's jacket on the sand
and invited Vita to lie down next to him. She studied him closely:
Diamante was smiling, loosening the collar of his shirt. His face was so
familiar—smooth and lean, with the dark shadow of a mustache above
his lip. She obeyed, sinking against the hard mattress of sand. "We can't
fall asleep." "I'm too tired to make plans," Diamante declared, even
though he would have liked to say many things to her. The sky was
black, there were too many stars, and he lost track trying to count
them all. Vita pressed the metal trophy with CONEY ISLAND 1906
against her chest—it was fake, and made a dull sound when she tapped
it with her knuckles. "Can we keep the puppy? Can we take him with
us?" Diamante responded that they had to give him a name. That way
they'd always be able to find him again.

"Let's call him Prince," Diamante suggested. He wanted to find a
way to properly immortalize the day of his farewell to New York.
"Prince, Prince—yes," Vita said. The seagulls screeched at the water's

edge, and one circled above them. Diamante, unusually lyrical, had the impression the bird was singing for them. Can I? What? Take your hand. Yes. He placed her hand on his heart. It was beating wildly. Strange because he was resting now and the tiredness, fear, and anxiety that had tormented him all day were ebbing out of him like the tide. A pleasant weariness came over them. No need to hurry. All the time in the world. Nights, days, years. They held hands, watched trails of pale clouds momentarily obscure the stars and then race east, where a glowing reflection lit up the night. Italy's in that direction—how far away it is tonight! Too bad there aren't shooting stars in April—he could have made a wish. He had one ready. They stared wide-eyed, hoping for an impossible shooting star in April, but the sky was a blurry carpet, a blanket without warmth. Vita's hand pressing against his distracted him; it was a strong hand, rough and riddled with pinpricks—a hand that made him ashamed for a moment. But one day, when we're married and I have an office job, she won't have to sew artificial flowers.

We'll get up now, catch the ferry, go to the depot on the Hudson, hide in a freight train and head west. We'll find work in the countryside—there's got to be countryside somewhere. We'll say we're brother and sister, put aside some money, and when we meet a priest we can trust we'll have him marry us. In church, though, or else I won't believe it. I want God as my witness, nobody less important. And then, only then, I'll take Vita—because that's the way it should be. And then? What'll we do then? We'll stay here. We won't go back to Italy. There's nothing for us over there. It's all here—somewhere, not far away.

"Diamante!" Vita cried suddenly, making him jump and tearing him out of the stupor that held him to the beach, his feet to the wind and his head sinking in the wet sand. "I saw it! I saw it!" "What did you see?" he murmured, confused. "The white star, the star with the tail." There was such elation in Vita's voice. How different she was, everything enthused her, everything—a lemon seed, the shell of a shrimp, she was even passionate about a blade of grass. He couldn't explain it, but all of a sudden, up there in the still sky where the stars seemed hung on invisible pegs or painted on the vault as in the apse of a church, something moved: a white light, a flash streaked across the darkness and sank into nothingness. It had a tail of light—yes, a tail, a star with a tail. Probably a balloon or a dirigible. They launched them from the airfield outside the city. Along with airplanes, hot-air balloons, and colored rockets. But Vita would never have accepted that the flash was merely the reflection from a piece of metal. "Now make a wish," Diamante said, "but don't tell me what it is." Then he kissed her eyelashes and looked her in the eyes. If a dirigible could be a shooting star, then Coney Island beach could be a cathedral. God was watching them that very night. God was their witness—here, now.

Star light, star bright, what did Vita wish that night? To forgive Agnello and accept him as he was? To buy his shop back and pass the day weighing potatoes and tomatoes? To have Lena come home? To discover her body's secrets, which she sensed but did not know how to find? To become Diamante's wife, cook him delicacies, and wait for him all day while he works in a skyscraper? Bear him children, and love him her entire life? And yet on the night of the shooting star, none of these things seemed important enough, truly important, decisive. She couldn't choose but knew she had to hurry because the wish has to be made right away, and the shooting star had already vanished in the fixed sky: she was cold and the sand was stinging her under her dress, in the spot where Diamante's jacket ended and the beach began. She sought a wish as big as the sky because she felt as though she had seen something immense, impossible—a shooting star in April, a star with a white tail—a comet.

She placed her gold chain with the cross, which her mother said kept evil away, around Diamante's neck. She closed her eyes and the phantom of the inspector with horn-rimmed glasses dissolved from the convulsive day that had just come to a close, together with Agnello's cursing, the pains in her hand where she had pricked her skin. She already felt the rumbling of the train on the tracks . . . As her worries vanished and Diamante came closer, eager to discover the taste of her kisses on this night, she searched and searched for a wish that could contain everything. Happy. To always be as happy as this evening.

"Are you asleep, Vita?" Diamante asked all of a sudden. She didn't answer him. He covered her with his jacket, reflecting that her sleep had saved him from committing a very grave mistake. God was not here this night. He had hidden himself to keep him from ruining their lives. Diamante stayed awake, too excited to rest. He felt ready to face anything, overcome any obstacle. With Vita, curled up asleep at his side. Soon she would be his wife. She had chosen him, had put the magic chain around his neck. From now on, everything would be different. Life opened up before him like an unexplored continent. Life for him began in this very moment, and everything finally had a direction, a goal. He smiled to himself as he sucked on the gold chain, pressing the cross to the top of his mouth. He built castles in the air as he studied Vita's legs sticking out from underneath his gravedigger's jacket. The world was at his feet, there to conquer just like her dark body. I won't be an errand boy or a porter in a grand hotel, not even an office worker. I'll be somebody, one day I'll become an industrialist, I'll build skyscrapers, railways, locomotives, dirigibles, rockets—or no, I'll be an artist, as Moe says, a great painter like Michelangelo, and they'll put my work in the museums on Central Park where you have to buy a ticket to get in—or something grander still, I'll learn all the words, I'll be a famous poet, Vita, like Dante—my books will be in the Lenox Library, that building that looks like a palace, where anyone can enter without buying a ticket, even people like you and me—people will know who Diamante is, they'll know my name, we'll go far away from here, I'll take you with me, I'll have my own house and I'll write you thousands of poems, I'll write about you as you sleep, as you dance, as you wake, as you think who knows what thoughts, I'll marry you in Saint Paul's Chapel, the first one we found here, even if it's not a real church and doesn't have a cross on the roof, and we'll have a house on Washington Square and you'll be my lady, and in the summers we'll go to Tufo, travel first class, and look at the sea and remember the night when a balloon became a shooting star, when we bound ourselves to one another forever, and you'll never regret having placed your gold chain around my neck, and we'll have children, and our children will be small like me because diamonds aren't big like bricks, and they'll have your gift and your imagination, and I'll be true to you, and you'll be true to me—Vita.

PART II

The Road Home

My Desert Places

Captain Dy joined the Fifth Army, led by General Mark Clark, in October of 1943. Having graduated summa cum laude from Princeton with a degree in engineering, he volunteered for service the day the United States entered the war. Even though his father, as a citizen of an enemy country, was suspected of unpatriotic activity and briefly placed under house arrest, Dy was nevertheless accepted by the Combat Engineers, a special corps destined to fight in Germany. Eager to erase the disgrace of his father (or perpetrated on his father, for later his opinion became less certain), for nearly two years he built aircraft bases, munitions depots, hospitals, hangars, lodgings, and every type of building, runway, bridge, or port, as crucial for victory as infantry or bombs. His war, spent among offices and construction sites, was pure abstraction. The metaphysics of mathematics. Great honor, no risk. But when Dy learned that the Fifth Army was preparing to attack across the Volturno River, he requested a transfer to the southern front. It was explained to him that he was committing a serious error that would compromise his career. The war in Italy was merely a diversion, given Operation Overlord. An ostensible theater, intended to draw as many Germans as possible onto the peninsula and thus keep them far from the English Channel, where the war would really be decided. There were no medals to be earned on the southern front. It was an inglorious mountain war—plunging into turbulent torrents and wallowing in the snow while under German artillery fire. Not a war of numbers but a war of dirt, water, fire, and mud.

Dy insisted. He was hardheaded and rarely discouraged by the endless refusals. Twenty-three years old in the autumn of 1943, Dy possessed a limited fear of death and only one certainty: he wanted to be among the first liberators to enter the village his parents had fled, where his grandparents still lived. The village he'd heard so much about, the village whose tastes and smells he already knew, a paradise lost and memory's inferno, which he'd seen only in a black-and-white postcard his mother kept taped to her dressing-table mirror. A remote land, a foreign name. A place he hated, for it reminded him of all that he was not. A place he wanted to destroy—so as to free himself once and for all.

This had been his desire ever since the day of the Harlem uprising. That day, for the very first time, he realized he wasn't a real American. He would always be an Italian in other people's eyes—even if in his own he wasn't and never would be. It was March 19, 1935. Dy wasn't even fifteen years old. He was the best in his class, which meant he didn't have many friends among his classmates, who were envious of his ability to calculate the square root of triple-digit numbers in his head and, more so, to hoard all the cash prizes awarded to the student with the highest grades. He had to make do with his two little sisters, whom he spoiled rotten. Even though his father had been ruined in the Depression, his mother had managed with her work to maintain the family's comfortable, dark brick house on the liveliest street in Harlem. Dy was his mother's favorite. On the whole, he could be considered a happy child. But then fear and the feeling of his own unworthiness were tattooed on his mind—like the sign of his difference. He wasn't sure how it all started. At a certain point he found himself on hands and knees under the desk in his father's office. On the sidewalk outside were hundreds of hotheads with crowbars and baseball bats. They were smashing everything, and as they shattered the office window they yelled "Hang them, burn them!" These were popular slogans, usually shouted at lynchings or executions. But this time *them* meant them: his father and him. Dy recognized one of his classmates among the demonstrators. More than a fear of dying, he felt incredulity and shame. His mother wasn't able to explain to him the reason for the uprising that had devastated the neighborhood and caused them to move in a hurry. She had spoken to him about Mussolini, about the fact that he'd gotten the idea to conquer Ethiopia, and that this had wounded the sentiments of the black community. But Dick was his classmate—they sat next to each other—and the only thing that Dy, who was rather taciturn, admired about Mussolini was his irrepressible garrulity. Other than that, he seemed like a flaccid, loudmouthed boor, just like his parents' compatriots—of whom, parenthetically, he was so ashamed he pretended not to know them at school ceremonies. *Burn them, hang them.* The office had been sacked and would have been burned as well if the cleaning woman, black like the assailants, hadn't stopped them. While Dy hid behind his father's swivel chair, the demonstrators smeared red paint on the walls. When they were done, the words FASCISTS—MOBFIA—FASCISTS—MAFIA—FASCISTS—MAFIA dripped on the white walls—like a wound carved in his flesh.

The scar did not heal. The insulting writing on the wall obsessed Dy for years. Like a message. A command showing him the path to salvation. The destruction convinced his father to close his real estate agency, which had been losing money for years, but it also had another, unforeseen, and much more devastating consequence. On that day, March 19, 1935, Dy stopped speaking Italian. He refused to answer to his real name, preferring instead the American nickname they'd given him at school. And without even realizing it, he began to hate his father, his mother—himself. In the autumn of 1943 he obstinately requested the opportunity to cancel that indelible writing on the wall.

His request was granted. He was assigned to the auxiliary units. And so the Princeton engineer ended up in the slum of a Combat Engineer battalion—building floating bridges in an exhausted infantry division of the American armed forces.

The weather was atrocious. It rained for weeks. Aviation didn't even attempt to take off. For days on end, all along the front, a fine, incessant drizzle fell over the naked, bare hills and mountains that provided no cover; the viscous wet mist turned to cold, cutting winds and then tempest, ice, and storm. The few roads were impassable, obstructed by debris and pocked with gaping craters; those not covered in snow became torrents of mud. The sluggish soldiers wrestled with weapons rendered practically useless by the most tenacious filth; even though they cleaned them constantly, they never functioned properly. It was an immense effort just to advance a few hundred yards along track or dirt road. The tactic adopted by the Germans during their retreat was the systematic demolition of bridges and buildings along the roads—and of houses in the towns and villages. The junctions, roadsides, and river escarpments were strewn with mines, and areas suited for bivouacking troops were littered with explosive traps. There was no respite: just an endless succession of skirmishes between patrols, as absurd as they were ferocious because, in a region such as this, whoever controlled a hill, a crest, or a ruined cottage had a greater chance of staying alive. It was also important to take prisoners and make them identify formations. The Germans hoped to find signs of the Allied offensive, and the Allies signs of the German retreat. But the offensive stagnated and there was no retreat. Day and night, both sides vomited out all the fire that was permitted by the shortage of artillery and ammunition. Dy thought this war of trenches was sinisterly similar to that of 1914 and started to suspect that this time it would be his turn to die, just as it had been Coca-Cola's last time.

How many times he had heard tell of that death—always with a mixture of incredulity and respect. To everyone's surprise, Coca-Cola enlisted in 1917. With the Americans because they have the strongest army, so you're guaranteed to win. The Americans had never lost a war. "Italy and the United States are allies, so Italy wins as well," everyone had objected. "But Italy wins less," headstrong Coca-Cola had responded. And so he joined the U.S. Army instead of Italy's Royal Army. They sent him to who knows what field in Belgium. All that remained of him was a letter, accompanied by a photograph in which he is not smiling, so as not to show his rotten teeth. In two unimaginative lines he expresses his satisfaction with the rations. The rest of the letter is covered in heavy black stripes, the work of the censors. In 1919 his remains were returned in a wooden box wrapped in the stars and stripes. The ambulance he was driving—he'd reasoned that after the war everyone would have an automobile, so driver was a profession he could carry on in peacetime as well—had come under enemy shell fire. Risking his life, Nicola Mazzucco had carried the wounded to cover, one by one; then, breathing in the green smoke of mustard gas, he had repaired the motor and driven the tottering ambulance through thick fog laced with poison to safety behind the lines. His lungs were burned and he died in the hospital shortly afterward, suffering atrociously. They awarded him the Distinguished Service Cross for special merit—"for exceptional courage and devotion to duty while acting under heavy enemy fire." That improbable soldier had become a hero even though he would never know it, unfortunately. He had died before Dy was born, so Dy had never met him. But he felt close to him—closer than to his own father. Coca-Cola had known how to choose the right side. But Dy didn't want to die as he did, an unarmed, defenseless target in a barren land all gray with mud. Dy would fall firing a machine gun. Or pulling out the ring of a hand grenade.

In November 1943 the Germans formed a line of defense from the Tyrrhenian Sea to the Adriatic, a line that cut Italy in two. Known as the Gustav Line, it rested on the only thing Italy had to offer in abundance: high ground. The westernmost part of the line included Minturno and a network of tumultuous rivers devoid of fords: the Rapido, Gari, and Liri Rivers, which flowed together to form the Garigliano. On the southern side of the Liri Valley rose the Aurunci Mountains, a mass of jagged ridges that served as a gnarled and precipitous bulwark. "In short," Dy concluded in his diary, "the entire line is constituted of a series of defenses, with no key point. It is impossible to deliver a decisive blow that would cause it to crumble: every mountain must be taken separately, every valley scoured, only to find ourselves faced with more mountains and another line that must then be broken with infantry attacks. Minturno must be taken first, however, at any cost." Many American and many German soldiers will perish, but Captain Dy will be the first to enter Tufo. He will liberate the inhabitants, slaves for centuries, and will show his father and those that suspected him how wrong they'd been: people like him are always on the right side of history. He wrote to his mother not to expect him back anytime soon. The road was long and difficult. Maybe he would fall. But he did not want to be mourned. It was his duty to die for America and for Italy. Only thus would their story have meaning, only thus would it be complete.

On December 19, 1943, Mr. Churchill, laid up in Carthage with pneumonia, reprimands his chiefs of staff: "There is no doubt that the stagnation of the whole campaign on the Italian front is becoming scandalous." The chiefs respond that they are in complete agreement, this stagnation cannot continue. Something must be done. In January, or at the latest February, of 1944 we must enter Rome. It is decided for a landing north of the mouth of the Garigliano—in the bay of Minturno. A diversion to attack the Gustav Line from the west. If the Allies manage to break through from the sea, simultaneously penetrating the center from Venafro, the Germans will find themselves caught in a pincer movement. But even if the maneuver fails, it is essential to engage the Germans on the banks of the Garigliano, because meanwhile the VI Corps will land at Anzio, outflanking the Gustav Line and implementing Operation Shingle. On January 17 the X Corps will force open a passage on the lower Garigliano near Minturno, establish a bridgehead on the dominant ground between Minturno and Castelforte, and then send a division along the Minturno–Ausonia road in order to attack north toward San Giorgio and enter the Liri Valley. What in the arid military lexicon is known as "dominant ground" for Dy has another name—Tufo. When the Allies press across the Garigliano, two kilometers southwest of Minturno, Tufo—his point of origin, there where everything is beckoning him—will be the first village in the line of fire.

The attack is set for 2100 hours on January 17, 1944. But Dy won't be there. The Fifth Army has suspended its attacks. It must reorganize and await reinforcements in light of the action it will soon be required to perform. The honor of liberating Tufo will fall to the English, Irish, and Scottish soldiers of His Royal Majesty King George VI. On the

Panorama Tufo di Minturno

evening of January 17, while the 5th Infantry Division is landing in silence on the beach it believes to be deserted, the engineer Dy is in the command office sadly contemplating the Gustav Line that winds its way across the military map. Tufo is a black dot on the despairing white of Italy. But if the attack is a success, if the surprise works, it will all be over by tomorrow morning.

Deafening silence, terrible weather conditions, piercing rain, a clammy fog festers on the surface of the water. The Garigliano plain has melted in the drizzle. A whole division struck dumb in absolute silence, ready to move without artillery cover so as not to ruin the surprise effect. Thousands of men crammed into forty-five assault vessels loaded with gangways, life jackets, rafts, pontoons, and supplies for throwing a Bailey bridge across the river. The shore is a flat, dark line. The Royal Scots Fusiliers will land two kilometers from the German lines, above the mouth of the Garigliano. Their task is to take the small hillock that goes by the romantic name of Monte d'Argento, Silver Hill. But the small contingents using landing lights to guide the DUKW amphibious vehicles have been swallowed up by the fog. In the darkness many DUKWs get lost and the munitions and anti-tank guns they are carrying—fundamental, essential, and indispensable equipment—land back on the shore they'd departed from. Chaos descends on the landing operation. Everyone's pushing, crowding, getting in each other's way. The landing craft vomit out hundreds of exhausted and exasperated foot soldiers onto the shore—they've been in Italy for 122 days, 115 of them spent in combat. Many of their companions are already dead, and all they want to do is lie down and sleep. The commanders had requested 4,686 fresh infantrymen to fill in the gaps in the ranks opened these last four months; they received 219. This is an illusory theater—incapable of diverting a single soldier from Overlord.

The German observation posts immediately detect eight landing vehicles. They have been betrayed by the sea's phosphorescent sheen. The first wave of foot soldiers venture onto the beach without realizing they are already in the sights of the German artillery nestled in bunkers. The columns begin their march in eerie silence. The Hurricanes and Spitfires do not bomb the German positions, and the Junker 88s do not hit the American support ships. The 17th Infantry Brigade is already two hundred yards from the shore. Then suddenly a trail of fire, a minuscule tapestry embroidered on the abyss of the night. One after the other, pinwheels of light descend two hundred yards above them. The soldiers lift their eyes to the sky. Phosphorescent jellyfish with white hair and rose-colored tentacles are swimming down toward them, floating in the dark as if in the sea. "Take cover!" a lieutenant suddenly shouts. They aren't jellyfish, but illuminating flares attached to parachutes. And they're not there to comfort but to expose them. An instant later, the German guns open fire.

The infantrymen race toward the pine trees. The mines are well hidden beneath the sand and don't explode the first time someone tramples on them. But the weight of two, three, twenty men makes the gears shift and the soldiers are blown up all at once. The platoon loses its officer right away. The moans of the wounded echo painfully in the dark, but the medics are unable to locate them. The beach is mined, mined is the path that winds among the earth-colored dunes, mined the whole strip of coast. They are trapped between guns and the sea, between invisible mines and illuminated parachutes, between the duty to advance and the fear of doing so. The battalion scatters—

without officers, without orders, disoriented, surprised by the unexpected storm of fire whose source they can't perceive, terrorized by mines they can't see. Company A begins a bayonet assault on Monte d'Argento, offering itself to the fire of the light weapons hidden at the top of the hill. Maybe the rise owes its name to the olive trees that cover it. But in war the only silver that shines is barbed wire. Metal thorns coil around ankles, bite at calves, and defy cutting shears. No. 9 Platoon communicates that the base of the hill is surrounded by a barbed-wire barrier more than two yards high, at least four yards thick—impenetrable. The survivors take cover in the shrubs. They send a patrol to circle the hill—maybe there's an opening in the wire somewhere. The patrol doesn't return. Three hours later, dense smoke rises from the eviscerated houses and the pine forest is in flames. The columns are pinned to the beach among the brush. The barbed wire shines in the firelight.

The Germans had been informed months earlier of the Allied intention to land in southern Lazio and outflank the line of resistance along the Apennines, so they had plenty of time to fortify the coastal zone. They set up artillery stations on the hills, mined every clump of earth on that bare plain devoid of natural defenses, strung out miles of barbed wire, garrisoned and blocked canals and watercourses, interrupted every road, mule track, and footpath leading to the villages. They deployed a rear guard all around Minturno. There's a howitzer on every peak, a machine-gun nest in every ditch. In these seven months of the Italian campaign, the Allied command has come to realize that the Germans will defend the southern front to the last man. General Kesselring, who had been given command of the German troops, explained to his men that every day the Allies are held back on the southern front is a day gained for Germany. This battle, which seems diversionary and eccentric compared to the heart of the war, in truth is primary. Every bomb the enemy drops on the Gustav Line is a bomb that will not fall on Hannover, Dresden, Berlin: on your homes. We must draw them to Italy, engage them, make them supply more troops, reinforce their lines, dismantle the eastern front, the northern front, the western front, keep them here. Envelop them in barbed wire. Force them to fight house to house. Stop them—even if we all must die in the effort.

But now the Allied artillery has broken the order for silence and started backing the disoriented infantry: at dawn the battalion is able to advance almost a kilometer. As the darkness dispels, the light exposes the soldiers, who look like actors on the stage of their own death. The more the day brightens, the more the artillery fire—reduced only by the shortage of ammunition that plagues the German shooters—perfects its aim on the exiguous beachhead. Keep the beachhead at all costs: this is the express order of the commanders. The infantrymen fear they will all die. One hundred and forty men have already been lost. Not one officer is still alive. The wounded have been abandoned, and survivors wander terrorized and bewildered among the dunes. The sea is calm, the color of pearl. The lapping on the beach is pacific, unreal. But the radio patters with the good news that, just as according to plans, the Second Wiltshires of the 13th Infantry Brigade have succeeded in crossing the Garigliano to the right, two miles above the demolished railroad bridge. The surprise was total. It is January 18, 1944. The Wiltshires enter Tufo at 8:00 a.m.

When Dy arrived on the Garigliano plain, the sky was gray and thick with clouds and the earth brown—the fields had just been planted. He tried to pick out the roofs of Tufo on the crest of the hill, but saw only the silver reflection of olive trees and a sharp hedge of prickly pear. The green of the pines, a palm tree ruffled by the wind. Up there, somewhere, was Vita's lemon tree, Diamante's well, Antonio's cistern, Ciappitto's shoe shop, Agnello's abandoned land. There was the lame old cobbler—Geremia's father—who hoped the Germans would succeed in tossing them back into the sea. Up there, somewhere, was Dionisia, the blind letter writer. She was waiting for him. Her last letter was from before the United States' entry in the war. "*Figlia mia*, my child, so now it's come to this. Now in order to hold you in my arms again I'll have to wait until we win the war, and I'll tell you quite frankly, I hope we don't." Dy looked at that miserable stone village clustered on the ridge—practically suspended in nothing. Surrounded by an efflorescence of red roses. It was so close. A miserable village set in an opulent countryside—mountains, hills, sea—a natural richness that had always ignored man, its beauty always illusory and indifferent. That fall the fields had been sown with mines. Every clump of earth could turn out to be a trap. The beauty of this place showed itself to be treacherous—deadly. After January 18, not even its illusory beauty would remain.

At ten o'clock, the tanks of the Hermann Goering Panzer Regiment begin moving along the Appian Way. The morning haze hasn't yet dissipated and the plain is hidden in the mist. The Wiltshires advance amid smoke and fog, unsure if they're moving in the right direction. For them, Tufo is merely a name on the map. And the map is not precise, the topography of the village confusing. These hamlets are senseless heaps of houses clinging to each other as if they were cold. The German cannons nestled in the highlands that have been bombarding Tufo for hours are what guide them. At ten-thirty the first Wiltshires, sent to clear the village house by house, fall to the snipers positioned on the roofs. The rest of the 13th Infantry Brigade seeks cover among the ruins. The tanks that are supposed to make their task less precarious don't arrive. But how could they? The Sappers are trying to complete the first bridge across the Garigliano, but it'll take hours, maybe the entire day, and the Germans are hammering so furiously it won't be operational for long. And the bridge on the Appian Way that the Royal Engineers are hurrying to make operational won't be ready before January 20, and even then it'll be too exposed to be used except at night. The truth is that all the tanks—the 30- and 32-ton Churchills and Shermans—are bogged down on the southern bank of the river. At eleven, the Germans pop out of cellars, shooting at anything that moves. The Wiltshires regroup behind broken walls, assess the situation, and withdraw—as orderly as they can—onto the high ground to the east of the village.

Artillery support for the brigade's attack was delayed ninety minutes—too long—but the Royal Inniskilling Fusiliers advancing immediately behind a curtain of fire sweep the German positions with bayonet assaults. When the smoke clears in front of them, the Germans suddenly emerge: they had been hiding, protecting themselves and awaiting their destiny in trenches three meters deep. Many surrender. They want to be taken prisoner. They want to stay alive. The British are finally able to take control of the high point to the east of Tufo, identified on the military map as Pt. 156. Everything seems calm.

On the evening of January 19 a signal flare indicates that the enemy has abandoned the hill. Monte d'Argento has fallen. The division now holds a line that runs from Pt. 413 to Ventosa and Castelforte and the elevated terrain toward the east. Simultaneously, the 5th Division has reoccupied Tufo and taken Minturno. Now ten battalions have crossed over the Garigliano and can push north toward the Ausente Valley. Despite grave losses and the partially failed surprise, the plan has succeeded. The Gustav Line has been perforated. But at this point the Germans stage a counterattack.

Von Senger telephoned directly to Kesselring from General Steinmetz's headquarters, requesting the immediate support of two Panzer Grenadier divisions being held in reserve. Kesselring consents. The 29th Panzer Grenadier division heads for Castelforte via Ausonia, while the 90th hastens south to attack along the Appian Way so as to reestablish the situation in the coastal zone where the Allies are threatening to outflank the German position. The advance along the coast is blocked, the tanks reoccupy a bit of ground north of Minturno, and the hill on which Tufo is located changes hands once again.

On January 21, forty-eight hardened soldiers from the notorious Waffen SS, who had been routed twenty-four hours earlier and forced to evacuate, realize that the occupying forces in Tufo are completely without cover and have advanced too far ahead of the rest of their army. They hurl themselves against them. The 13th Infantry Brigade vacillates—it pulls back, is driven into retreat. In the streets of the village, the SS boast they have killed four hundred soldiers and captured two hundred prisoners.

"What's happening?" asks Dy, who has been urgently summoned to the operations room of the U.S. XII Air Support Command. If the Boston Light Bombers and Kittyhawks don't take off, the entire operation is in danger of failing. Bombs on top of bombs, it's hell down there. Germans everywhere. And the civilians? Have they pulled out? Abandoned their houses? "No," says Joe Parodi, Dy's Anglo-Genovese friend who had dreamed of marching up the peninsula to Genoa and instead was in Tufo risking a bullet to his head. "Where were they supposed to go? This is their land. They waited for us, welcomed us with tears in their eyes, and begged us with tears in their eyes not to abandon them to the SS—not to pull out." "And you pulled out?" Dy shouts. "Tufo is indefensible. They were hitting us pretty heavily from the mountains."

They fight for four days straight—from house to house, hill to hill, stone to stone. Every position has to be taken with hand grenades or bayonets. The tanks, blocked by craters and ruins, still can't enter the action. And the jeeps and light trucks have been halted: too many have exploded on land mines. The enemy lurks behind the corner of every demolished building, in every cellar, cistern, and well, and fights for every heap of debris. Smoke, fog, dust. Two whole companies of Royal Scots Fusiliers have gotten lost, wandering on the hills. *"Tufo Road,"* they yell, searching in vain. "You're on the wrong hill—the wrong hill! You're out of the battle!" crackles a voice over the radio, and then the communication goes dead. They end up in a ravine and then back at the camp they'd departed from, screaming to their sentinels not to shoot at them. The German artillery bombards Minturno from the hilltops, and an entire street crumbles as a Scottish platoon passes along it—they just barely escape being buried alive by an avalanche of ruins. The fog hinders the flight of the infallible American bombers, makes the air strikes imprecise. The 1500-pound bombs the Bostons drop and the 1600-pounders from the Kittyhawks fall like hail, blindly destroying the vineyards. The British 46th Infantry Division is annihilated attempting to cross the Garigliano at Sant'Ambrogio. A massacre. Three hundred twenty-nine dead and 509 taken prisoner. The Oxford students who had come to Italy as if they were going on a picnic, annoyed at being confined to the Spaghetti League, left hundreds of dead on the battlefield. Corporal Fisher takes a bullet in the mouth and heroically drags himself off Monte Natale—Christmas Hill—on his elbows; vomiting blood and teeth, he beseeches his superior to with-

draw the troops, give the order to fall back onto Minturno. Tufo
Road—the romantic, solitary road that winds its way through rose-
bushes to the village—is the German artillery's preferred target: they
let a company advance until all the men are perfectly in range, then hit
them squarely with just one barrage. Whoever escapes the direct hit
dies from the shrapnel. The Scots count the wounded and missing.
Those still alive are trapped on the riverbank and terrified of being bitten by a mosquito and dying an inglorious death from malaria. The
nurses are overflowing with atabrine and quinine. But in January the
anopheles haven't laid their eggs yet. They do that in the spring, and
we cannot possibly still be bogged down in this land then, not for any
reason in the world.

On January 22 Dy rips up the map and curses his college degree. If
he were a pilot, he would guide his twin-engine over the tank turrets
hidden among the rubble and crash into the Panthers. He'd blow them
up, at least the load would be good for something. But he's an American engineer. They ask him to calculate the margin of error of the
bomb drops, factor how many pounds a Boston A20 can carry. His
Royal Engineer colleagues are asked to devise a system for ferrying
tanks across the river. They need to get as many men as possible onto
the north shore or the infantry holding on the hills will be annihilated,
and the losses have already been considerable. Headquarters is outraged
that they haven't advanced one yard on this damned front in four days.
We have to break the line. Now.

During the night of January 22, the Fifth Army lands at Nettuno,
but the German artillery continues to pound the infantry on the
Garigliano and pin them to the crag of the hill. The villages are an
uninterrupted line of smoke. Everything is smoking—the ruins of
Minturno Castle, Saint Peter's Cathedral, the cemeteries. Houses,
chicken coops, stone quarries, arms depots, gas pumps, trains—
everything has been eradicated. Train tracks, roofs, damaged tanks, the
hedge of prickly pear, even the Roman ruins on the shore of the
Garigliano. When the Royal Scots Fusiliers crossed over to the north
shore, they wandered about as in a dream on the steps of the am-
phitheater and among the columns bearing Latin inscriptions—guns
level, shooting crazily at upturned memorial stones and Ionic capitals,

fearing that desperate phantasms in black uniforms would pop up among the ruins. But no one was there—nothing but the eerie silence of a city abandoned two thousand years ago.

What's happening in the villages? Shooting. People hiding in grottoes, cisterns, wells. There are bodies in the street, even in the churches. There is nothing to eat because whoever dares to venture into the fields to pick some greens or roots is either blown up by a land mine or taken out by a sniper. Four Churchills advancing along the road for Minturno are hit by anti-tank artillery and ignite with a roar that makes the earth tremble. They burn among the thickets of reeds and the untimely bloom of a wisteria bush. It starts raining again. A heavy downpour, with thunder, lightning, and blasts of cold wind. Electricity scars the night sky. The winter, which had seemed to be holding back so as not to compromise the victory, now suddenly unleashes its wrath. The flood flagellates the earth, ripens the mines, penetrates the cottages with fallen roofs where the commanders are encamped. They wait in the mud, sink in the turbid mire that imprisons boots, weighs down backpacks, clouds the mind. A thick haze hovers on the horizon, swallowing up targets and boundaries. They fight with cold steel amid ghosts of homes. Advance guard and rear guard clash with the same determination—the one so as to be able to rest after weeks of battle, the other so as not to have to evacuate. This war is no longer an abstract calculation. Men kill staring each other in the face, unload entire magazines into enemy bodies, sink bullets and plunge knives in flesh, claw at faces, legs, eyes, dog tags. On the night of January 22 the Germans receive orders to ease the counteroffensive. The Americans have landed at Anzio and will have the honor of liberating Rome. But engineer Dy dreams of fighting in the front line on the southern front. The British are down there instead. Personal motives do not exist in war. But it's nothing personal, I've never been here before. I'm an American.

Southern front. It's not possible that we're still pinned on the ledges of these hills at the end of January. We throw ourselves against the lines again. They shoot at us from Scauri Hill, from the trenches, from the mountains. They bury us under tons of bombs. I see Joe Parodi die, hit by shrapnel; he slides on the crag of the hill, tries to cling to the rocks, his bazooka slips from his hands, I lose sight of him. We advance. I see John Zicarelli's tank explode. We stay together. Why isn't there air cover? There's so much dust we're all coughing as if we'd been gassed in a trench. We advance for ten kilometers, practically blindly, and push too far ahead in the smoke and chaos. A German loudspeaker assails us with tremendous insults in broken English. The disembodied voice seems to come from the heavens. "Cowards, chickens, what are you waiting for? Forward!"

We're coming, we're coming! We feel its nearness. The objective. I see the houses of Tufo. No, they're not houses, they're stumps of houses, tottering walls, roofs caved in. I see bodies in the street, I see an abyss—we are pushed back toward the railroad.

For hundreds of miles on every shred of land between the Tyrrhenian and the Adriatic there is fighting. We have to break through somewhere, anywhere along the front, but we sustain considerable losses. The Germans don't want to lose Rome. Symbol outweighs strategy or logic. But they've already lost it. This is the great battle for Italy and I'm here. Southern front, January 23, evening. *Mamma, I'm fine. I can't tell you where I am. But if I say I'm where you'd like to be, do you understand? Kiss the girls for me. I think of you every moment and it gives me courage. Dy.*

On January 24 Liberato Saltarelli, the Carabinieri brigadier accused of spying for the Allies, is shot at Tufo. On the same day the Germans suspend their counterattack. The war moves north—to Cassino, the beaches at Anzio, the road for Rome. The penetration of the X Corps on the other side of the Garigliano is stabilized. Now the German line is unstable, wedged in; it retreats, contorts, withdraws behind the highest points. The southern front moves like a serpent—a poisonous stingray.

By May 12 the Minturno-Scauri front has become elastic. A sieve or a colander. The pincers open and close, ruins are occupied, then abandoned. We haven't seen any civilians for weeks. But they must be there, somewhere. Before the war, Minturno had at least ten thousand inhabitants. A thousand or so in Tufo. When I look at Tufo through my binoculars, all I see is smoke. Is anyone still up there? Finally a U.S.

Navy cruiser approaches the Minturno beach in order to shell the German artillery positions that are out of range of the Fifth Army artillery. Some German JU 88s try to intervene in Minturno, determined to help their ground troops, who are exhausted by this point. The single-seater twin-engines dive-bomb, drop so low they almost graze us with their wings. I can see the pilots in their cabins as they dive over our positions. The British left for the Channel in mid-February. Our moment has finally arrived. In the end it's up to the American divisions. By now our entire army has crossed the Garigliano. An immense silence has returned. I plunged my hands in the river. There were reeds with plumes of feathers, hydra floating on the current, a majestic white water lily, dragonflies with transparent wings, and a mysterious bird I'd never seen before, with a tall crest and a long black tail. It was beautiful. A strange fear came over me. I knew I would survive.

In early June the JU 88s are called back to France. All that remained of the German divisions flee. Finally we infiltrate for miles and miles, open a deep wound in the southern front. The fascist press admits to the infiltration—and justifies it by claiming they had created a "fluid zone." I weep, for now I know the Gustav Line no longer exists. The Fifth is at the gates of Rome. And I, too, am at the gates. I'm on my way home—too late perhaps. There's nothing left. My desert places. Where are you? *Southern front.* We've broken through.

The Son of the Lady Tree

And so he forged the lances, pliers, horseshoes, and all the other instruments the Narts needed, but then the god Lhepsch began to get bored. He went to seek advice from Satanay, the woman who knows everything. And Satanay said, "Now go and walk the face of the earth. You shall see how other peoples live, so as to gather new wisdom and new knowledge to bring back with you. And if God does not abandon you, you may discover some interesting things and learn some stories along the way." And the god of the blacksmiths asked, "What do I need for this voyage?" "You do not need much," the prophetess responded. "Prepare some comfortable clothes and then begin your search." So Lhepsch made a pair of boots of the most resistant steel, put them on, and off he went. He was so swift that in one hour he covered the distance men can travel in a day, and in a month what would take them a year. He crossed the highest mountain in one strong stride, the widest river in a single bound. Walking and leaping, jumping and flying, he crossed the seven seas and soon arrived at the coast. There he uprooted hundreds of trees, ripped off their branches and bound the trunks together to form a raft; he placed it on the water and set sail. The sea was infinite, and Lhepsch navigated for weeks. When he reached the distant shore, he saw a group of girls playing. They were so beautiful he instantly fell in love. He reached for them, but they slipped through his fingers and he wasn't able to catch even one. He chased and chased, but to no avail. And so finally he begged them, "For the love of God, tell me who you are. I have never seen anyone like you my entire life. No one has ever refused me before." "We are the handmaids of the Lady Tree," the maidens replied. "Come, our Lady will receive you and hear your requests."

So he followed them to the strangest creature his eyes had ever seen. She was not a tree, nor did she have a human form. Her roots penetrated deep into the earth, and her hair floated in the sky like a cloud. She had human hands. And her face was glorious. All gold and silver. The Lady Tree smiled at Lhepsch and welcomed him graciously. She received him with magnificence and then sent him off to bed. But Lhepsch awoke in the heart of the night. He found the Lady Tree, seized her, and tried to rape her.

"This is most discourteous," Lady Tree protested. "No man has ever laid a hand on me before."

"But I am a god," Lhepsch replied. And then he made love to her.

She liked it so much that she fell in love with Lhepsch and asked him to stay with her. Lhepsch declined her offer. "It is not possible," he replied. "I must go my own way. I must find the ends of the earth and then bring back all I have learned to the Narts."

"Lhepsch," said Lady Tree, "if you leave me you will be making a terrible mistake. I can give you all the wisdom the Narts will ever need. My roots penetrate to the depths of the earth. I can confide to you all the secrets enclosed in her womb. My hair reaches to the eye of the sky. I could tell you everything about the planets and the thousand suns. You do not need to roam the earth."

Lhepsch would not let himself be convinced.

"To everything there is an end, but not to the earth. Stay with me. I will show you all the stars in the sky. I will offer you all the treasures of the earth."

But her prayers fell on deaf ears. Lhepsch preferred not to believe

Lady Tree, and so he departed. He wore out his steel boots, and his walking stick was whittled away and grew smaller than his pinky finger. His threadbare hat dropped around his neck like a ring. He journeyed and journeyed, but he could not find the end of the earth.

And so he returned to Lady Tree.

"Have you found the end of the earth?" Lady Tree asked him.

"No."

"What have you found?"

"Nothing."

"Then what have you learned?"

"Now I know that the earth has no end."

"And what else?"

"That the human body is stronger than steel."

"What else?"

"That there is nothing so tiring and distressing as traveling alone."

"All this is true," said Lady Tree. "But have you discovered something that will improve the lives of the Narts? What new wisdom and what new knowledge will you bring them on your return?"

"I have nothing to bring them."

"Then your search has been in vain," said Lady Tree. "Had you listened to me, you would have brought your people a wisdom that could have served them always. You Narts are an ignorant, stubborn race. And this trait will lead to your annihilation. So be it. But I give you this," she said, and offered Lhepsch the most beautiful baby boy. "Take my son. I have taught him everything I know."

Lhepsch returned home with the baby.

One day the child asked the Narts: "Do you see the white path in the sky—the Milky Way?"

"We see it."

"When you are far away, look at it always; this way you will never lose your way home," he said.

"By God! How wise he is," the Narts remarked. "When he grows up, he will provide us with fabulous ideas. We must raise him with care." Seven women were assigned to watch over him so that he would never be left alone.

But one day as the child played with the women, he got lost and disappeared.

The women searched for him everywhere, but he was never found again.

When the Narts were informed of what had occurred, they mounted their horses and began searching for the child. They found people who had seen him, and they found people who had met him, but they could not find him.

"Perhaps he has returned to his mother," the people said.

So the Narts sent Lhepsch to Lady Tree. But the child had not come back to her.

"What are we to do? What hopes have we of finding him?" Lhepsch asked Lady Tree.

"There is no hope for you," she replied. "When the moment is right, he will return on his own. But only God knows when that will be. If you are alive when he returns, then fortune will smile upon you again. But if he does not return, then may weeping be upon you, for this will signify the ruin of you and your people."

Lhepsch returned home enveloped in melancholy.

Many years later, as the truck bounced over holes in the road, jarring him from a mindless sleep, Captain Dy thought about this story. He was seven or eight the last time his mother had told it to him. She would recount it to him in Italian, and at the end, he would always ask her the same thing: "And does the child come back?" His mother would shrug her shoulders. She didn't remember. Her father's woman had told her this Circassian fable many years before, and she'd forgotten to ask her about that detail. Somehow it didn't seem important to her. Dy had imagined two different endings. In the first one, Lhepsch forges an enchanted shoe for the horse of a young stranger, and only as the stranger rides off toward the hills does he realize that this was the child they'd been waiting for. In the second, the land of the Narts is devastated by famine. The grain refuses to grow, the rivers dry up, the fruit will not ripen. The gods have abandoned them. But precisely at that moment, the saddest in their entire history, the child returns. He plucks the sickle of the moon from the sky and teaches them to scythe the grain, so the Narts will never be hungry again.

"This is it," they said to him. The truck had stopped in front of a depot. An unruly line of boys, ragged women, and unshaven men were waiting for the distribution of free bread. Dy grabbed his back-pack and, before getting out, checked to make sure the documents he needed were still in his jacket pocket: his pass for a ten-day leave with all the appropriate stamps from his superiors, and the piece of paper the Minturno postman had scribbled on for him. After thirty months of war, eight hundred miles, a wound in the leg, a promotion, the fu-nerals of many of his companions and all his illusions, Dy had finally arrived in Rome.

The captain moved closer in order to decipher the badly faded street number, checking it against the scribbles on the scrap of paper he'd been carrying in his pocket. It was already dark, but not one sign was lit along the entire street. Besides, the piece of paper had been folded up in his pocket too long, and the Minturno postman's arthritic scrawl was nearly illegible. He lit his lighter: the army issued the soldiers an infallible model that neither rain nor wind could extinguish. Dy had given dozens away and had sold a few. Yes, the address was correct: Via Ferruccio, 30.

It was a six-story building with hundreds of windows but no bal-conies. The plaster was a dismal potato color. He would have liked to speak to the doorman first so that he could be announced—he wanted the moment to be solemn—but didn't see anyone to ask. He ducked into the gloomy entranceway, its low ceiling barely illuminated by a feeble little bulb, like the ones you find in cemeteries. The perpetual light glowed beneath a tiny Madonna in blue wax. In the back was a warehouse selling cloth wholesale, but its metal grate was mottled with rust. Clearly it had been closed for a while. Probably went out of busi-ness during the war. An impossibly steep staircase led upward, but it was covered with floating dust balls and disappeared into darkness. He heard a door slam, followed by dozens of voices. A radio was on somewhere, playing a syncopated rhythm he thought he recognized.

He went into the courtyard. Against the wall was a fountain with a red terra-cotta mask and a pool covered in moss. Water dripped on his collar, but it wasn't raining. Lifting his head, he saw that the courtyard looked like a seaport filled with white sails. Dozens of sheets were hanging in the void, pinned to a spider's web of iron wires and swelling in the breeze. Underwear, pillowcases, socks, aprons; the building must be jam-packed. The apartments were small, crammed eight to a floor. The only spaces the builders had left empty were the landings. Each floor had a vast open gallery decorated with squat, square pillars and a white wooden railing. But the paint was already peeling. This building looked like all of Italy—it had once had a certain dignity, now lost.

On the second floor, behind the railing, sprouted a forest of plants. Basil, sage, rosemary, geraniums. On the third floor a swarm of little children squatted around a soccer field drawn in chalk on the tiles. In the dimness Dy was able to make out that they were using corks for the players and a bottle top for the ball, which they kicked with a flick of their fingers. One team's corks were red, the other's blue. The children had stopped playing and were staring at him. Their eyes shone. They hadn't asked him for anything, but Dy felt around in his pockets for some chewing gum or chocolate. He didn't find any, though; it was already evening and Rome was full of hungry children. On the fourth floor a man in his undershirt sat smoking in front of the door to his apartment. He threw him an indifferent, slightly hostile glance. Dy faced the gallery and looked down. From here the sheets didn't look like sails and the courtyard seemed like a deep, dark well.

On the fifth floor, a woman leaned against the peeling railing and stared at him. She evaluated his uniform with a practiced avidity, seeming to count the stars on his shoulders, and then threw him a smile. Dy knew that smile; all Italian women were for sale. Not just for sale—on sale. He pretended not to see her. The name he was looking for was not on any of the four plaques to the right of the stairs. He had to walk past her in order to read the others, and the woman ostentatiously ran her hands through her hair. She was young, twenty maybe. Thin, with chapped hands and opaque skin—finished. The pungent smell of broccoli filtered through the door. Dy obstinately turned his back, but he knew the girl was still staring at him. Her face was all painted, but she wasn't a whore. In a certain sense there weren't any more whores in Rome. "Lookin' for somebody, Joe?" Her voice was sweet and inviting, but Dy shuddered, afraid she was the daughter of the man he sought. He read the names on the plates: Moriconi, Di Cola, Feliciani, Scarabozzi. "A man who lives here," Dy responded. "On the fifth floor."

When he and his men were about to leave Tufo, a toothless old man with a face browned like pork rind approached him. He had been the Minturno postman thirty years ago. He remembered the address because during the war—the first war, Captain, the one against Franz Joseph, Emperor William, and the Great Turk—a letter would leave Tufo for that address in Rome every day. A certain Miss Emma lived there. Maybe she was a poet: she wrote a letter every day as well. The postman didn't know exactly where Via Ferruccio was, somewhere behind the Termini station, near the train depot. The Piedmontese had built the neighborhood, so it must be elegant and stylish.

The girl shook her head and said nonchalantly that no man lived in that apartment, and no "Miss Emma," either, because she lived there now—and her name was Margherita. Dy rested his pack on the railing, discouraged. He couldn't even remember how long he'd been searching for him. Ever since he'd landed, even before. He was a mysterious man, a recurring phantom in his parents' conversations, and they would lower their voices when they noticed he was listening. An unreal yet fabulous figure, like the knight Guerrin Meschino, who fell hopelessly in love with the princess of Persepoli even though he abandoned her, promising to return in ten years—just like the god Lhepsch. He wouldn't, couldn't, leave without finding him. Or else everything—the bombs and ruins, the destruction, the entire war— would have been pointless. The sun was setting. Above the open gallery with its potted geraniums and sheets hung on iron wires, the golden roofs of the Esquiline Hill set the horizon ablaze as far as the eye could see, until they blurred with the blue of the distant hills.

He understood he was going to have to pay her. Nothing's for free, and that's the way it should be. He opened his pack. In anticipation of the encounter, he had brought razors and blades, stockings and soap, cosmetics and a duffel coat. Nothing so useful as the sickle of the moon, but he hadn't come across anything better. He handed the girl the stockings and hand cream. They were worth quite a bit on the black market, so Margherita had no trouble remembering that the inhabitants of the apartment had left in '31. Evicted. Dy's face must have looked worried because the girl laughed. "It's no disgrace to be evicted from a building that's falling to pieces, Joe. I'd say they were lucky." "My name's not Joe," Dy protested, but the girl said all Americans are called Joe. She didn't know where they'd moved to—maybe to public housing. Which public housing? "What do I know? They're all the same. Why you lookin' for them, Joe?" Dy had no desire to explain. Besides, he wouldn't have known what to tell her. He had to find him, that was all. "Don't you think it's destiny you found me instead of that guy? Why don't you come in and tell me where you're from? Hey, has anybody ever told you you look like that actor—what's his name, Dana Andrews? You're so handsome. Why don't you stay awhile, Joe?" Dy hoisted his pack on his shoulders and told her again that his name wasn't Joe.

In the village, the old men barely remembered him. They sat in the ruins smoking Dy's aromatic American cigarettes and trying to understand what he wanted from them. They couldn't believe this captain from the United States Army had come all the way to Tufo to find an old cobbler and a blind letter writer who were dead and buried, and the son of Mantu, the most unfortunate man in the whole village. That boy who died from a mosquito bite? The carabiniere? No, no, the other one—the one who went to America. The old men looked out across the plain and pointed toward a shimmering tangle of metal in the distance that spoke of the existence, and not so long ago, of tracks, railway ties, trains. What they told him surprised him. Except for his convalescence, he had never come back to Tufo. He had gone to Rome.

It made an odd impression on Dy, their talking of Rome as if it

were some faraway place, even farther away than America, where most
of them—or at least their brothers, fathers, sons—had been. Rome, on
the other hand, was something foreign, unknown, and powerful to
those old men. Whoever was in Rome had to be important. And so it
was for the son of Mantu. Important, foreign, and unknown. As long
as his mother and father were still alive, he would come back to Tufo
in the summer. Always well dressed, sweet-smelling, and with a red
carnation in his buttonhole—a real gentleman. He'd become head
clerk. The townspeople were green with envy. He had married a Roman wife, about whom the old men recalled nothing other than her
hair—what a lot of hair that woman had!—and her particularly offensive habit of wearing her city shoes to go walking in the countryside.
Dy couldn't say why, but he didn't like the fact that he had a wife. He
would have liked to go back to America and tell his mother he had
never married. Then Mantu died and he never came back to Tufo.
"How can I find him?" Dy asked. Eh, *paisà*, how could you expect to
find him? Rome's a very big city.

He lost time searching in public housing. In the 1930s many Romans
were evicted from their homes, by either the authorities or the owners, and dispersed in a thousand different directions—transferred,
deported, or simply "moved." Most of them ended up in housing de-
velopments on the outskirts or farther out in the countryside. But it
turned out that Dy was on the wrong track. It's true that Mantu's son
was assigned to public housing, but he'd refused to go. He was obstinate, irascible, and damned proud. The fascists were about as pleasura-
ble to him as a fishbone in the throat, so he refused to take anything
from Il Duce. Castor oil purges and beatings were the only things he
would accept from him. Dy tried to evoke that vivid blood-red writing on the walls of his father's office . . . FASCISTS—MOBFIA—
FASCISTS—MAFIA . . . but couldn't remember the white walls or the
paint or even the exact words. The writing had faded and no longer
offended him. Dy was pleased; he had always known he would behave
this way. As a little boy, when Dy observed his father's wildly hairy
body, his ear bitten by the fire, and his dead arm hanging at his neck
like a cadaver of the past, he imagined he'd merely been loaned to

him—because in truth his father was someone else. A seductive and invincible hero, a voyager—a god. A mysterious man who would come back to get him one day.

He searched for him in the social centers and party meeting halls. Yes, they said, they remembered him, but he didn't come regularly, had never signed up for a party membership card—neither during the years of hiding nor after the liberation. He was a loner. Someone remembered having seen him asking for information about the trials. "The trials?" Dy asked. The American captain probably didn't know anything about the trials, didn't even know what the word *epuration* meant, but for Italians this was a serious matter. The victims were seated in front of their persecutors, the oppressed in front of the oppressors. "Men are responsible for their behavior and must assume responsibility for their actions, you understand, Captain?" "I'm afraid not." Dy smiled. "I don't know what was happening in Italy all those years." I know what's happening now. The ruins. The dust. The misery. The music. The girls. "It can't all just end with an amnesty, *capisci*, Joe?" There's no forgiveness without justice. Otherwise it'd be as if anything—any behavior, vileness, violence, horror—were legitimate. After justice has been served, then this country will be able to start again. It will be reborn. But if justice doesn't come, Italy will have sold her soul—and it will be lost forever.

"It could be that your man was called to testify against his superior in front of the Epuration Commission," the old man concluded. He would have the right to request compensation for the injustices he suffered—withheld pay, a denied promotion, vacation time not granted, demotion to the most demeaning and worst-paying tasks. He certainly would have the right to receive reparations. But if he testifies, it won't be for the money. You see, it's more about obtaining some sort of compensation for moral persecutions. Something—even if it's purely symbolic—that can cure the resentment. Heal the wounds, the offenses. The injustices. The humiliations. "But he was head clerk," Dy objected, rather perplexed. What humiliations would he need to be compensated for?

His time in Rome passed too quickly. He had already received notice of his departure date. He was to take off his uniform, to which he had given four years of his life and his dreams of a brilliant career. He was to return home, to his work as an engineer, for which he had studied so diligently and which he hadn't been able to pursue. To his family. And yet he was saddened when he received the news. He had to leave Italy, Rome, and all that he could not—or did not know how to—find. The man had disappeared. For all Dy knew, he hadn't ever written so much as a postcard. So much time had passed. He probably didn't even remember his mother. Dy had already learned that very few things survive the wear and tear of life. It seems as if they will last forever, and instead time erodes them bit by bit until, when you turn around, you realize that nothing of the past remains. Despite everything, he decided to spend his last day in Rome in the Prati delle Vittorie neighborhood in order to verify the information that a carabiniere who had been a colleague of the man's brother had given him. He'd advised him to take a look in the area around Via della Giuliana.

The carabiniere knew him when he was young, but later lost track of him. He remembered the funeral at the Verano cemetery, though. The man hadn't attended—they hadn't even given him the day off so he could accompany his wife to the cemetery. "His wife?" Dy interrupted. The Roman woman, the "poet"—Miss Emma? "She died young, poor thing," the carabiniere said. "The illness claimed her in less than a week. It was a long time ago, maybe in 1936 or 1937." Dy clenched his fists and bit his lip. A confused relief was slowly growing in him. The carabiniere said it was a sad and squalid story. His boss had accused him of trying to exploit his wife's death because his colleagues had taken up a collection in order to help pay for her funeral. It took four of them to hold him down, because even though he was past forty, he had started punching his boss, as if he were still a kid. He broke the guy's nose and yanked out his devilish-looking goatee, but he still didn't get the day off. Instead he was suspended from work for six months. "A collection?" Dy interrupted him. Why in the world would an important man like him need them to take up a collection? The carabiniere must be mistaken. He'd confused him with someone else.

He decided to go to Via della Giuliana anyway. Across the Tiber was a neighborhood of plane trees and spacious, deserted boulevards, in the middle of which boys were chasing balls made of rags, using the tree trunks as goal posts, the passersby as referees, and the girls as targets. On the facade of a 1930 condominium building was carved the motto DULCE POST LABOREM DOMI MANERE. A pleasant place to rest after work. He stopped in front of a rather tall building. Seven, maybe eight stories jammed into a canary yellow facade. And yet the carabiniere's information turned out to be correct. The wine seller confirmed that he really did live there. Dy removed his dark glasses and studied the third-floor windows. I've found you, he thought to himself. And you don't even know I exist.

The shutters were closed. No one was home. It was nine o'clock in the morning; he should have realized that people are at work by this hour. But he couldn't come back this evening. He had to report to the barracks before sunset for the farewell ceremony. Three kids pointed out a petite figure walking quickly toward Viale delle Milizie and said she would be able to help him. He ran after her. They formed an odd procession: he tall, squeezed into his impeccably ironed uniform, hair closely cropped and boots shining, and the boys with filthy bare feet and dusty hair. Dy didn't turn back to look. If he had, their eyes full of hope and their strident requests—pen, notebook, dollars, take me with you, take me to America with you, Joe—would have haunted him for days. He'd been in Italy for two and a half years, and had gotten used to forgetting things he couldn't remedy.

The girl was a brunette, slender, and in a hurry. She didn't stop when he caught up with her, but eyed him amusedly, as if he were a figurine or an actor in uniform. Was he really an officer in the U.S. Army? She'd never seen one up close before. Her father didn't let her go out: American men are more dangerous for girls than German measles. She apologized for not being able to stop, but she was in a terrible rush, as she had to punch in at the office at nine. "The office?" Dy exclaimed, surprised. At fourteen? She must mean at school. The girl laughed. Alas, she was already twenty-one. If she didn't look her age, it was because time had forgotten her. He had knocked on her door, but she hadn't opened. Dy smiled. He would have liked to say something more, but his rudimentary Italian didn't permit it. For the first time he regretted having forgotten it. The girl walked very quickly, almost at a march. When he asked her where he could find him, she wanted to know why he was looking for him. Dy replied that he had a letter to give him, from someone in America. A lie. There was no letter. And no one knew Dy was looking for him. The girl said he could find him at the Cassa Nazionale degli Infortuni, Piazza Cavour, number 3. Dy stopped to take off his jacket, but the girl soldiered on and didn't wait for him. Dy started to call out to her, but he didn't know who she was, and hadn't even asked her name.

He quickened his pace and the girl stopped abruptly. If he wanted to go to Piazza Cavour, he should head down Via Lepanto. She, on the other hand, was going straight. "*Buona fortuna*, Captain. If you happen to meet him, please don't tell him we have spoken. He's an old-fashioned sort." Dy brought his finger to his lips and promised to keep their secret. But then he grabbed her by the wrist and said: "Whose secret? Who are you? What's your name?"

Dy froze in the middle of the street, stunned, with the sweat running down his temples. His heart skipped a beat. Now it was pounding loudly against his ribs. The girl walked away quickly. Narrow shoulders, a fine head. She was dressed like a student in a gray skirt and white blouse. Without an ounce of makeup. She probably had never been to the hairdresser's or had a boyfriend. For an instant Dy thought he could fall in love with her. Lots of his friends were going back to America with their Italian girlfriends. He could go back with her. It would be as if he had fought in the muddy plains, the ruins of Tufo and the hills of Italy, as if he had scoured the streets of Rome for her— just to find her again.

That spring morning, seated behind an ugly, scratched desk, the usher kept watch over the entrance of the Cassa Nazionale degli Infortuni, the National Fund for Injured Workers. It was ten in the morning and the employees were at their desks, secretaries clicked away on their typewriters, and visitors streamed toward him, each with his confusion or problem. In a year like 1946, the office had thousands of cases regarding accidents and injuries to process. Through the doorway, he could just barely make out the palm trees swaying in the breeze in Piazza Cavour, the very young worker sweeping the entrance to the

Adriano Theater, and the sleepy waitress opening the shutters of the trattoria. He distractedly directed a cripple to the fourth floor and a widow to the third. Then a uniform appeared before him. A uniform of the U.S. Army, with the stars and rank of captain. One of the many officers of the Fifth Army who seemed stranded in Rome, unable to leave now that the war was over. They wandered among the moral ruins of a defeated country with the gaiety and arrogance of those who have always been right. The usher admired them—but he also hated them, without understanding why. "Is this the Cassa Nazionale degli Infortuni?" the stranger asked in a heavy foreign accent, emphasizing all the wrong syllables. The usher lifted his eyes and was met with a pair of impenetrable dark glasses—Ray-Bans, standard issue for American officers. He listlessly replied in the affirmative. What did he want? Did he have an appointment?

Dy barely looked at him. He nervously studied the staircase. The disoriented crowd wandering among the offices intimidated him. Once again, he felt lost. He asked himself what he should say to him. What words he would use to explain to him. "I am looking for someone," he chanted, articulating every syllable so as to make himself understood by the little man hidden in the shadows of the entranceway, a tiny Italian with a graying mustache and formidable blue eyes. "Please tell me whom you are looking for; perhaps I shall be able to help you." The usher spoke automatically—he has responded to similar requests thousands of times a day for thousands of days. For twenty-six years. Watch over the office for eight consecutive hours, repeat a hundred times a day senseless phrases—*Buongiorno*, sir, do you have an appointment? Fourth floor, the elevator is down the hall to the right, fifth floor, thank you, you're welcome, where are you going, please? Do you have an appointment?—point visitors in the right direction, polish the desks, empty the wastepaper baskets, clean the ashtrays, and then, long after everyone else has already gone home, make a final round of the offices, now strangely empty, his footsteps echoing in the deserted corridors, turn out lights and walk in the dark to the electricity meter and disconnect the current. This last conscious gesture of his day is so insignificant, yet it never fails to fill him with anxiety. "Could you repeat the question?" he asked, worried that he had not understood correctly. Pronouncing clearly every word, the American officer repeated: "I am looking for Diamante Mazzucco."

The usher fixed him with his clear blue eyes. The American was tall, brown-haired, tan. Probably around twenty-five. Why was he looking for Diamante? What the heck did he want from him? The arrival of a stranger—someone who descends on you with no warning, with no introduction—is never a good sign. The prudent diffidence cultivated during those sordid years of dictatorship made him protective. "He's on vacation," he explained. "When will he return?" Dy asked hurriedly. Insistent. Inquisitorial. "Oh, he won't be back for a while," was the usher's evasive reply. The American let out a moan, leaned with all his weight on the desk, and took off his Ray-Bans. Such dark eyes. Long eyelashes, a straight and peremptory nose. A regular, square face, impervious to melancholy and introspection. And yet what flickered across that face was neither disappointment nor vexation, but something much more profound—violent, even. A boundless delusion. "You have no idea how I have searched for him! I've pursued his trail through all the places he's lived . . . but Rome is a big city. I found someone who had seen him, someone who had spoken with him, but I never found him. And now I must return to America . . ." A twenty-five-year-old American. The usher asked himself if he had seen him somewhere before. But of course not. His face said nothing to him. "Do you know Mr. Diamante?" Dy asked in an anguished tone. "By sight," replied the usher, who would have liked to throw the American out, in part because a line of cripples in need of assistance had formed behind him. "Too bad. He's an extraordinary man, you know. A hero. There aren't many like him." The usher was curious but also rather alarmed. "Really!" he laughed. "I never realized."

"Just think—he traveled to America all by himself," said Dy, who had the sensation he was recounting something inconceivable—a legend. Like Hercules, who strangled serpents in his crib, or Billy the Kid, who killed his first man at age twelve. "He was twelve years old. In order to support his parents, who were so poor their children took turns wearing pants because they only had one pair. Just think—he had the courage to go up against the Black Hand thugs, all alone, just a boy, when the whole neighborhood kept silent, terrorized and obedient. He was so brave he climbed into a dead man's tomb and stole his shoes. He challenged the railroad bosses, crossed America without a penny to his name, paid for his parents' house with his kidneys, and ill as he was, even volunteered for the army." The usher realized he had never considered Diamante in that light. The Diamante he knew was a little man, stubborn and proud, violent, and a liar. An ordinary person, whom no one was particularly proud of—and who certainly didn't go around feeling proud of himself. "It's a real pity he is on vacation," Dy continued. "I so wanted to meet him. It was really important to me. If you see him, could you please tell him I was looking for him?" Dy put on his Ray-Bans and turned toward the exit. His slim, athletic figure cast a dark shadow on the usher. "If you would tell me your name," the usher mumbled confusedly, "I will do my best to track him down. Just a minute so I can write it." "You don't need to write it," the young man smiled, lifting his shoulders. "My name is the same as his. My name is Diamante Mazzucco."

The usher would have liked to say something, but surprise turned his throat dry. That officer who was no longer a boy had spoken of him, an absolute stranger, with familiarity, admiration, affection, as if he had known him all his life. And he knew things—facts, episodes—that he had never told anyone, and that he himself no longer remembered. By the time he recovered from the shock, the other Diamante was already striding across the vestibule. He stood up and was about to follow him, but then he sat down again. The captain had come looking for a hero, not an usher. As the American who bore his name crossed the blinding light of the piazza and disappeared into the crowd hovering in front of the courthouse, Diamante realized he was Vita's son.

Good for Father

s we were putting my father's correspondence in order after his death, I happened to come across a packet of airmail letters from New York. As the sender was THE ELEXPORT CO.—MANUFACTURES' EXPORT MANAGERS, 14 Liberty Plaza, New York 6, N.Y., they didn't seem particularly significant and I put them aside. I had no idea what would inspire a company that sold electric supplies to contact my father. When I started to write this story, however, I recalled that those letters had all been sent during the period from October 1947 to the spring of 1951. Because that time—the archaeology of my father as a young man—was completely unknown to me, I unearthed them from the sea of paper in which my attempts to reconstruct his life had been buried, and opened them. The owner of the Elexport Company wrote in an eager yet uncertain Italian. His name was Diamante Mazzucco—yet he signed his letters Dy. His name took me by surprise, and spawned a series of questions and queries no one could answer anymore. Who was he? What did he have to do with *my* Diamante? Was he somehow connected to the rich *americana* who had showered us with care packages? Was that woman the little girl from the steamship? I opened the letters sent from Liberty

Plaza. I now know that, on the other track of history, Captain Dy—
Diamante II—could have been my father.

My two fathers did not meet, not even fleetingly, during the time
when Dy scoured Rome in search of the man who bore his name. In
October 1947, Diamante II was twenty-seven, Roberto twenty. Diamante II was an engineer, a captain in the U.S. Army who had served
in the German campaign and fought on the southern front with the
Fifth Army; Roberto's war experience was as a student at the Mamiani
High School and observer and victim of the black market and other
restrictions that depreciated his father's already pitiful salary. He had
been born in Rome, and considered himself Roman. Like his mother,
his maternal grandparents, his great-grandparents, and so on. As for
what had happened in his father's village, all he could do was read a
few suggestive articles in the papers of the day. The *Messaggero* opened
1944 with an article entitled "American Landing at Minturno Fails."
On January 20 the headline read "Bloody Clashes in Tufo." For the
first and only time, the village without a past, which didn't even appear on the maps, landed on the front page. As happens to all men
and women without a story, it landed there dead, assassinated. On
March 3, the *Popolo di Roma* published a dirge for the death of
Minturno penned by the Arcadian writer Americo Caravacci. A canti-
cle for a village destroyed, the literary lament did not even allude in
passing to the war, but wept for the knoll "enveloped in luminescent
air" and the lost homeland of the nymph Marica—"goddess of land and
sea, mediatress between the waves and our mountains." In 1947
Roberto was already in his third year of university, studying history. He
felt obliged to graduate ahead of, or better than, everyone else. Nothing was less appreciated in the family than mediocrity—nothing more
expected than perfection. He wanted to become a professor. He started
working for some newspapers—the first was *Il Minuto*—and began
looking for a job that would earn his keep and pay for his studies.

Roberto and Diamante II seemed so different—antithetical. Yet
they shared the same dream: to become rich. Really rich, by taking
advantage of the great upheaval at the end of the war. How? What do
an American engineer and a Roman college student have in common?
Exactly what they are. They will sell Italy to the Americans and Amer-

ica to the Italians. With the mathematical simplicity that characterizes him, Diamante-Dy explains in article 3 of a memorandum dated January 1949: "You will offer American goods on the Italian market and I Italian goods on the American market."

Dear Mr. Diamante, allow me to introduce myself. I am Roberto, Diamante's son, and I write regarding your proposal. Papà is extremely busy and so is not free to devote himself to another activity; however, if you are not opposed to the idea, I would be eager to give you a hand. Naturally, it would be necessary to clarify more precisely what exactly my responsibilities would be. For example, I am not sure if you need a list of companies and factories or a list of stores. Are you looking for manufacturers whom you would supply, or rather merchants who would sell prepackaged products? As soon as you clarify your requests, I will be able to satisfy you. Further details will be necessary, outlined article by article, perhaps even a catalog with explanations regarding operations, prices, etc. And I trust you are up to date regarding all the complicated but necessary formalities for importation and customs in Italy. I would be pleased to collaborate with you and eagerly await your response. Best regards. Sincerely yours, Roberto Mazzucco.

They will found a company; Dy will be the owner and Roberto the only representative. They will import, export. What? What one has in excess and the other lacks. Electrical supplies, spaghetti, plastic razors, cement, blenders, iron rods, umbrellas. But also words. Dy, sure that "in all my letters, there clearly are grammatical errors; therefore, please do not think you offend me if you correct them. On the contrary, I would greatly appreciate it if you would be so kind," humbly sets out to learn Italian; Roberto teaches. Curiously, the story of their parents repeats itself, but in reverse. Apart from their grammar and their ages, however, their roles are the same. Unfortunately, each is destined to shatter the dream of the other. Diamante II suggests electrical supplies. Roberto explains it is impossible to export electrical supplies because of government prohibitions. Roberto discovers that medicines such as penicillin, streptomycin, Chloromycetin, and Aureomycin are in great demand in Italy. Diamante II verifies that they are not allowed to be imported freely to Italy. Diamante II proposes plastic razors. A very popular item in America. He proposes an entire catalog:

PRICE REF.

STYLE OR MODEL	DESCRIPTION	PRICE
B-2	Black plastic	$12
S-2	Black plastic	$12
	Colored handle	
AAI	Brown plastic	$9
D-2	Black plastic	$13
	Metal handle	
D-3	Ivory plastic	$13.50
	Metal handle	
C-5	Nickel	$19
	Plastic handle	
MOUNTING PAPER	Plastic with packet	$14.50
	of five blades	

Urea is a special plastic, harder than the metal traditionally used in the handle and a mix of aluminum that will not rust.

The PRICE is per GROSS, consisting of 144 complete items.

On July 27, 1950, Roberto responds to Diamante II's hopeful precision by stating that

during the war there was significant expansion in the Bakelite razor market, but they are no longer sold, and merchants no longer accept them. As for the nickel metallic razor Model C5, your offer is about 80 lire a piece. If you add import duty, which is high, and transportation, you will see that your price is significantly higher than 120 lire a piece, the average price at which Italian factories sell to merchants. Without even mentioning that the Italian products are of better quality. I have seen beautiful metallic razors on sale to the public for 300 or 350 lire, a price which would be impossible to meet with the proposals in your last memo. And that's not all. Importation *of blades and almost all razors* is prohibited in that they are manufactured products.

Therefore, if another proposal is not possible, the deal is destined to fail. I will give the packet to your mother when she leaves.

The project—between one bureaucratic delay and another—does not take off, and in the meantime the Korean War breaks out. Roberto becomes inflamed with politics, as is the tradition in his mother's family; he demonstrates against Eisenhower and the imperialism of the United States, takes some blows to the head and is carted off to police headquarters along with many others his age. He discovers he does not love what America represents in precisely the same moment America comes knocking at his door, offering him the eternal dream of an earthly, material, possible happiness. The correspondence continues nevertheless, albeit tested by Roberto's ideological crisis. Dy asks for steel, which is scarce. Roberto proposes cement. Even though he is wasting his time, he collects information and elaborates proposals: "Here's the latest. The BPD factory with plants near Rome produces these types of special cement: (a) super-white cement, $36 per ton, resistance 680 kilograms; (b) white cement, $30 per ton, resistance 500 kilograms; (c) Ari cement, $36 per ton, special, extremely resistant."

He goes on: "Point 5. I found out that in America you need men's silk umbrellas and silk handkerchiefs. If you think we could do something, I'll let you know the prices right away." Unfortunately, seduced by the immaterial fragility of silk, he lets drop the proposal—a lucrative one—to export iron rods and plates. And when Diamante II finally announces he has received permission to export penicillin, the major pharmaceutical houses in Italy are already producing it.

Dy disappears for a period. He resurfaces in February 1951. One senses that there have been some unexpected changes in his life. "I've been away from home since late August and didn't write to anyone for a while. Thus my silence." He does not provide his new address. He advises Roberto to send letters to a company in Tonawanda, New York, "because I can't say what type of work I'm doing—all I can say is that I am head of construction for the company on the envelope, which works for the government." What is a construction company making in such great secret for the U.S. government? A prison? Fallout shelters? Arsenals? Bombs? The only certainty is that Diamante II picks up the thread of their dream as if nothing had happened, and once again asks Roberto, "What goods could be of interest in Italy today?"

My father, in the first and only stroke of commercial genius in his life, responds: *televisions*. "In a few months Italy will start using the television. Why don't you try to obtain the exclusive rights to export the better brands to Italy? This could become a great business." Unfortunately, visionaries are always ahead of their time. And they do everything possible to not realize their intuitions. There is nothing more despairing than a dream fulfilled. A few months later he adds, "It's still premature for the television. They are only now conducting the first experiments. I am following the situation and as soon as something is decided I will let you know."

But he will not let him know anything. Diamante II and Roberto will not get rich together. Or on their own. Roberto, who in the meantime had graduated in history, renounced his dream of becoming professor: he won a post at the State Railway, where he will discover the twentieth-century abomination of white-collar existence. Diamante II closed Elexport and allowed himself to be swallowed up by the mysterious activities of the Lepori Company. He disappears, vanishes into thin air. Why? What happened to him? What does it mean for an engineer—a former captain of the Fifth Army—to do construction for the government? Did he receive an irresistible offer? Did he join the CIA? In any case, when they stopped writing at the end of 1951, their paths had already gone in different directions. Dy was working on some secret project for the U.S. government, and Roberto inventoried locomotives in an office above the railway depot at Rome's Termini station. Like his father before him, he watched the trains pass. Perched over a labyrinth of rails, switches, stoplights, and ties. The rails that had swallowed his father's future had seized him as well. And just as it happened to Diamante I, the American dream of searching for earthly happiness had become odious to him. Roberto will never try to make money again. He will come up with an idea worse than that of distributing Bakelite razors in 1950. He will start writing.

The Elexport story was his apprenticeship in failure, just as America was for his father fifty years earlier. Now, and for the thirty-nine years of life left to him, his only interest will be in what doesn't work or is destined to perish. What reveals itself to be obsolete, unreal, in decline. Nations condemned to defeat. Peoples confined to the margins of history. Races in extinction, like his own. The voices of those who have been silenced. Lost causes, missed opportunities, unrealized dreams. In the office, he scraps locomotives and archives outdated models. At home, he writes theatrical works in a country that believes it's avant-garde to proclaim the death of theater (and the playwright). The newspapers that finally take him on as correspondent do not have a wide enough distribution to survive the postwar start-up market and are annihilated by the competition. The removal of his spleen and pulmonary emphysema caused by a villainous driver, instead of providing him with compensation, cost him greatly in reparations to the person who ran him down, thanks to the corruption of his lawyer. The cooperative he joins in the 1960s will go bankrupt after gobbling up his down payment, and fail to build the house of his dreams. The political cabaret he opens in the early 1970s in a wine cellar near the San Francesco a Ripa Church in Trastevere, an initiative that promises to finally bring him fame thanks to an outrageous piece entitled *Vilification and Other Ridiculous Affronts*, will lose its license due to the lack of a proper security exit. The gibbous hill infested with snakes and wild boar he purchases in Tuscany will never be declared suitable for building. The land in Tufo that his grandfather and his father dreamed of owning belongs to a woman who prefers to keep it untilled rather than give it up to the son of someone who left. The novels he writes in the 1980s stall due to his advanced age; he is deemed too old for a debut.

Even the freight car we choose in the San Lorenzo depot, excited by the audacity of our plan, will never be transported to the top of our hill not suitable for building. Every now and again we talk about how we will decorate it, remove the battens to make windows, and camp there, thus gaining savage solitude on our land—we who never had land and who feel connected only to the asphalt of Rome and the strident verses of the seagulls who hover like vultures over the Tiber. We will have a house on wheels, the only one appropriate for us, for you and me. At age sixty, he will serenely say to me, "The best thing in life is a moderate failure." I will ask myself if he is right. Perhaps. Yes. He is loved—surrounded by his friends and respected by his enemies. Perhaps in a moderate failure anyone can recognize the results of his own illusions and the betrayal he has experienced in life. At any rate, his moderate failure will kill him soon after. In one of his short stories, "The Real Reason for Commissioner Sperio De Baldi's Resignation," published posthumously in 1991, he wrote, "I didn't know anything about the psychology of the vanquished, who seems to become extraneous to himself."

In 1978 Roberto went to New York for the first time and practically against his will. Diamante II read his name in the newspaper, among the "Italian men of theater" invited to a conference, and went to find him in his hotel. Since at the time I didn't know who that Diamante with our same name who lived in New York was, I didn't think to ask Roberto if he had found the time to meet his "brother"—his twin, or the man he was not. There was only one way to make up for my error. When I returned to New York in 2000, I looked in the phone book. There I found Daniel, Diana, Donato—the usual plebeian abundance of Mazzuccos—but no Diamante. He would have been eighty that spring. I could picture him—serene and content in a suburban house in New Jersey with a garage and a nice lawn. I was not mistaken. I recently discovered he did in fact live in New Jersey, in Hazlet. But I would not have been able to meet him. Diamante II died in January 1996. I am sure he never regretted not having sold televisions.

Of all his passionately bureaucratic, pragmatically winning, and naively optimistic letters, the sentence that most sticks in my head is the one he wrote to involve my father in his American dream. This, I imagine, was the lesson he would have communicated to me. "I believe," Dy affirms, "that we two are embarking on an enterprise that will bring us great profit, always with the help of God and with OUR OWN ENERGY AND STRENGTH. Because he who seeks, finds."

With this sentence in mind, I flip through their correspondence again. 1948. 1949. 1950. Roberto wants to give the Bakelite razors back to Dy's mother. What does this mean? Where is Vita that summer of 1950? And then my eyes fall on the marginal note of May 30. Those few intimate and affectionate words are the sign I have been looking for. I knew that Vita would keep her promise. She would have kept seeking because she wanted to. Thirty-eight years after saying goodbye to him, thinking she would see him again after thirty-six months, Vita crossed the ocean to find Diamante. Roberto writes, "Your mother stayed with us only for one day, but we hope she will return from Tufo soon and stay in Rome for a while."

RAGAZZA ITALIANA SPARITA

Italian Girl Missing

A line of patient pilgrims are waiting to cross the threshold of the Holy Door. The sun beats heavily, reducing the shadow of the colonnade and transforming the piazza into a dazzling pool of light. A group of sweaty nuns in white habits and young Dominican friars are admiring the Egyptian obelisk brought here by Caligula, wondering whether it is right to transform pagan symbols into Catholic ones. They conclude that it is—the gods, if they die, are reborn, such is the essence of their eternity. The cupola glistens like an onion in the sun and the balcony swarms with tiny tourists, industrious as ants. For many of them, the Holy Year is an excuse for an affordable vacation, and they are in good company. Prince Schwarzenberg and Jennifer Jones, Eleanor Roosevelt and King Leopold, Prince Pierre of Monaco and David O. Selznick, the King of Nigeria and the Foreign Minister of Lebanon, Prince Baudoin, the poet Paul Claudel, and Princess Henvianne de Champonny, descendant of Queen Jeanne of France, have all been here, and who knows how many others will come. It is an homage that displeases no one and satisfies everyone—the devout, shopkeepers, hoteliers, souvenir vendors, peddlers of plastic and bone rosaries, parishioners from five continents, members of every religious order, and certainly also Our Lord. The audience with the spectacled pope will not begin until eleven o'clock, but the basilica is already full—and only those with reservations are admitted.

A group of flashily dressed American pilgrims stands out against the white Dominicans like a handful of Jordan almonds on a tablecloth. They are all women. Some have been waiting years for this moment— the sight of the Holy Father, Saint Peter's, beloved Italy so far away, and on and on—and tears roll down their cheeks. Others, less sentimental, rustle synthetic fans and chatter animatedly as they take turns rendering each other immortal with their automatic cameras. Their hats are shaped like disks or bombs or zucchini, their gloves are of lace, satin, or suede, and their dresses candy pink, watermelon, citron, or lawn green. Only the last in line, a petite woman in a pair of daring dark, butterfly-shaped glasses and a lace veil that mercilessly punishes her exuberant hairdo, is dressed in black. The woman looks around as if she were expecting someone, standing on her tiptoes to scrutinize the sea of heads that fills the piazza. As if she were looking for a needle in a haystack she knew she would never find. She is the only one who turns her back on the Holy Door.

Half an hour later, when the contrite and subdued Americans enter through the Holy Door and take their assigned seats in the center of the nave, they realize that the president of the Association of Italian Women of New York is no longer with them. No one saw her leave, so her disappearance causes a flurry of agitation. They confer. She was right here, then I turned around and she was gone. Could someone have kidnapped her? The words of Pope Pius XII fade in the alarmed buzz. One of them says not to worry, she must have gone to take a walk, she's probably hot, poor thing, dressed all in black, and in this sun! She probably went to get an ice cream. But she was so looking forward to the papal audience. In fact, it was she who contacted the parish last year in order to organize the trip. She certainly isn't terribly devout, who has ever seen her at catechism? She must have taken a vow, and vows must be kept. What vow? Signora Vita wanted to come back to Italy and took advantage of the occasion. It's not exactly easy for a woman her age to pick up and say, I'm off to Italy. What would people say? What would her children say? Signora Vita couldn't care less what people say. That's always been her problem. At any rate, let's not sit here worrying about her. She knows how to take care of herself. Let's pray and then go enjoy the day while it lasts; it's too hot and will rain soon. You'll see, she'll be waiting for us in the hotel.

But when they return to the hotel, the key to her room is hanging in the wooden frame. The doorman conveys the message in broken English. Mrs. Mazzucco apologizes, but she had an urgent appointment. She says not to wait for her.

The young man had dark, kinky hair and the look of a Saracen. He was tall, thin, and squeezed into an ugly suit much too small for him, like the sapling at the nursery that has grown too big for the ring with its name on it. The jacket had patches at the elbows, and the trousers had the threadbare and hostile air of garments that fear they will end up in the rag bag. The Moor was staring at her so insistently she thought he was planning to snatch her purse—middle-aged American women are the ideal victims for Roman thieves. They had already tried to steal her wallet three times since her arrival in the Eternal City, taking advantage of her confusion and foreign accent. She learned to keep quiet and smile absentmindedly, clutching her purse close to her chest. In any case, she had left her jewels in the hotel safe, so she smiled absentmindedly at the dark-skinned young man and kept her eyes on the colonnade, expecting at any moment to be pierced by the arctic blue gaze of Diamante. She hid behind her dark glasses, afraid of being incinerated. But Diamante was decidedly late. She began to fear he would not come. Perhaps the seven basilicas, the whispered prayers, the anxious checking of her watch, the very new God she had converted to—perhaps it was all for nothing. Diamante was dead, just like the Christian martyrs, or remote, petrified, and unreachable like the angels on the Castel Sant'Angelo bridge, those ghostly sentinels of a past now reduced to ashes. When the young man furrowed and arched his eyebrows discontentedly, she blushed—and for a minute she couldn't breathe. She slipped away from the line and wormed her way through the nuns' habits until she reached him. She tugged his sleeve. He didn't look like him at all. But he had that same fugitive glance, the same independent nose, the same exquisitely beautiful lips—the same shyness that anyone else would have mistaken for arrogance. This young man must be about the same age he was when they had arranged to meet again. And then she realized that, absurd as it seemed, the person she had been waiting for was this tattered and proud boy, not some middle-aged man weighed down by aches and pains, who might even walk with a cane.

"My father sends his apologies," the boy was awkwardly explaining to her, "but he is terribly busy and was not able to come. He sends his greetings and thanks you for all the trouble you have taken over us, we received your packages and are very grateful." Grateful? she thinks. And what am I supposed to do with gratitude? I would cover you in gold, I would buy you the moon if only you could give me back my Diamante. The boy fell silent, exhausted, as if he had completed his task. But Vita had taken his arm, and working her way through the crowd pressing toward the Holy Door, she was already dragging him into the sun.

"If your father cannot come to me," she said nonchalantly, "then I will go to him." Roberto wondered what this tiny woman with the butterfly glasses wanted. There were far too many women who hovered around Diamante, and he didn't like it. A father is a father, not a man. But Diamante would orchestrate dissonant scores of lies to meet women. A son should not know these things, but he does. When a father has consumed all the love in a family, not much is left for the children. The oldest got married when he was quite young, to the first girl who smiled at him; the second doesn't want to get married at all, and he, at age twenty-three, has not yet fallen in love. But this tiny lady was not like the other women. For one thing, she was older: the others were young enough to be Diamante's daughters. And she wasn't poor, a seemingly fundamental prerequisite for Diamante's senile adventures. And she was American. "My father is at the office at this hour," he tried to explain. Vita scrutinized him diffidently. "I thought he was already retired," she said with a wicked, infantile smile that contrasted surprisingly with the wrinkles adorning her neck.

"True," Roberto confessed—and then, as if to justify him, added, "but only recently."

The streets were flowing with tour buses with foreign license plates, flocks of pilgrims on foot, crippled beggars, automobiles dented by the years, too many bicycles, and scandalously overcrowded city buses with passengers crammed onto the running boards. Indolent trams basked in the sun among the palms in Piazza Risorgimento. The half-moon face of Totò, faded and weather-beaten, hung on a torn poster. The myopic gaze of Anna Magnani chased by a volcano emerged from the remains of the poster beneath it. Men in outmoded shirts whistled generously at any creature of the female gender under ninety years of age who happened to cross their line of sight. The entire city had a nostalgic air, as if it were mourning vanished glories and awaiting better times. The boy was no exception. He had already revealed to her his desire to become a writer, but explained that he had sought a job with the railway because at home a certain Calvinism of work reigned (he said it just like that, and Vita wondered what he really wanted to say), and everyone, as soon as he was able, was required to earn his independence, or survival, or freedom.

"The railway?" Vita flinched. "Of all places." The boy said he had always loved trains. Vita asked what Diamante's opinion was, and Roberto responded that his father was the one who had encouraged him to look there. Vita pressed her butterfly glasses closer to her eyes; she didn't even want to imagine that Diamante had become one of those fathers who inflict the very failures they were unable to liberate themselves from on their own children. The boy said that ever since his father had retired, he was erupting with projects. He had even revived his dream of buying a house in the countryside, in Tufo; all he wanted now was to spend the rest of his life staring at the sea and growing lemons. The thorns of the lemon tree can be quite painful, but it is the only citrus that gives fruit the entire year. The same plant can simultaneously bear flowers, sour lemons, and mature fruit. The lemon tree is practically the only plant that doesn't know winter or old age.

"The rest of his life!" Vita exclaimed with ill-concealed hostility. Young people think a fifty-nine-year-old man is a walking cadaver. But according to the recent statistics from the board of health, prominently published in *The New York Times*, the life expectancy of a Western male is as high as seventy. A woman—an American woman—can expect to live to seventy-five or more. With a bit of luck, Vita and Diamante could still have twelve years to live, to take back a good bit of the time they had lost. "What house does Diamante want to buy?" she asked cautiously as the boy leaned on the bus stop marker and peered down Via delle Fosse di Castello to see if a bus was coming. "Yours, Signora Vita. Your family's, I mean." "It doesn't exist anymore—it was bombed." "Then maybe he means the house in the countryside that belonged to my grandfather, or to yours—I'm not quite sure. But it's just a dream. He wouldn't be able to buy it, and I don't think he really wants to, in the end. We never go there, to Tufo." "Do you like it?" Vita asked. Among Rome's faults, she counted the pockmarked roads with their loose paving stones. Imprudent bicycles bounced over them, their bells incessantly tinkling. "To tell the truth, no. I hate small villages. Their conventionality, their apprehensions. The acrid surveillance of walls, windows, bell towers—do you know what I mean?" Vita laughed. "Your father hated them, too, when he was your age. And you know something? I detest them as well. We belong less to the place we come from than to the place where we want to go."

"And where is it you would like to go?" Roberto asked. Vita narrowed her eyes and stared in alarm as a sputtering wreck that dared call itself a bus approached them. "Home."

It was, in fact, a bus. It maneuvered past the spectacular flower stall, practically brushing against the proliferation of waxen calla lilies, gardenias, and brightly colored carnations in metal pails, and exhaled black clouds onto the half-asleep customers lounging in front of the cafés. Near the stop the bus slowed and the accordion door folded in on itself, revealing the sweaty uniform of the ticket-taker and the hostile faces of passengers clinging to leather loops that swayed disrespectfully. Roberto gestured to her to climb aboard. The ride was really quite short. And the bus would stop right in front of their house on

Via della Giuliana. "My son"—Vita held him back, her hand clutching his sleeve—"I didn't work for forty years to be squished to death like a sardine. We'll take a taxi." "It's quite expensive," the boy warned her. "And I am very rich," she laughed, amused. "Richer than I ever dreamed of becoming, and I have more money than I need."

The elevator was in use. The stairs received a lackadaisical cleaning once a week, and the decoration of the landings was left to the good-will of the tenants. Clearly Diamante and his children considered ornamental plants a superfluous luxury. And clearly Diamante was as poor as Italy. On the plane Vita had read an article in *Life* that shocked, disgusted, and dismayed her. It stated that one in four houses in Italy is without running water, 67 percent are without gas, 73 percent lack toilets, 70 percent a radio, 90 percent heating, and 93 percent a telephone. At the beginning of 1950, barely six hundred thousand Italians had phone numbers. Diamante was not among them.

On the front door was a plaque engraved with his—their—name. She recalled that one of the reasons she had married Geremia was the dowry he brought: their harsh name, like a stone flung from a slingshot. Maybe Roberto should at least have rung the bell, but he didn't; he was afraid his father would not have opened the door. Diamante didn't appreciate surprises. He was a methodical man, cautious, and hostile toward any novelty. He fooled himself into believing he could negate the passing of time by freezing it—emptying and thus deceiving it. He had advised Roberto to accompany Dy's nice mother—that strange girl I knew in America, I think I told you about her—to see Rome's glories: the Sistine Chapel, Castel Sant'Angelo, the fountain of the Four Rivers (remember to tell her they are the Ganges, Danube, Nile, and Rio della Plata, and not the Mississippi, Hudson, or Ohio), but do not bring her to Via della Giuliana, not for any reason. There's nothing worth seeing there.

The apartment was dark. The corridor was long, narrow, devoid of windows, and anonymous, as in a dream; forgiving shadows masked the yellowed wallpaper and the peeling plaster floral motifs on the ceiling. A vase of flowers stood on the 1920s console, but the drooping red carnations were dead; no one had thought to change the water.

Vita and Roberto were greeted by the austere smile of Giacomo Matteotti and a poster for Luchino Visconti's *Parenti terribili* at the Teatro Eliseo—a relic from the firstborn Amedeo's passion for the theater. On the dining room wall Vita was met with a brown-haired woman wearing a striped dress and black shawl. She had a huge head of wild, wiry, and willful hair barely contained at the nape. She was plump and maternal—a brunette Madonna with knitted brows; big, distant black eyes; and a mild, kind, slightly awkward gaze that seemed to be staring at something that disturbed her. Diamante's wife, evidently. Dy had said her name was Emma.

There was a faint odor of dust and old books. Books—the only things in abundance—were piled up on shelves, stacked in leaning towers, heaped on tables and chairs. Everyone in this family loses themselves in other people's stories so as to forget their own, Vita gathered. All of a sudden, the fragrant perfume of tomatoes bubbled up through a half-open door at the end of the hall. "My father's convinced he's a great cook," the boy explained. "Don't disappoint him, please." Vita said she hadn't crossed the ocean in an airplane that vibrated like a mosquito with malaria, had not left her comfortable home, her restaurant on Fifty-second Street, her apprehensive children and adored grandchildren, in short, she hadn't come all the way to Rome to disappoint Diamante.

Diamante wielded a wooden spoon, which he dipped in a bubbling, brightly colored sauce. His lips grazed the red liquid clotted on the spoon and he closed his eyes for a second, savoring the taste. Nodding with satisfaction, he turned off the burner and picked up the pan. Then he saw her. "Oh, Madonna," he exclaimed after a pause, thus summarizing all his wonder and greeting in one expression. It was not the only word that came to mind. Twenty pounds too heavy. More like thirty. That hairstyle doesn't suit her, the color is too strong and makes her look pale—eccentric. She seems smaller, her eyes are shaded in violet, her skin has lost its bronze glow. The moment he had evoked in his mind for almost forty years was as simple as a blow. Vita is clearly and definitely a widow. "When did it happen?" he exhaled. He was referring to Geremia, naturally. But since his children were standing behind her, ready to catch the slightest weakness, the question sounded invasive, intimate and allusive.

Vita didn't reply. She was standing on the threshold, staring wide-eyed and severely, almost hostilely, as if he were an offensive imposter, a thief who had taken away the man she had come to find. The man she loved. Diamante should not have been surprised like this—wearing a faded plaid dressing gown, a pair of terry-cloth slippers, and an apron stained with sauce in this mess of a kitchen—caught in the act. Emma died almost fourteen years ago, so he is the one who cooks now, who washes the dishes and does the shopping—he has become a housewife, his own unloved wife. He wished the floor would open up and swallow him. He didn't even have time to take off his apron because Vita had already insinuated herself in the narrow space between the table and the stove, she was coming toward him, taking his hands. "Oh, Dio, Vita, if only you had warned me . . . ," he began. Her hands were soft and sweet-smelling now, her nails painted an opalescent pink. The gold band on her ring finger. Diamante was wearing two wedding bands, one on top of the other, both tight—both now a binding and final memory of Emma. Surprised, Vita said, "Diamà, what did you do to your hair?" But he hadn't done anything. Which was why it had gone all white.

Diamante offered her the choice of a chair that looked like it came from a hospital and a three-legged stool that leaned to the right when Vita rested her not insignificant weight on it. Strange: even though her beauty was truly obscured, he realized with melancholy—and desperately late—that she still looked like the "Italian Girl Missing" the shopkeepers on Mulberry Street had hung in all their windows, whom the customers dreamed of finding if they could keep her as the reward. He was the one who was supposed to find her again. But he hadn't. He poured a glass of water and downed it in one gulp. His throat was dry, he was dying of thirst. Certainly from these powerful emotions. He didn't want to think of the doctor's prophecies about dryness of the mouth. He was tired of his nephritis. Today he will be healthy. He will put on his best clothes—a flecked gray flannel suit, which will smell faintly of mothballs—his wing-tip shoes and silk tie with gold squiggles. Because the Italian Girl Missing is here. Because she was mine—then.

"Put out the good plates today," he ordered his daughter, who docilely slipped away. His only daughter had narrow shoulders, a fine head, and was wearing a gray skirt and white blouse. She had not been given the name of his mother, Angela, or that of his wife's mother. Her name was Vita. Emma was the one who had chosen the name; she was a woman of rare sensitivity and intelligence. Diamante probably didn't deserve a woman like her, but chance, or whatever hides behind it, had given her to him—and then quickly taken her away. Vita's namesake had not even looked her in the eyes, for the shadow of their guest had always darkened their kitchen and her name had always reminded her she was not who she should be.

"The good plates for me?" Vita laughed. "To honor our guest," Diamante explained, embarrassed. "Am I a guest?" she asked. Diamante didn't answer. He studied her, running his eyes over her face as if it were a map that could help him orient himself—those dark eyebrows she had never plucked and that framed her jet black eyes, her lips twisted into a perpetual expression of strained curiosity, the white part in her hair, recently moved to the left side of her head, the mole on her right cheek he could almost feel with his fingertips. He popped an ice cube in his mouth and cracked it. That way she wouldn't realize that his teeth were chattering as if he had nearly drowned.

Vita noticed that his eyes had completely lost their color. They were as transparent as a glass window. "No, of course you're not a guest, my house is your home." But he realized it wasn't much of an offer, fifty square meters in one of the new buildings on Via della Giuliana. People say Vita owns three apartments in Manhattan and a restaurant on Fifty-second Street, recommended in all the guidebooks. Diamante never did have much to offer her. He was never able to imagine, not even now, that all she wanted was him.

Since the service of good dishes had been sold during the war, the settings were mismatched, the glasses different sizes—some fluted like petals, others with horizontal stripes—and the gold rims of the plates were faded and cracked from the heat. The table trembled on wobbly legs and every now and then Diamante would grumble and kneel down to insert a wedge. A racket rose from the street: two- and four-wheeled vehicles, panting buses, and street vendors offering to sharpen knives, scissors, and blades; repair umbrellas; or sell lupines, olives, sweets, brooms, or wine by the liter. After the first bite—extremely salty—Vita felt she was back in the kitchen on Prince Street. Even the tomatoes had that same sour, slightly dusty taste American tomatoes had long since forgotten. Diamante didn't say a word, and a heavy silence fell over the table; it became embarrassing to chew because they could hear the intense activity of everyone's jaws. Vita was not the cause; Diamante's children said he had always been this way, the most laconic father in the entire city. It was as if he had nothing to say to them, or didn't know how to communicate it. Vita liked to think he had forgotten the words and needed to learn new ones. Who knows if he still remembers—men never look back at the past. Vita had mulled over those words that were now irreparably useless, had worried them like rosary beads for thirty-eight years.

"Will you stay?" he asked when they moved to the living room. "The house is small, but it's all yours, Vita will give you her room, she can sleep here on the couch." She didn't know how to tell him she had left her own children on the other side of the ocean and hadn't come here looking for others. Diamante seemed convinced she had come to stay. But now Vita only wanted to get away, to be alone, to ask herself if she had really come to Rome to look for this measured and taciturn man who didn't show the slightest sign of having thought about her in all these years, who didn't seem to remember what had gone on between them, who didn't even try to engage her in conversation. The only argument they were able to share was their common civil status—widowhood. Geremia's tumor and Emma's enigmatic, sudden, and premature death.

Diamante told how she had been operated on for a kidney infection. The doctor had shown him his wife's diseased organ. The diagnosis seemed a nightmare to him, a grotesque error. Emma's kidneys were perfectly healthy; he was the one who was sick. The kidney in question was an insignificant, rust-colored sac in the doctor's hands. So that's what it looked like—a heap of entrails destined to end up on the scrap pile at the butcher's. The kidney was his enemy; it had tormented him since his time in Denver and was poisoning his blood and drying out his throat. The incision in Emma's side made her look as if she'd been stabbed. His Emma: drugged, lying there with her hair tucked under a paper cap, her head on a pillow, her face wearing an indecipherable expression either of iron sweetness or supreme indifference. As he looked upon that face, so essential and solemn, a chilling thought gripped him: Emma had taken his illness into her own body, pressed it into her own flesh. The doctor assured him that the operation was a complete success; as he spoke, the infected organ he was holding dripped pus onto the open wound. Hypnotized by the sight of that insignificant, rust-colored sac oozing onto the inanimate body of his wife, Diamante kept asking himself why. As if she had wanted to send him a message somehow. To save him. Liberate him. The next day, the infection had spread. Emma died without ever regaining consciousness. He realized then that when he went home he would never see her again sitting where she had always been, in the soft halo of the lamp, bent over the hem of a garment, sewing or relining her clients' coats on her Singer sewing machine. Often the only noise in the silent house had been the self-important buzz of the bobbin welding stitches in cloth. Emma had been a seamstress in a coat factory, but she also wrote poems, verses, and stories, and perhaps she would have liked to go on doing so. But after her wedding, she dedicated herself exclusively to Diamante, just as he had wished. She had lived for him; he became her entire world. So she took in work at home. Never again would Diamante hear the buzz of the bobbin. His wife, his sweet wife, *had died for him, in his stead.* Or so he thought.

Vita couldn't explain to him the sensation that came over her the night Geremia left her. That emaciated body in the bed, that distressing and distressed presence she had accompanied to all the best hospitals, where he was tortured with cures as painful as they were useless, had only revealed to her how healthy her own body was. Geremia didn't know the word *resignation*; he was always convinced he would get better, would pull through—he had survived the fire in the elevator shaft, the loss of all his assets and his wife's love, two heart attacks, and the humiliation of house arrest as enemy of the country in which he had chosen to live—but in the end he didn't make it. She stood at the door of their bedroom, holding the tray with the dinner Geremia had never even tasted, and felt neither pain nor gratitude. Instead she felt dismay at still being alive. Her muscles, tendons, veins, joints, bones, and heart all cried out the same thing. I'm alive. I'm alive. Alive. Alive. Alive. Before her opened a terrifying abyss of years, twenty maybe, that she didn't know what to do with—an inherited wealth she did not deserve. Twenty years! More time than many people are given for their entire lives. An empty, absolutely useless, almost desperate time. Unless. Unless Diamante still exists, and is still who she has believed him to be for so very long.

But all of this was sucked up by the silence that accompanied their coffee—strong, bitter, and covered in dust like a memory. Was he? Was this man with the transparent eyes really Diamante? Was this the same boy who appeared in her mind when she thought on the past—a real live boy who came to join her in the lifeboat, who spent the night in her arms? Diamonds are precious; they sparkle and can cut glass, but they only shine by reflecting light. They aren't worth anything in the dark.

Diamante stared at her triple-buttoned jacket, her stockings just showing under her skirt, hemmed at sixteen inches. He read ladies' magazines out of love of women, and had learned that the rules of fashion dictated that elegance be measured in this way, counting the distance from the ankle to the hem. Black jacket, black skirt, black stockings. Widow's weeds. Vita is alone. Vita is free. We are both free. So desperately late.

"I'm not staying," Vita said to him, avoiding the eyes of her young namesake, in which she would have read a sign of genuine relief. Diamante placed another ice cube on his tongue. He forced himself to dig up some topic of conversation. So as not to speak of themselves, he spoke of Eisenhower, Korea, the hydrogen bomb a thousand times more powerful than the atom bomb, too powerful, so destructive that to use it against people would be like shooting a mortar at a baby sparrow—nuclear weapons will destroy this earth, which might not turn out to be such a bad thing, as the human race is the most dangerous of all, which proves that natural selection is an inefficient criterion of progress. He spoke of Ingrid Bergman, who had come to Italy to give birth to her love child, which, given the puritanism of the public, probably meant the end of her career, don't you think? Of Piero D'Inzeo and his horse Destino, who won the World Cup a few days ago, did you go? He didn't, even though he would have liked to, he's always loved horses, they have such strange names, horses do— Uranium, Aladdin, Umbrella. Of Benny Goodman, who played in Milan, and Duke Ellington, who will play in Rome, but he won't go hear him because he doesn't understand this new music—*jungle*, is that what it's called?—he still listens to Enrico Caruso and *Aida* and your beautiful sky I would like to give back to you, the sweet breezes of your native land . . .

Vita wondered whether all Diamante's talk was intended to hold her there or distance her definitively. Words had always been their currency. But it was an obsolete currency, no longer in circulation, valid only in their land. And that land now seemed as pockmarked as the moon—a desert of craters from a war long over. An uninhabited satellite that continued to rotate in the void, diffusing to the end of time the pallid splendor of a reflected light. But which light? Diamante spoke of Rome, a city he loved for all it once was and is no longer, for all it never was and never would be—a city without the sea, without a port, without a world around it. Of Via Ferruccio, where he had lived for years, that neighborhood of travelers where lost objects ended up, things no one remembers to claim accumulating on office shelves until they're finally sold for almost nothing, to whoever wants them. Where else could he possibly have lived? He who had been a lost object for so very long. He spoke of the seagulls that follow the Tiber and throng on the roofs of the city, their cries that sound of the sea. They always seem out of place, or in the wrong place. Which is how Diamante often felt.

Because I could never really go home, Vita—he would have liked to add. I didn't have a world to come back to—not a landscape or a place. Not even the memory of those things. Just their names. There was no longer a group of people who were *my* people. I no longer had anything in common with my relatives. Their naïveté astounded me. Their avarice irritated me because it reminded me I had lost my own.

Their ignorance offended me. I couldn't share in their projects. I no longer knew my parents. I still loved them and would have thrown myself into the flames for them, but my love had become nothing but compassion, pity. Who was I? A stranger. A *foreigner*. I kept going back, but always ended up leaving again. It was as if the ship I was sailing on never arrived in port, as if I were still wandering on the ocean, suspended between two shores, without a destination, without a way to go home. I tried to be part of something, I tried with the financial police, the marines, the war—but they didn't want me. My illness kept me at a distance. I tried with politics—but it didn't do any good, I merely discovered how many people are ready to whistle to point you out to the ones waiting to kill you . . . And yet I got what I wanted. America made me into someone respectable, a bourgeois. I got a job in an office. They *accepted* me, Vita. But I was always somewhere else. Until finally I wasn't anywhere, and if I never managed to kill myself, it was only because I was already dead. Dead like all the other dead people who jostle on the tram, elbow their way in the office, on the streets, at the movies, in church. Who exchange the usual greetings, but don't know and don't want to know. Who think they've survived their dead bodies, dead souls, dead thoughts. I was killed, Vita, assassinated by poverty, mediocrity, and bullying, by the tyranny of necessity and need. Yet never—not once—did I wish to retrace my steps.

Vita did not interrupt him, not when his children withdrew, leaving them alone, facing each other on the armchairs nibbled by dust, or when the light began to fade behind the shutters. She let him talk, and senseless words flowed like the hypnotic, irregular lapping of the surf. The shadows in the dining room had swallowed up the dead carnations and Emma's bewildered gaze, and all of a sudden she seized his hands and covered them in kisses. Diamante let his fingertips caress her nape. Time fused, crumbled, melted. It was already dark when the street vendor shattered their oblivion with his mournful voice: "Umbrella man—got a broken umbrella that needs fixing? Umbrella man . . ." His arrival meant it would rain soon.

He could have asked to go with her to her hotel. But the eyes of his children seemed more severe than the eye of God, and more dismayed than Emma's. The proposal would have sounded ambiguous, improper. They were past the age of hotel rooms. Ingrid Bergman might be forgiven, her sin forgotten, and perhaps she would be able to continue acting, but she was an immortal goddess of the silver screen, while they were just normal souls. They would not be forgiven. He made do with escorting her down the stairs and onto the street, walking beside her for a few blocks. Both of them were silent, reflecting on all that had been said that day, said without ever being uttered. They were amazed by this sudden knowledge of what exists in the silence between words, astounded by the complexity of human discourse. Then Vita stopped, said she was tired. "Would you mind calling a taxi, dear?" Diamante recognized the mournful umbrella man, always dressed in black, hunched over his repairs in a doorway. Spread out in front of him were wooden handles and rubber linings, irreparable metal ribs and torn fabric. Diamante shuddered at the sound of his monotonous call.

"What are you planning on doing?" he asked as Vita adjusted her veil and studied herself in the darkened pharmacy window. She had gotten used to letting her skirts out every six months, to recognizing that the stout woman reflected in the windows was herself. She did not look away. She had never lived in the past. She liked the past, its darkness, the comfort of knowing it has nothing to teach and will be lost, its satiated fullness that asks nothing—but she had always liked the future better. And there she saw a silent and poor man in a dressing gown and slippers who walked on water without leaving the slightest trace.

"I'm going to Tufo," she replied as she searched his transparent eyes for a blue reflection. "I might buy a house in the countryside, spend the summers there. The restaurant can survive without me by now." Diamante arched his eyebrows, unsure if it was charity, a gift, or simply a coincidence. He wasn't used to good news. The voice rang out again: "Umbrella man! Umbrella man!" "When is your return flight?" Not that he wanted to send her back to New York, quite the opposite. All of a sudden, he knew he was seeing her for the last time. Vita smiled, resting her gloved hand on his puckered lip with its ancient scar. "I haven't bought my return ticket yet."

Diamante opened his shirt collar. He felt short of breath. It happened, now and then. He swallowed hard. Perhaps he had been set on fire, he was burning up, was already burned—only his blackened skeleton remained and was about to crumble, only his skin held him together, the precarious fragility of his epidermis was all that kept him from collapsing. And if she did buy that house, Vita was saying, would he come? "I would buy it for you, for us, I mean. I want you to come live with me, to die with me, to do everything with me." "You're crazy, Vita," he said. "Think about it, Diamante." She probably didn't even realize she'd shattered his life. Sliced it open like a tree struck by lightning. All that remained was the trunk, upright and planted solid in the ground, the split trunk where moss grows, where birds make their nest—but that could never be born anew. Even the roots have rotted, and it falls over, raising up to the punishing heavens a tangle of twisted branches.

"It's not possible, Vita. Out of the question." "You really wouldn't come?" she asks as she turns up his jacket collar. The wind that comes before the rain. "Just tell me you'll come." "No, no." "Why?" Diamante clings to the translucent opacity of her veil. He is losing her: before his eyes appears a radiant little girl, nine years old, sitting on the side of a lifeboat, intent on polishing a silver knife with her breath. The glimmer of that knife in the gray surrounding him is all the light that remains. She hasn't yet realized he's found her. Her back is turned, her disheveled hair on her shoulders. Black, dark. *Don't leave me, not for any reason, do not leave me.* If he stretches out his hand, he can still touch her. But he can't manage to keep her.

"Are you telling me no?" Vita asks.

Damn! There are never any taxis in this city of valiant pedestrians, everyone complains they have to wait for hours, and instead here one comes, heading from Piazzale delle Medaglie d'Oro. It catches sight of the two silhouettes standing side by side near the crosswalk. In the deserted evening street, the man with white hair and the woman with the veil—facing each other, rigid, almost petrified—are as visible as statues. The taxi's headlights cast patterns on Vita's stockings, illuminate her face and reveal the hunched figure dressed in black behind them. The taxi pulls up and stops. Vita opens the door, and since Dia-

mante has retreated, sure he would not survive the slightest contact
with her lips, she climbs in, settles herself in the passenger's seat—
excessively long for just herself—and pronounces the name of her
hotel in a shaky voice. She adjusts the veil over her face. Italian Girl
Missing. Diamante places his hands on the glass; the raindrops shimmer
like crystal—he has nothing more to add, and everything still to say.
Vita tries to open the window, but the handle must be broken because
she can only open it a crack. All he can see is her mouth—the shimmer of white, perfect square teeth. American teeth. "Diamante," that
mouth is saying, "life is so long. It's one hundred sixty-six kilometers
from this corner to Tufo. In another age, it was a long journey, uncomfortable and complicated, but not today. It only takes three hours
by train. Travel those one hundred sixty-six kilometers. Come. Everything will be different, and we'll be happy forever."

The taxi driver doesn't realize what is transpiring in the life of his
passenger and the white-haired man leaning on the door; the glass between prevents him from understanding her words, which to him are
merely a rustle. "I'll stay all summer. So, okay, not tomorrow, not even
the day after, but maybe in a week, a month, sooner or later, come and
live with me. You must give me—give yourself—this chance." The
taxi meter clicks noisily—the driver has already pressed the accelerator,
and the black, beat-up, 1930s Berlin spits smoke down the center of
the street. *"Arrivederci,"* Vita promises her Diamante. We'll see each
other again. The driver turns on the windshield wipers and they
squeak across the glass; they are quick and efficient, but unable to wipe
away her tears. There he is, struggling to open the umbrella—the last
thing she sees in the rearview mirror, just before the curve, is a mass of
white hair sprinkled with rain. In the shadows it shimmers like diamonds.

At the end of September, Vita boarded a Pan Am flight to New York.
In January, Roberto sent her a two-word telegram: DIAMANTE DEAD.

PART III

The Water Line

Water Boy

In the photograph, taken in the late autumn of 1906 when the first snow dusted the forest white, there are nine of them, lined up together in the middle of the tracks. As if they were trying to bar the path of an oncoming train and block out the horizon. But behind them there is nothing—no railroad line, no road. That's precisely why the nine men are there: to strip the forest and build the railway. All that can be seen behind them are fir trees and a load of rocks held aloft by an invisible hoist. They are all wearing the uniform of the American worker: blue-jean overalls and checked shirts. Different sorts of hats—coppolas or berets. One of them wears a knitted wool cap. The men have Mediterranean features and dark skin. They are Italians. Strangely, only three of them have mustaches, in contrast to the caricature of the dago in newspapers of the day. None are over thirty. Tired but strong-willed, they all sport muscular builds and concentrated expressions. The last one on the right, standing on the rocks slightly in the background—the one with the wool cap and the only one beyond the tracks—still has smooth cheeks. He's rather small and his shoes are falling apart, but he looks defiant with his hands at his sides and a pout on his face. The faded photograph is black-and-white, but you can tell he has light-colored eyes.

The photograph appeared in a 1907 Baltimore & Ohio Company publication vaunting to shareholders progress on the internal sections of the line. The Baltimore & Ohio Railroad, the oldest and one of the most popular railroads in the United States, linked up with the Atchison, Topeka & Santa Fe by way of Cincinnati, Saint Louis, and Kansas City, and reached all the way to Los Angeles. Farther north it joined with the legendary Union Pacific at Toledo, Chicago, and Omaha, and went all the way to San Francisco. That boy with the different hat just might be Diamante. He was most likely in that area. When he was about fifteen, all the world's water glimmering in his destiny was suddenly drained into the wooden pail he found himself lugging along the tracks. Without intending to, he had become what he had always dreamed of: he's the one who brings together what's far apart, who lays a bridge between two distant points. The water carrier. In America they call him water boy.

His job consists of quenching the workers' thirst. Put that way, it seems easy, and in fact Diamante gushes with happiness when the foreman tells him he's been hired for at least as long as it takes his team to finish building the section assigned to them. He is allotted a horse blanket and two wooden pails linked by a sort of yoke. The foreman warns him that they are Company property, if he ruins them he'll have to pay. It seems to Diamante that there's little to ruin; the pails are older than his grandfather, and not even a horse would want to use the blanket. But since the foreman is armed with a sinister mug and a rifle, Diamante is quick to smile and assure him he'll be careful.

Placido Calamara's team is at Camp 12. Diamante had drawn the short straw. On the railroad, the numbers work in the opposite direction from New York: the high numbers are the unlucky ones because you start counting from the base nearest the city. Pasquale and Giuseppe Tucciarone are at Camp 6 with fifteen other boys from Minturno, but they didn't need a water boy there. Diamante climbs on the supply cart next to Placido Calamara. Bossy, squat, and slick as an olive, Placido reminds Diamante of Nello and takes an instant disliking to him, even though he hopes Placido will find reason to like him. They travel for thirty miles on an increasingly wild trail through an immense forest. Diamante has never seen so many trees. In Tufo the charcoal merchants and shepherds have cut them all down, and the Aurunci Mountains are bare. When the cart halts, it's already dark and there's nothing to see except an old freight car, left behind from when the trains ran on wood. Well, this is the camp.

Diamante slides the door open and enters the freight car. It stinks of dog and mattresses. "Greetings, mates," he says cheerfully, "I'm the new water boy." The only response he gets from the already reclining workers is a raspberry; this is no salon. When you're in the middle of a forest thirty miles from the nearest settlement, it's better to act like a wolf. Diamante blinks. Twenty, maybe thirty men with long beards and haggard faces. The wooden benches lined up crossways in the car must be the beds. Diamante aims for the bench farthest from the door and the drafts and trips over a large rusted can. The vilest insults come hurtling at him from the dark because that can is their stove and they'll freeze to death in here without it, *porco demonio*. Diamante apologizes. He sits on the straw mattress. A voice like nails on a blackboard shouts stridently, "Hey, boy, you can't stay here, go find yourself another spot."

"Awright," Diamante sighs. He understands immediately that the water boy in the railroad camp is the same as the cabin boy on a ship: the bottom of the heap. He settles himself on the mattress near the door, where he'll be raked by drafts and powdered with dust. With all these trees in Ohio, it probably rains a lot, too. Not worth getting undressed. The mattress is black with dirt and stinks as if there were a dead body inside. No use being squeamish about it, though—he's got to sleep on this straw for at least seven months. Since he's to start work tomorrow at dawn, he lies down. The mattress is as lumpy as a mountain range, with razor-sharp stingers as hard as wood that poke out of the holes and cover him with bruises. But Diamante's not sleepy. He's so happy to be in fabulous Ohio, to have found a good job and to be starting a new life. Unfortunately, his body heat warms up the mattress and an entire army of crackling, ravenous bedbugs descends on him.

He moves again. He brushes the trash that has accumulated on the floor—hazelnuts, seeds, sawdust, mouse droppings, fly shit—under his neighbor's bench, unfolds his horse blanket and stretches out. He tries in vain to get rid of two cockroaches that insist on crawling on his nose without bloodshed, but loses his patience and squashes them with his fist. He takes out his knife and carves two notches on the wall. When he leaves Camp 12 in November, there will be 510 notches. Diamante will have exterminated an entire colony of cockroaches. He'll even have eaten quite a few. The American cockroach has a floury taste, similar to chickpeas.

Fifteen hours a day, for 190 days, Diamante travels back and forth along the tracks. To go from the camp with the freight car dormitory and the well to the work site, first he uses a handcar he calls the elevated—in part to remind himself of New York, in part because he likes to imagine he's flying over avenues, automobiles, markets, and buildings. When he reaches the end of the tracks, he gets off and keeps going on foot, the pails full of water skillfully balanced on his shoulders. It isn't hard because people from Tufo can carry all sorts of things on their heads—a basket full of eggs, a bale of hay, even a casket. It's not a good idea to empty the pails along the way because if the foreman thinks you're being clever, he'll wallop you so hard your face will be disfigured. The downside is that the shovelers work constantly and only catch their breath when they stop to drink, so they guzzle water like buffaloes and drain the pails immediately. Which means that Diamante is forced to fill them constantly; to get to the well, he pumps the handcar along the tracks, back and forth, again and again, sweating, toiling, getting stiffer and stiffer and wearing himself out. The sun never sets. It burns his back, his shoulders, his neck; blisters quickly cover his skin, which then peels away like a boiled potato. In a month it's as black as the workers'. When it's windy, it's like being whipped in the face because in America the wind comes straight down from the North Pole without anything to block its path. When it rains they are soaked all night long, and the freight car sounds like a hospital ward with all the coughing. But Diamante is fifteen; the summer sun, the north winds, and the Ohio rains only tease him. And so from dawn to dusk he walks with his pails. The water sloshes against the wood, the

car creaks on the tracks, the silence and songs of mysterious birds sur-
round him—and he's happy; he has a secure income, and soon he'll
put aside enough money so he can leave here with Vita.

He gets paid $1.80 a day. Less than everyone else. But the others are
shovelers, real virtuosi who know every secret of wood, iron, and
stone. They excavate, dig, push wheelbarrows full of stones, level the
ground, carry ties, align and arrange them, and screw down the tracks.
The Company pays them for the maintenance and construction of
railroad lines and wooden and stone ballast, consolidation, clearance of
natural obstacles with dynamite, laying and expansion of track. The
water boy is small but robust, and if he wants to, next year he, too, can
saw wood and split rocks with a sledgehammer. But Diamante has calculated he will earn $10.80 a week. In six months it'll add up to a
good $280. So next year he'll already be someplace better—with Vita.

Unfortunately Camp 12 is isolated, far away from the Japanese
teams, who have cooks. There's no choice but to buy food from the
foreman's shop, which everyone calls the "pluck-me store." It takes
Diamante a week to figure out why. Calamara sells rotten anchovies,
rancid cans of tomatoes, and moldy tins of beans that cause dysentery,
all at exorbitant prices. Diamante comes down with a violent attack on
the seventh day. Since there's no john, you go wherever, in a stinking
hole dug in the earth and covered with a rotten plank. But your mates
whack you with the shovel if you shit anywhere near the freight car
and make you go deep into the woods. So after a while, between the
dysentery, the lousy food, and the exhaustion, you go as soft as butter
and can't manage to drag yourself off your mattress in the morning.
The foreman prods you with his rifle, not a pleasant way to start the
day.

Diamante prefers to make the best of things rather than complain,
and stops buying food from the company store. He fashions himself a
slingshot and strips the bark off a branch and makes a club. After work,
while his mates gather around a table covered with old newspapers and
eat and fart—their intestines are shot—Diamante heads out in search
of prey. He kills squirrels and moles with a bite to the head. He fells
woodpeckers, quails, and chaffinches with his slingshot, applying the

same deadly precision he'd learned as a boy. He gathers mushrooms, acorns, and snails in the damp gorges. The others are horrified at first, but he learns to make himself some pretty tasty stews. Only the prairie rat has a foul smell that neither blueberries nor mustard can disguise. The dormouse is excellent. The pheasant is so greatly prized he even sells some. Osprey meat tastes like chicken. Diamante chews with satisfaction and wishes Vita were here. Or that she could see him, at least. She would be proud of him; she likes boys who know how to make it on their own.

He hasn't heard from her since the day he left—she was running along the tracks, balancing on the metal rail, her blue dress blending with the blue obscurity of the dawn. Vita ran alongside the car he was hiding in until the train began to pick up speed and swerved at the switch. Then, just as they had agreed, she went home. As soon as he found work, Diamante sent her a postcard with the name of his railroad company, begging her not to tell anyone—in case the vindictive Cozza was contemplating some sort of punishment. They still hadn't given him her reply. The mailman never came to Camp 12. Next Sunday, Diamante will go and protest to the Company agent. With the four words he still remembers, he'll somehow make them understand it's just not right to make the workers wait so long. It's bad enough they're living in the middle of the woods, but if they don't even get news from home, their morale will bottom out. He doesn't want Vita to be worrying. Everything's going just splendidly.

On payday he realizes they've subtracted seven dollars for "company store purchases." "But I didn't buy anything at the store," he protests. "I went hunting." Calamara stares at him in disbelief. He still hasn't decided if the water boy is incredibly smart or incredibly stupid. He hawks and spits on his boots. "You have to pay anyway, even if you don't buy anything," he clarifies. "No," Diamante insists. "It doesn't say that in the contract. I accepted to work for a dollar eighty a day. I'll pay you what I owe, and nothing more." "You didn't understand, then," the foreman says as he rises to his feet. "You're the one who doesn't understand," Diamante rebuts. "If that's the way things are, I'm leaving."

When Diamante opens his eyes, Santo Callura is pressing a towel to his face. He's all wet, but not with water. He's bleeding from the neck. Diamante now understands that Calamara's rifle isn't good just for controlling, threatening, and prodding his men. "You can leave when the snow comes and the river ices over. We'll all leave then," Callura explains patiently. "Nobody can leave the camp without permission or before their contract's up. If you escape, Calamara'll come find you and bring you back. And if you keep on busting his balls, he'll report you for stealing and the Company agent'll throw you in jail." Diamante moans weakly from the pain. "But we're not prisoners," he murmurs. "It's not like they've deported us to some forced labor camp." Callura shrugs his shoulders and keeps packing the wound. "How long you been working for the railroad?" Diamante asks suspiciously. Callura dries his hands on his jeans and doesn't answer.

In July, when the sun inflames the freight car so it's like sleeping in a furnace, a Methodist spinster shows up, eager to teach English to these "men of bronze." Diamante asks if he has to pay. Miss Olivia Campbell states that the course is free. The generous parishioners of Lima want to help the foreigners integrate themselves into our nation. Diamante explains he'd sign up, but he's Catholic. Baptized and first communion. Not confirmed, though, because he came to America. The spinster smiles. She must be about forty. Skinny as a twig, red hair. She sure has nerve coming here all alone to track dagoes, whom the Americans consider to be hardened rapists. Diamante explains that he's not really very Catholic and hasn't set foot in a church since the day he left. Miss Campbell replies that we are all Christians. Diamante signs up. The lessons are held in Camp 9, so he has to run ten miles through the forest to get there. Thirty show up for the first lesson, piled into an old car that stinks of cow manure. The seventh lesson there are ten of them. The fifteenth, Diamante finds himself alone with Miss Campbell. Unfortunately, the dagoes don't show any interest in the advantages the American language provides, and she will be forced to offer her treasures to the Ukrainians, Hungarians, and Finns down the track. "Oh no, Miss," Diamante implores, "please don't go. I'll convert to Methodism." Miss Campbell smiles. She hadn't come to buy the soul of a water boy. But she gives him a book. Not the Holy Bible, which they had just started to study. This book is written by a certain London Jack, *The Call of the Wild*. It's the story of a dog who is sold, beaten, and humiliated, and becomes a wild and ferocious beast, and Miss Campbell thinks Diamante will really enjoy it. Diamante works like a dog to understand the story, but gives up on page 47. For years he will be curious to know what happened to the indomitable Buck.

The mail sack finally arrives in mid-August, but there's no letter for Diamante Mazzucco. Maybe Vita never received his postcard from Cleveland. Or maybe she wasn't satisfied—it was a bit mean-spirited, after all. He should write to her again and not be ashamed to tell her how much he loves her. His more experienced camp mates say women need words the way men need impure acts. But when Diamante picks up his pen, he discovers he can no longer bend his fingers. His hands have stiffened into fists from constantly gripping the ropes. Maybe that's why he always feels like punching somebody. He uncurls his fingers. From now on he'll do exercises every night so he won't end up with rheumatism and crippling arthritis.

Dear Vita,
I can't have you come out here yet, but I'm saving up and will be ready soon. I promise I think of you always and never forget for a second that we are betrothed. I can't wait to be with you, and we'll never be separated again.

Forever, your Diamante

Autumn air filters through the cracks in the freight car walls. When the icy wind from the North Pole blows, the car shakes, sways, and trembles as if hit by an earthquake. But the mail sack they deliver at the end of October contains no letter for the water boy, either.

Crocefisso Cassano insists that the best letters from women never actually arrive. Somebody steals them first. The Company wants to keep the men from becoming too nostalgic. If you have the money, you can buy them back. If not, you have to resign yourself to the fact that somebody else is reading your letters and going around boasting he has a girl waiting for him somewhere. "But she's *my* girl," Diamante says. Crocefisso contradicts him: "It looks like she's Giobatta Reato's girl now." Diamante coughs up three dollars for Vita's letter. Reading it makes him melancholy and brings tears to his eyes. But the letter is addressed to a certain Pietro from a certain Assunta. When Diamante complains and demands to have his money back, Reato refuses. He claims he did him a favor because there wasn't any letter signed Vita.

At the end of the season, Diamante is fiercely determined to quit the railway and take any job he can get in Cleveland. But he hadn't calculated correctly. Once expenses are subtracted (housing, wear and tear on the horse blanket and work tools, food items, fines for infractions and tardiness according to the unfeasible work plan devised by the foreman so as not to be liquidated together with all his men in favor of another, even more desperate group), not only is there nothing left to send to his parents or put aside so he can go back to Vita or ask her to come out, but he finds himself indebted to the foreman who'd hired him. There's only one way to pay off the debt: work for him for another season.

He wintered in Calamara's mother-in-law's boardinghouse, a lurid boxcar stranded on uncultivated fields behind the Cleveland freight yard. A place of whistles and signal lamps, filled with the sounds of trains, of metal against metal. Determined to earn the money he needs to free himself of the foreman, Diamante hit the dismal Italian quarter wedged between 119th and 125th Streets, but they told him to try down at the port, at the Standard Oil refineries and paper mills. The pay didn't even cover the rent. He worked in a foundry and a shipyard, and sold hemorrhoid creams and blister ointments. In an exhilarating thirty-floor tower he was in charge of the elevator cuspidors where the workers spit out their disappointment. Then he gave himself over to letters: he deciphered and wrote them for illiterate Italians, trying to imagine what the recipients in Italy would want to hear. After a while he substituted for the mailman. Delivering the mail brought him an indescribable joy. When he loaded that bag full of envelopes on his bicycle, he had the sensation it contained all the words in the world, including the ones written for him. *Dear Diamante, I'm glad you're well.*

I'm fine too. I won't say much because I've always found writing a chore, but I am, as always, your loving Vita. Diamante would pedal past the Italian neighborhood, far from the tracks and the smell of trains. Sometimes the watchdogs in front of the blond people's suburban villas would rip his trousers. He hardly noticed, though; soon Vita's letter would arrive. But then the regular mailman returned, and after that other people's letters nauseated him.

And so he found himself back among the railway slaves. Chained to the tracks, even in winter. Wrapped in the frozen fog, bent over the switches with a broom, sweeping away the snow that buried the ties as signals blinked intermittently. The locomotives emerging from the smoke were nothing more than a vibration in his veins—he couldn't even see them. Phantasms exhaling iron and rust. Men without women. Violent, lost men. People called them migratory birds. But they didn't mean it poetically—these were birds of prey, sinister creatures. Yet even migratory birds know how to find the way home when winter is over.

When spring came, Diamante discovered his debt to the foreman had doubled. He had to start all over again. Three hundred miles farther west, in a new state, a new group, a whole new landscape. He had no idea where he was. It was already dark when he arrived in camp on a lead-lined car penetrated by only the thinnest ray of light. All he saw during the day were tracks shining among stones, a flattened universe without form or dimension, disappearing into blue sky. Again the railroad. Again the boiling freight car, the rotten anchovies, the thousands of steps with the yoke on his shoulders, the water sloshing in the pails. Again the wavering sight of a line of men stationed along straight tracks and the skinny shadow of a boy lugging two wooden pails.

But Diamante was happy to be the water boy. He was like water himself. Tasteless, odorless, with no apparent qualities, independent of earth and sky, malleable, fluid, and ready to assume the form of whatever contains him—but in truth unmoldable, resistant, dangerous even, and *necessary* in any event. The people from his village were afraid of water, though—water and death are always waiting behind the door, the old proverb went. All they had ever had from water was invasions and diseases, Saracens and malaria. His mother had often told him about the last incursion, which had made 1860 an inauspicious year. The pirates had come ashore at Scauri and made their way up to Minturno and the surrounding villages. They plundered and pillaged, killing men and children, so that the streets of Tufo, even Via San Leonardo, ran with rivers of blood and wine. Angela, who was six at the time, had saved herself by hiding inside a basket. She never went down to the sea again, though it was only a few miles away. The water was also the treacherous enemy of Antonio's hopes. He'd suffered terrible seasickness in his two ill-fated transatlantic crossings, while the city he was destined never to reach shimmered on the sea like an unrealizable dream. But Diamante had never believed all this. For him water was merely the reflection of his restlessness—his way of escape.

Water sought him out, and he would search for it wherever it was hiding. The stagnant water of the swamps, where opportunistic larvae wallow and irascible frogs splash. The clear, still water at the bottom of the well. The deep green waters of the Garigliano, flowing without banks and without obstacles across the parched plain to the sea. The blue waters of the Mediterranean, which had always beckoned him to faraway places, to departures, to freedom. And finally the great indigo waters of the ocean, cloudy and infinite under the Atlantic's dusty stars. After all, blue was the first color Diamante had ever seen; Angela had given birth to him in the fields of the Garigliano plain, where, despite her advanced pregnancy, she had gone at dawn to pick chicory, a basket balanced on her head. According to the people of the village, this was the reason mother and child had blue eyes while everyone else's were black. And now Diamante loved the American water that sloshed about in his pails, a prisoner reflecting the merciless clarity of the sky. But bit by bit he began to dream of running away, of abandoning his pails, the shovelers, and the rails. Of truly becoming a bird of passage, a migratory creature guided not by hunger but by the rhythm of the seasons—free. He dreamed of riding one of those trains whose lacerating whistles always startled him as they cut through the distance.

His dream train would take him to Penn Station. He would exit, cross streets that were now more familiar to him than the one his parents' house looked onto, walk through the city with the gold chain and cross between his lips, letting himself be guided by his happiness until he suddenly recognized the rancid smell of the Prince Street courtyard. His daydream would always end on the stairs—it always broke off before Vita appeared. He didn't want his radiant fiancée to share his nights in the freight car with the dog shit, lice, and rails. He wanted something better for her. As he trudged on, hunched under the weight of the water as his companions shouted and sometimes insulted or beat him for being late, he wondered how he could present himself to his girlfriend. Not a penny to his name, clad in rags like a vagabond, and turning feral like the dog Buck. Unable even to speak his own language. This time his team was made up of mountain people from the North who kept to themselves and were the pride of the Scottish inspectors. He didn't understand the Calabrese workers' dialect, so as evening set in and dark settled over the freight car, the best he could do was exchange a few words in their lingua franca—American. In the end he was reduced to hoping he'd be accepted by the Celts, and begged their respect.

One day an inspector sent by the Italian government to see about the conditions of the railroad workers asked him where he was from. "Torino," Diamante replied. The inspector asked if he was related to that old Federico Mazzucco, the watchmaker on Via Lagrange, and Diamante decided to take a chance. He said Federico was his grandfather. At that, the inspector invited him to drink a glass of cordial and launched into a reminiscence of old Federico Mazzucco; he'd been one of Garibaldi's Thousand and nearly got himself killed so that those scoundrels from the South could be called Italians, and now they had come to America and were making Italy seem like a country of tramps. It would have been better if they hadn't bothered to unite Italy and had left everything as it was. Diamante suffered inside, but told him he was right. When the inspector left, Diamante felt ashamed for having sold his fierce pride to the Great Northern Railway Line.

From then on he began to be assailed by the fear he had sold something even greater: his future. In those moments, he would hold Vita's chain in his lips to try to reassure himself. At night he would put it in his mouth and run it over his teeth. He had sold everything ex-

cept his stubborn determination to somehow make it. He wouldn't go
back to Vita empty-handed.

Diamante keeps the chain in his mouth because he's afraid of the
crooks, ever since they broke into the dormitory on payday to steal
their stipends. Since the shovelers weren't willing to be robbed, a huge
fight broke out in which the water boy participated with furious rage
and indisputable talent. But it was pointless; the thieves were armed
with axes and daggers. When they finally left, there was blood everywhere, and several of the workers had broken hands, noses, cheekbones. A poisoned silence, bristling with rancor, fell over the robbed,
beaten, and defeated men.

And yet Diamante's most precious possession wasn't stolen by the
crooks from the other camps. His own workmates took it. The northerners always say southerners have no class spirit, which is the reason
they're so backward. Diamante had never heard of this class spirit, but
he learned that your so-called comrades are capable of splitting open
your skull and tossing you in the river for a pinch of salt or a cap. Vita
had knitted that wool cap for him. They stole it at the end of the second season. The cold is merciless out on the plains. Two days later, the
cap reappeared on Raffaele Rotundo's head. Along with the talisman
chain and the blurry photograph from the automatic camera on Coney
Island, that cap is all he had left of Vita.

Diamante takes it back. He steals it while Rotundo is asleep, slipping it off his head with the ability of a trickster. He curls up under his
horse blanket and presses it to his face, searching for Vita's scent in the
musty wool. Vita smells of rosemary, sage, and pine nuts, of field balm,
sugar, and lemon verbena. She never wrote him. Not even one line.
Her letters must have gone astray; she's not a girl who's at a loss for
words. Diamante is maneuvering the handcart when they jump him.
They'd hidden behind a row of poplars. No one can save the water
boy. They stomp on his pails, crushing them under their boots. Then
they drag him into the grass, where they kick and punch him until he
finally decides to pull the ball of wool out from under his overalls. Rotundo jams it in his mouth, shoves it down his throat. Diamante can't
breathe. Vita's cap is choking, suffocating him. "Is this her?" Rotundo

taunts him, waving the photograph from Coney Island. "Is this your girl?" Diamante stretches his hand out, but someone nails him to the ground and he can't move. They pass the photograph around, making comments, but Diamante can't understand what they are saying because his ears are filled with blood. When Rotundo slips Vita's photograph into his jeans, Diamante breaks free and hurls himself at him. If he can't have it, then he'll destroy it because here in the camps a woman's image is even more precious than a gold cross. Men are capable of jerking off staring at the neck of a bottle or the wrinkled ass of Calamara's dog—just imagine what they'd do with the face of a smiling girl. But he can't get it. They hurl him onto the cart. He'll never know who landed the kick that split his lip.

The cut bleeds for hours, swells, and gets infected. Chewing is as painful as getting a tooth yanked. The rough scab cracks open all the time, so he can't smile anymore. Not that he has any desire to. All he feels is a furious rage—at the world, destiny, his employers, capitalists, the cowardly imbeciles they exploit, the crooks, and the losers. After a while, his mouth assumes its regular shape, and his rage, too, diminishes. But his lip remains slightly puckered, as if he were constantly unhappy or disapproving of something. Not even time will erase that scar: the only indelible sign of his years in America.

On the plains, time passes like the wind—there's no resistance. The year 1907 passed, as did 1908. Lots of people went back to Italy, but Diamante headed in the opposite direction. The rails dragged him farther west. Much farther west than he would have liked. Much farther east than what was awaiting him. Panic was spreading. America was going through one of its recurring "physiological" crises: companies closed, businesses quoted on the stock market failed, and the railway teams were forgotten at the end of the track. At the end of 1908 Diamante's team was abandoned in a forsaken camp somewhere in Minnesota. When the Company had announced it wouldn't renew the workers' contract, the foreman left with the last month's pay. The stock had dropped 50 percent in the Wall Street crash. Work was halted. They had to wait. It was election time. Maybe the crisis would pass quickly. The Republicans promised to take measures to repair the damage that was the legacy of eight euphoric years of Roosevelt's presidency, and Theodore's optimistic grin was swiftly abandoned, along with his spectacular wolf and wildcat hunts and his bombastic promises to destroy the power of the trusts who were secretly financing him. William Howard Taft was elected president—a politician whose incredible girth promised opulence for all. The men of bronze couldn't wait for the recovery. By the thousands they flooded steamships of the Veloce Line, Lloyd Sabaudo, and Navigazione Generale Italiana. They fled. Among them was Giuseppe Tucciarone. When he arrived in Tufo in 1908, he brought Antonio a letter from Diamante. *I'm well, I have work, and I'll send you something soon. Don't worry about me.* Diamante did not return. There was still something for him somewhere in America. He didn't know what it was, but he intended to find it.

He held on. Remained. He didn't become a shoveler or a foreman. Just as he wasn't able to whistle in front of Prophet's house, he wasn't able to threaten or beat his fellow workers. He would have never wanted to. He lacked the ambition, the desire. Diamante didn't move up in the camps. He was still a water boy, even when he turned sixteen, seventeen, eighteen. He became a master in the art of carrying water. A quick, steady pace on the way to the men, his body countering the weight of the water, the yoke parallel to his shoulders like a cross, back straight, knees bent, fingers firm and low on the ropes, five hands from the yoke. He learned a few tricks, such as pricking a tiny hole in the bottom of the pails so that they'll constantly get lighter along the way. On the way back, carry the pails differently. Don't stiffen your back, let your numb arm muscles relax, let the blood circulate, walk slowly, save energy—that's the most important thing— take advantage of those brief moments of freedom before you have to bend under the weight of another load. Every now and again, halt the handcar at a point equidistant from the campsite and the work area, stop and look at the sun, deep red in the sky like a swollen bruise.

The ties were awkwardly spaced, either too close together or too far apart, so Diamante danced along the tracks. His mind was blank, far away from everything and everyone. He listened to the sounds of silence, to the steady drip of water seeping through the cracks in the wood, the wind beating against the grass, the rain pelting the rails. Sometimes to keep his rhythm he would swing the pails and chant the words Vita had taught him so very long ago. The memory of her would summon up an ancient pain, deep, lacerating, and irremediable. It was a salutary pain. He eventually developed such an automatism that body, pails, water, handcar, tracks, yoke, ropes, and ties all merged into one. His body had memorized every movement and would remember them forever.

At the beginning of 1909, he still hadn't found a way to escape the inevitability of those rails, which knew neither curve nor deviation. The relentless straight line of the tracks told him there was no future in the railway. It was a life sentence.

Diamante was completely cut off from the world all those years. Just as he knew nothing about Vita, Nicola, and Geremia, he knew nothing about what was happening at home in Italy. The news of Amedeo's death never reached him; he would learn of it only years later. For a long time Diamante continued to carry water in his name, thinking on his future, and when he started writing to his father again, he suggested he send Amedeo—the favorite, the younger brother—to join him in America. Diamante wanted him here with him. Antonio didn't have the courage to write back explaining that Amedeo would never be able to join him because a mosquito bite had taken him when he was thirteen, poisoning him with malaria as he swam in the backwaters of the Garigliano one summer afternoon. Diamante didn't even know about the devastating earthquake in Messina. Only one piece of news reached him out on the great plains, and with the force of a dynamite explosion. He read it on a filthy scrap of newspaper in which the pluck-me store had wrapped his sardines. The news had nothing to do with him, but he was astonished nevertheless, and it made him feel inexplicably uneasy—a mysterious warning.

Enrico Caruso, the idol of the masses, the man every woman wanted to love, the star who every evening received aroused, hysterical women in his dressing room who were prepared to do anything in order to catch a glimpse of that impetuous Italian (and ready to report him for improper behavior if he didn't comply), had been cheated on by his own woman. By the only woman who mattered to him. While he wore out his voice singing in theaters all over America, the woman he'd lived with for almost ten years waited for him in Italy—in the Tuscan villa Caruso had bought as soon as he had struck it rich, as any Italian man in his position would have done. The woman, a soprano endowed with a certain talent, had given up her own career, as every Italian woman would have to do, and as Diamante hoped his woman would do one day, and decided to live only for him. To sacrifice her world and ambitions, if she had any, in favor of his. Caruso could spend only the summer months in that monumental villa, pompously christened Bellosguardo and crammed with baroque armoires, Renaissance trunks, and papier-mâché figures from nativity scenes. In May of 1907, an anonymous letter writer was pleased to inform him that his beloved was living with another man as husband and wife. A certain Cesare Romati. The chauffeur.

Caruso refused to believe the gossip. He didn't give a damn about the rumors that crossed the ocean and knocked on the door of his apartment on the fourteenth floor of the Plaza Hotel. He would believe only her. He departed. Ada met him at the Milan train station. Caruso decided to be magnanimous. Despite and because of her betrayal, he loved her even more than before and was ready to ignore all that had transpired. They could carry on, or start again. On one condition, however. She had to send the chauffeur away and never see him again. Ada agreed. They were reconciled.

In the fall Caruso said goodbye to his rediscovered Ada and left for a tour in Hungary, which ended in a fiasco. He sang in Vienna, Leipzig, Hamburg, Frankfurt, Berlin, and in November returned to New York. The following spring, as he was on his way to Italy, he received the atrocious news that Ada had grown tired of waiting for him and had left with the chauffeur. Caruso spent the month of July indecorously and pathetically pursuing them all over Italy and France. In vain. He wrote a desperate letter to his friend Marziale Sisca, director of the magazine *La Follia* in New York. "They have broken my heart in the most beautiful moment of my life! I have wept much, but those tears have not helped in the least. I hope that with time my poor, brutally shattered heart will heal, and life will seem brilliant once again."

The news of the "troubles of a tenor" received enormous play in the newspapers because everything having to do with the star—even the cut of his whiskers—made its way onto the front page. But perhaps, too, because the story clashed with the image of the Italian male as a great lover that had begun to take hold in the American imagination. The *Daily Telegraph* and even the austere *New York Times* concerned themselves with his "broken heart." A Montevideo newspaper sent a reporter to ask him how he was feeling. He replied bleakly: "My only hope is not to die old. In general, death is preferable to life."

The blow was deadly. Caruso canceled all his contracts and wanted only to disappear in some forsaken corner of the world—alone. He went to Tunisia, Naples, Leipzig. Then he returned to New York, and naturally he kept performing—the show must go on. He sang, even if every spectator in the upper galleries knew his whole sad story and studied him in their opera glasses to see how he would mask the anguish of abandonment. Poorly, it seems, even though he was a good actor. He sang and sank into a vertiginous melancholy from which he never recovered.

At the end of January 1909, the fugitive Ada presented herself—with no warning—at the Knickerbocker Hotel, where Caruso had moved so as to forget the Plaza. Caruso flew out of the bathtub to chase her away. Grooms, elevator operators, doormen, neighbors, curious bystanders, and his fans listened with the greatest of pleasure to his screams and her sobs (and vice versa). The insults they exchanged. Ada left again, this time with a check (reputed to be for a miserable amount because she hadn't come to ask for money) and a ferocious desire for revenge. Caruso remained with his rage and remorse. Shortly afterward, he suffered an emotional collapse, the first of many which would recur frequently over the years. He developed a hypertrophic node on his larynx, possibly malignant. He was unconsciously attempting to destroy his only truly precious possession—his voice. Surgery was necessary, but it was impossible to say whether he would ever sing again. They cut his throat with a scalpel. Even his most fervent admirers were saying that Enrico Caruso was finished.

Diamante mulled the news over for months. The moral of the story was not to leave a woman alone for too long; betrayal is only waiting for the right moment. And sooner or later, the right moment presents itself. He absolutely had to find a way to leave the railway and get back to New York.

The Right to Happiness

The phallus rises up against the muggy, whitened sky, soaring above their heads like a votive candle. Who knows if it is begging for fertility and hardness or giving thanks for having achieved one and, especially, the other. The throng of people on Mott Street trembles and pulses with excitement, then lunges and sweeps her forward. Vita is swallowed up by the procession. She stands on tiptoe, she elbows and shoves, but to no avail. Beyond all the backs, bodies, and voices of the crowd, there is only the statue, suspended in precarious equilibrium on dozens of shoulders. The majestic phallus bends forward, as if offering a blessing, then totters back as if it were about to fall, leans to one side, then straightens up, steady. And then it disappears.

Hundreds of paper flags—green, red, and white—are waving in the air. They have been distributed by associations eager to transform the saint into a patriot. But the real reason the crowd waves them so wildly is to make a bit of breeze. Even though it's only ten in the morning, the air is heavy and oppressive, like mucilage. Curious onlookers who have come downtown to experience for free the enactment of "authentic Mediterranean folklore" stand out with their reddened faces, but there aren't as many of them as for the Feast of San Gennaro. The Americans uptown have left the city by August 16. But nobody from this neighborhood leaves. Not one of the kids has ever missed a procession in all these years. Not because of their devotion to the saint, but for the phalluses. On this day, whoever manages to touch the wart sprinkled with holy water is guaranteed his virility. If Diamante is back in New York, she'll find him here among the crowd.

The saint has a gentle look. His mouth is painted carmine and his hands ochre to make his skin look presentable, but he is the patron saint of the sick and the plague-stricken, so blotches disfigure his cheeks and nose. This makes him the favorite saint of the boys, who suffer from acne every day. He's the only one Coca-Cola calls on when he contemplates with terror the pimples on his forehead. Or maybe the saint is so popular because he's the protector of convicts. At any rate, he is an understanding saint, for he has suffered greatly. And so whenever they carry him out of the Church of the Transfiguration, people scramble to kiss his pestilent swellings. Petards, Bengal lights, and fireworks paint the white sky with cherry-colored smoke; the rhythmic drum rolls are deafening and unleash frenzied dancing, transforming the procession into a sweaty wave of contorted bodies; yet everyone still prays devoutly, and even those who don't believe in miracles find themselves making the sign of the cross. For all of us are wounded, contaminated by some sort of plague, even if we don't know what it's called.

On Mott Street nothing has changed. There's still the tavern run by Elmer's father, with mismatched tables and tin plates. At the corner of Spring Street, Gennaro Lombardi's bakery sells pizza, the only one in the whole country to do so. There's the Chinese emporium where years ago Diamante bought her a silk shawl. At number 178 there's even the sign for Doctor Vincenzo Cione's office; he distributes the *fosfymbine* of Professor Carusi of the Royal University of Naples, which is capable of radically curing functional impotence. The Prince Street boys used to have a grand time hurling indecent epithets at the humiliated souls passing through that door. Back then Vita didn't even know what functional impotence was. Not as if she knows all that well now. The procession drags her in the opposite direction, prevents her from heading down Prince Street and climbing the stairs, trusting that greasy rope, to see if the horn that wards off the evil eye is still on the door of her old home. But the past will only return when the cows come home, and cats begin to talk. There's no point in looking back.

All praise for Saint Rocco, who heals us of typhus and tuberculosis, syphilis and nephritis, raging insanity, trachoma, silicosis, and the rest. Those who have prayed for his mercy and those who have been granted it swarm behind the statue, offering up their thanks. A cedar leg carved by the best woodworker in the neighborhood, for which someone has spent all his savings; a wax breast with a rosy nipple, which initially inspires ecstasy and then disgust in the two reporters from the *World*; a foot that seems to be made out of some organic substance; a lung, a cloth heart, and then, bringing up the rear, a whole range of phalluses made of wood, stone, porcelain, papier-mâché, and clay. She has found it again. Vita's gaze fixes on a dazzling white marble phallus. The woman who holds it is not looking at anyone and is not interested in anything else. She merely smiles and utters a prayer only she knows.

All of a sudden, amid the confraternity of men bent under the weight of holiness, drenched with sweat and done in by the heat and exertion, Vita recognizes him. He is so tall that the corner he's carrying rises up and makes Saint Rocco seem about to trip. His arms are muscular, used to lifting heavy things and unloading ballast. He's dressed in a dark, double-breasted suit with six pockets, rather outrageous compared to the miserable outfit the saint is wearing. His hair is greased back, his cheeks smooth, and the eyelashes shadowing his dark eyes are so long it looks as if he's wearing mascara. That serene and distant look, the mystical smile of Merluzzo. Vita starts, steps back, and tries to hide, but it's too late. Rocco, his head bent to one side so as to better offer his neck to martyrdom, has already seen her. His face registers surprise, amazement, and, she would say, a certain pleasure. He smiles slightly, just as he did six years ago when he met her for the first time in that crowded Prince Street kitchen.

But where is Diamante? Could that be him, that slight figure leaning against the church door? Oh God, it looks just like him. Yes, it's him. But no, on second thought, he doesn't have blue eyes. He's just some pickpocket, come to earn his bread. The whole neighborhood is here, gathered behind the saint. Until recently, this was simply the festival for the people of Lucania, but now it belongs to everyone—saints, like vagabonds, don't have a country. Vita recognizes her old neighbors from the apartment across the hall. She sees the street vendors, shopkeepers, pharmacists, doctors, obstetricians, charlatans, undertakers, the coffin maker who works for Cozza, even Mr. Bongiorno himself, complete with Panama hat and bamboo walking stick, as well as the black errand boys and friends of friends. And there in that crowd of people praying, dancing, begging forgiveness, weeping, moved by desperation or nostalgia, is Rocco, who certainly has come to expiate some mortal sin. But no Diamante.

"He never shows up on Prince Street anymore," the newspaper boy tells her after begging her to buy his last copy. She recognizes him, too—Giose Cirillo, known as Cherry, one of the boys who peddled the *Araldo* with Diamante years ago. The last time anyone saw Diamante was in Oaio, he was working as a water boy for the railway. "Ohio?" Vita snorts. "Even I know that. But where is he?" Smitten, Cherry studies Vita and fans himself with a newspaper. She's going on fifteen. Her black hair falls over her ears, framing her voluptuous neck. Her striped dress fits her well, and the thin cloth highlights the eloquent curve of her breasts. Cherry is overcome by a powerful passion and takes advantage of the festive confusion to press against her. He savors her firm flesh for a moment. "I dunno, Vita," he answers blissfully. "Somewhere out West."

The procession follows the statue into the Church of His Most Precious Blood at 115 Baxter Street. There isn't room for everyone and lots of people are hovering outside, thronging in the street. Others flow back toward the booths, hoping for some shade under the shop awnings. Vita already knew Diamante had gone to Ohio. Where else could he have gone? Other boys from home were out there. But why didn't he answer me when I wrote that I wanted to join him, just as we'd planned? I had even scraped together some money sewing linens for the school. Maybe he was mad because you took so long to write him back, she thinks. Ten days after he left, he sent you a postcard with a picture of the great Ohio River, but you didn't get it until a year later because nobody lives at Prince Street anymore. How you longed to join him at the end of the tracks! You wanted to live in a freight car and become the girl bride of a water boy. But maybe Diamante preferred things this way. He was sure you wouldn't go anywhere, that all he had to do was come back. He'd find you right where he left you, on the tracks of the train depot along the Hudson River, where the trains you'll never take leave from.

Vita elbows her way into the church among the women dressed in mourning. In the dim light she makes out the statue, the priest in his holy vestments, and behind the altar, Merluzzo, who wipes the sweat from his forehead with a silk handkerchief and adjusts his tie. Then she witnesses a scene that is as absurd as seeing Nicola in a millionaires' club or herself in a nun's habit: Rocco is singing in the choir, singing the praises of God. Jesus, it's all true. What's happened to you? What's happened to me? As she watches him, looking devout behind the altar in his dark blue double-breasted suit, she remembers how Geremia used to get up early on Sunday mornings and sneak down the stairs; Rocco would make fun of him because the only people who go to mass are lice who are content to cling to the hair of a prick; they hang there, miserable and uncomfortable, while the prick has fun and enjoys himself. Now Rocco's voice rises above the other members of the choir. A clear voice, sincere and in tune.

"Merluzzo's generous, he always buys my last copy," Cherry murmurs, pulling on her sleeve. "But you, Vita, what you waiting for? Don't you remember how it works? Come on, it's my last one." As she rummages in her purse for change—she wants to buy that damned newspaper—Cherry whispers that Rocco's tight with Don Casimiro now, ever since he took that confirmation class. "Isn't he a bit big to be confirmed?" Vita laughs as she fishes out a quarter wedged between her horn comb and the kissproof lipstick that her girlfriends at the school had given her to celebrate her return to the real world, but that she still hasn't gotten up the courage to use. "Yeah, but what kind of man are you if you haven't ever been confirmed? You couldn't even get married in church—they wouldn't have you." "But Merluzzo doesn't want to get married," Vita smiles. "People only get married when they have no other choice, or because they're desperate, or so as not to lose someone they can't live without. Besides, revolutionaries and bandits don't have women."

Cherry eyes her, hesitant. "He didn't have time for women before," he declares. "And now he does?" Vita inquires cautiously as she places the coin in his grimy palm. The newspaper boy doesn't respond. He foists the last copy of yesterday's paper on her and disappears triumphantly, abandoning her in the midst of the devout ecstasy of the crowd, staring bewilderedly at Rocco singing the *Ave Maria*. Despite his crooked boxer's nose, his blasphemous words, and the bones he's broken all over the neighborhood, he still looks like an angel. And he stares at her as he sings, not even pretending to look elsewhere—as if she were the only woman in the world despite all those others armed with marble legs, nipples, and phalluses. He runs his eyes over her, measuring how she has changed in these last three years, and the smile hovering on his lips tells her he's pleased with what he sees. Vita, without knowing why, is flattered. She should go before mass finishes, go back to Harlem, where Agnello has holed up. Agnello has forbidden her to see Rocco, and she wants to try living with her father now—to start all over again, as if she had landed only today. But she doesn't move. Instead she waits for who knows what, and when the choir stops singing and mass is over, she lets him approach her. She lets him squeeze her hips with an intimacy she should not permit.

Vita finds herself licking a vanilla ice cream and walking next to him in the muggy streets; it's noon already, and the sun is high in the sky. They head toward the elevated stop and Vita blushes when Rocco says, "What a fetching little kitten you've become, Vita, a princess. And that striped dress suits you real fine." Vita had sewn it herself when she was in school, out of scraps from the Newark factories. She fans herself with yesterday's newspaper and waits for the train, cursing herself for having come to the Feast of San Rocco, but also pleased that a young man like Rocco—how old must he be now? Twenty-three? Twenty-four?—has noticed she's grown up. Rocco's so spiffed and polished now he looks like one of those American benefactors who used to bring us gifts on Sundays. She curses herself again, but at the same time she's glad the train hasn't arrived so she can dally at his side a few minutes longer while kids squabble over who gets to shine his shoes and women toss him little smiles as they walk by. What is Rocco like? Reassuring. Yes, that's it. Protective. So big and tall, he makes you feel safe. And even though it sounds strange, he's sweet. Like vanilla ice cream.

Everything about him oozes a brazen-faced affluence, an insolent supremacy. He's made it. He's arrived. Who would have thought it? Rich, he'd wanted to become rich. But nobody believed he would succeed. They all thought he'd end up in prison, but she was the one who'd landed there instead. When she asks him where he went to live after Agnello had to close the boardinghouse, he says he stayed in a bunch of different places, but nothing was as good as when they were all together. Agnello shouldn't have run off, he should have confided in him. Rocco would have helped him, would have gotten him out of trouble and kept those gossiping ogresses from dragging her off to the Children's Aid Society. If anybody wants to harm Agnello, Rocco'll put them six feet under because Agnello's like a father to him and Vita is like his little sister. But that's how it went, you can't change the past. Rocco lives in a real house now—with heating, a bathtub, running water. He doesn't want to tell her the address, though, and merely says that it's somewhere near Eighth Street. Vita knows Eighth Street is above Houston, which means that Rocco has crossed the poverty line and really lives in America now. Then, without the least bit of irony, Rocco boasts that he now directs Mr. Bongiorno's place. "You mean you're a grave digger now, too?" Vita interrupts him, laughing, and Rocco nods vaguely because it's both true and not exactly true, but how can he possibly explain this to Vita, who spent three years in a reform school for bad girls? Surely they must have brainwashed her.

Vita meets Rocco's enveloping gaze without the least embarrassment, and when he finally gets to the point and asks about Diamante, she tells him they're engaged. She explains that Diamante went to work for the railway, but they've kept in touch all these years with the power of their thoughts. Distance doesn't matter. She can always tell when Diamante's thinking of her, and she helps the moon to paint her features on clouds and train windows. That way Diamante won't forget about her. But he's coming back now. "You remember how my eyes could move things, Rocco? Well, they still do. Only now I don't care about locks and knives anymore. Now I want him. I'm calling him—and he's coming." Rocco nods skeptically. An unemployed man comes to ask him for a loan; Rocco keeps him at a safe distance but fishes in the pocket of his jacket and neatly produces a dollar bill, just to show he's always ready to help those in need. "I'm glad Diamante has a girl like you," he murmurs. "I've always loved Diamante." Vita's not sure he's telling the truth. Rocco got into a lot of trouble because of Diamante, even though she can't remember why exactly, or maybe she never really knew.

Rocco notices that her eyes sparkle when she talks about Diamante, and he begins to understand how a girl like Vita could survive three endless years of reform school. Diamante gave her hope, somehow. The vision of what could be. And she gave it to him. When the train doors close, Rocco waves to her as if she were leaving for a long voyage and he might never see her again. Vita stands at the window and doesn't even realize she has blown him a kiss.

Things Vita learned at reform school:
1. There are very few bad girls under sixteen. In all of 1906, only 1,011 of them were brought to trial, as opposed to 9,418 boys. One hundred thirteen were sent before the court because they were morally depraved or in danger of becoming so because of their environment. Forty-four were accused of running away from home. Thirty-one of petty theft. Four of robbery, but they were acquitted for lack of evidence. One of attempted suicide.
2. All the girls in for petty theft are Italian.
3. Vita was locked up in order to remove her from "a degraded family environment." And to offer her an education. For her own good, in other words.
4. In America everyone's a foreigner, and everyone becomes an American. Even the Statue of Liberty is a foreigner, French to be precise. There was a competition for who would write the poem. A woman won. Her name was Emma Lazarus.
5. The poem goes like this:

"Keep, ancient lands, your storied pomp!" cries she
With silent lips. "Give me your tired, your poor,
Your huddled masses yearning to breathe free,
The wretched refuse of your teeming shore.
Send these, the homeless, tempest-tost to me,
I lift my lamp beside the golden door!"

6. No one remembers who Emma Lazarus is, but Vita had never read a more beautiful poem. No one had ever explained to her that you can learn to read not just to decipher the labels in the stores and the price signs stuck on top of a pyramid of tomatoes, but to read poems that seem written just for you.

7. Anyone can become president of the United States.

8. The right to happiness is provided for in the Constitution. Everyone has the right to be happy.

In the fall of 1909, Rocco developed the habit of taking a Turkish bath with Cozza at the Ansonia Hotel. They would get undressed in the same room and stretch out on the tiles, covered only with a white towel. Mustachioed employees would massage and rub them down. They always arrived at the same time, and when they'd sweated enough, they'd recover their strength dining in the hotel restaurant. By now many people thought they were father and son. Even though one was as thin as a skeleton and the other big as a tree trunk, they had started to resemble each other—the same seraphic gait and the same dignified and cautious manner. They were very generous with the waiters; as a result, they were always served first, even if they arrived last. At the end of the meal, Rocco would go to the bathroom to fix the wave on his forehead, which time and the inexorable liquefaction of brilliantine had caused to droop. And while he was there, he would take advantage of the adjacent door to look in on the kitchen.

Vita would have preferred he not see her in there; thirty people were whirling about simultaneously, tending to pots on the stoves, to sauces and steaks, and she was the newest and the least regarded of all. In the din, their exchanges were false and affectionate as between two relatives. Vita kept him up to date on Nicola's sudden job changes: until September he'd been a porter at the Ansonia Hotel, which is why he'd been able to recommend her to the man overseeing the kitchen. Unfortunately Coca-Cola was scatterbrained; he mixed up the room numbers, spoke a garbled, indecent American that horrified the guests, and fell in love with the room-service waitresses, leaving suitcases in the elevator to go chasing after them. In short, he was fired, leaving her alone in this smoky Babel where everyone spoke a language all their own and didn't understand anyone else, or even try to. Vita wanted to leave, too, change jobs, but these were hard times, a recession, there wasn't any work, so she had to hang on to her place at the Ansonia. At school they'd found her a position in the house of an American doctor who lived with his wife and two small children on Madison Avenue, and she'd really wanted to take it; she was curious to get to know an American family close up. But Agnello put his foot down: it was a bad idea to send a girl as naive as his daughter into the home of strangers. The Poles and the Irish can do these barbaric things if they want, but not the Italians, and he wasn't about to let his daughter go work for strangers. Agnello is so backward he doesn't realize the Ansonia is much worse. The Greek scullery boys repeat to her the only American words they know, words that describe the female anatomy; the Basque waiter gropes her when he places his orders; and the Romanian maître d' follows her home. Vita stays glued to the other women in the kitchen for fear that the maître d' will jump her even though he's past fifty. She has no choice but to stay put at the Ansonia for now, while Coca-Cola, thanks to Agnello's pleading, got a job with Rizzo selling bananas at a store on 126th Street.

Rocco was sympathetic and offered to find her a less tiring job with some friends in the neighborhood, such as taking care of the children of one of the Bongiorno Bros. But Vita couldn't accept because Agnello didn't know she'd started seeing him again. She begged him to look out for Nicola instead, who was miserable selling bananas, and asked him what Nicola had ever done to him to deserve his indifference. Coca-Cola was hurt because Rocco shunned him as if he had the mange, when he would've gotten himself killed for Rocco. That was precisely the reason, but Rocco couldn't very well tell her, so he lied, inventing some excuse. And all the while he would shift his massive body to make room for the waiters, who swung through the double doors balancing trays stacked with dishes without even spilling a drop of the wine left in the glasses. They shouted their orders, left slips of paper on the shelf, railed against the slowness of the service, demanded urgently their *filets saignants, escargots,* or *civet de lapin,* while counting their tips. Not that they had any intention of sharing them. Even if the customers were satisfied, the tips never made it to the kitchen.

All of this filled Rocco with repugnance. He couldn't explain to himself why he kept going back to the restaurant at the Ansonia Hotel, where they served French food, besides. Respectable people ate French cuisine as a mark of distinction. But French cuisine is all sauce, a strange concoction useful for covering things up. Rocco prefers things—and people—that don't hide themselves, that are what they seem. Maybe because they're the opposite of him.

He had to go already because Bongiorno was waiting for him at their table, and Vita couldn't even say goodbye because her hands were covered in flour and smelled of frying oil and sauce. The stink of frying clung to her clothes and penetrated her skin, as did the grease and scraps of chewed, picked-over remains abandoned on dirty plates. Soap wasn't enough to wash it all off her hands, face, and hair. Even on the street you could recognize someone who had just left a kitchen because they walked enveloped in a cloud, a nasty stagnation. All the perfumes, colors, and tastes remained on the other side of the door—in the dining room, where feathery laughter and polite manners fluttered, where jewels and necklaces sparkled. On this side there was only the smell and the exhaustion.

Not that Rocco even noticed this suffering. His gaze lingered instead on Vita's white apron, her bare arms as they rolled out dough, her face aglow with a mysterious light. He couldn't tear his eyes away from that face; it was so absorbed and concentrated—as if the only thing in the world were the dough she would never taste. Vita could grow distracted and concentrate with the same intensity, lose herself in you when she talked with you, and forget herself and you with the same denial. That ability to forget yourself is the secret of all spontaneity, its greatest mystery. That perfect and extraordinary state of being within yourself. He could have told her he'd killed a man or changed his name, his history, his past, that he'd sold everything he'd ever loved in exchange for something that he wanted even more but that at times seemed like nothing more than a flimsy illusion—but Vita would not have heard him. There was nothing as beautiful as watching someone so concentrated in herself. Vita knew how to transform illusion into reality. This world was not to her liking, so she invented another one. Perhaps the people who make this world livable aren't those who try to change it, as he'd believed in doing, but the ones like Vita. Maybe this is what it means to dream. Rocco put his hands in his pockets and reluctantly tore himself away.

And then he was gone—his dark head floating behind the glass in the dining room aglitter with lights, his huge frame weaving among the tables, slowly moving away from her. He bent over Mr. Bongiorno's shiny baldness, helped him into his overcoat, and then preceded him out into the treacherous obscurity of the night.

At that moment Rocco finally understood why he kept coming back to the Ansonia Hotel. He was in love with the love that Vita radiated for another man.

On the day of Vita's fifteenth birthday, Rocco offered to see her home. He saw that Vita was expecting his proposal and kicked himself for having waited so long. Maybe she'd been expecting it since that first day at the Feast of San Rocco. He's never been able to understand women. Not when they invite you and not when they reject you. All he knows is how exhausting a woman is, how much attention she demands, how much of you. And the worst thing about women is that they expect you to fall in love with them, or at least to say you have. But Vita declined. She always went home with the other women in order to avoid the attentions of the Romanian and the other suspicious characters who roam the streets of New York at night. "But I can give you a lift in Mister's car," Rocco insisted. He knew everyone admired Cozza's new Hudson Touring with its silver wheel rims, slim briarwood steering wheel, padded seats, convertible top, its windshield to keep out the dust, its roaring engine and huge headlights towering above the hood as on a ship. Rocco navigated brilliantly amid the anarchic traffic of New York. He honked to warn unfortunate pedestrians to get out of the way and sped up and down Mulberry Street humiliating the old-fashioned carts pulled by horses and donkeys. But he was generous and farsighted; he let the shoe-shine boys polish the body and the street urchins climb on the running boards to take a look at the complicated system of levers and gears. He'd never given anyone a ride, however. But ever since he'd seen Vita again, he'd wanted to have her climb in beside him.

Why had she told him no? After twelve hours wasted closed up in the kitchen, certainly she deserved a ride in the evening air? And Rocco was so dignified and mysterious in his double-breasted suit, his hair all shiny; he fascinated her and she was always disappointed when he didn't come and say hello. She wasn't sure if he was really the crook Agnello said he was—maybe Agnello bad-mouthed him out of envy, because things were going well for Rocco but not for him. But it didn't affect her, no matter what. Cowboys shot and killed, too, and the public applauded them. Vita's day off was invariably spent at a movie theater in Harlem, chewing popcorn, hating the sheriffs, cheering for the gunslingers, and dreaming of being kidnapped by a lone knight who would carry her off into the desert with the sky for a roof and a saddle for a pillow. If Rocco were an American, he'd probably be a cowboy.

Agnello never wanted to hear his name again. Didn't want to have to ask him permission to survive. He had a cart now—he sold coal in the winter, ice in the summer. Rain or shine, Agnello peddled his wares all day to the Harlem shopkeepers. The blocks of ice would melt, leaving a wet trail as if to mark his way home. All he wanted was to live in peace with his children in a neighborhood where no one knew anything about his store, a Circassian woman named Lena, a certain Coca-Cola who played with fire, or Vita's having spent three years in a school for bad girls. Where no one had to call him Uncle Agnello. Rocco was done with the past as well. He still felt a flicker of affection for the man who'd been a second father to him, but now there was Mr. Bongiorno. Vita wasn't interested in Rocco's plans. She'd stopped making plans and didn't want to live in the past or the future. She lived in the present, as always. Vita studied Rocco's broad shoulders, his snub nose, his lips, red and dark like a French wine. He was leaning stiffly against some shelves in the kitchen amid clouds of steam, an absent look on his face. Everybody said he only loved Soot; that women were less important to him than his cat. But Vita didn't think of herself like other women. "Okay," she said. "I'll come."

She crossed the streets of Manhattan standing up, leaning on the windshield, oblivious to the rain drumming on her head and running down her face. Even on a Sunday evening there were people everywhere. On the sidewalks, and waiting in line in front of theaters. In November the contagious Christmas spirit had already begun to spread through the city, tempting people to spend money and have fun. This infuriated the puritans, whose bellicose proclamations proposed closing the theaters and movie houses in order to sanctify the holiday and force New Yorkers to pray. Fortunately, they were unsuccessful. Movie houses remained open on Sunday, seeing as how they earned millions, especially if they showed real box-office attractions—films with cowboys and Indians, shoot-outs, and chase scenes. Rocco clutched the steering wheel with his gloves and couldn't bring himself to head uptown to Harlem. He swerved, turned back to Fifth Avenue, headed downtown along the darkened park, drove under Christmas lights strung in festoons above the streets, accelerated, scaring pedestrians and street vendors, and then braked suddenly so he could see her startle with fear and cling to the windshield. So he could see her smile and hear her bright laughter. Vita didn't realize how beautiful she'd become, how deep her eyes had gotten. How attractive a woman unaware of her own beauty is. Vita has no faith in her charm because she doesn't know she has it—she only trusts her convictions and feelings. This state of grace is so brief—and so precarious. He wanted to pull her toward him and bury his mouth in her hair.

After half an hour, they were nearly frozen. He couldn't suggest they celebrate her birthday in his beautiful apartment complete with fireplace. Instead he slowed in front of the Café Boulevard, a cheery Hungarian beer hall on Second Avenue and Tenth Street, patronized predominantly for its cabaret and a Gypsy orchestra, where astute Italian dockworkers went to pick up stunning Hungarian girls with green eyes. A place for sailors, thugs, and whoremongers. Not suitable for

Vita—but what place was suitable for Vita? Rocco'd always had the feeling he didn't really know her, that she had never really let him see what she was capable of. She had never made objects move for him, set a rival on fire, turned in her father. She had never called him. He had a better idea. He picked up speed again, drove a few blocks, and pulled up in front of the darkened funeral home. Vita said she didn't want to disturb the dead. But Rocco was thinking that, with all the people who don't mind their own business, at least the dead can't gossip.

In the hall where the wakes were held, Rocco lit a candelabra and some votive candles thick as logs. He pulled the curtain to hide the catafalque looming in the chapel, turned the crucifix to the wall so he wouldn't be pierced with rebuke, and put Enrico Caruso on the phonograph. Now he knew who Cavaradossi was and why he was dying in such despair. He knew *Rigoletto, Aida, Carmen*, and *L'Elisir*, and had even been to the Metropolitan Opera House a few times. The opera per se bored him, because it was all papier-mâché and rhetoric, make-believe and pomposity—nothing authentic. But if he closed his eyes and lost himself in Caruso's passionate, masculine voice, he felt he was back on Prince Street with all the other kids, with Geremia cranking the handle, Coca-Cola getting his fingerprints on the records, and Diamante not understanding a thing about the music but too proud to admit it. With Lena, her shawl around her hips and the American son in her womb, telling them stealing is a sin, and Vita, all sleepy and bewildered because her secret father had found her. The applause made the opera house shake and told him Enrico Caruso had triumphed once more. But the kitchen on Prince Street no longer existed.

Vita started feeling edgy—it was late, she shouldn't be out at this hour. And never, never, never with a man. The waxed floor creaked under their feet. The empty chairs rebuked her for her boldness. Here where people came to weep for the loss of a loved one, she had come to celebrate having found someone again. But not the one she wanted. Rocco wasn't Diamante. He couldn't be more different. She should have been ashamed—and yet she felt no trace of shame. Rocco put his arms around her and Vita, instead of telling him to leave her alone the way she wanted to, felt her knees tremble. Rocco placed his mouth on hers, and when their lips touched, she felt she was sinking into a dream and didn't want to wake up. Rocco sensed that Vita did not want a tender, cautious, and respectful kiss. She wanted to be kissed for real. And so he kissed her with an amazing sweetness, lingering, exploring, sucking, nibbling—and she forgot all about the funeral home and the smell of fried food and wilted flowers that infiltrated the hall. They stayed there in the flickering candlelight, standing still and kissing in the middle of that too-silent hall surrounded by empty, spying chairs, until her tongue was dry and her lips began to hurt.

The Track Gang

In the summer of 1909 one of Diamante's mates, a jovial type who played the harmonica in the evenings and in the day talked about how beautiful his wife was, how he missed her the way someone else would miss his own lung, proposed that they make themselves permanently disabled. Agosto Guerra had heard that the Company would compensate anyone who suffered a serious injury while working. Substantial compensation. Up to fifteen hundred dollars. But you had to lose a hand or a foot at least—something that truly prevented you from working. Agosto had decided to make himself disabled. Fifteen hundred dollars could alter his destiny. He would open a construction company. Based on what he's seen, America is still half empty. They've got to fill it somehow. Whoever dedicates himself to building houses won't ever be short of work. Not only that, in ten years he'll be a millionaire. Since Agosto was generous and liked the laconic water boy, he confided in him and suggested they go in on it together.

Diamante was enticed, and started asking himself what exactly he could do without. A foot was out of the question. Walking and running were as essential to him as breathing. On Sundays, when his companions went up to the first camp to get drunk and scuffle with the men from the other teams—it was a way of working off their frustrations—Diamante would head out across the plain, walking over the arid and barren turf until he was swallowed up by land and silence. He always came back after dark but never got lost. He could reach the other ocean on foot, just following the sunset. Could he give up an ear? He didn't understand a thing about music, after all, and no one had ever taught him. He'd been the only one on Prince Street who wasn't crazy about the phonograph, and the only time he whistled was when he had to be the "lighthouse." When Agosto Guerra played his harmonica in the freight car, Diamante would hide his head under his blanket because the melody evaporating in the dark reminded him of Vita and his vanished dream. But he liked to listen. He picked up everything—conversations, nuances, news, prejudices, allusions, noises. He could identify the rumble of a storm miles off and the rustle of a serpent in the grass. Even the gurgle of water at the bottom of the well. No, he couldn't give up an ear. A hand? But a one-handed man can't hold a woman. And even though it had been three years since he'd held one and he had almost forgotten how to do it, no memory was so sweet as that of tracing a woman's velvet back with both hands, caressing her breasts with all ten fingers. He'd wished he'd had a hundred fingers then. Or would nine be enough? What if he lost a finger? But Agosto warned him that according to the Northern Pacific a finger was only worth five hundred dollars. And five hundred dollars isn't enough to change your destiny. An eye. All it would take is the tin fork with the crooked tines he used to stir his beans. With one eye you can still see colors and distances. But the sky had fallen into Diamante's eyes and he didn't want to throw away the only piece of sky he'd ever been given. Lungs are indispensable. So are the heart, brain, liver. Maybe his spleen. Or a kidney. He could sacrifice a kidney. But how? "With a shovel," Agosto suggested. "I'm an artist with the shovel. I know where your kidney is; it's in your back, low down. I'll crush it in one blow." Diamante accepted. In exchange, he would cut off Agosto's left leg with the hatchet. Afterward, they would say it was the train.

One evening on the way back to camp, Agosto climbed onto the handcar with Diamante. They pumped for a few hundred yards and

then at the switch let the handcar run on the wrong track. Everything was still. Only the orb of the sun moved, grazing the edges of the earth and setting them ablaze as it descended. This was all Diamante knew of America. It didn't look like anything, but had its own barren beauty. There wasn't a hollow or tree where they could hide. No obstacle to temper the light or alter the profile of things. They were as visible to their teammates as Indians to the sentinels in the desert; their unbroken shadows caressed the horizon. They let the handcar roll on until the backs of the men returning to camp were a mere glow in the distance. The handcar glistened in the stubbly grass. Diamante blocked the wheels.

Agosto thrust the shovel into the earth, sat on the blade, and took a sip of grappa from his flask. He must have perceived some hesitation on the water boy's face because he said, "You should never turn back in life, you have to be prepared to make sacrifices in order to move forward." He, for example, what did he need a leg for? He always had the other one. Instead of keeping a leg that had never carried him anywhere, and Diamante a kidney that was only good for filtering piss, they would build houses ten stories tall, with real windows. Casements, not like the ones in this fucking America, where you can't even throw open the window in the morning but have to stick your head out under a guillotine. They'd have their families come live in those houses. They'd bring their parents, their brothers, and most important, their women. He'd bring his wife and Diamante his girl—he had a girl, didn't he? Being eighteen, he must. "I have a girl," Diamante said. "With tiny hands and eyes as black as coal."

"Let's go, boy," Agosto interrupted. It was pointless to stand there dreaming. Diamante slid the hatchet out from under the handcar, where he'd hidden it the night before. A rudimentary hatchet with an irregular blade, like a saw. "It'll hurt, you know. Are you sure?" he asked doubtfully. "I'm sure. Another month here, and I'll hurl myself in front of a train. I'll get a wooden leg. My children will walk for me—I've already walked enough." Diamante hesitated. The diffusing light confused him. Agosto stared at him—his eyes were the color of a rotten banana peel. He was decidedly ugly. But those eyes shone with hope. Diamante thought of Agosto's children; he had six. He must be a good father. He never fought, never got drunk, was a man of solid principles. How could he cut off the leg of a man like that? "Okay," said Agosto. "I'll do it myself. I'll put my leg under the wheel, you don't have to do anything. Don't worry, we'll still open that business together." Agosto grabbed the shovel. Diamante took off his shirt and shivered. His back was tanned, his muscles rippled under the skin. He dropped his suspenders and clenched his cigarette between his teeth. I'm not afraid. What's a kidney? It must be like a cow kidney—a rust-colored sac, soft and disgusting. The gleaming of the handcar on the tracks blinded him. He smelled dust. Immense expanses, such as he'd never seen. Everything was exaggerated here, enormous. Grandiose. Just the way his dreams and ambitions had been once. "I don't want to sell a kidney to the Northern Pacific," he said, turning around. "So you're staying?" Agosto commented disappointedly. "I'll take my leg off myself, then."

Agosto Guerra was not compensated. The fabulous sum he believed he would obtain by mutilating himself was only a legend—a mirage, nursed by disgruntled men in the obscurity of a railway car or during the interminable hours of labor as they laid miles and miles of ties that would never take them anywhere. Nobody had ever received fifteen hundred dollars for a leg. Achille Serra, who lost a foot in 1908 while working for the Missouri Pacific Railway Company, had to settle for two months' pay.

The story didn't go exactly the way Diamante told it. Diamante didn't run away from the camp because he didn't want to sell his kidney to the Company. He fled because he saw his companion die, saw that his life was worth less than the water trembling in his wooden pails. It wasn't summer, but October 1909. And on that day, Diamante realized that his life was still worth something.

The name of Agosto Guerra—which means August War, at once so sunny and bellicose—stayed in my mind, as it had in Diamante's. It's unlikely anyone shared it. When I came across his case in the Historical Diplomatic Archives of the Ministry of Foreign Affairs in Rome, I knew right away it was the same person, one of the last of 378 names that comprise the "summary of activities of the Italian Consulate at Denver's legal office through the second semester of 1909." Among those who told the investigator that the Company's official version of the accident was false—an invisible presence, a person without a name, without a face, for the wheels of bureaucracy and history—was there also Diamante?

The recently established legal office battled against the indifference of the ministry and a depressing lack of means: even typewriters were in short supply and the consul had to stoop to justifying the use of a rented Remington because he couldn't very well give his own Smith Premier to the secretary. In 1909 the office functioned briskly, however, sustained by the humanitarianism of the new consul, Adolfo Rossi, a former waiter and journalist who strove to erase the obscene conduct of his predecessor, Cavaliere C——. Said individual, in addition to letting old cases get moldy, had also embezzled the (miserable) compensation owed to miners and railroad workers who had lost their lives on the job, thus robbing, without the slightest twinge of conscience, widows and orphans back in Italy who were waiting in vain for money that would never arrive. The legal office dealt with sad stories: compensation in case of death, reparations in case of injury, burns, or amputation in accidents occurring in a territory ten times larger than Italy. In 1909 the Denver consulate's responsibility included all Italians spread over ten states and two Indian territories: Colorado, Utah, Wyoming, Kansas, North Dakota, South Dakota, Nebraska, Idaho, Oklahoma, Montana, New Mexico, and Arizona. New states, brand new. Desolate, uninhabited spaces, rich only in tracks and mines. Agosto Guerra's file states that in October 1909 he was in the middle of the Great Plains of North Dakota. That stack of papers, held together by a rusty paperclip—378 lives in thirty lines typed on a Remington by the secretary Ferrari—is a sort of *Spoon River*, a heartrending sequence of names, crosses, and graves, an anthology of shattered and worthless lives.

Lorenzo Lucci was eighteen like Diamante and, like him, a water boy. His father in Eveleth, Minnesota, obtains two hundred dollars from the Company for his son's life. Zeffiro Mugnani's widow and her baby girl, "against whom is pending an interdiction for illegitimacy," obtain nothing. Nothing for Giuseppe Addabbo's heirs, either, after his death in Sheridan, Wyoming, in 1906, or for Giuseppe Bacino's family after his death in Helena, Montana, in 1908: the Burlington Company and the Northern Pacific Railway Co. refuse any indemnity. Giacomo Motto is number 88 on the list. "There were continued efforts to obtain benefits from the Company, but to no avail. In June 1910 the mother of the deceased again appealed to the Consulate in hopes of obtaining reimbursement for funeral expenses at least, but the Company refused to consider the request." Antonio Ferrari, number 107, is seriously injured. The Company offers him two hundred dollars, which, given his permanent disability, he refuses. He sues. Eleven of the twelve jury members vote to condemn the Company to an indemnity of three thousand dollars, one votes for acquittal. Having demanded a unanimous verdict, the court finds the Company liable and sets damages at one dollar. The consulate appeals this "shameful verdict," but nothing else is known of the matter. Michele Sanna, number 172, is found dead in Berwind, Colorado, on March 3, 1909. He had been killed in a brawl, beaten to death with a club by some fellow workers, and not, as it seemed, crushed by a falling beam. The Company was found not responsible. Carlo Fossen dies of smoke inhalation in the Liberty Bell Mine in Telluride, Colorado, on August 9, 1909, while attempting to rescue his fellow workers who were trapped by a fire in the mine. It is shown that he was "not carrying out Company orders, but rather performing a heroic act on his own initiative. Therefore the owner cannot be considered responsible for his death." He leaves behind a pregnant wife in Telluride. On September 23, 1909, Domenico Lunardi is seriously wounded in Oak Creek, Colorado. He is taken to the hospital, where "his right leg is amputated and several teeth removed. Thanks to the immediate intervention of the Consulate, the Company, despite its poor financial status, was made to pay his hospital and medical bills, provide a sum of cash and false teeth. It also contributed significantly to the repatriation expenses of the injured to his country of origin." Francesco Doglio, injured on April 9, 1909, at Spring Gulch, Colorado, also had his right leg amputated. He was in the hospital for several months and turned to the consulate too late to collect witnesses. All he was able to obtain was $159.65 for his artificial leg. Michele Garbo, number 276, is injured on June 27, 1909, in the notorious mines of Starkville, Colorado. In October 1910 fifty-five workers on the night shift, thirteen of whom are Italians, will die there. Garbo is admitted to the hospital in Pueblo in grave condition— a broken vertebra—and is considered incurable. The Company offers to pay for the invalid and a companion's voyage from Pueblo to Palermo. Compensation? Nothing. Alms of one hundred dollars in cash. "Garbo would be willing to accept the offer, but has not yet found someone to accompany him."

Men die in the railway camps as well. Fifty-nine-year-old Alfonso Miulli dies of intestinal inflammation on September 5, 1909, in Culberston, Montana. He worked for the Great Northern Railway Company and had probably eaten rotten food from the pluck-me store for years. The Company pays twenty dollars for the coffin and fifteen for the funeral cart, but as Miulli was expecting only $30.45 in pay, nothing is owed to his heirs. Train men often die of pneumonia. Raffaele Brandonisio, number 277, dies on March 24, 1909. Spring hasn't yet arrived in Missoula, Montana; the winter lasted too long. But in Green River, Utah, you can still die of pneumonia on May 31. The deceased had a wife in Turin and a girl in town. He leaves both "with no means of support." Men die of typhoid fever and tuberculosis, or are burned to death in dormitory cars, as happens to Giuseppe Caringella on August 16, 1909—the Feast of San Rocco. The car belongs to the Chicago Milwaukee & Saint Paul RR Co. Someone from his hometown pockets Caringella's pay and vanishes. Or they're electrocuted by a power line when two trains collide, as happens to Martino Pollu on the Denver & Rio Grande line in Dostero, Colorado, on

September 18, 1909. But more frequently they are run over by trains—like Giuseppe Mangiaracina in Cheyenne, Wyoming, on September 19, 1909. "The coroner's inquiry concluded in a non-suit against the Union Pacific Railroad Company." Salvatore Bellanca is killed on August 30, 1907, while repairing track in New Mexico. "The Union Pacific Railway Co. insisted that no worker of that name had ever worked for them or been killed in Dawson, New Mexico." Giuseppe Scappellato is found dead on the tracks in Omaha, Nebraska, on January 19, 1909. He leaves a wife and four children in Carlentini, Siracusa. Eleven companies make use of those tracks. It might be possible to take the Union Pacific Railroad Company to court. Maybe. The investigation was unable to prove that the train that hit him was owned by the "above-mentioned company." Cesare Recchio is killed in Fargo, North Dakota, on November 30, 1908, while clearing snow from the Northern Pacific Railway lines. Rocco Carchedi is hit and killed by a Great Northern Railroad train in Belmont, Montana, on October 4, 1909. No indemnity. The Company maintains that at the time of the accident the deceased was not in service and, furthermore, was inebriated. Men also die falling off handcars, as happens to Luigi Ungaro, number 365. "While traveling at full speed on a handcar of the Denver & Rio Grande RR Co, for which he worked, he imprudently leaned over in order to grab a pail that was sent flying by the motion, and fell, mortally injuring himself. The Company cannot be held responsible for the accident. It paid the journey of his widow and two children from Salida, Colorado, to New York." But Ungaro couldn't let that pail fall, for it was precisely the reason he was riding that handcar. Ungaro had tuberculosis, and so at age twenty-five he was still a water boy.

Trains unhinge the mind, and the monotonous clatter of the wheels provokes anxiety, and makes obsessions and fears explode. Costante Dolcini, number 329, leaves San Francisco on August 28, 1908, in order to return to Italy. Something happens. All of a sudden "he goes mad" and is admitted to the Norfolk lunatic asylum. "Deportation procedures are advancing, as in agreement with the American immigration authorities." The trains—funeral cars clacking across interminable spaces of nothingness—seem the ideal place for meeting one's death. Giovanni Massa, number 350, dies of tuberculosis as he travels on the Union Pacific. They unload him in North Platte, Nebraska. He was on his way back to Italy, and his waiting relatives know that he is carrying 150 silver dollars in addition to his deadly disease. But the body is washed by the coroner and funeral home employees, after which the authorities declare to have found "four dollars in silver, a knife, a watch and a small amount of undergarments." Trains are also a place of suicide. Pietro Pompeo Zambelli is on his way from San Francisco to New York in order to embark for Genoa. He decides not to complete his journey—there's no way home—and throws himself under an approaching train in Gallup, New Mexico, on April 12, 1910. "A trunk belonging to the deceased, recovered by the Consulate, contained dirty laundry, which was burned for hygienic reasons, some worthless papers, and a few photographs, which are being held for the widow to claim."

The trains of the Northern Pacific Railroad Company kill as well. It is October 15, 1909, the setting is Taylor, North Dakota. Today it is a tiny point (the equivalent of 163 inhabitants) on the map; a hundred years ago it was nothing but a dot. North Dakota is a nightmare of monotony and solitude. The men are working in the middle of nowhere. A furious wind blows. It's raining buckets and they shouldn't still be out there because their contract stipulates they should be in the dormitory cars at that hour. But the team is probably behind on the work plan they agreed to with the contractor; it's already late autumn and they haven't yet finished the section of track contracted to them. The workers are heading back to camp. Maybe they passed it: it's already dark and the car lights could have been obfuscated by the rain. The train suddenly leaps out of the night and thunders down on them. Only one of them is unlucky: he is run over and dragged for several hundred yards before getting stuck in a switch. "The eighty-five dollars found in the pockets of the deceased were consigned to the authorities to be used for funeral expenses." Eternal shame on the undertaker who earned eighty-five dollars for burying a man in North Dakota. "It was impossible to obtain any compensation, for the Company denies any responsibility for the accident." It affirms that the de-

ceased was drunk at the moment he attempted to cross the tracks. His
fellow workers swore the deceased was a teetotaler. But most of them
are nowhere to be found on March 19, 1910, and so cannot repeat
their claims at the trial. Not that it would have made a difference,
however, because the legal office is here to show that the Northern
Pacific has excellent lawyers. "He is survived by his elderly parents and
five children (ages 11, 9, 7, 4, 3), who are also recently orphaned of
their mother, and an adopted little girl." The deceased was thirty-one
years old. His name was Guerra. Agosto Guerra.

Diamante preferred to remember him as he was during that summer they'd spent together. Nostalgic and daring. A dreamer. Ready to
cut off his leg with a rusty hatchet in order to offer a future to his six
children. The bureaucracy didn't consider that adopted girl his, but
Guerra did. Maybe because he'd told the story that way, Diamante
ended up believing it really was true. No train came barreling out of
the dark and the rain. No body mangled by the wheels and scattered
across the tracks. No hasty burial by some common thief in a grave no
one could ever visit, in some noplace on the Great Plains where no
one will ever know who he was. Diamante ended up believing there
was no investigation, no slander, no lie. That both of them had gotten
what they'd wanted. Agosto Guerra his money. And Diamante his
freedom.

He escaped from camp during the night. His companions were asleep
in their bunks, wrapped in blankets. He knew what they were dreaming, if they had the energy to dream. He would never see them again,
nor would he ever want to. They would have reminded him of the
taste of rotten anchovies, the itch of lice, the endless fornication fan-
tasies around the stove, the tales of indemnities for self-inflicted
injuries—there wasn't anything good to take from camp, no happy
memory. You need to know how to forget the bad so as to hold on to
the good. Otherwise even the good fades, becomes overwhelmed and
poisoned. The door to the foreman's car was slightly ajar. The foreman
was out—probably working with the Company on the official version
of the accident in which Agosto Guerra was killed. Or maybe he was

only getting drunk on rhubarb liqueur with the foreman of the next camp. It was upsetting to him, too, when he lost one of his men. He knew it could have been him.

Diamante walked in darkness along the tracks, guided only by the glow of the rails. If water could talk, there'd be some trace of all these years. It would tell of all it had taught him. How the lightest, most transparent things are heavy. How much effort it takes to contain what cannot be held; water runs through your fingers, so you find yourself empty-handed and still thirsty. But as water has no memory, no trace of his rage and loneliness will remain. He has lost these years forever. The car remained visible for a long time—an unnatural protuberance jutting out of the plain. The feeble light filtering through the planks illuminated it like a Chinese lantern suspended in the dark. Then it disappeared, and he found himself alone, guided by the steady repetition of the ties. He adjusted his stride to their distance, let them set the rhythm. He ran, dancing practically, jumping from one to the next, balancing on the iron. Parallel paths, chained together. Tracks that would like to flee to opposite ends of the earth, but can't. Bound together forever. Sometimes not even dynamite can separate them.

At dawn, he was still in the middle of the empty, silent plains. There wasn't a sound—not a rustling of grass, no twitter of birds, nothing that spoke of nature awakening. The sun rose on the plains as on the ocean. An ocean of light after an ocean of darkness, with that profound, ineffable silence all around him. Waving grass without end, the immense sky, nothing to protect him from sun, wind, or storm—it all reminded him of the ocean. A mute and formless seascape, without time and without history, for miles and miles. The frozen rails glistened in the first rays of light, like phosphorescent fish in the sea. And no end in sight. He felt dazed, disoriented, frozen by the solitude of that continuous line. It robbed him of his sense of direction, his body, himself. A tumbleweed on the prairie, uprooted by the wind, lost. But tracks always lead somewhere.

The distant protrusion that puckered the monotony like a comma on a blank page turned out to be a station—a wooden shed, the paint on the sign still wet. It was already surrounded by a heap of makeshift houses piled one on top of the other that got to be called a city only because places like this bloomed at regular intervals along the railway lines. A city would spring up in three days, named after the first thing that crossed the railway engineer's mind—the name of his wife, his son, a city somewhere else that he held dear, some person he idolized. Taylor, Howard, Winfred, Canova, Cavour, Ipswich, Seneca, even Rome. Diamante recognized the billboards strewn along the route, the same one he'd taken out to the camp months earlier. He passed the beer ad towering over a solitary expanse of stones, then the poster for Karo corn syrup, the tin of Sanitol tooth powder—its mute reflection in a bug-infested puddle informed him that antiseptic and oxidizing Sanitol produces cleanliness as quickly as a breath of pure mountain air—25 CENTS EVERYWHERE. EVERY DAY, AS YOU GO.

And then he was alone again. A world without curves or depth. Barren, empty. Diamante was stupefied by the discovery of his own minuscule irrelevance as he trembled from the cold and anxiously studied the clouds building above his head, threatening a furious downpour he would be unable to escape. Every now and then he would be surprised by the unmistakable whistle of a passenger train, so similar to the horn on a steamship—a puff of smoke on the measureless vastness that soon dissolved without a trace. But he let it pass. That train was not for him. He was waiting for a freight train loaded with grain and cattle and headed for the Chicago slaughterhouses. A train for animals and things.

It was already afternoon when the first one made the ties vibrate. Diamante stationed himself on the embankment and waited till it came near—smoke, noise, wood, coal. Then he ran alongside the lengthy convoy for a hundred yards or so, letting cars thick with soot race past until he found a handle and grabbed it. He swung in the void for a long time, his feet grazing the embankment. If he'd slipped, the wheels would have mangled him, made mincemeat of his legs, and he would have become the umpteenth nameless body dragged until nothing was left of him. But Diamante managed to climb onto the roof. The wind painted his face black with coal. The storm drowned him mercilessly. He had nothing to eat and thirty dollars in his pocket—the miserable fruit of four years of forced labor. His undeserved imprisonment. Or maybe he did deserve it because back in New York, it's hard to say exactly when, he had erred, had denied all that was important to him. He had gone astray.

Diamante didn't know where the train was headed, or what it was carrying. The cars were sealed. America was immense, scored by millions of miles of rails, laced with metal even where there was nothing else. But no matter where all those rails were heading, they all ended up in the same place: New York.

The Hesitations of
Amleto Attonito

During the winter of 1909, Rocco and Vita met whenever possible in the Bongiorno Bros. hall after her shift at the Ansonia Hotel kitchen. They would kiss standing up because the chairs had a mournful air and the lugubrious couches seemed soaked in tears. They unbuttoned coats and clung to one another, body pressed against body, so as to forget the chill of this room intended to accommodate bodies that felt neither cold nor ice and were less inviting than the cold walls and floor, less than winter itself. Vita knew what she was doing was profoundly wrong. She remembered clearly the intensity of her love for Diamante. But if she was here, clearly she also loved Rocco. So much so that despite strict orders forbidding her to go to the Mulberry District, on Sunday mornings she would pin on the fur hat he had just given her, button her coat, a recent gift, too (there was no end to the presents, as if every day were her birthday), duck into the elevated, and dash over to the Baxter Street church just to hear him sing. She couldn't bring herself to tell him to stop, and didn't tell him to put her dress back down or quit ex-

ploring her body. She had always considered it fenced in, a garden
where precious fruits were maturing but not yet ready for picking, as if
awaiting the return of their legitimate owner. With the same obstinacy,
she now offered her body to Rocco so that he could discover and reveal it to her. Her memory of Diamante had not diminished; in fact,
she could imagine his imminent return more realistically now, and
thought of him during the long hours in the kitchen as she prepared
desserts and sugared pastries, as she sliced open the wrapping of
Rocco's latest gift, even as Rocco drove her toward the Bowery or
knelt in front of her, sinking his face against her prohibited triangle.
But now when she thought of Diamante, she also thought of Rocco.
She loved both of them with the same heated intensity even though
she'd never imagined such a thing could be possible—and maybe it
wasn't. But she didn't feel worse or different from before. She only
hoped she wouldn't have to choose; she wanted to be able to keep
closing her eyes, trembling, and listening to the voice of Enrico
Caruso rising out of the phonograph horn in the unnatural silence of
that hall. Then all of a sudden she would say, "Stop—take me home."
She always interrupted him in time, because she wanted to marry Diamante, not Rocco—or maybe both of them, though no law had yet
been invented that allowed it.

Rocco didn't insist, because he was confused as well and wasn't sure
what was happening to him. After dropping Vita at her door at three
in the morning—her clothes disheveled, her hair ruffled, her eyes
aglow, and a knowing smile on her lips—and he was alone, he would
tell himself that was enough, the last time. He really had to quit going
to the Ansonia. The car was not his, nor was the funeral home for that
matter, and Bongiorno called him "my son." Rocco had married his
daughter Veneranda, who went by the flattering nickname Venera, last
spring. Because he was ambitious. Because he was tired of being considered merely a faithful bodyguard, a dull-witted and insensitive machine. A gorilla. An underling, only good for action and dirty work,
but whose opinion is never asked. The functioning of the organ called
his brain wasn't taken into account and was considered superfluous and
harmful, like a kidney stone. But Rocco had a brain. He wanted to

take charge of the funeral home and the money that old-fashioned and narrow-minded Bongiorno didn't know how to invest. He wanted to buy trucks, excavators, cranes; he wanted to become what his boss was incapable of becoming: a businessman.

He'd only seen Venera once, after he'd saved Cozza's life by taking a bullet in his thigh. As soon as he got out of the hospital, Bongiorno had rewarded him by inviting him to lunch. While Bongiorno lauded Rocco's courage in front of his wife, daughter, and the Bros., Rocco ogled the fireplaces, carpets, Chinese vases, antique furniture imported from Italy, and windows that gave onto Saint Mark's Place, and decided to make that house his own—at any cost. He had always thought he wanted to destroy everything and never own anything. He'd never desired money or beautiful things. But he had never seen such beautiful things before. Nor had he ever gotten close to a young woman like Veneranda Bongiorno before: slender, diaphanous as tissue paper, her copper-colored hair swept up in a chignon, her dress a pale gray as in an old etching, her voice as light as a sprinkling of talcum powder. At the time Rocco was still living in a boardinghouse run by a greedy shrew who charged an arm and a leg for foul-smelling dishwater and threw him wicked looks when he used her embroidery thread to sew up his cuts. The Bongiorno home became an obsession. Mr. Bongiorno, his protector, became the enemy to expunge from the fortress in order to expropriate his earthly happiness. Veneranda had studied with nuns and knew nothing of her father's dealings and friends. She would have spurned Rocco had she known that when they shot him, he had just been released from the Blackwell Island prison. However, since he'd had the good sense to provide a false name when they arrested him for shaking the monthly payment out of a Brooklyn hotel owner, they'd locked him up as Amleto Attonito. But obviously no one told her these things. Venera found the dignified young man with the angelic face fascinating, and thought his reserved behavior meant he found the company of her father's mustachioed friends vulgar. As did she. The young guest didn't say a word the entire meal, not even when Bongiorno invited him to select some music for the phonograph. He merely looked over Cozza's considerable collection—he owned a full set of Victor and Columbia records—and chose a sad and languid Neapolitan song: *Ah! che bell'aria fresca, ch'addore 'e malvarosa e tu durmenno staje* . . . And as it was in the song, so it was in the house. Bongiorno's daughter was indeed quite asleep, soothed by all her reassuring certainties. When the singer shouted *I' te vurria vasa', I' te vurria vasa'*—I long to kiss you—Rocco let his gaze linger on the girl's copper hair. And Venera knew she was in love.

Whenever Rocco drove her father home, Venera would spy on him from behind the curtain, letting it fall as soon as she was sure he had seen her. Rocco would raise his hand to his hat and make a slight bow. He didn't dare speak to her because Pino Fucile had once told him that his way of talking and gesticulating agitatedly would make him a laughingstock in good society. Rocco had taken it very poorly; after making sure he wasn't being followed, spied on, or watched, he entered a bookstore. When the salesclerk, fearing a holdup, asked him how he could help, Rocco whispered his request: an English dictionary and a book that teaches you what to do and say, and what not to do and say. A book of manners. The book and dictionary cost him ten dollars, but it was money well spent. Bongiorno obviously had something completely different in mind for his daughter than to sacrifice her to his hotheaded bodyguard, but Rocco organized it all with the same efficiency he used when planning punishments in Bongiorno's name. Rocco punished Bongiorno.

With Venera's consent, he kidnapped her as she came out of her piano lesson. They took shelter in the church of a priest friend and waited until Bongiorno's murderous rage had spent itself. After which Rocco communicated to the father that he was willing to marry the girl, thus restoring honor to father and daughter both. Bongiorno contemplated a massacre, but finally relented, probably because he adored Venera. In truth, Rocco did not have to restore Venera's honor, because he had never touched her. He hadn't desired her before he kidnapped her, and he certainly didn't desire her afterward. He would have married a locomotive if he thought he could get something out of it. Theirs was a happy marriage even though Venera complained she didn't see very much of him. "Travel for work," Rocco explained. Venera, who had been raised to become a businessman's wife, accepted his lengthy absences and mysterious disappearances. She pretended to believe that the precautions her husband took with the police had something to do with his allergy to taxes—he confessed he'd never paid them and had no intention of doing so in the future. Even though she was only twenty-two, she was incredibly wise, and the cocoon of lies in which she had been raised had taught her not to ask herself or others too many questions. To seem to be the naive girl everyone desired her to be, even though she wasn't. Rocco was sincerely grateful, and would never have wanted to hurt or wrong her. He didn't want to make his only ally unhappy. Consequently, he had no intention of entangling himself in a clandestine relationship. Time to cut things off.

But the thought of Vita—fresh, wholesome as a windy day, and hopelessly in love with Diamante—tormented him all day long. The unfamiliar intensity of it annihilated all the rest. He grew distracted during meetings and hid behind a gaze even more absent than usual; he performed his duties hastily and carelessly, even started finding them repugnant, and fidgeted restlessly until he could take his father-in-law home. Then, instead of leaving the car in the garage, he would go to pick up Vita. He would drive in silence to the funeral home, spring the lock, and tell her to wait outside in case there was some catafalque threatening to overshadow her happiness. Then he lit the candles, turned the crucifix to the wall, removed her coat, and held her in his arms, rejoicing in her soft exuberance. He touched his lips to her breast, immersing himself in the smell of fried food and candles and wilting flowers, sinking into the velvety, firm oblivion that was Vita.

Perhaps Rocco envied Vita the feelings she never hid and that he would never know: her force, certainty, lack of doubts—her obsession. There had always been an invisible wall between himself and other people, the weight of words not spoken and thoughts not defined—a coldness that tightened around him like a vise and made him invulnerable. He couldn't even remember the last time something had moved him. Vita was like the strong but delicate thread of a spider, suspended in the corner and brushed by shadow, heat, and sun; the slightest breath of wind makes the thread vibrate, but it is elastic, bright, and simple, and does not break. The terse luminosity of the void is cut by a shimmering line. We are used to valuing complexity. We look for strength in knots and entanglements, consider it impossible to join simplicity and greatness in the same soul. But complex things are opaque, wretched, and dull, while the soul is as simple as this thread.

And so he would whisper, "Vita, are you still thinking about Diamante?" "Yes, always, yes," she would answer sincerely. "Diamante is my fiancé, we're betrothed. I called him, and he's coming back." Until one night. "He's not coming back, I am free." Rocco put his hand in the candle flame that was fluttering in the draft. He wanted the pain to convince him he was happy. He didn't feel any pain, but convinced himself anyway. "I don't care about Diamante anymore," Vita said, unhooking a stocking from her garter. To love and not be loved in return is time wasted. Her head was on fire. At a certain point she realized she might not even recognize him if she ran into him on the street. She couldn't remember his mouth, the color of his skin, the shape of his nose. She had lost his face, his voice. She had forgotten. His name had become a cold, distant echo, the whisper of a vaguely remembered story lost in the past, in their childhood. "I should marry you, then," Rocco concluded thoughtfully. "You'd have to kidnap me first," Vita laughed. Rocco blew out the candles. "I already have."

A Ticket for Ohio

Sacrifice is a woman's most precious virtue and her reward is not of this world, but eternal Paradise. Vita knows this. And if she forgets, her neighbors remind her: women who spend interminable days shut up in two rooms on Broadway sewing buttonholes and eyelets for Levy & Co., surrounded by swarms of malnourished creatures who don't yet know how to talk. Serene existences made up of stacks of dishes to wash, sheets to straighten and iron. Stable existences that unfold against the same landscape of laundry and landings, with the same consoling view out the window of the street heading for the horizon. There are no curves in New York: everything is straight and unrelenting. Everybody said Lena was crazy. But if she was, then Vita has gone crazy, too, living for years with one dream that wouldn't return, and for months with another that took her to a funeral home to make love on couches soaked in tears. Vita never cried there, though, not even on the night she was kidnapped. Her laughter refused to die, ringing out in the silence of that hall filled with candles, catafalques hidden behind curtains, and crucifixes turned to the wall so as not to witness the forbidden happiness of human beings.

Rocco would constantly say that Vita, *his* Vita, shouldn't waste her youth in a place like Harlem amid ignorant, brash, and brutal people who scorn happiness and beauty and turn ugly with toil and regret, all the while dreaming of unattainable wealth—not that they would know what to do with it if they ever obtained it. Rocco wanted to take her away from there—*to move her.* Which is precisely what Vita longed for him to do, so when he proposed they run away together, she accepted. She wanted to change, to free herself from the suffocating chains of duty and the gray fog of unhappiness hanging over her. They fixed an appointment at the station, right on the platform so they wouldn't be seen together—*never, not for any reason.* It was the spring of 1910. Vita hurried out of the house and ran to the station because she was afraid that remorse would follow her.

Rocco did really intend to marry her. It had never crossed his mind to deceive her; just as Vita had said straightaway she was engaged to Diamante, he'd always wanted to start off by saying he was already married. But the moment for confessing slipped through his fingers. He knew he would lose her—and he couldn't resign himself to the idea of life without Vita. He cursed the Children's Aid Society for saving her from her ignorance and telling her her rights, or those she believed she had. He cursed himself for letting her imagine a luminous way of escape. For months he had lived two mutilated lives, both of them risky. Between one clandestine appointment and the next, rumors began circulating; out of respect, they were immediately reported to the funeral home director. At first Rocco listened with pleasure, but then his blood froze. "You know Vincenzino Vadalà, the guy who washes the dead bodies?" his consumptive gravedigger Fagiolino asked him one day. "Well, one night he forgot his house keys at work. So he goes back to get them. It's midnight. He opens the back door and hears an excruciating death rattle coming from the hall. His hair stands on end—he's terrified of ghosts—but he's got to get those keys or he'll have to sleep in the street, so he plucks up his courage and goes in. He tiptoes into the hall, doesn't turn on the light. The sighing is frenetic now, and he drops to his knees, ready to beg for mercy. But you know what it was? You'll never believe this one. Two lovers going at it in one of the coffins."

And Filomeno Scaturro swears it's all absolutely true. He heard it, too, saw it, knows what was going on. The woman was naked, dark skin, well-turned thighs, black hair. A girl, really, but the foul demon comes in the guise of innocence to seduce the world. Rocco feels something cold crawl up his spine. Scaturro's the coffin carver, a devout, hunchbacked little fellow and a faithful Bongiorno Bros. employee. He comes to the office to tell Rocco all this, asking him obsequiously to intervene and put a stop to this obscene defiling, this horrendous profanation. "And the man, did you see him, too?" Rocco asked, struggling to control the unseemly urge to grab the coffin carver by the throat and break his neck. "The man," Scaturro responded, staring coldly at Rocco, "is young and strong, but if he keeps it up, he'll find himself at the bottom of the river with a block of cement on his feet and the instrument of his sin cut off."

Scaturro was found in the dump a few days later, his neck broken. But the funeral home went back to being what it had always been for Rocco—an anonymous, depressing place full of coffins and cadavers to bury at Calvary or send back across the ocean at the family's expense, a place where people came to keep watch over or plot death. He felt uneasy, dirty, and dissatisfied sitting on those straight-backed chairs. He was consumed by the desire to spend a few hours with Vita, but didn't know where. It wasn't enough to park his father-in-law's car on the deserted docks and snatch a few minutes in the darkness of the warehouses. This wasn't what he wanted, not for Vita. Maybe he should become a bigamist: Veneranda's husband in New York and Vita's in some other city.

In February Rocco had decided to surprise her. Yet another present. He took her to the Metropolitan, and after the performance he led her to Enrico Caruso's dressing room. Just like hundreds of other real or bogus admirers who boasted they were from Naples, Campania, or Italy at any rate, Rocco had approached Caruso several times, hoping for a stack of tickets he could then scalp at ten times their price in front of the theater. Vita had a hard time connecting that fat and sickly melancholy creature with the velvet voice to the man she had idolized for years, dreaming he was her father. Overwhelmed, she peered at the sad little tenor; he seemed both familiar and lost, like the happiest part of her own past, but she couldn't find the words to tell him. Rocco asked for Caruso's autograph—on a picture of him as Canio the clown. He even dictated the dedication, an effrontery Vita found shameless. "To the most beautiful girl in America." The tenor seemed to be of the same opinion, for he was bewitched when he looked into Vita's dark eyes. Everybody knew Caruso was looking for a girl to console him after his had abandoned him, so to ward off any further intimacy Rocco took Vita by the hand and led her away. As she was about to leave the dressing room, she turned back to the tenor and smiled. Rocco had acted most imprudently in taking her there. Caruso did not forget Vita. He would not forget Rocco, either.

Some weeks later, three men showed up to collect fifteen thousand dollars. After a terse and threatening correspondence, Caruso gave in and declared he was ready to pay. He would leave the money wrapped in a parcel under the stairs of a factory on Van Brunt Street in Brooklyn. But, like everyone else who had nearly died of hunger once, now that he was rich Caruso furiously protected the money he'd never dreamed of having—ready to give it away to all sorts of people, but not to let it be taken from him. So he wrapped up some scrap paper and included two dollar bills, just to insult them. He sent the police to the appointment. Two underlings were nabbed, but the third managed to escape. Antonio Misiani, importer, and Antonio Cincotta, liquor distiller, were locked away. Bail was set at fifteen hundred dollars. The police wanted to identify the senders at any cost, but the two behind bars weren't talking. Their friends tried everything to clear their names and throw off the investigation. On March 17, the police received a letter full of errors in which a supposed Genovese lady accused herself of the blackmail. "Signore Caruso," the letter read, "I is the women that wroted them 2 leters to yu becuz I love yu and becuz I cant love yu as I is amarried I wroted them leters to make yu friad so yu not come back in America and so the arrestid man are innocenti. Save the innocenti. BHSOD." The clumsy letter had no effect, despite the abbreviation in the signature (Black Hand—Society of Death). Given the fame of the victim, the detective on the case was hoping for a clamorous success and was determined to get his hands on the third man. He showed Caruso a hundred mug shots of suspects who'd been arrested in the past for threatening letters or extortion. When Caruso came across the enigmatic smile of a certain Amleto Attonito, he recalled that giant who had come to see him with a luscious young lady named Vita.

On March 19 Misiani and Cincotta were let out on bail. Eugenio Gentile, a Carroll Street liquor distiller, and Pasquale Porrazzo, a Hicks Street barber, had posted bond. Frank Spardo warned Rocco that a desperate search was on for Amleto Attonito. The police were looking for him, and so were two furious underlings who felt betrayed and wanted revenge or indemnity for the years they'd have to spend in jail from the man who'd hatched the plan. Rocco had to disappear, get out of the city—now.

They took the train for Saint Paul, sitting in different compartments. Every hour, jolted by the wheels and shaken to the marrow by the rasp of the whistle, Rocco Attonito would get up and pretend to head toward the platform, but he really just wanted to make sure she had really run away with him. Vita was wearing a dark sailor dress with a large square collar. She didn't have anything to do but look out the window. How vast America is. Endless. The forced separation bored her. When she saw Rocco's reflection shimmering in the window, she turned and offered a smile that was anxious yet brimming with desire. As if she were saying: When will we get there? When can we finally sleep together? Wake up in the same bed? That smile, the candid and absolute intensity of her desire, pierced Rocco, for he was unable to reciprocate. How did I manage to get myself into such a mess? Where am I taking her? He hurried onto the platform and smoked cigarette after cigarette, until his throat burned. When Vita, as if by chance, happened to come out, they leaned over the railing together, their hands just touching, and stared at the landscape disappearing into the night. America slipped away alongside them like someone else's dream.

They put up in the only luxury hotel in the Flats district, a room with flowered wallpaper that looked out onto the Great Northern and the Chicago & Omaha tracks. Rocco was used to hotels and their fake splendor, but Vita had never seen a real hotel room, and certainly had never slept in one. She felt like a princess. Oh, such a big bed! Oh, a bathtub! Oh, hot water! Oh, a lamp on the nightstand! He smiled at her joy and would have liked to buy her a house on the ocean outside New York—maybe Orchard Beach. He'd only been there once, but he still ached with the memory of the shore's romantic solitude. He'd buy her a maid, a car, silver, paintings, Chinese vases, a dog—anything. Everything her heart desired, things she couldn't even imagine existed. Vita was the tenacious thread keeping him connected to the most authentic part of himself. He had never felt so close to someone in his whole life.

Vita ran to the bathroom and slipped into the nightgown Rocco had given her. A rustle of mauve-colored satin, just like in the movies. Like the ones in the window at Macy's. "How do I look?" "Stupendous," Rocco told her. Vita curled up on the bed, but Rocco stayed by the window. She couldn't understand why he didn't even try to kiss her, so she asked him what was wrong. Didn't he like her anymore? Rocco finally said it. He started off by telling her he had another wife.

Vita said she didn't believe him. Rocco swore it was true. He hoped she wouldn't start to cry or try to shoot him or decide she wanted to go home. Vita didn't say a word. They spent the night in silence, each one staring at a different flower on the wall. When Vita turned on her side, her mauve-colored nightgown rustled with disillusionment.

They were wed in a house by a friend of Rocco's, a guy with a haunted look who claimed to be a priest and know Latin. John Palmieri had once been a priest for real. He'd been kicked out of Mother Church because he'd taken a serious liking to heroin, thanks to his frequenting the Chinese quarter in order to convert them to the true faith. When he started robbing his parishioners to buy the powder, he was forced to remove his frock. But since nobody wanted to go to the Midwest—for a priest it was like being condemned to forced labor—John Palmieri went out to the railroad camps, Gospels in hand. Even though he was no longer a priest, he consoled the men with parables and the mail delivery. This was their wedding: Vita was dressed in white and Rocco was naked from the waist up. The priest, or former priest, told Vita to write the letter *V* in ink on Rocco's

heart. *V* for your virginity, which you have given me, *V* for the violence I'll use against whoever tries to harm you, *V* for the victory of
our love over those who want to thwart it. *V* for Vita. I will wear your
name on my heart forever. Then the priest brandished a mattress needle and tattooed the letter on Rocco's skin while Vita held his hand.
They were now joined until death do us part. For Rocco it counted as
a real wedding. Even though he hadn't married her in front of God,
whom he didn't believe in, or in front of men, whom he despised, he
had wed her with blood and in front of his conscience; thus their bond
was indissoluble, for conscience was the only guide he respected and
obeyed. His conscience knew he had never meant to deceive Vita and
truly desired to make her happy. He repeated his vow and squeezed
Vita's brown hand in his large paw. "I will protect you from danger. I'll
take care of you. No matter what happens."

Rocco went out at night, like a bat. During the day they'd hole up in
the room, making love until they were exhausted. With the passing of
time their room's shabby decadence, hidden beneath the pretentious
patina of luxury, was revealed: the wallpaper stained with humidity,
the blood of swatted mosquitoes, and every type of organic liquid;
the mangy carpet; and the sheets full of ancient cigarette burns. The
clothes Rocco had bought her rustled and were the latest fashion, but
Vita quickly grew weary of them. The bed was soft, but it remained
hostile and extraneous—a temporary bed. Waiters dressed in livery
brought her breakfast in bed and called her "ma'am," but the hotel
guests looked like crooks and probably were. And the view outside the
window didn't allow for any illusions: it displayed a social realism without embellishment. Everywhere there were hovels made of wood, cor-
rugated tin, old jam boxes. Pigs, goats, scrubby gardens. Dirt roads
overrun with weeds. Factory smoke. Ghosts contorted by poverty and
hunger. Industrial and human wreckage. Trash. Desolation. A muddy
river and a bridge that looked impassable. And tracks—hundreds of
train tracks cluttered with forgotten, abandoned, dilapidated cars.

So this is what being with Rocco meant. Make-believe. Distance.
Something they were unable to say to each other, that kept them apart,
and would keep them apart forever. Something that maybe not even

they could recognize, but that insinuated itself in their embraces and settled into their silences. Solitary nights and immobile days, incapable of going anywhere, like those detached train cars on dead tracks. Waiting for something that will never come. Isolation. The feeling of never being loved for what we are, but for what we make others believe we are. The world reduced to one body, and that body reduced to one damp part. A few shared moments and an infinite emptiness inside. On the seventh evening, when Rocco went out on "business," Vita crossed the tracks, trudged over to the office, and asked for a ticket to Ohio. The ticket man tried to explain to her that Ohio is not a station. What was her destination? Where did she want to go? "Oaio," Vita insisted unflinchingly, and deposited five crumpled dollar bills on the counter. The man told her that five dollars wouldn't get her anywhere near Ohio.

When she got back to the room, Rocco was still out. The suitcase was still on the top shelf. The curtains were closed. The flowers still multiplying on the wallpaper. Rocco's tie knotted on a hanger, along with his suits, too loud, too gaudy, too clingy. His sweet, musky odor everywhere. She wished she hadn't married Rocco, even though it wasn't a real wedding. She wanted to go home, even though Agnello would never take her back because by now, after having ruined Lena's and her father's lives, she'd also ruined her own. She wanted to go back to the Ansonia kitchen and waste her youth amid steam, pots and pans, and sugar for the desserts, even though she'd lost her job by running away with Rocco and would never be rehired. She wanted to write to Diamante and beg his forgiveness—but didn't know where he was. She wanted to leave Merluzzo to his mysterious business and to his wife, who probably put up with his reticence. She wanted Mr. Bongiorno to be riddled with bullets so that Rocco would be free to leave the funeral home, redeem himself, and become a normal person—if he was capable. She wanted to board a train, any train, any of the ones that made the walls of her hotel room shake, before disappearing into the night, to be swallowed up by America like those trains. She wanted to be different from who she was. She wanted to die tonight, here in the Flats district of Saint Paul, drowned in Phelan's Creek.

Rocco carried a pistol in his belt, and when he slept he slipped it in his shoe. That night, after a long time, Vita found herself calling out to that pistol. Shoot me, shoot me. Looking at it until every other object ceased to exist, until the room and the entire world disappeared, sucked up by that metallic gleam. Staring at it until the pistol slid out of the shoe, raised its barrel as if it were weightless, and floated in the air. The metal glittered in the shadows. She didn't even have to stretch out her hand to pull the trigger. It would fire by itself.

But that's not how it went. The pistol dropped heavily to the floor, and no matter how she called, it stayed there, inert. Maybe she wasn't able to make things move anymore. Just as she hadn't been able to call Diamante, now the pistol refused to obey her. Maybe she could no longer desire with the intensity she'd once had. She'd lost the gift. She'd become just another girl with vague desires and a weak will, her gaze limited to the superficial, cold reality of things. Or maybe she didn't want to die so badly she would put a bullet in her head. She only wanted to die a little. But also to live and be happy—the kind of happiness when there's nothing left. Happy. She fell asleep thinking to herself: It's not true, nothing's happened—tomorrow I'll wake up and find it was all just a bad dream.

Italian Girl Missing

Nine months passed between Diamante's escape from the Northern Pacific Railway Company camp and his seeing the towers of Manhattan again. He'd walked for two thousand miles and had jumped on and off dozens of freight trains. He weighed eighty pounds, had a shaved head, a nagging pain in his back, and chronic hunger. When he finally limped onto Broadway, he looked like one of the countless hoboes who thronged the streets in those recession years. It was the summer of 1910. He wore an undershirt blackened with grime and a pair of military pants he'd acquired trading with a Negro veteran who'd traveled with him for a while. The first message that greeted him on his arrival was written on the wall of the Salvation Army meeting hall, where he'd gone to fill his stomach: WHEN IS THE LAST TIME YOU WROTE TO YOUR MOTHER? Diamante hadn't written to Angela in years. He'd turned out to be a disappointment to her and the whole family. They'd sent him to America to make his way and open a path for the rest of them. And instead here he was, more dead than alive, no future in sight. He'd been by himself for so long he'd forgotten the sound of his own voice, and in the America of Americans for so long that hearing Italian in the Mulberry Street shops and taverns moved him terribly.

He hasn't seen any of his friends—or enemies—in ages. Lots of them had gone back to Italy, others had moved to different parts of town. They'd gone out to Brooklyn or East Harlem, abandoning the streets that hope forgot to the most powerful and the most recent arrivals. He learned many things, some insignificant and others that lacerated his flesh and made him wish his heart were made of stone. Tom Orecchio was dead, his skull split open in an inn in Tenderloin. Nello was in jail, and if things went awry, he'd end up in the electric chair. Merluzzo sang in the Baxter Street church choir and went around in a double-breasted suit, bills of different amounts in each of his six pockets, from which he would produce a one, a ten, or a fifty, depending on the importance of the supplicant. Plainly put, he'd become a big shot—or big shit, you might say. Cousin Geremia had lost his job at the anthracite mines where he'd slaved away like a mole and was vegetating in a boardinghouse on Humboldt Street waiting for a new contract. Coca-Cola sold bananas for Rizzo up in Harlem and still drooled after dancing girls, frittering away his measly salary, much to Uncle Agnello's annoyance. Still the same stupid good-for-nothing he'd always been. Moe Rosen no longer photographed the dead; he'd gotten in with some folks from the movies and had gone out to Colorado, where he cranked the camera for westerns starring Broncho Billy, the lone horseman with fancy leather chaps and boots. Vita had disappeared, and Agnello, like the parents of hundreds of other girls who disappear every year in New York, had put an announcement in *Il Progresso*:

> Vita has been missing from home for seven days. She went out in the morning to go to work, but never came home. It is unknown where she may have gone or been taken. She is five feet tall, weighs 110 pounds, and when last seen, was wearing a dark dress with black stockings and shoes. Her father is an honest man and does not have any enemies he knows of. Whoever can provide information regarding the whereabouts of his daughter will be performing a good deed. Her father fears he will go mad with grief.

The announcement was accompanied by a photograph. Posed, taken by a professional: maybe for her mother in Italy. Or maybe it was taken at the reform school, because in the photo Vita is twelve or thirteen at most, not fifteen and a half, which is how old she was in the spring of 1910 when she went "missing." She's dressed in black, an austere outfit that could well be a uniform. Her long dark hair is parted slightly to the left and pulled back over her ears. She is holding her hands in front of her, her ring fingers resting under her chin. She's not looking at the camera. Not looking at whoever is looking at her. Her dark eyes, slightly in shadow, are looking at someone who probably isn't there—or at nothing. She's not smiling. Her expression is thoughtful, melancholic, unusual for a girl her age. It was a Vita whom Diamante didn't know, a Vita who hadn't yet come into existence when he'd set out, and who he'd hoped would never exist.

Under the photograph was written: ITALIAN GIRL MISSING.

The page with the announcement was still hanging in several neighborhood taverns; Vita was photogenic, and the men who came to drown their sorrows liked to get plastered dreaming they'd be the one to find that missing girl.

Diamante also learned that Vita hadn't simply disappeared. She had run away with her lover, and this lover was none other than Rocco, even though everyone pretended to know nothing about it because Merluzzo had sworn he'd break the neck of whoever so much as dared to utter Vita's name—and he was pretty convincing. Diamante listened to it all feigning his usual indifference. Even, or above all, about Vita's escape. That's how it is when you grow up in the streets: you have to pretend you couldn't give a shit even about things that really matter.

That same day Diamante went to Moe Rosen's father's pawnshop and left him Vita's chain and cross. He had guarded it all this time, even going hungry in order to keep it—for nothing. It had been his talisman and the only tangible sign of the vow they had exchanged. Instead, with the money he got for it, he gave himself another chance. ITALIAN GIRL MISSING. Missing for everyone, but for him most of all. He never wanted to hear her name again—and America was big enough to grant him this oblivion. He had the curly-haired old man write down Moe's address in Denver, Colorado, and sent his old friend a telegram. THERE IS A JOBBA FOR DIAMANTE? I DO EVERYTHING.

Then he went to Geremia's boardinghouse. He shared a bed with his cousin, just as they'd done for years. Feet to face, face to feet. Symmetrical, identical, inverted bodies. They didn't say a word about the years that had passed, for both of them were eager to forget about them. But they found each other greatly changed: Geremia all hairy and wild, his skin the color of a dirty shirt collar, typical of people who hadn't seen the light of day for years; Diamante like a galley slave with his shaved head. And a furrow between his eyebrows that hadn't been there before. On his lip, the puckering of a scar that hardened his smile. They spent only a few words on Vita. Diamante merely grumbled that he wasn't surprised. That's the way things go.

Geremia refused to believe the lies buzzing around the neighborhood. Couldn't believe that Vita, Diamante's girl, who was so adorable and so passionately adored, could fall for that delinquent Rocco, who couldn't even marry her besides, because he was already married to Bongiorno's daughter—and fall so madly in love she'd run away with him. It was more than he could fathom. He'd known Vita since she was a little girl, and couldn't match his image of her with such a stupid, futile, and cruel story. Because he'd been alone for years in the mines without even the thought of a girlfriend to comfort him, this distressing news inspired in him a great compassion. He took pity on Diamante, whose excessive pride prohibited him from expressing what he felt and forced him simply to bear it—or feign to bear it much better than one might have expected. And the more he felt sorry for his cousin, the more Geremia despised Vita; the mere thought of her was repulsive, even though her image had occasionally appeared to him in the dark of the mines: a warm, luminous vision of childlike innocence.

In the summer of 1910 there were already a good number of automobiles in circulation, even though a used 1909 Fiat cost forty-five hundred dollars. *Il lampionaro di porto*, *Rosa la pazza*, and *Masaniello* were playing at the Teatro Garibaldi. A new phonograph cost a mere twenty-eight bucks and was no longer a privilege of wealth or theft. On July 3 the fight in Reno between the white boxer Jeffries and the black boxer Johnson was transmitted live at Madison Square Garden. The monthly bulletin of the State Department of Health reported that in June in New York there were 116 suicides, 53 homicides, 146 drownings, 145 train mortalities, 86 deaths by fire, 46 by horse- or electric-powered vehicles, 7 by lightning, 15 by tetanus or poisoning, and 2 as a result of explosions. Most of the suicides chose illuminating gas. So many people killed themselves that the newspapers had a regular column just for them, with titles like "Life Deserters," "Tired of Living," or "Death's Volunteers." But if you don't succeed, you can be arrested for "attempted suicide." Eighteen of the homicides were committed with a firearm, 7 with a knife, and 19 with various other instruments. During the month of June in the city of New York there were 17,727 births and 10,865 deaths, so that in just one month the population of the metropolis grew by 6,862 souls. And in just one week 31,000 foreigners disembarked. On April 12, the steamship *Madonna* had unloaded 1,174 Italians and 5,670 northern Europeans. On April 20, 2,047 Italians from Genoa and Naples had disembarked from the *Celtic*. In six months, 843 children died in the city: 4 were bitten by rabid dogs, 12 fell off fire escapes, 5 were crushed by carts or trains, 2 were hit by stray bullets while playing in the street. In less than three months, from January 19 to March 29, 15 girls disappeared, never to be found again. Nineteen people disappeared in the twenty-four hours from April 5 to April 6. A law was promulgated prohibiting the distribution of alcohol on Sundays and holidays. A city ordinance forbade rummaging in trash cans and dumps. Transgressors ran the risk of being fined and arrested. One individual was arrested for stealing pigeons, another for setting a Jew's beard on fire, another for pushing cocaine to elementary school children, a fourth for stealing claws from a dead bear, a fifth for making off with two hundred dollars' worth of rubber heels. Nicola Maringi and Francesco Ceccarini were executed in Norristown for the murder of a cobbler in August 1909. Workers formed associations for mutual assistance. Strikes flared up and burned out all over the place, in clothing factories, ports, construction sites, and mines—forty-seven thousand miners were on strike in Ohio, a hundred thousand in Pennsylvania, eighteen thousand in Indiana, five thousand in Colorado. They were demanding a half day on Saturday and a raise. The most astonishing thing was that a bourgeois newspaper like *Il Progresso* backed the miners and supported the strikes with an unprecedented press campaign.

So much had happened in the world while Diamante was stranded in those freight cars on a dead track. Like the trade unions and socialist propaganda, the Black Hand had also become more efficient. Crime had doubled. Now they used sticks of dynamite to blow up stores, fruit stands, restaurants, and even entire buildings. It sounded like a war zone out there, and the explosions made it impossible to sleep at night. The Italian newspapers kept a scrupulous count from the first of the year and printed headlines like "Bomb Number 24!" The journalists were ashamed there were so many. They might make it to fifty this year. Blackmailers would demand you brought a thousand dollars to the Brooklyn Bridge or the zoo. In the bars where Diamante hung out waiting for Moe Rosen's reply to arrive at the Mulberry Street post office, people spoke respectfully of the Black Hand. "You're all a bunch of idiots, you respect them and they blow you to smithereens," Diamante would bark. He didn't give a damn if they reported what he said. On the contrary, he wanted them to come ask him to pay for his words. He longed to prove to himself he was ready to buy his liberty with a stabbing—or his life. The more you respect them, the more they call you losers, they'll crush you. And if they wanted the money delivered to the zoo, it just went to show they were nothing but wild animals, even if they dressed in double-breasted suits.

He didn't want to see anybody. Nevertheless, in those days of the summer of 1910, Diamante found himself hanging around in the part of Central Park where he knew Enrico Caruso enjoyed strolling while he memorized his parts. Diamante felt close to the tenor because they had endured the same type of offense, wound, and melancholy. Their lives had run on parallel tracks. They'd both arrived in New York in 1903 and risked getting caught in the gears of American bureaucracy in 1906; both were betrayed and abandoned at the same time, and now both were stagnating in a morose convalescence, trying to simultaneously heal and punish themselves for an annihilating and shattering defeat. But Enrico Caruso had become ill, whereas Diamante was still on

his feet. He looked for Caruso's now-heavy figure at the lake and on
the parched lawns. He longed to meet him. Or at least see him from
afar. See himself reflected in the other man's story, read in his face the
courage to pull himself together. No such luck. Enrico Caruso didn't
come. He was in Italy. The paths through Central Park reminded Diamante of Vita. Their first day in America. Diamante swore to himself
he'd get over this, as well. He wouldn't let himself be taken by a tumor
in his throat. He wouldn't destroy the most precious thing he possessed. He would not crumble.

COME AMICO MIO JOB FOR BILLY'S REDEMPTION GOOD PAY CASH X
RAILROAD FOLLOW SOON. When Moe's telegram arrived, Geremia,
who felt lost in this city of tumult and upheaval, began asking himself what he could do to keep Diamante here. Could it really be that it
was all over? Diamante would get all excited when he explained to
Geremia the importance of the bituminous coal miners' strikes and
why he should refuse to accept the boss's offer to break the strike. Becoming a scab, that's what Diamante called it. You can slave like Uncle
Tom, live like a rat, you can collect garbage, even steal the shoes off a
dead man. You can steal a ride on a train and accept charity. Because
your benefactors are really only giving back a small portion of what
they've stolen from you. But become a scab—no. That you can't do.
It's like stealing bread from a starving man. You have to show class
spirit.

Geremia sensed in his cousin a need he knew all too well—to become passionate about something, to argue about some question that
in truth was irrelevant, in order to silence the unbearable, intimate
thoughts in your head. "This one's on me, cousin," Diamante said as
he slid a beer mug across the bar. "Let's drink to Broncho Billy, who's
paying my way to Colorado." "And Vita?" Geremia murmured. Diamante raised his glass. "To her health." Geremia looked doubtfully at
the turbid liquid foaming in his glass. They call this beer, but it's all
head and leaves a bitter taste. "If you see her," Diamante added with
a wink, "tell her she was and remains free, and I hope she finds
happiness."

"But it's absurd," Geremia dares to say. "You can't leave like this, without even talking to her. What if it's not true? You can't believe everything you hear—people say all sorts of things." "True," Diamante grumbles bitterly. "And even if it were?" Geremia slips in. "When I would gripe that we should get out of Prince Street because Lena wasn't a serious woman, you used to defend her, saying you have to forgive a woman who makes a mistake." "But I never said I would be able to forgive her myself," Diamante explained, resting his forehead on his mug. "Should I go ask Agnello for Vita's hand, be understanding, something like that?" he started yelling bitterly. "Sure, that's really noble, but I don't go picking at Rocco's leftovers. I spit on Rocco's plate." He downed his beer in one gulp. "If you want to be my friend, don't ever talk to me about her again." Geremia clinked Diamante's glass as a sign of agreement. He bought another round, and they kept on toasting—to friendship, liberty, fidelity, to the women who are waiting for us—in every bar they came across on the way to the station. In the end they were so plastered their sides were splitting with laughter, though they were a truly sorry sight. But Diamante was still laughing when he hugged Geremia and said, "Goodbye, Uncle Tom. Be good, maybe we'll see each other again soon," and Geremia continued laughing on his way back to his boardinghouse—until it sank in that Diamante was really gone.

Vita was sewing in the microscopic living room. When Geremia saw her from the doorway, he was stabbed by her indifference. She had lost weight and was pale, but she wasn't the least bit ashamed, humiliated, or embarrassed as he might have expected. She didn't get up to welcome him, nor did she thank him for coming to see her. When Geremia settled into the armchair, she smiled slightly, that smile of detachment and suspicion that only disappointment can paint on a face. She looked at him without really seeing him, her eyes asking him one thing only: Are you with me or my father on the Rocco story? Geremia didn't exist in his own right. In truth, he never had. He was the serious cousin, the Uncle Tom. Vita didn't justify herself. She didn't bother to lie or deny anything. Things rot if you hide them. Instead she stabbed her needle into her embroidery and asked if he had news of Rocco, if something had happened to him. Geremia turned red and said bellicosely that nothing at all had happened to him, that nobody talked about Amleto Attonito anymore. Enrico Caruso was far too generous, or maybe he was just scared. He bravely testified against Misiani and Cincotta—something few would have dared do—but then asked that they be pardoned, saying that in the end they were really just "boys who'd made a mistake." But sooner or later Rocco would be made to pay for his lies and betrayals, he'll be killed like a dog in the street, which is just what he deserves.

Vita dropped her embroidery on her lap and looked at him, surprised. A tense, unpleasant silence filled the air. Vita harbored neither hatred nor rancor for Rocco, but no one would believe her if she said so. He'd betrayed her—but she had begun to suspect that the ability to betray people is a lot like the ability to lead them. Every one of us has to be abandoned sooner or later, left helpless and alone to experience betrayal inside of us, on our own. Everyone has to discover what it is that sustains him when he's no longer able to sustain himself. Only in this way can he acquire an indestructible force. That is what Vita experienced in that Saint Paul hotel room the night she didn't know how to die. But neither Geremia nor Agnello would ever have understood it. She waited until Coca-Cola disappeared into his room to ask hurriedly, not even naming him: "I know he's back. Have you seen him? How is he?" "He's managing," Geremia explained, embarrassed. "Diamante's tough, you can't cut him with a knife, not even with dynamite." Without looking at him, Vita said, "You're his cousin, he'll listen to you, tell him to forgive me."

Nicola, all decked out and wearing a cologne to turn your stomach, grabbed Geremia by the arm and whispered that his girlfriend was waiting for him around the corner. Her name was Joyce, she worked as a chiropodist in the barbershop downstairs. She lived on the same floor. That oaf Agnello had whacked him with a frying pan when he found out, but he didn't give a damn and wanted Uncle Tom to meet her because Joyce was a real knockout. Next to her Nicola looked like a cadaver. Because Joyce was black. "Sure, wait a minute, I'm coming," Geremia responded, astonished. He didn't know how to tell Vita that Diamante had already left. He was afraid she'd attack him for not knowing how to convince him to stay. Maybe in her naive, sixteen-year-old ignorance of a man's heart, Vita was fooling herself that they could start over again, patch things up, heal the wounds. "I know it's all over between us," she lied, her voice low so that Agnello wouldn't hear. That subject was prohibited in the house on 112th Street. As was the name of Rocco, the memory of Lena, and Coca-Cola's unpresentable girlfriend—in other words, just about everything that mattered to them. "I'm sorry I hurt him. Tell him to forgive me. For everything."

Geremia looked away. It was a narrow house, wallpapered with pictures torn out of newspapers. Views of the Grand Canal in Venice, Saint Peter's, the Milan cathedral. But it was respectable, a real house. Vita must spend hours madly scrubbing the floors, at least as a way to pass time. Agnello kept her locked up and told everyone his daughter had bad lungs. "Think of me as a friend," Geremia dared say. He was anxious to be going; it was a mistake to have come up here to 112th Street. When a sweater starts to unravel, there's no stopping it. "I'll be here until the twenty-seventh, then I'm off to the coal mines. They're making me foreman." He obviously didn't mention the strikes or scabs or Diamante's ideas about class spirit. They'd offered him a considerable salary, and he didn't give a hoot about the miners out on strike. Everyone has to take care of himself, make his own way. He would have liked to earn more, too, when he worked in Pennsylvania, but he'd been careful not to express his opinion. The disastrous experiences of his first years in America had taught him patience and forbearance—a bird in the hand is worth two in the bush. And all things considered, by living on nothing, not allowing himself anything, he'd managed to save more than he ever imagined possible; a few more years and he could go back to Italy satisfied. "When I settle in I'll send you my address," he added, twisting his hat in his hands. "You never know. If you need anything, some advice . . . You can count on me."

"Advice!" Vita laughed. "About what?" Geremia avoided her gaze and stared at his nails, still blackened despite his constant washings. The coal dust had gotten under his skin, permeated every pore—he'd never be rid of it. "Well, you're so young and all, all your life ahead of you. You'll have to make some decisions, and maybe you don't have anyone to count on . . ." "What decisions should I be making,

Geremì?" Vita smiled sadly. "I've already ruined everything." Her dark eyes stood out against her pale face like the anthracite veins on the terrifying walls of the mines. Geremia would grope for those anthracite marks in the dark. They were his bread, his future. The most precious thing—the only thing that mattered.

"If I weren't what I am," Geremia muttered as he got up and hurriedly took his leave, not even shaking her hand, his eyes glued to the tips of his shoes, "if I were the most attractive, strongest, most intelligent guy in the whole city, and if I had enough money to raise a family, right this instant I'd kneel and ask for your hand and your love, Vita."

Bomb Number 53

He'd never been to Da Agnello before. He knew Vita well enough to know she'd have made him leave. She didn't want to serve him or take his money. Rocco only showed up once at the tiny restaurant—just ten tables—on 112th Street and Third Avenue. It was July 5, 1911. He glanced at the blinking sign. AG EL O—some of the bulbs must have burned out. White curtains feebly attempted to shelter the dining room from the confusion of the street. The blackboard behind the cash register announced the daily specials: PIZZELLE WITH ANCHOVIES, SPAGHETTI WITH MEATBALLS, CLAM RISOTTO, FRIED MOZZARELLA, RICOTTA PUDDING. He pushed open the door and entered ahead of Bongiorno, just as he always did.

Three workmen were noisily slurping their soup. A boy wearing a rather uninviting apron was pouring wine from a flask. All of a sudden the floor began to shake, the windows to tinkle, and the bottles to dance on the tables. A deafening roar drowned out the voices—and then just as suddenly it was gone. The elevated train. It passed every ten minutes. So much the better, thought Rocco. Nobody'll hear the shots. The boy gestured for them to take a table. The restaurant was half empty, so they had their choice. Rocco knew that Tony Viggiani, Nicola's nutty deaf-mute friend who'd never laid eyes on Rocco, waited tables here on Wednesdays. And that Vita wouldn't know he was there until dinner was over. She had the habit of coming out of the kitchen and going from table to table, asking her customers if they were satisfied and had enjoyed their meal—or what had gone wrong if their plates weren't completely empty, the last drop of sauce wiped up. She would do the same thing this evening as well. But since the end of this dinner would never arrive, Rocco didn't worry about it.

He'd come with his most trusted men and his father-in-law. And dressed as if he were going to a party, in an oil-colored suit with a white gardenia in his buttonhole. He'd driven Bongiorno's car—just as he'd done for years—because, even if nobody would've blabbed his license plate, he wasn't taking any chances. He preferred things to be clean and simple. No frills. No complications. He'd had enough already. Rocco was wearing a black tie. Bongiorno hadn't asked him why. Venera had already told him with amusement that the death of the decrepit Soot had greatly distressed him. Rocco, whom no one had ever seen ruffled, not to say moved, had actually wept for that squint-eyed, skinned cat. He'd had it embalmed and buried in a marble tomb and had commissioned a sculpture to adorn it. Bongiorno hoped the birth of a son would console him, but the infant persisted in refusing to come into the world. But Rocco wasn't in mourning for his cat.

They chose a table in the back near the kitchen door so they could escape out the rear if there was an ambush. Table number 3. Bongiorno had the privilege of sitting with his back to the wall. Pino Fucile thoughtfully pulled out his chair, and Rocco helped him take off his jacket. Despite the creaking fan, which Viggiani moved closer to their table in hopes of a tip, the air was stuffy and intolerably hot. Monday the temperature had risen to 105 degrees. A real record. It was the hottest July in the last forty years. Bongiorno was leaving the next day for the shore. The dining room was adorned with festoons and watercolors, and there were flowers on the white tablecloths, but decorations couldn't conceal the room's modesty or the ordinary simplicity of the silverware and glasses. So this was the place Vita had preferred to come back to. This the existence she'd chosen for herself.

Frank Spardo studied the other customers. They were all inoffen-
sive-looking, tenants from the nearby boardinghouses. Only then did
he relax a bit and loosen his tie. Black like Rocco's. They chatted
lightheartedly about the tragedy. Rocco—very serious—observed that
in the end Soot had led a good life. For a mangy stray he'd even had
the good fortune to die in a nice house in the same neighborhood
where a bunch of street brats had tried to set him on fire nine years
earlier. Not everybody's so lucky as to take a long journey and then
end his life on down pillows when destiny arrives to send him back to
where he came from.

Tony Viggiani immediately identified Sabato Prisco, Pino Fucile,
and Frank Spardo: flamboyant figures who worked the Mulberry District. But when he approached the table to take their order, he recognized the bald old man with the dyed mustache as well. He would
have liked to genuflect for the honor they had done him in coming to
Da Agnello. He was about to tell Vita so she'd cook as if the King of
Italy himself were here. But he refrained. Vita was too wild; she didn't
like having people like that around—even though Nicola said it wasn't
as if they could ask to see their customers' police records. They'd
opened the restaurant just three months ago and hadn't yet acquired a
steady clientele. Some evenings they just sat around staring each other
in the face among ten empty tables. The five flamboyant characters at
table 3 were relaxed, or at least it seemed that way.

They didn't want to hear the daily specials. They said there are only
two occasions when men shouldn't be in a hurry: in bed and at table.
They ordered Neapolitan garlic soup, *capponata di melanzane*, and cod
alla marinara. Rocco knew Vita enjoyed cooking cod—*merluzzo*. In all
sorts of ways. In foil, au gratin, fried, in a mousse, stewed. Maybe it
was a warning—her bizarre revenge. Or perhaps just a coincidence.
Vita's cod alla marinara had even made its way to the pages of the *Telegraph*, in an article by a journalist who enjoyed "haunting the sweaty
taverns of the Italian lowlife where you can taste exotic southern Italian cooking." Those were his words. He'd nonchalantly appropriated
the recipe, copying down the instructions Vita had given him:

Choose a good soaked cod and boil it slightly so it will be easier to peel
and bone. Be careful not to break it into pieces. Meanwhile, lightly
brown finely chopped onion, marjoram, and parsley in good oil in a
pan. Add the cod, salt, pepper, and spices, and stir. In another pan put
some white vinegar, a ladle of fish broth, and two bay leaves. Add a bit
of flour to thicken. Stir well. Remove the bay leaves and take the pan
off the burner. Prepare fried croutons and layer them in a bowl. Then
arrange the cod on the croutons and pour the sauce over the fish.

Vita didn't mind. Even if somebody else makes that recipe, she'd said
serenely, it'll never taste like mine. Dishes reflect their maker. Even if
you cook and sift and stir and flour and salt the same ingredients in the
same way and for the same amount of time, the result will never be exactly the same. Rocco had never tasted that recipe. Vita never would
have cooked it for him.

Frank Spardo wrinkled his nose and closed his eyes, a beatific expression on his face. He had just caught a whiff of the *ragù*. So Bongiorno called the waiter over and told him to bring them ziti with *ragù*
as well. Fettuccine, Rocco corrected. He was hungry, but not nervous
or preoccupied. It had always cost him more to lie to his wife than to
act. More to console a widow than to kill her husband. He was disappointed that no other customers had arrived. If Vita had wanted, he
would have bought her a place in the theater district. On Broadway. A
real restaurant, frequented by artists and actors. Millionaires curious to
glimpse the other half of the world they'd never actually set foot in.
University students. Boxers, pilots. If only she'd revealed to him that
this was what she wanted. If only she'd asked. He avoided picturing
her checking on the boiling water and browning the cod in that tiny
kitchen. You ate well, but Da Agnello was a greasy spoon, a place for
workers. For everything he never wanted to be. Bongiorno was already asking him why the hell he'd brought them to a place like this.
"Because the food reminds me of home," Rocco said absentmindedly.
Then he corrected himself. "It reminds me of how it all began."

Bongiorno was very relaxed. In July an unwritten code had
brought peace to the city. Everything would be tranquil now till the
end of August. Even problems were put on hold. And there were lots

of them. Someone was selling the Bros. out to the police. In the last twelve months, a good number of them had ended up in jail or in Calvary cemetery. Bongiorno was still alive but was losing control. He was lord of a realm under siege that had dwindled to the block where his funeral home sat—but he was not ready in the least to retire. He went on about his projects, which Rocco had already listened to, or pretended to listen to, dozens of times. Bongiorno had heard it said that Caruso was returning to the theater this fall. The resurrection of Caruso made him think of the events of last spring. It was a good thing he'd found his voice again because that boy had a lot to be forgiven for. Did Rocco remember all that? How in the world could that cuckold have recognized Attonito? It was something that had never been explained. Rocco merely nodded—he didn't want to think about last spring because if he hadn't gone to Caruso's dressing room to introduce Vita, Caruso would never have remembered him; there were tons of people who scalped his free tickets. But there were few girls like Vita, maybe only one. And if he hadn't had to run off to Saint Paul, maybe things would have been different. But Bongiorno insisted. Those two Sicilian guys, Cincotta and Misiani, got caught in the middle. In spite of all his diplomacy, he'd never been able to make things right with the Sicilians. Bongiorno shook his head, disgusted. What did they expect? Caruso was a commodity to be shared, you couldn't let just the Sicilian Mafiosi enjoy him. Caruso was from Naples, after all. Rocco inadvertently touched the bulge of his pistol. He could have ordered Frank Spardo or Sabato Prisco or somebody else to do the job. But he didn't want to dishonor Bongiorno. He'd always respected him. He was an important man, or at least he used to be, years ago. Even if now he was just a relic from a bygone era, an old pedant incapable of understanding that the time had come to enjoy his retirement, Rocco had to concede him the honor of dying by his hand.

The waiter came to take away five perfectly cleaned plates. Bongiorno agreed that you ate well in this dump. And drank well, too, he said, lifting his empty glass. "Bring another one." Rocco didn't drink. He wanted to stay clearheaded. Enjoy every instant of this evening for which he'd been waiting for almost ten years.

Bongiorno was back on Caruso again. Maybe the time had come

to put a bomb in his dressing room. Or kidnap his son. Make him really scared. "No, not his son," Rocco interrupted, struggling to conceal his disgust. "Kidnappings don't work anymore. If anything, we'll
hoist his jewels." Bongiorno stared in astonishment. "Honorable people have never stolen jewels. Even the police agree on that." "Just because something wasn't done in the past, that's no reason not to do it
in the future," Rocco shouted over the rattle of the train. "Risk pays
better than nostalgia. You shouldn't be afraid of innovation." An indis-
creet smile crossed his face. "That boy's accumulating jewels worth
thousands of dollars, maybe even a hundred thousand. Diamonds,
rubies, pearls, emeralds. All insured, so it wouldn't be a great loss for
him. He could buy them all over again in a few years: he makes a hundred thousand dollars a season. If you touch his kid, though, even a
peaceful man becomes capable of murder. But a man doesn't cry over
a handful of jewels. He can resign himself to having lost them, in part
because they're insured so the money's not coming out of his pocket."
"Such arguments are not worthy of you, my son," Bongiorno said.

Rocco lit a cigarette. He pretended to be interested in the tablecloth. When he scratched it with his fingernail, a white dust came off
on his fingers. The stains had been camouflaged with powder. Evidently Vita wasn't making enough to be able to change the linens every
evening. That miserable trick irritated and offended him. If he hadn't
come here tonight with another plan in mind, it would have moved
him. But Rocco hadn't come to Da Agnello to admire the resourceful-
ness of the girl who'd left him high and dry in a hotel in Saint Paul.
Nor her late repentance, which was manifested in a savage devotion to
the family she had previously abandoned with no regrets. And he
didn't want to talk with that pain in the ass of a father-in-law anymore.
It was pointless, besides. He was obsolete, outdated, and dull-witted,
unable to move with the times and adapt. Too brutal. Rocco'd had
enough of bombs and violence. Excessive greed is no good for anyone.
It simply impoverishes people and makes them hate those who are hitting them up for money. All people want is security and protection—
they had a right to do their business in peace. Merluzzo would give
them just that. And the shopkeepers, bakers, hotel, restaurant, and bar
owners, street vendors, shoe-shine bosses, and newspapermen would

pay him gladly; they would even be grateful. The Bros. didn't agree.
Like brigands stationed at the crossroads, they wanted everything right
away, wanted to hit the first guy who passed by, even if his purse was
empty. They didn't know how to think ahead or choose the right enemies. The neighborhood was an empty casket. Under siege by the Chinese who were spreading from Peel to Mott Street, swallowing up the
old shops one after another and turning them into laundries. The
neighborhood was growing old because the new arrivals preferred
Brooklyn and East Harlem. And turning poor. Business was in sham-
bles. Everything was in a state of agony. There wasn't much left to take
there. The old Bros. didn't understand the unlimited opportunities offered by the transformation of the construction business in the city, the
alliances with unions, the control of the port and the ice, coal, and gas
trade. They kept on milking a dead cow. Everything had to change.
And Rocco would be the one to do it. He would transform the funeral
home into a shipping company. His caskets would no longer carry dead
bodies. He would put down death once and for all. "You have to learn
to distinguish between a diamond and a piece of glass," he said, stub-
bing out his cigarette in the remains of his cod. "There's no more place
in this city for hick bandits from the countryside."

The dining room was nearly empty when the waiter served the
coffee. It was late, but the customers at table 3 lingered and didn't ask
for the bill. Vita had told the waiter to start clearing the table so they'd
realize it was closing time. Bongiorno smoothed his mustache. It was
as black as a crow, but only because he dyed it. Those jet black
whiskers clashed with his bald head and wrinkled face, revealing his
real age. Despite all their tricks, the makeup crew at Bongiorno Bros.
would never be able to give him back an acceptable smile, because this
man would never smile again. He wouldn't have lips, whiskers, a face.

The old man had never met Vita. And Vita would meet him only
when he was dead. Deep down, Rocco hated him. The man he was
about to liquidate had been the boys' idol when they were young—the
man who loved errand boys and taught them to make themselves respected and feared—but he was also the man who attempted to control his life, their lives. All things considered, he was the man who had
separated them. In his own way, Rocco had come to pay homage to

Vita, to allow her to contemplate Bongiorno's cadaver. Like a cat who
brings the mouse it's just torn to pieces to the person who feeds it or
whom it wants to conquer. Rocco asked the waiter to send his compliments to the owner, and if she had nothing against it, he would
come back again. Then he slipped fifty dollars into his apron pocket.
Tony went away beaming, galloping off to collect Vita's praises because
if he'd merited such a generous tip, it meant that the evening had truly
been unforgettable for the men at table 3. And Vita strove to teach him
exactly that, to make the evenings spent at her place unforgettable. To
make people happy, even if only for a few hours.

"What were you getting at with that line about hicks from the
countryside, my son?" Bongiorno asked him. Rocco started to say it
was about time he stopped calling him that when he realized the
waiter was returning. Viggiani handed him the fifty-dollar bill, gesticulating that the owner was making him give it back because it isn't
right to accept such a big tip: it means someone wants to buy you.
And we are not for sale. Frank Spardo and Pino Fucile clapped with
glee. Rocco had no intention of taking back his fifty dollars, and Tony
smiled as he made the bill disappear in his pants pocket. "Where's
the bathroom?" Bongiorno asked, getting up. Viggiani pointed to the
door next to the kitchen. He remained standing in front of the table, a
foolish grin on his face. Rocco waited until he turned away before following Bongiorno.

For a second, he stood at the kitchen door, looking through a window like the porthole on a ship. The kitchen was so small you had to
dance about so as not to bump into plates and burn yourself on pots of
boiling water. He made out a shadow near the stove. Vita. Her hair
tucked under a small white cap, revealing the brown nape of her neck.
Her skin glimmering in a cloud of steam. He placed his hand on the
swinging door, but hesitated. There were so many things he wanted to
say to her, entire poems to recite, words just waiting to be heard. I
cannot touch your life, much less save it. I still have a lot to do to save
my own. But he didn't tell her anything. When it seemed as if Vita was
about to turn around, he hurriedly pushed open the bathroom door.

Bongiorno's legs were spread wide and a flowing torrent hit the
urinal. "Did you eat well, my father?" Rocco asked, closing the door

behind him. "Like the Pope!" Bongiorno replied without turning around. He shook himself slowly. He was dressed in black—as always. The floor beneath his feet began to shake. This was the moment. The train arrived with a deafening roar. "Turn around, look me in the face. I don't want to shoot you in the back," Rocco heard himself say. "What did you say?" Bongiorno asked. He turned. Perhaps he caught the metallic reflection of the pistol pointed at his face in the shadows. But he didn't have time to say anything more. Rocco pulled the trigger. The bathroom was so small that Rocco had to get out of the way as Bongiorno fell. He shot twice more—until the body was still. He heard confusedly the rumble of the train heading downtown, the tinkle of bottles, and the echo of chairs scraping against the floor in the dining room. He rinsed his hands; he felt as if someone had thrown a pail of dirty water in his face. When he went back to the dining room, the light hurt his eyes. The room was empty. A chair was tipped over—as if whoever had been sitting in it had suddenly run off. Pino Fucile was holding the door open and told him to hurry up. But Rocco fished in his top pocket, remembering to pay the bill.

A few minutes later, Vita came out into the dining room. The moment had come to ask the customers at table 3 if they'd enjoyed their evening. It might seem a humiliation to whoever doesn't work at a stove to expose yourself to the judgment of every idiot who may have ruined his palate with a cigar, have dyspepsia, or be in a foul mood. But Vita knew that if you open a restaurant you cook for other people, not yourself, and so it is essential to satisfy them. She hoped they would go away happy, not regretting having spent their money there. The room was deserted. Everything in order, but not a single customer. Escaped—flown. With their glasses still full. On table number 3—in plain sight under the wine bottle—was a hundred-dollar bill. It didn't make sense. Then she pushed open the bathroom door. It was blocked. She leaned against it with all her weight, and then she saw him. He was stretched out in front of the urinal, his pants still open, disheveled, caught in the instant of most extreme weakness, in the most indecent, most human moment. She recognized him immediately.

When the police arrived, it was impossible to track down even one of the thirteen people who had dined at Da Agnello that night. Tony Viggiani was still overcome with emotion at having served the boss— and with wonder that someone had the unimaginable courage to kill him like that. Nicola had the day off and Agnello had gone to a neighborhood committee meeting in defense of Italian tenants; the landlords were evicting them in favor of blacks, whom they charged three times as much rent. Whoever shot Bongiorno knew that on Wednesdays Vita was alone in the restaurant with the deaf-mute. The police officers covered Bongiorno with a tablecloth. The waiter was no help whatsoever: he just stared at the officers with a bewildered, slightly idiotic look. The young owner displayed a disturbing coldness and was in a hurry to wash the bathroom floor. Vita told the police she hadn't gone out into the dining room, didn't know who the four young men were who had come with the old man. The waiter who served them had never seen them before. They weren't regulars.

Only when Vita climbed into bed several hours later did she realize she knew perfectly well who had dined with Bongiorno. And why he had brought him to her. He had had him eat his fill of all her specialties, devour entire plates of potato croquettes and *mostaccioli* to the point of indigestion—and then in the end, and only at the end, when, satisfied and satiated, he went to relieve himself, he shot him dead. Not in the dining room. In the bathroom. With his pants unbuttoned. In all his baseness and decadence. These things are done in person. The more the target is worthy of respect, the more indispensable it is to render him honor. It would be a vulgar sign of disrespect to unload him on a hit man. Whoever killed Bongiorno did not lack respect for him. The gesture showed he'd been well nourished, but now the time had come to present the bill. Vita turned cautiously on her side. She couldn't sleep. She kept seeing Rocco—big, uneasy, and unreachable, as he said: *I am afraid of growing old. I am afraid of becoming flaccid, resigned, vile, and obedient. I am afraid of ending up knifed by someone like me.*

When she was summoned to the police station, Vita didn't appear. She had developed an atavistic distrust of authorities, who only came looking for her in order to imprison her—first in school, then in a sort of nursery for recalcitrant and morally corrupt girls. And yet she wanted them to be able to nail Rocco. Punish him for what he'd done to her as well as for what he hadn't done, but also for what she chose to believe he could do. Destroy his hypocritical facade of bourgeois businessman, his sophisticated American wife, take away his automobile, his house with the fireplace, the evenings in a box at the Metropolitan, the vacations on Long Island—everything he had. Maybe because she had never realized how much she coveted the automobile and all the rest, how much she missed them. Or precisely because she'd never desired that life, whereas he hadn't wanted anything else and had sold or given up everything he'd believed in to get it.

Five days after the killing, the police came to pick her up. An anonymous letter had been sent from the post office in East Harlem. It suggested investigating a certain Richard Maze. Vita was the only witness to the homicide with faculties of comprehension. She had declared she hadn't seen anything, but maybe she had something to hide. Or maybe she was actually the author of the letter and only wanted to be encouraged to cooperate.

Vita was wearing her Sunday dress, a rather tight-fitting, lobster red tunic with a fringe—she nibbled a bit too much while she cooked— that highlighted the imperious curve of her breasts. Gold hoops in her ears, a vaguely cone-shaped, bottle green hat. Lace-up shoes with worn heels but rigorously polished. Her best smile.

At the Harlem police station, no one speaks Italian, and Vita, who can chatter away fluidly with her brother's American girlfriend if she wants, feigns a spurious accent and limited vocabulary, which contributes to aggravating the reciprocal mistrust. The witness swears she never left the kitchen? Swearing falsely is a crime.

"What is your occupation at the restaurant?"

"I am the daughter of the owner. We have a restaurant license."

"If you are the daughter of the owner, what were you doing in the kitchen?"

"I am also the cook."

"Why did you lie when I asked you if you had come out of the kitchen?"

"I didn't lie."

"What are you afraid of? Have you received threats?"

"I didn't leave the kitchen. I swear on my father's head."

"Did you know Lazzaro Bongiorno?"

"Who doesn't know him? He ran the most famous funeral home in the Mulberry District."

"Have you ever seen this letter?"

"No."

"You didn't write it yourself?"

"I don't know what you are talking about. I don't know any Maze."

"You do not know the aforesaid Richard Maze, also known as Rocky?"

"No."

"That's strange, because he has your same last name."

"My name is not Maze."

"This man is not an American. Or rather, he's an American now. When he was naturalized, he changed his name."

"Oh."

"He's Italian. He was born in your country."

"This is my country."

"He's known as Merluzzo, and it seems that he also went by the name Amleto Attonito. But he's really named Rocco. Do you know whom I am talking about?"

"I think so."

"Would you be able to recognize him?"

"Yes, of course. I know who he is."

"Who is he?"

"His profession is funeral director and undertaker."

"When was it, in your activity, that you heard his name for the first time?"

"I don't understand the question."

"When did you meet him?"

"On April 13 or 14, 1903. I had just arrived."

"Under what circumstances?"

"He was a tenant at my father's boardinghouse."

"Do you have ties to this individual?"

"No."

"When was the last time you saw him?"

"Years ago."

"Could you be more precise?"

"Well, I don't remember exactly. We moved away from the neighborhood. I came to live in Harlem in the summer of 1909."

"And you never had any relations with him?"

"He was a tenant in my father's boardinghouse."

"But he was seen in your restaurant on the night Mr. Bongiorno was killed."

"Not as far as I know."

"So according to you, this man has nothing to do with the homicide?"

"As far as I know, he didn't come to the restaurant."

Faced with such obstinacy, the detective starts to get suspicious and asks her if she is aware of the criminal activities this individual is suspected of performing, and so on. Vita is starting to feel more and more uncomfortable. Her anger rising, she responds that all sorts of legends have always floated about regarding Merluzzo, that he was a thief, some type of bandit, a knight, a pirate, and whatnot—but she had never paid much attention to them because Rocco—that is, Merluzzo, or this Maze—was a very generous tenant, good in every way, and she didn't believe he could be capable of doing anyone ill. On the contrary, he did good because he bought everyone gifts, helped his friends in need, and said Jesus Christ prefers the last, that he will open the doors of heaven to them and not the rich. Merluzzo wasn't part of any group, and hated associations, gangs, and rackets. He was for himself and against the world, and this gained him quite a few enemies even though many people admired him.

"Can you confirm that this individual possesses a gun?"

"How would I know?"

"Therefore, you affirm that he does not possess a gun."

"He may have had one. The neighborhood where we lived was rather dangerous."

"As opposed to this neighborhood?"

"All neighborhoods where the people are unhappy are dangerous."

"Have you ever heard talk of the Forty Thieves?"

"The band of Forty Thieves?"

"The Italian and Jewish thieves and criminals that have infested Harlem."

"They're cutthroats."

"What can you tell me about the Car Barn Gang?"

"What can I say? It's a gang. There are a bunch of them."

"It appears that these gangs exact a percentage of the earnings of all the owners in the restaurant business."

"They have never come to us."

"Could it be that they never asked you for a cut because someone ordered them not to?"

"I never thought about it."

"Doesn't it seem strange to you that yours is the only business on the street that hasn't been worked over by the mob?"

"We opened three months ago. We don't have many customers."

"Your neighbors have testified that lately the place is always full."

"Then it must be that the Forty Thieves don't appreciate my cooking. I enjoy experimenting with new recipes."

Vita interrupts herself to ask for a glass of water. She remembers perfectly well Rocco's pistol. She can see it there, tucked in his moccasins, floating in midair—called up by her desire—wavering, gleaming in the shadows of that hotel room in Saint Paul, and then dropping back with a thud. She remembers perfectly well the first time Rocco sat down at the table with a pistol in his belt instead of a knife. On New Year's he would shoot out the streetlamps from the window, and when he was in a bad mood he'd go up on the roof and fire at a putrid pig's head stuck on a stick—but most of the time he used it for holdups. She'd heard him tell Nicola that the best moment was right as people were coming out of the Metropolitan. Women go to the opera house so covered in jewels, they look like a jewelry-store window. Rocco had the bracelets and necklaces melted down at the jewelers on Grand Street. He had a real passion for gold and sparkling stones. Sometimes he'd wear the jewelry himself, and when he was eighteen he wore earrings, just like a pirate. Or like a girl. Vita sips the water, her throat parched. She's been under the suffocating glare of the detective for half an hour. She holds his gaze—and says exactly the opposite of what she would like. But what would she really like to say?

"In conclusion, according to you, the individual whom we are talking about is not a member of the Black Hand?"
"No."
"Have you ever known anyone who was a member?"
"No."
"Do you know what the Black Hand is?"
"It's a legend."

In short, the witness protects an individual she says she has known for a long time, but only superficially. She claims not to know he is suspected of criminal activities—she merely knows the rumors about things that took place years ago, when she was just a girl. The detective feels he's being taken for a ride by the curvaceous young woman stretching indolently in her chair, tormenting him with her abundant breasts and her provocative sensuality. He goes back to the fact that she and the suspect have the same last name.

"We're not related. I remember my father saying that he had entered America with one of my cousin's passports. My cousin sold it to him."
"And why didn't he use his own passport?"
"I don't know. Maybe he'd been in trouble with the law."
"Do you know—or only suspect—that he'd had trouble with the law?"
"He was too young to have been in trouble with the law. He came here as a child."
"So why did you suggest he might have been in trouble with the law?"
"I seem to recall that his father had troubles."
"What sort of troubles?"
"In those days lots of people in Italy were in trouble with the law.

There was an economic crisis, lots of strikes, occupation of land. As-sassination attempts. My mother used to tell me about it. My mother knows how to read."

"The Italians granted passports to all criminals; they invited them to expatriate. They dumped the dregs of their prisons on us."

"But here they didn't want to admit anyone who'd participated in the land movements. Anarchists, subversives."

"And this Rocco had participated in these *movimenti*, as you call them?"

"No, I told you he was just a boy then. But maybe his father did."

"You don't remember anything more specific?"

"He'd been accused of stealing a sheep."

"A sheep?"

"His father was a butcher of sorts. The one who slaughtered pigs. They only worked from December to March. The sheep belonged to his boss. He took it and killed it and gave it to his children to eat. There was a trial. He ruined his police record for that sheep. Or so they told me. I wasn't even born then."

"So this Mr. Maze's first name isn't even Rocco."

"But he has always celebrated on the Feast of San Rocco."

The detective is resigned. He notes everything, dismisses Vita, and files her declaration. Italians prefer not to report on other Italians. Unless there's some personal issue involved. As there clearly is in this case. And yet he wasn't able to get a word out of the girl in the lobster-red dress about her true relations with the suspect. She was clever, tripping over her English words, but never losing control of the conversation and vaguely relating only the details she chose to reveal. The girl went all stiff whenever the topic of the argument was broached, and denied everything. She'd even deny the evidence. It's clear, however, that she didn't write the anonymous letter that noted the presence at Da Agnello on July 5 of this Richard Maze, alias Rocco, funeral director and undertaker at the Bongiorno Bros., 207 Bowery, son-in-law of the deceased, for whom he organized three days of memorable funeral rites, complete with a procession of thirty automobiles and a ton of white gardenias. Even if she knows him intimately. As is proven by the strange declaration found in paragraph 3, which is highlighted in red pencil.

"All sorts of jobs. What matters is to advance, he used to say. He always had a great deal of initiative. Each one of us has a talent, and his was for business."

"Don't you think that if he had applied this talent for the good, instead of ending up being suspected of a hateful crime, he would have become one of the most respected men of this country, a worthy representative?"

"For what good should he have applied himself? *He looked out for himself. For me, that's his real crime.*"

The ambush of Lazzaro Bongiorno didn't get much coverage in the newspapers: it was taken to be simply the latest episode in the war among various groups aiming to control the business activities of the city, who would even strike upstanding citizens who chose not to give in. These episodes did nothing to improve the already terrible image of the Italian community, and since it was impossible to silence the news, it was at least worth underlining the difference between the blackmailers and the blackmailed, and attempting to sympathize with the latter. Richard Maze, "esteemed undertaker," confirmed in an interview that "Lazzaro Bongiorno's funeral home, of which he is director, had been targeted by blackmailers, but they hadn't taken the threats very seriously because they had faith in the law and in justice." "From this," the author of the article concluded, "one can see clearly that the murder was the result of professional jealousy. It is superfluous to add that no arrest has been made." To the best of my knowledge, no one was ever investigated for the homicide of Lazzaro Bongiorno. To the best of my knowledge, no one ever connected the homicide with the bomb that exploded on Sunday, July 30. No arrests were made, and it was never determined who had thrown the bomb or why.

According to the count compiled by the *Araldo*, it was the fifty-third bomb of 1911. According to the acid comment in *The New York Times*, by December there would be seventy, "a number that beats all records." Bomb number 53 merited a mere fifteen lines. The news of the day was otherwise: cholera was raging in the city. Dozens of people had already been admitted to the quarantine hospital on Swinburne Island. The virus had disembarked from one of the ships from Italy. Where else? From Naples, to be precise. It was an unwanted guest, a clandestine, a Neapolitan. No reference was made in the paragraph on bomb number 53 to Bongiorno's murder, which had occurred in the same place a few weeks earlier. The article conveyed resignation and bored contempt: "ANOTHER BOMB! Here we go again! After a period of inactivity, the attacks have started again. The explosion occurred at 11:45 AM, in broad daylight, in front of the Italian restaurant Da Agnello. Panic spread, and the entire block of residents abandoned their homes and fled. Police officer Walfert, who was on duty in the area, verified that the explosion was extremely violent." No one was killed, and the restaurant was closed at the time of the explosion. It was completely destroyed, however, and never opened its doors again.

Richard Maze and Venera Bongiorno never had children. I was able to trace down only one distant relative, the grandson of a cousin of hers, who lived in C—— and who still had some letters Venera sent to her grandmother across the ocean. The brief letters, written in a hesitant Italian, coincide with occasions such as birthdays, saints' days, Easter, Christmas. They never mention the people whose story I am trying to reconstruct, and instead refer to other individuals who are completely unknown to me. There is nothing in them that alludes to a life anything less than legal, bourgeois, and conventional. Venera seems to be a woman with a discreet education. She doesn't ever have much to say to her correspondent, whom she doesn't know and has never even seen. She refers to her husband only three times—always away on business. At Christmas of 1926 Rocco is running a shipping company; no further details are given. In April of 1935 he owns various import-export businesses and a construction company, and runs a taxi cooperative. It seems that after the Second World War he retires and moves with his wife to Florida, where he builds a modest villa with ten rooms and an ocean view. In 1949 Venera comes to C—— to meet the cousin, but Rocco refuses to accompany her. At least according to what Venera writes, he has no memory of Italy and nothing to look for over there.

The correspondence breaks off after the visit. The cousins probably discovered they had nothing in common, and nothing more to say to each other. When Venera died in the late seventies, Rocco was still alive. The grandson of Venera's cousin doesn't remember when he died, but it must have been in 1984 or 1985. He was almost one hundred years old. The Italian grandson, being the closest living relative, had some hopes of inheriting the villa, not to mention his collection of paintings and coins—in short, something of Rocco's "fabulous riches" the family had always dreamed about. All he got was a handful of jewelry worth a few thousand dollars. I naively ask if by any chance "Richard" had named a certain Vita Mazzucco or her descendants in the will. He informs me that Richard Maze did not leave a will. But how can that be? Certainly a man who is almost a hundred when he dies had plenty of time to arrange his affairs? Then I remember Agnello's outrage in a letter he wrote to Dionisia in 1907, one of the last he sent her. Agnello is talking about Rocco: "But that one doesn't even want to offer his bones to the world beyond, does he?"

And so it was. Rocco asked to be cremated. Nothing remained of his considerable fortune. All he brought to the world beyond was a handful of ashes.

No other information survives today that can reveal whether Rocco ever saw Vita again after the summer of 1911.

I was unable to find any photographs of him. The New York Police Department files are systematically destroyed after fifty years. Only brief yellow sheets were kept at the various stations, but they are destroyed upon the death of the criminal in question. Some examples are preserved in the Police Academy Museum, but none pertaining to "Rocco" or Richard Maze. At the beginning of the 1900s, when the crime world called itself by the fabulous name the Black Hand, newspapers only published the photographs of famous men, and crime was not a guarantee of fame for an Italian. Everyone knew the deformed face of Monk Eastman, head of one of the principal gangs of New

York, but no one had ever seen the monikers of the far more fearsome Ignazio Lupo, known as Lupo the Wolf, or Giuseppe Morello, alias Gray Fox, heads of the Prince Street gang. Or that of Salvatore Arrigo, head of the Black Hand in Ohio, or Vincenzo Sabatesser, head of the Connecticut Black Hand. The Italian underworld was spoken of with that kind of exaggerated terror inspired by strange phenomena: "human butchers," "bunch of bananas," savages who cut out their victims' tongues and cast spells on their ignorant fellow citizens, reducing them to silence. Lupo the Wolf, who starred for a time in horror literature, was defined as a "pathological killer," but what really aroused the morbid interest of readers was his "murder stables" in Harlem, outfitted with a meat hook for torturing his enemies and a furnace for burning them alive. Sixty homicides and 548 crimes, the lightest of which was "bomb planting," were attributed to him and his group at the time of his arrest. Yet he was quickly forgotten. The first novel about the Black Hand dates from 1905 (written by Adolfo Valeri, it appeared in the *Bollettino della sera*), the first film from 1906, the first record— *Pasquino membro della Mano Nera*, cut with the European Phonograph Co.—from 1920, but only in the 1930s did the gangsters with Italian names become stars.

In the State Central Archives in Rome, I found a file from the Judicial Police division of the Public Safety Office of the Interior Ministry entitled *Expulsions and extraditions from the United States*. It pertains to the "undesirable individuals" reported to the court or arrested by the New York police. In the majority of cases, the consul merely informed the ministry of their impending expulsion, but sometimes the American authorities asked, via the consulate, to investigate the possibility of compulsory repatriation. The reply was usually negative because there was no record of the subject's previous conviction, nor was his entry into the United States in violation of immigration laws. Therefore, once he had served his time, he had every right to remain in America. According to the response in the archives, this was true in the following instance: "The subject has no previous history according to this office's records, nor does his name appear among the list of wanted criminals directed to this office."

The file contains the fingerprints of a certain "Amleto Atonito."
The card looks like this:

These fingerprints, the unwilling shadow of hands placed on the ink pad and then rudely pressed onto paper, may be all I will ever find of Rocco. I try to align my fingerprints with his. The hands of the man who was supposed to have been a giant seem strangely tiny. They correspond perfectly to mine—to the hands of a woman. Looking at them again, those fingerprints on the yellowed paper look more like the paws of an imprudent and indolent cat who has walked slowly and cautiously across the floor, inadvertently leaving his tracks in the dust.

Postcard from New York

I first saw the copper postcard in my childhood, on a day now impossible to identify precisely. I had asked my father to show me something of his father's. He pulled out a shoe box containing a pair of reading glasses without lenses and Diamante's correspondence with his fiancée: 458 picture postcards and letters varying from bashfulness to lies, from threats to passion, folly, and indifference, that sum up the entire repertoire of the amorous discourse. Out of respect for my father, I read them only after his death. There was also a black leather case that had gone brittle with the passing of time. The case contained a brass plate.

Since the plate was signed "Geremia" and therefore did not belong to Diamante, I put it aside. "Is that all? Nothing else?" My father replied that Diamante was very reserved and never said more than was necessary; he had tried to cover his own tracks by systematically concealing himself, taking refuge in a silence that became ever more impenetrable over the years.

I couldn't even begin to imagine him: he died fifteen years before I was born and left behind very few photographs, all from the last years of his life, when he was suffering from nephritis. A middle-aged man,

always impeccably dressed and attentive to his appearance: curly hair, a perfectly clipped gray mustache, and extraordinary pale blue eyes. With a tough, authoritative air, an explosive dynamism painstakingly suffocated beneath a composed and well-controlled expression. The oldest photograph of him is pasted on his transportation pass, number 12.313, issued in 1920 by the Tramway Company of Rome, and dotted with monthly renewal stamps costing thirty cents each: he must have been a faithful rider of public transportation. His curly hair is severely parted on the right, his face is at three-quarters, as if he were avoiding the lens, his eyebrows imperceptibly furrowed, his eyes fixed on an imprecise point in front of him, his nose straight and decisive, full lips. A meticulous dark mustache forms an isosceles triangle over his upper lip. His concentrated expression is both hardened and distant. Diamante is wearing a sailor's uniform, which means that the photo was taken in the summer of 1915; after Italy's entry into the war, he was called up by the Royal Marines and shipped off to La Maddalena island to learn torpedo-boat navigation. He was twenty-four when he posed in front of the camera lens. At that point he'd already lived through America, military service, various hospital stays, long years of solitude, escapes, voyages, fights, follies, exile, and return. And yet the image of this sailor in uniform is all that remains of his youth. Celestina, Spilapippe, little Diamante, the vital, anarchic, unbridled Diamante who went to America, left no visible trace; it was as if that life had been sucked up by the very words that recalled and transformed it forever.

Only many years later, as I was attempting to glean some clue from the few objects he had forgotten (or decided not) to destroy, I discovered that the brass plate was actually a postcard. As with all postcards, the writing—or in this case engraving—was on the back.

New York, April 1, 1936
Dearest Diamante
My very best wishes for a Happy Easter
                              Geremia
We will raise high in America
The name of our beloved Italy

I didn't know who this Geremia was, but I could no longer ask my father, who, when he passed away, had left me in turn a mountain of papers, a pair of reading glasses, and the tarnished plaques of his trophies.

I would later discover that, according to the Ellis Island passenger lists for May 24, 1902, this Geremia had traveled on the same ship, the Anchor Line's *Calabria*, with Filippo and Genoveffa Tucciarone, Nicola Ciufo, Antonio Dell'Anno, Luciano Forte, and Ferdinando, Tommaso, and Antonio Mazzucco, Diamante's father. Geremia and Antonio were questioned together by the immigration officials. They declared they were going to join the same person: a relative of theirs by the name of Agnello, resident at 18 Prince Street. Geremia, like Antonio, claimed to be able to read and write. Like him, he claimed to be in possession of twelve dollars. Like him, he declared he was a laborer, in other words, an unskilled worker or farmhand. The officials rejected Antonio, placing a fatal black mark next to his name, but they let Geremia pass. Antonio never saw that fifteen-year-old boy again, the putative son whom he had accompanied to America—and who remained there in his place, and in place of his own son.

As I turn the tarnished postcard over in my hands, I wonder what the date in the seal alludes to. November 18, 1935. The war in

Ethiopia? Searching through the newspapers of the time, I discover that November 18 is the day on which the great powers—the United States among them—vote in favor of sanctions against Italy. On that day Italy begins its autarky, or self-sufficiency. On that day the two countries pull away from each other, and only the war, with its interminable Italian Campaign of 1943–44, will bring them together again. Then I learn that the Italians in America sent hundreds of thousands of postcards just like this one to Italy: a total of two hundred tons of copper. They were part of an underwriting campaign in favor of the war. The copper postcards were a way of helping Italy obtain the metal that the sanctions were denying it. What was the receiver supposed to do with it? Hand it over? Melt it down? Donate it?

Diamante hid his. November 18, 1935, was not a good day for him. After returning from America he had become a socialist, and after 1922 viscerally antifascist. He was beaten up on the street twice because he dared stroll about with a red carnation in his buttonhole; they broke a tooth and dumped black paint on his clothes. He almost lost his job and was demoted to the lowest of positions. That day, which for Italians in America was a day of redemption, must have made him feel dangerously on the wrong side.

What did those words engraved in the seal mean: BETTER TO LIVE ONE DAY AS A LION THAN A HUNDRED AS A SHEEP? Were the Italians of America sheep turned into lions, now taking revenge after years of humiliation to their dignity and national pride? Were the Italians of Italy the sheep who, with the conquest of an empire, had become lions? Perhaps that's what the people *on the other side* believed. But Diamante probably interpreted these words as if they were written expressly for him. The sender was saying that Diamante had preferred to be a sheep instead of a lion.

The envelope is still in the leather case, folded several times so as to be almost invisible. It preserves the address of the sender:

Geremia Mazzucco
322 E. 82 St.
New York

I don't know if in 1936, Eighty-second Street on the Upper East Side was already what it is today: an elegant street near the Metropolitan Museum of Art in the most respectable neighborhood of New York. Probably. Only now do I realize that the copper postcard is a message and that Diamante kept it, despite how bitter that message was to him. He probably slid the postcard back in its black leather case, where the verdigris started to dapple the edges and cancel the words. Every now and then he probably took it out and stared at its gleaming surface. For a second he would imagine himself in Geremia's place, imagine that he was the one sending the postcard to the other who had come back. He imagined how his life would have been if . . . He imagined himself a different Diamante, without nephritis and a missing tooth, without patches on his elbows and paint on his pants. Before his death he destroyed everything that could have preserved for his children—as well as for those who would come after him—the other Diamante, the one he had been and had chosen not to keep being. He didn't want to be shadowed by any regrets or doubts that he had made the wrong choice. He had built his life and his family on the necessity of his return. Among the few pieces of wreckage from the other continent, he left us a box of razor blades, some newspaper clippings, a handful of exotic words, his stories, and this piece of sharp metal.

I realize that I still don't know who this Geremia was. An Italian in America who in 1936 lived on Eighty-second Street, someone who'd made it, and just wanted Diamante to know. And be tormented every day and every night with that knowledge.

The World of Dreams

At twenty-four, Geremia Mazzucco became ugly, so terribly ugly his destiny seemed either despicable loneliness or mercenary company. He considered himself the ugliest man on the whole continent, but this was because he had never taken a good look around. Then again, for the past ten years, he hadn't even had a minute to do so. When the men in the nearby hospital beds asked him what sort of work he'd been doing in America all this time, Geremia smiled and said, "I made money." No one found this a contemptible occupation, whereas they would have been ashamed to share a room with him if he had confessed he'd been a sewer digger, manual laborer, or coal miner. All told, he'd lost a piece of an ear, an arm (the left one was lame), and his hair (reduced to a moldy moss)—and had made seven thousand dollars. At times it seemed to him the balance sheet was positive—it was the reason he'd come here, after all—but more often he was assailed by atrocious doubt and asked himself if it had been worth all that suffering just to make some money. No one knew about the seven thousand dollars; distrustful as he was of banks, bankers, and strangers in general, he kept the money hidden, sewn into his shirt. Unfortunately, his ugliness was there for all to see. But since Geremia had always been positive and little inclined to regrets—a craftsman of the soul—he knew the money would cancel out his scars. He decided to return to Italy and buy himself not a farm in Tufo as he'd dreamed when he left, but a wife. He would have liked to find a wife capable of loving him and not his money, but he realized that as things now stood—his already noteworthy ugliness had only been aggravated by the accident and his flawed ear, dead limb, and moldy hair— objectively it would be rather difficult. But in the end love is just a word; you can't eat or drink it. Money is all that counts. He would buy himself a wife, a fertile and pretty virgin, and he'd be rich and happy forever.

Geremia passed through New York in January 1912. The ocean in the dead of winter, with its gales and mountains of ice, frightened him. But he was in a rush to go back home and would have flown there if he could. He felt as if he were about to be born again. He was about to see his father, mother, sister, and brothers again; they had all preceded him to America and had all gone back a while ago. His father's shop, bristling with nails, hammers, and wooden feet. The dark kitchen where his mother prepared unforgettable fish soups. The tavern where his uncle served coffee laced with anisette. And what was his place in that picture? Would he purchase a license to open a tobacconist's shop and sell salt and cigarettes? Or wines and liquors? Or would he start a construction business? There were good stone quarries in Tufo. But hard as he tried, he couldn't manage to picture himself there. He kept seeing the adolescent, intimidated Geremia again, hanging on every word of the thug who was supposed to stamp his passport. Not the twenty-four-year-old man in a tailored pinstriped gray suit who was peeking into the windows of a musical instruments store in Brooklyn. A trombone was leaning against a stool. With a mouthpiece of inlaid horn. The brass shone like gold. It was infinitely more valuable than the one he'd sold years ago to go to the mines. He could already hear its sound. And now he could afford to buy it. Buy it, yes, but he didn't have an arm anymore. He would never be able to play it.

As he was contemplating that trombone, filled with a burning desire to raise it to his lips and move the slide—just one more time—he saw a poster in the shop window for a conference on the war: ITALY IN TRIPOLITANIA. Open discussion. In fact, "as the topic is of great interest, all fellow countrymen are encouraged to participate." The poster promised realistic descriptions of life on the desert front. Geremia had never been interested in the fatherland and only realized he had one when he lost it. But since he was about to return, he decided it wouldn't hurt him to catch up on the news. He tore himself away from his desperate contemplation of the trombone, pulled his hat down, and headed off toward the Italian Socialist Federation meeting hall at 1915 Third Avenue between 105th and 106th Streets. Given that he didn't know where Libya was and couldn't imagine why Italy had to conquer it, he was happy not to be at the front. The rest of his generation had flocked there, however, and if it weren't for the mines, he, too, would have to go. Even Coca-Cola and Diamante would have to go if they were called.

He had received fragmented and bitter news about Coca-Cola from Uncle Agnello, who claimed he'd always known his son was an idiot, so much so that even "that black monkey" had managed to swindle him. Of his cousin Diamante, on the other hand, he'd heard nothing for months. Then a few weeks back they started writing again. In an allusive symmetry of destiny, they were both in the hospital: Diamante in Denver, Geremia in Pennsylvania. Both alone, ill, and incurable scribblers. But the strangest part of the story was Diamante's saying he was known in Colorado as Shimon Rosen, so he had to write to him as if he really were that other person. Geremia couldn't figure it out. Diamante's letters didn't seem as if they'd been written by Diamante or Shimon Rosen, but someone else altogether. Even more confusing, those melancholy and depressing letters revealed a disgusted aversion to imperialism and the rhetoric of governments, but also an ardent patriotism completely new for someone who was so ashamed of declaring himself Italian that he'd changed his own name. His was an abstract, cerebral patriotism: desperate. In his most recent letter, whoever Diamante was explained with chilling impersonality that he'd written his will (in the case of death, it could be found on page 47 of a certain Jack London novel), because wars offer a very noble way to die for those who haven't decided how to commit suicide. Geremia had never thought about committing suicide. Having survived—a miracle—a catastrophe in which thirty-six men his age or younger had lost their lives, he was pretty convinced that a tranquil and long-lasting happiness awaited him as compensation.

That day in January 1912 is of some historical interest because of the bloody Bedouin assault on a column of the 52nd Infantry, the 1st Grenadiers, Sappers and guides of the cavalry regiment near the Gargaresch oasis. As they marched tranquilly and imprudently out of their forts toward the stone quarries—they'd received orders to construct two redoubts to protect the quarries essential for the construction of the port—they were attacked and killed. That day was also of epochal importance for Geremia. Ignorant of the Bedouins and the massacre, he marched along Third Avenue toward Harlem, eager only to vindicate his injuries. Work had always been his war. The mine was his trench. Vita suddenly appeared on the crowded sidewalk, materializing from behind the elevated train pillars. She was coming toward him, bundled up in a man's overcoat and so absorbed in thought that she walked past without recognizing him. So deeply immersed in herself as to barely notice the sleet icing her hair, the traffic, the hard times. She seemed invulnerable. That girl had a strength he had never known. A grace he lacked. She was the dark and blinding vision of a possible happiness—different from all those offers of domestic felicity he was about to buy himself. Geremia passed the meeting hall and the crowd flocking to the conference. It didn't even cross his mind to stop. Vita turned right. He limped after her, block after block, until she became enveloped in a dense fog and her figure appeared and disappeared like a mirage near the river. He didn't know how to speak to her. He was missing an earlobe and his nose was still bandaged. And he feared a gust of wind would whisk his hat off, leaving him bald and naked before the demanding gaze of the girl he didn't even dare dream of. He settled for breathing in the perfume of dust her disheveled hair gave off, contemplating the harmonious, graceful pace of her overcoat. All of a sudden Vita stopped, quickly turned around, and asked him with a laugh, "If you don't have anything to say to me, Geremia, why are you following me?" She didn't ask him what had happened to his nose, for which he would be forever grateful.

Vita lived in an immense redbrick construction facing the East River;
it had once been a beer factory and still smelled of hops. Agnello had
bought it a few months ago and transformed it into a warehouse.
Agnello wasn't there, though; during the day he worked as a mover
with his handcart. When Vita pushed him under an enormous stone
arch into a vast space wrapped in shadows, Geremia didn't remove his
hat—sinusitis, he said as a way of excuse. He whom fortune smiles
upon, who is born with a nose of modest proportions, a full set of
teeth, and a wholesome complexion will never know the spasms,
cramps, and atrocious entanglements of entrails caused by other people's stares. The evasive stare of the person who, more than anyone else
on the face of the earth, you hope finds you handsome, fascinating,
adorable. Something that, unfortunately, didn't happen. Vita looked at
him with the interest she would have paid to a lamppost, and then
rushed to warm her hands on the woodstove.

A strange hodgepodge of disparate objects began to emerge from
the shadows, like the ruins of a shipwreck. Draped in stained, dusty
cloth. Trunks, bookshelves, birdcages, gas machines, hatboxes, ladders,
couches, desks, even an entire movie theater: rows and rows of chairs
covered in purple velvet. Agnello hadn't wanted to open another
restaurant. He didn't want to see his daughter slave for other people,
sacrificing her life to create something that was consumed in a minute.
Faced with one last attempt to figure out how to make a fortune, he
found he didn't have the energy. But Vita had an idea. Americans are
constantly moving. There's nothing stable in their lives. Not in their
cities, which changed appearance every day, or in their precarious jobs,
or in the social classes, variable as the stock market. Not even in their
successes. Not in their marriages or divided and dispersed families.
And least of all in their homes. Americans migrate to follow money,
opportunities. They move to other neighborhoods, other suburbs,
cities, states—incapable of settling down, being satisfied, staying put.
These days, everyone was moving frenetically, constantly demolishing
and constructing villas, palaces, skyscrapers. The whites were leaving
downtown, the Irish the East Side, the Chinese were migrating from
the West, the Germans moving up to Midtown to the houses left

empty by Americans who were moving near Central Park. The Italians crossed over to Chelsea and Bryant Park, the Jews to the West Side, the blacks down to Harlem, the Puerto Ricans were installing themselves in the basements abandoned by the dagoes, the artists in the garrets in Greenwich Village, the clandestine immigrants in the dilapidated wooden houses abandoned on the Bowery. Since Vita stayed put while everyone else moved, she suggested to her father that he make a living giving shelter to other people's homes.

Vita removed the sticky geometry of a spider's web hanging from the canopy and disappeared behind a monumental bed. She told Geremia to make himself at home, for this was their house. Their furniture had been ruined by the explosion and they'd sold the pieces as firewood. Now, in compensation, they had various living rooms, dozens of bedrooms, and five bathtubs with bronze feet.

So as not to lose the girl that Diamante couldn't or wouldn't keep, Geremia poked around among the objects piled up in that immense warehouse. It was full, so Uncle Agnello must be back on his feet once again. Geremia thought they were rather similar. They didn't let anything get them down, and had even frightened death. Vita said she didn't need to invent lies anymore because they came true, or to move objects, for now they came to her. This was the world of dreams. They inhabited hypothetical spaces, possessed hundreds of lives. They had houses full of antiques and rubbish from hurried moves, grandfather clocks, paintings, rugs, and globes. Entire libraries and stuffed owls. She moved from one life to the next by simply taking a step: she could live like a princess and take tea amid the furniture from a house on Fifth Avenue, a place she would never enter—but as there was no difference, it didn't matter. Geremia brushed his hand across a cloudy mirror, which kindly refused to reflect his image. Houses, houses, houses. But none for you and me.

He felt as if he were wandering in a gigantic storeroom for lost objects, a dump for dreams that had been returned, parked, or failed. Yet in those shadows, the name of the real missing object—Diamante— had not yet been uttered. Geremia thrust his fist in his pocket, fearing that at any moment she would simply ask him outright: And your cousin? Where is he? How is he doing? Does he have another girl? But

Vita didn't ask. Geremia thought it best to keep silent about the fact that Diamante had written to him. That he was ill. For Geremia had been ill himself, probably still was, and he knew other people's compassion is unbearable. He wouldn't have known how to explain to her that Diamante had found the time to ask about Nicola and even Agnello, but not about her. In fact, when Geremia had suggested they sail together from New York, Diamante had said that if he ever decided to go back to Italy, he would leave from Boston or Philadelphia, or Canada even, but he hated New York and had no desire ever to set foot in that city again. Geremia had understood right away, with an irksome anguish, that when Diamante wrote *New York* he was thinking: Vita.

So he merely mentioned that Diamante had gone to Colorado. That he was bloody-minded, ornery, a misanthrope—an idealist. He sought out battles he was sure to lose and always found merciless enemies to lay him low—in truth he had become his own worst enemy. Vita didn't display the least interest in Diamante's fate, and Geremia was relieved that theirs had simply been an adolescent love, profound but now forgotten. What could he know that afternoon? Vita had let Diamante's name drop like a stone in a well. It drowned in silence. She didn't seem unsettled. She was still the same old Vita—dynamic, a bit confused, distracted. Luminous. Beautiful. "I'm not like my cousin," he added with apparent modesty. "You're Uncle Tom," Vita laughed. "Perhaps," Geremia answered. "But you know something? Uncle Tom has his feet on the ground and a roof over his head." Vita shrugged her shoulders. All this keeping one's feet on the ground means human beings have lost their wings.

The speaker at the Avanti! Club was at that moment showing slides and moving the audience with the necessary horrors of war, but Geremia continued to roam among the furniture of houses in which he would never live so that Vita wouldn't throw him out in the sleet. When he did finally leave the warehouse, he didn't go to the steamship company to buy his return ticket. He kept thinking he wasn't made to store up other people's failed dreams, but to make them come true. And if Diamante preferred to die in some hospital in Denver instead of admitting he couldn't imagine a life without Vita, and if Agnello lacked the energy, means, and imagination to construct new houses in new neighborhoods, he had seven thousand dollars sewn into his shirt under his left pocket, close to his heart.

If anyone had asked him why he was still freezing himself in the fierce New York January when he could already be strolling down the street in Tufo and choosing himself a wife and a new house, Geremia would simply have explained that he hadn't found a place on the steamship: he would only travel second class, not third, because he was determined to show everybody back in Tufo how far he'd come since leaving that mud hole. But no one asked him. Vita, with whom he spent his last lazy American afternoons, didn't ask him anything. Appreciative of his discretion, she let him help her reorganize the files and billing. Geremia was precise, orderly, and silent.

At first she couldn't understand why Geremia didn't go out around town and enjoy his final days in America. She wasn't interested in him; she'd lost interest in men in general. She considered them arrogant, vile, and egotistical. She didn't want to become somebody's wife and have to depend on the moods and whims of a husband. She already had a family, and didn't want another one. She didn't need anything to be happy; in fact, she had come to the conclusion that happiness lies in self-sacrifice. Because when you try to satisfy your happiness egotistically, that is, by chasing after love, comfort, wealth, or who knows what else, the circumstances of life may arrange themselves in such a way as to make it impossible to satisfy those desires. No, happiness consists in living for others. Strangely enough, her father did not oppose her wish even though she had feared he would be prepared to make any sacrifice in order to buy her a husband to cancel her shame. He had taught her that a woman alone is something wretched and wasted. But Agnello had quite willingly accepted the idea that his only daughter dedicate herself to caring for him in his imminent old age. It was what he had always wanted, the reason he'd called her to America.

Besides, Vita didn't have much opportunity to change her mind. She had lost touch with her old friends from reform school, and didn't know anyone in New York. She was almost always alone. Several bachelors did happen by the warehouse—lawyers, doctors, and notaries about to move to some other city along the coast, Italians as well as Americans: the first with whom she'd ever exchanged a few words who weren't policemen or social assistants. She was curious about them, as she was about the roadrunners that wandered around the Brooklyn Zoo—exotic animals, a different species. Some of Nicola's friends had come around as well, as had a few fellow countrymen determined to get themselves an Italian wife. They were discouraged by her indifference and vanished after a few visits and went around bad-mouthing crazy Vita, proud Vita, Vita the whore. But Geremia Mazzucco endured that indifference. He would stay put on the edge of the couch, rigid and distractedly scratching his cheek. His beard traced a wild shadow on his jaw, but it wasn't sufficient to make him look tough. Geremia didn't look like a cowboy or a vagabond, just a hairy Italian who needed to shave twice a day. Even though it had been months since he'd been down in the mines, his skin still looked unhealthy and his black eyes stood out against his yellow flesh like two seeds in a shriveled apple. He'd bought himself new clothes, but he wore his new suit with the same awkwardness as if he'd rented it from Max Willner's store. And yet he was neither arrogant nor violent nor stupid nor false and mellifluous, nor proud, irascible, or stubborn.

When Vita felt his eyes on her hands and lips one January afternoon, she thought she could feel his heart beating. To ask him to leave—to forget her—would be like severing the elevator cables and letting him fall into the flames. She realized Geremia was asking her to accept the burden of his life. But she could not accept his burden. She was not at fault for what had happened to him. She had already accepted her own. The weight of other people's recriminations that carved an abyss inside her. The desire to be punished, to punish herself, to *sacrifice herself*.

Vita asked him if he remembered what he had asked her two years before. Geremia blushed and nodded. Okay, she would accept his proposal. She would consider him her friend. "Friend?" he repeated, uncertain. "The rest comes and goes on the winds," Vita said. "Friendship is forever."

To hide his scars, Geremia wrapped himself in thick scarves and coats and always sought out the comfort of shadows. But for Vita, those scars were the most fascinating element of his appearance. That face, which had once been banal, like millions of other faces, had now become unique, unmistakable, special. She couldn't tell him that, naturally. Her last memory of Lena was of a white hand sticking out from under the sheets at Bellevue. A hand scrawled with mysterious signs, like a sheet of paper. Vita knew she was the one who had decorated that hand, and couldn't tear her eyes away. She wanted to grasp it, hold it tight, shake it—but she didn't. She couldn't bring herself to ask Lena to come back home or to forgive her. Lena had turned her face to the wall, but left her hand in view for a minute. Then she withdrew it under the sheet. Vita had searched for her for years, all over the city, but had never been able to find out anything about her. She'd lost her. And with the passing of time, Vita developed the absurd conviction that those who had crossed through the flames and managed to come back knew a secret they didn't want to share. The secret Lena had promised to reveal to her, but never had: how to live beyond pain. How to bear it.

One afternoon, as Vita was dusting the furniture and Geremia bustled around trying to help her, they bumped into each other by accident, and Vita wasn't able to avoid touching his lame arm, all pink and gray, like a mouse's paws. Geremia started and pulled away, but Vita stretched her hand toward the lump sticking out beneath the handkerchief and slid her fingers under the cloth. It was the first time someone had touched Geremia's skin since he had been discharged from the hospital.

The affectionate way Vita had of caressing his lame arm taught him he still was able to cry. He was absolutely certain Vita would not push him away, and knew that one day he would tell her what had *really* happened in the mine, something he hadn't told even himself. He relived the accident in those moments when his consciousness drifted off, when he was half awake, or after two glasses of wine or an intense emotion. Then he was back at the end of the tunnel again, after the explosion—a dark womb invaded by shouts and moans. Trapped three hundred yards underground, buried with bodies and mud in a shaft, in the most desperate darkness. Alive and crazy with terror, his headlamp broken and his face lacerated by the rocks that had flown at him when everything exploded. He ran, slamming into walls, falling, hurting himself, banging his head, stumbling, yelling, using his own voice as a

guide. Then somewhere far away, at the end of the darkness—a red
glow. At first he thought it was the sun. The mine had opened up,
restoring the light of day to him. But it was fire. Everything was burning. An asphyxiating heat was dissolving metal, taking his breath away.
He runs toward the fire, because in that blinding light he had caught
sight of the way out of the shaft—the elevator that deposits them there
every morning at seven so they can penetrate the bowels of the mountain. He's the foreman so always goes down last, counting his men
first. He runs toward the elevator, fearful that the others, who have
somehow managed to climb on, won't wait for him, perhaps out of
vengeance for some tyranny, demand, or abuse on his part, will push
the button that will lift them to safety, leaving him to burn in the flaming mine. He shouts—Wait for me, brothers!—runs, trips, falls, weeps,
sees his last hope slipping away, the elevator has already started, it's already climbing, oscillating two yards above the floor. He holds out his
hands—Don't leave me here, don't abandon me. The others recognize
him, many are his men—Jump, boss, jump!—they yell and grab him
by the arms, hands all sweaty, bloody, slippery, they almost drop him,
they don't let him go, hang on, they hold on tight, he rises up hanging
in the void as the fire blazes in the well, flares toward the oxygen coming down the shaft, bursts up toward the men. He's on the platform
now—clinging to the iron cables along with the others. They're all
yelling, faces turned toward the sky, as if they could hear them up
there—Get us out of here, quick! It's no use, because the speed of the
elevator is set and can't be modified. The iron cables creak, the flames
are licking at the platform. The blue sky up above them is as far away
as a painting. At minus ninety yards the heat attacks their feet and
melts their boots. They press together, pushing, going mad, and in the
panic someone tries to break open the cage and hoist himself up by
the cables. Another falls, dropping into the abyss. At minus seventy
someone collapses, vanquished by the heat. Geremia tramples on him,
they all do, so his body will block the fire, so his flesh will shield
theirs—the sparks spray and dance in the swirling winds, the flames
coil around their ankles. The roar of the fire drowns out their shouts,
at minus fifty his arm is on fire and he crushes up against a man who
has fainted, tears off his overalls, spitting on himself, as if his saliva

could put out the fire, at minus forty the flames engulf the platform—like a funeral pyre, a tornado, a whirlwind—it burns less intensely at the center, the cables burst into flames, and those who had managed to gain a few meters by scuttling upward now fall back with charred hands, the skin burned off to the bone—at minus thirty his skin is blazing like a torch, his hair is screeching, his body emanates an odor of burning embers, of roast chicken, and he stops yelling. He falls.

Seventy days later, when they declare he's out of danger, the first thing Geremia asks for is not a mirror—he doesn't want to know what is left of his body. "The others?" he whispers. "My team? My boys?" No one answers him. Thirty-six men died in the explosion. The most catastrophic mining disaster since the days of Pittsburgh and Marianna, which left 139 dead in November 1908. Or Cherry in 1909, when 200 died. They never found all the bodies: when the walls caved in, they were buried somewhere in the darkness of the earth. "The ones on the elevator?" *Jump, boss, jump!* "The men on the elevator?" When he leaves the hospital seven months later, he is bald and his hair is just starting to sprout again, like down. One arm is lame, impotent, dead, his right nostril collapsed, his right ear missing at the top. Light hurts his eyes, and smells nauseate him. When the elevator arrived at the mouth of the mineshaft, the firemen turned their hoses on the engulfing flames, creating a cloud of black, oily, oppressive smoke that enveloped the rescue workers' clothes and faces. When the smoke cleared, there was a clot of fused and charred bodies, melted limbs—they were all dead. And on that heap of ashes and flesh, one blackened body was smoking. It was you.

Vita lightly touched the edge of his ear nibbled by the flames, his crumpled nostril, the skin on his neck, smooth as a baby's, perfectly white. She smiled at him. Geremia didn't say a word. It was a clear day and the wind had transformed the sky into blue enamel. The sun's rays flooded the windows of the old factory. Here it was dark, but there the light traced illusory, evanescent presences on couches and coat racks. When Geremia left the warehouse, instead of going back to his boardinghouse he headed toward the wharf. He took a yellow envelope out of his coat, in which he jealously kept the photographs of his wives.

Ever since he'd become foreman in the coal mines, dozens of women in Tufo itching to share his wealth had sent him photographs of their daughters, nieces, or goddaughters. The girls competed in appealing to him. Country girls, simple—and faithful. Virgins who dreamed of an invalid but well-off husband. With the money the mining company had to give him as compensation for the burning elevator, but even just with the seven thousand he'd saved, in Italy he would be important and prosperous, a man to know. Forever, because in Italy social status is permanent, and nothing—not the end of a kingdom or a war, not even death—can change the way things are. This was the reason he'd come to America, and this was the reason he'd never leave Italy again. He smiled, looking at the awkward smile of an eighteen-year-old niece of who knows which relative, godfather, or buddy of his. She was staring at the lens as if she were looking for him. That sweet, docile look told him how ready the girl was, how predisposed and resigned to loving him. But he didn't know what to do with a wife like her. He turned the sepia-colored packet over in his hands. He wouldn't marry them. He didn't even know their names. He had survived. He would never be able to accept again the life he'd left behind on the fiery elevator. He wanted the other one, the one he'd glimpsed in that blue frame ninety meters above his head. The woman he could speak the truth to, the woman capable of bearing it. Instead of putting the packet back in the worn yellow envelope, he ripped it up and threw the photographs in the river. His wives drifted amid apple cores and oil stains, slid on the turbid water, rocking, revealing their old-fashioned hairstyles, white scarves, and plump hands to the sailors operating the timber barges downriver. They revealed his future in Tufo—his return—to the indifferent, clear January sky. Then they were sucked into the wake of a steamboat, flipped over, and disappeared. Geremia stared at the dust specks floating in the sunlight and vanishing by the steep sides of the steamships. In the world of dreams there was also a place for him. He had passed through the flames unscathed—like the heroes and warriors of the legends of his youth. The most coveted prize was his. Vita was his.

The Wreck of the *Republic*

The real estate agency that Geremia and his partner, Celestino Coniglio, had opened on Lenox Avenue was closed on Saturday afternoons, and after lunch he would slowly make his way to the warehouse. He would tell himself he'd wait until Uncle Agnello finished playing cards at the bar and came home, but then his impatience would get the better of him. Vita and Geremia would go to the movies, for their daily encounters had exhausted all topics of conversation. The darkness of the theater favored silent colloquia and offered them both a pleasing intimacy: Vita had her thoughts, and Geremia her nearness. They would never have been allowed to go out together alone in Italy, but here no one thought anything of it. There were hundreds of movie theaters in New York. They saw comedies, dramas, stick-ups, even Milano Motion Photograph's version of Dante's *Inferno* at the Fair Theatre on Fourteenth Street. They saw dozens of westerns: *Broncho Billy's Heart*, *Broncho Billy's Promise*, *Broncho Billy's Mexican Wife*. Vita liked imagining that as Broncho Billy rode off into the sunset, somewhere behind the screen was Moe Rosen, the Jewish boy who had once painted a window for her and Lena on the blind kitchen wall.

At the Bella Sorrento Theatre on Thompson Street, with continuous showings from nine in the morning till midnight (entrance fifteen cents), they were playing the "cinematographic scenes that portray the entire life of the brigand Giuseppe Musolino." Geremia hated stories about brigands. It annoyed him that the only way Italians knew to get themselves talked about in this part of the world was when they opposed the state and went up against law and order. Something that happened to one in a hundred, while the other ninety-nine, himself included, never even got noticed. But when Vita chose Musolino, he accepted. It was not the only sacrifice he was willing to make for her. He had calculated that a friend would take several months, at worst a year, to become a husband. He must check the attacks of other men whom chance will send into her arms, demonstrate by his actions that he is preferable, always maintaining the strictest moral code, which foresees only the utmost loyalty, devotion, and faithfulness. Then they saw the sinking of the *Republic* and Geremia realized he had erred in all his calculations. His hair will turn white first. He will become a businessman, owner of the real estate agency of which he now possesses only one modest branch, and Vita, nearly thirty, will have consumed every drop of time in waiting, becoming so used to solitude that she'll want to share it. It would take him years to find the path that leads to Vita.

It was during a dismal documentary on Italy entitled *News from Home*. But whose home? The film offered the shocking images of the earthquake at Irpinia—the devastation of Sant'Angelo dei Lombardi, Lioni, Calitri. The departure of soldiers for Libya. That February afternoon as she sat in the dark next to Geremia, Vita tried to imagine which part of the port of Naples they had used to film those images, and for the first time in many years, she thought about Tufo. There was little left. A few fragments, noises, such as the cry of the clam vendor—big fresh clams!—who shook his basket as he climbed through the village, or the rustle of the rain on the roof tiles of her house, the whistle of the train as it sped across the plains, racing over the Garigliano bridge in a cloud of smoke. The clatter of a cart on the Via Appia lined with pine trees, the murmur of the olive trees in the countryside, intermingled with the chiming of the San Leonardo

Church bells for vespers. Some faces: the liver-colored visage of the prison guard, the herder's face the color of goat droppings as he came down from the mountains amid throngs of ferocious, shameless dogs. Some smells: the incense in the small church, a just-peeled mandarin. A freshly picked lemon.

The bitter perfume of that lemon tasted so long ago summoned a vibrant image from the most remote corner of her memory where it had been hiding: a lemon tree leaning over an ancient stone well. She remembered clearly the rope disappearing into the icy obscurity of the well. The splash of the pail in the invisible water. Someone had picked that porous and compact yellow fruit from the lower branches and sliced it with a knife. Placed a transparent slice on her tongue. She drank icy water from her pail, sucking on the lemon slice. The water tasted sour and wild. That someone was Diamante. His blue eyes pierced the guilty depths of her memory.

Those eyes are so close she longs more than anything else to touch them, but hesitates; somehow she knows that if she puts her arms around him she will embrace cold air, her hands will pass through him and he will vanish in the fog, light, and smoke. All of a sudden Diamante has disappeared. A heavy weight suffocates her heart. *No, no, no!* cries a voice inside her head. She calls him. And when she opens her eyes, her heart pounding like a crazed metronome, she finds herself in a Harlem movie theater staring at a lifeboat swaying off the port side of the *Republic* and an empty lifejacket floating on the waves of the Atlantic, the words *White Star Line* already worn away by the salt.

Images of the shipwreck of the *Republic* passed across the screen. On January 23, 1909, a foggy day like today, between six and seven in the morning the *Republic* was rammed by an Italian ship seventy miles south of the Nantucket lighthouse. The prow of the *Florida* penetrated deep into the hull of the English transatlantic steamer. The marvelous *Republic* began taking on water. The machine room was completely flooded in fifteen minutes. The telegraph operator tapped out the SOS. The crew had orders to evacuate the ship. The coast guard sent a tug to tow the ship to safety—but there wasn't time. The *Republic* leaned to port, the stern was already underwater. The ship was full of sick passengers; they traveled in groups and almost always returned in the company of pneumonia, tuberculosis, syphilis. The 250 first-class passengers were evacuated first, among whom were numerous American millionaires on their way to the Costa Azzurra for the winter, the countess Pasolini, and the writer John Baptist Connolly. Then the 211 third-class passengers—on their way back home. Numb with cold, they huddled on the bridge. Sailors folded back the tarpaulins. Lifeboats were being filled and lowered into the water. Passengers were putting on lifejackets. *Those* lifejackets—with the white star printed on the cloth. *That* lifeboat—with the pointed prow ready to brave the waves for the first and only time.

Geremia wasn't following the terrible sinking of the *Republic*, pride of the White Star Line. The ship, now desolately abandoned, the captain alone on deck, raised its prow to the stars, and sank to the bottom of the ocean. Geremia let the film flash onto the dumbfounded faces of the spectators. That ship meant nothing to him. He was watching Vita. Alarmed, she asked him if she had spoken in her sleep. Geremia swallowed but said no. He pulled out his handkerchief, leaned toward her, and dried the tears streaming down her face. She hadn't even realized she was crying. Then Vita remembered calling out his name, and that her dream had made her cry. Diamante.

It was our ship. The one that brought us here. It was new, wonderful—intact. Now it has sunk to the ocean floor. Ripped open by the violence of a blow it couldn't foresee. Broken in two. It must be all rusted over by now. Battered by the currents. Penetrated by every wave, every storm, every tide.

"Why are you crying, Vita? It's only a reconstruction, poorly done at that. A toy model in a swimming pool. Manikins." "Don't you understand, Geremia? Diamante and I sailed for real in that lifeboat—ten years ago." We wanted to stay together, so after the third bell we didn't separate, we stayed together all night long in that lifeboat, clinging to one another in the cold. I was nine years old and didn't know anything, we didn't do anything wrong, or good, I don't know, we should have gotten out of there, should have knocked on the windows of the first-class saloon. Someone would have heard us, there were dozens of waiters in there, even at night. They would have opened the door for us. They wouldn't have punished us. I would have cried a bit and they would have been indulgent with a little girl. We couldn't stay there, it was too cold and there was a storm. The cables creaked. Those lifeboats weren't very secure. It could have come unhooked, could have fallen below. But we didn't go. We didn't want to go back inside, back under. Closed up like in a prison. So we made do. We liked that place, so we stayed. Huddled up against the side of the hull. The life-jacket smelled of mold and sea—and ever since then, that is Diamante's smell to me. That night, Diamante decided he wanted to become a sailor someday. Try to picture us there. Alone. A child with inky-colored hair, filthy hands, grimy cheeks. A flowered dress stained with coffee and sauce, darned socks, a shawl full of holes. A little boy who owns nothing but his cap, a pillowcase full of odds and ends, and his smile. We had nothing to lose and everything to find. All of a sudden we burst out laughing because we realized why we couldn't find the white star in the sky. We were wearing it, stamped on the lifejackets. Nothing could happen to us, no danger touch us. We stayed huddled in the bottom of that boat, seeking warmth, he fitting perfectly against me, curved along my back. I discovered that night how two bodies can complete one another, so that they seem mutilated if separated.

They found us the next day, suffering from exposure. A dog, you know. One of the first-class passengers' dogs smelled us and started to bark. The officers came and lowered the lifeboat onto the bridge, and there we were. The frost had condensed and frozen, forming a thin, hard crust on the lifejackets, our hair and clothes. The night had been bitter cold, below zero—we were off the coast of Newfoundland. But what did we care about geography? For us there was just one coast and then the other, with the water in between and us suspended there. If it weren't for that dog, we might have died like that. And the strangest thing is that today I was thinking that if the dog hadn't started barking, we would've stayed there in the bottom of the lifeboat, at the beginning of everything. We were so close that night, Diamante and I— inside an empty universe, full of possibilities and space, the two of us inside that universe, whole and untouched—and I wished we'd never been discovered, never been found.

Geremia was silent. What could he possibly say? He didn't feel like taking her back to the warehouse. He said he was tired, he'd been working lots. He didn't have the energy to stay by her side. He only had one heart, and it was in pieces. Vita squeezed his good hand— a handshake between business partners, brusque, energetic, and hurried—and headed off. He stood there staring at her overcoat, her dark wavy hair tumbling over her shoulders. Turn around, turn around, *turn around*. Vita didn't turn. She disappeared around the corner, swallowed by the sea of people.

But Vita didn't return to the world of dreams. Tousled, beaten, and harassed by the winds sweeping through those unnatural streets devoid of curves, deviations, or surprises, she headed toward the port. She stopped along the docks and stared at the incessant movement of men unloading cargo.

The warehouses cast dark, black shadows onto the East River. An icy damp oozed from the very walls of the city, this city to which she felt she belonged, but where nothing anchored her. Vita was invisible to the inhabitants of this country. Vita the guest. Unknown Vita. Iridescent, oil-colored waves sloshed against the banks, set in motion by the passing boats. At times a strange prison encloses us and we cannot see the walls, vents, doors. It's hard to escape from a prison like this.

Dozens of ships were crisscrossing the river that March afternoon. Steamers, cargo boats, and barges called out to one another, their whistles signaling their routes. The mist floated like smoke on the water. A donkey was flying through the air. Hanging from a winch, bound to the cables, crazy with fear, he was twisting wildly, flying through the thick fog. A bit farther beyond, a coast guard vessel was combing the water with a searchlight, as if it were looking for something or someone. An agitated crowd on the docks was gesticulating, pointing to a rag jostled by the current. The searchlight whirled about, illuminating first the river, then the crowd, the coast guard vessel, then Vita. Her head was spinning. She tried to hang on to Diamante's image, but couldn't. Her mind could no longer reconstruct him. He was like the breeze blowing on the water, dissolving into tiny circles, quivering and melting on the surface of her consciousness. She had to see him again.

Even just once. To know. To ask him why—what had made the

paths of their existence diverge, where had those tracks welded together forever come apart? Or perhaps no. What did it matter now
to ask, explain, justify herself? Embrace him, behold him, touch him.
His name was surrounded by a shimmer, and that shimmer was his
absence—but to her it seemed like light. It was just the searchlight,
though, illuminating everything as it moved away—fog, ships,
winches, and water, every rag and every passerby, every window and
every wall.

I'm Writing to You from a Place You've Never Been

On the bungalow's outer walls horses with thick green tails galloped, white birds soared across a deep red sky sprinkled with black stars, and floating brides danced in the abyss of a violet ocean. Moe Rosen had painted these fantastic figures in order to cover the nakedness of his dwelling and to satisfy every desire of the woman who was to come here. Over the years his painting had erased the plain wood and absorbed the windows, transforming his shack into a densely populated and subversive world in which everything seemed possible—every coming together sensible, every encounter happy. When the rain beat against the boards, it filtered directly from the ocean onto his cot, and the snow fell on the horses' manes. That shack sheltered him from reality, keeping it distant.

When Diamante returned from work, he would sit on the wooden stairs—even these were painted blue—where the paradoxical freedom of that universe comforted him. It made him think that everything has a reason if it is turned upside down and observed from a different perspective. He sat scouring the horizon in silence, until darkness de-

voured everything and he forgot he existed. He often wondered where
Moe Rosen was now, and if he'd ever paint images like these again. A
few months after Diamante's arrival in Denver, Broncho Billy's company moved farther west, to California. Now the paint was peeling,
the eyes fell from the floating brides, and the ocean was fading away.
Diamante would have liked to touch up the colors eroded by the Denver sun and cold, but he didn't dare; that house had not been dreamed
for him.

When Moe Rosen departed, so did Diamante's only friend, and
the only American—new, recent, voluntary—he had ever known. Lit
by a violet sunset, they had shaken hands at the garden gate on the
dusty road that descended the hill. How beautiful this area was! Lots of
people said it looked like the high plains of Italy. But Diamante had
never seen Italy. His Italy was Tufo, and Minturno on Saturdays, market day. Moe had lifted his tanned hand to shade his eyes, that ironic
yet trusting smile of his hinting at an awkward farewell. The painted
females had already started to flake by then because Moe had thrown
away his colors and brushes one day. He didn't want to paint anymore,
didn't want to become a great artist—it had been a liberating fantasy,
but it faded when he no longer needed it to escape from his past.
Art—either it's real or it's not. And Moe had decided he wasn't the real
thing, even though Diamante didn't agree. Just like the brides, the
horses, too, would soon be eaten by the wind, for Moe had gone to
Niles with a bunch of actors who merely pretended to be cowboys.

"Thanks, Moe!" Diamante said, waving his hand. "What for?
What are you saying?" Moe cut him off. Then he turned and walked
slowly toward the street. Only then did Diamante notice that Moe
walked with his knees slightly bowed, as if he'd just gotten off a horse.
He'd started to look like Broncho Billy. Clumsy, naive, and unshakable,
just like him. Diamante stood there yelling "Thanks, thanks," even
though Moe couldn't hear him anymore. And so he left—slowly, awkwardly; alone, too. Lena hadn't come to Colorado. Moe Rosen had
combed New York for her and in the end he'd found her. She was
working at the Haymarket, a famous dance hall on Sixth Avenue. Men
could rent her for a dime a dance. She was the most popular. Moe had

asked her to marry him and Lena had said yes, she just had to sort out a few things first. But she never arrived. Moe became a shadow, stretched by the sunset until he finally swallowed up his colored house. He was wearing boots, a gaudy handkerchief around his neck, and a hat. A cowboy hat.

Diamante was supposed to join him in Niles on the road to San Jose as soon as he'd saved up the money for the ticket. He liked Moe Rosen's friends, those dream catchers for whom he'd nailed together backdrops and painted scenery. He could have become one of them. Busy people, inured to reversals of fortune, the brevity of triumphs, and the consequences of failure. But Diamante never went to Niles. For months, his only company was the painted images on Moe Rosen's shed. His was an isolated existence, silent as a tree. He responded in monosyllables to his employers—brick factory owners, managers of nightclubs and resorts for wealthy loafers—for whom he delivered packages, unloaded trucks, painted walls, or watered gardens and lawns. The starry silence of the Denver night and a dizzy, deep sleep were all he felt he needed. Lots of girls came to Moe's shed, but none of them stayed. The doctor never came, either, because Diamante was convinced he wasn't sick, just tired. He didn't take care of himself. He thought he simply needed to find the right lime or cement to put back together the thousand scattered splinters of his wounded and shattered pride.

Sometimes, when the mute company of the painted figures distressed him like a broken promise, he would go into the city, to a theater, where for a handful of change he could watch the comic yet pathetic show of a slapdash company of low-level hams, fleshed out by flabby trapeze artists, decrepit clowns, and unknown comedians, whose awareness of their inability to make people laugh only made them more vulgar. By now Diamante understood the punch lines they tossed about and managed to have a bit of fun despite everything. In the winter of 1912, he went to a show by an English company whose name he'd forgotten to notice when he entered. The theater was frozen thanks to the drafts coming from the stage. The place was half empty. The star of the show—who might have acquired a certain fame in cities on the East Coast, but was completely unknown here—played an old drunkard. While the actor concentrated on performing his number with the utmost professionalism, ignoring the icy stare of all those empty seats dotted here and there with a few frozen silhouettes, Diamante realized his throat was parched and he was incredibly thirsty. His muscles, tendons, bones, even his veins ached, and he clearly had a high fever. So high that his thoughts jumbled confusedly in his brain and his body trembled uncontrollably. He felt more drunk than the drunkard onstage. Hiding his face in his coat collar, indifferent to the laughter that was shaking the audience, he slumped in his seat.

When the workers came to turn off the lights and close up the hall, they noticed a young man stretched out on the seats fast asleep. They tried to wake him, shaking and tugging, but all in vain. The agitation that spread through the empty theater reached the dressing rooms, where the actors learned that a spectator had died during the performance. Theater people are highly superstitious. Such an accident could cast a dark shadow over an entire career. The star of the show took off his fake nose and removed the cotton padding from his pants. He'd looked seventy onstage, but he really was just over twenty. Shaken, he went back onstage. Half of his face was still white with wax. The other half revealed black whiskers and a bright blue eye.

The spectator's body was stretched out on the floor, his head resting on a carpet of popcorn and roasted peanuts. Glimpsing a pair of black pants—too long—and broken shoes with gaping holes in the soles, the young actor was struck by a terrible foreboding. Irresistibly drawn to the ominous shadow the dead man would cast over his future, he jumped off the stage and kneeled over him. He realized with horror that the young man was more or less his age. And that he had light blue eyes, black whiskers, and the fine features of a prince. His expression—tender and ferocious, clever and defeated—illuminated his melancholy, serious face, too serious for someone his age. The man didn't merely look like him—he seemed really to be him.

The theater workers rummaged in Diamante's pockets but didn't find a cent. Just a piece of paper covered with strange words:

I'm writing to you from a place you've never been
Where the trains don't stop, the ships
Don't sail, a place out west,
Where silent walls of snow . . .

The English actor watched the inanimate body being dragged toward
the entrance. As the door opened, a cold blast blew in. The theater
workers dumped the vagabond in a pile of snow on the other side of
the street. It had been snowing for two days straight. Flakes like hard
white sand covered the stranger's face. The English actor was thinking
that if that young man died, so, too, would his hope of one day leaving behind the wobbly boards of these low-grade American theaters.
His hopes of meeting someone who understood him and would invest
in his talent, someone courageous enough to take a chance on an unknown, proud foreigner who knew he wasn't the mediocre individual
everyone thought him to be. What struck him about America, where
he'd been floundering for months, was the dismissive hurry with
which people got rid of things, gestures, and people, which made him
feel so desperately alone. But he'd also been struck by the hope for
change here, and he had carried that uneasiness with him when he returned to England. There he realized that he would simply keep tumbling down the rungs of the social ladder with no chance of ever
picking himself up. His destiny would have been one of manual labor,
forever. And so he decided to leave again. He went back to America.
But on that Denver evening, his hope of saving himself—of being
saved—was dying along with that young man.

He crossed the street. He was still dressed in his tattered old drunkard's costume, and when he tried to hail a carriage, the coachman
whipped the horses and filled his shoes with mud. He practically had
to get himself run over in order to make one stop. He climbed on the
box and ordered the driver to take the young man to the hospital. And
to make sure he would actually get there, he paid in advance.

The theater company stayed in town another three days. The English actor went three times to ask about the young stranger's health.
He was told that he hadn't regained consciousness and that he was a

foreigner. But the only document they'd found in his pockets was a sort of poem.

> I'm writing to you from a place you've never been
> Where the trains don't stop, the ships
> Don't sail, a place out west,
> Where silent walls of snow surround every house,
> Where the cold beats the naked body of the land,
> Where people are new, and memories,
> When they come, arrive in letters
> Unwelcome like ghosts.
> This is a place where the sun doesn't warm,
> But at night I melt like ice in the blazing room of dreams
> To pluck the pleasures that rise up from the past—
> Days torn like pages from a book
> And I search for the black cat, long tables that never end, the off-key
>   chorus of our song,
> Amazed.

The English actor was a stranger in Denver as well. He said he would pay for the young man's treatment and not to be stingy with the medicines, for he didn't have economic difficulties at the moment. He was the star of the company, after all, and his contract was good for a few more months. On the fourth day, he had to catch a train west and continue his tour. More low-grade theaters, more wobbly floorboards, once again the stock character of the drunkard. For how much longer? Forever? The doctor told him that the man had recovered and was improving. Did he want to meet him? The English actor asked if he was out of danger. Yes, they assured him. The actor smiled, nodded, and added that it wasn't necessary to disturb the patient. Relieved, he left some money to cover his bills. He told the doctor, who was eyeing him strangely, that he would come back. Of course he never did.

When Diamante asked what had happened, they explained he had fallen ill during a performance and that his brother had brought him to the hospital. "My brother?" Diamante exclaimed, surprised. "Why, yes, the one who played the drunkard in the English theater company at the Sullivan and Considine Theater." Diamante didn't say a word; he was too confused to think. Much later, when he left the hospital, nobody remembered the English company anymore. They couldn't tell him the names of the clowns or the old drunk. No one had noticed. They were low-grade hams. Lots of them passed through Denver every season. But the cashier was sure that the young English actor was named Charlie or Chas—no, Charles. His last name started with a C. Something like Chaliapin, Chapin—Chaplin.

We used to have a whimsical, beat-up projector for showing eight-millimeter films. The screen was made out of some rough plastic substance that magically unfurled from a metal cylinder and hooked onto a little gray ring with slots set on an extendable pole. On Sundays, when my father surfaced from the studies that stole him away from me during the week, he would transform the living room—too grand a word for this space, which also served as dining room, library, and study—into a movie theater. We didn't have much of a selection of films, probably because we were both extremely loyal and obsessive in our passions; we always watched the same ones, shot fifty years before I was born and a good many years before his birth as well. They were shorts, comedies from the silent era. We started watching them one afternoon in 1971 and continued all through 1972 and 1973, at which point I stopped enjoying myself and Roberto lost the desire to show them. To me those Sundays seemed interminable and empty until the movies began, while for him they were all too brief; Sunday meant family time, something he allowed himself little of during the week, constrained as he was to work to feed us and simultaneously feed himself—that is, to write. But I didn't know that then. I only knew that my father's occupation aroused in my schoolmates a mixture of perplexity (because they'd never heard of it before) and envy (because he wasn't a butcher, policeman, or lawyer), and in me uneasiness (because he wasn't successful despite my worshipping him) and later amazement, when I found out that he kept working for the railroad even though he was a writer. I also knew that there was another type of film than what we watched on Sunday afternoons. With music and words, editing and color: he had taken me to see *2001: A Space Odyssey* and other such novelties. But at home, *film* meant the films of the 1910s and we never asked or told ourselves why.

The images trembled, the projector sizzled, screeched. At times the film jammed and caught fire and the screen would be invaded by an alarming vision of a small hole burning bigger and bigger. The image of that ever more ravenous hole devouring in a blaze the stories we loved so much was tremendous. Over the years, the films became unusable—eroded and broken by flames. The screen ripped and the images appeared inexorably more distorted, the faces ruined by a deep scar that lacerated the screen. Finally the projector burned out; it was impossible to repair, for the company that made it had gone out of business and the first video recorders were starting to appear on the market. I never again saw those shorts my father used to show me, and for a long time I didn't even worry about where they had ended up. They had simply disappeared along with those Sundays of the early 1970s, along with his and my solitude, the questions never asked, the choices never explained—along with our distancing and definitive separation. Along with him. When I went back to look for them, I only found one, still in its case. The label portrays a vagabond with his unmistakable too-big shoes and cane. The man is either coming or going—at any rate he's moving and seems about to leave us—a black figure on shiny white paper. I never sought out an eight-millimeter projector from a collector because I didn't want to see that film again. It would have been unbearable without him. But I didn't need to see it. I still remember every frame. The name of the film was *The Immigrant*.

The film was distributed in Italy in 1917. It opens with Charlie Chaplin on the ship that is taking him to America. Loaded with immigrants, the ship rolls and sways, making him seasick. On the third-class deck he meets a girl and her mother, poor shabby wretches like himself. The mother has been robbed. In a poker game, Charlie recovers from the thief the sum that had been stolen and presents it to the girl, thus risking being mistaken for the thief. The first image they see of America is encouraging—the Statue of Liberty. But right under that statue the immigrants are fenced in like animals and put through the discouraging disembarkation procedures. Charlie and the girl lose sight of each other once they get to New York. Somewhat later, Charlie, who is starving just as he did on the ship, is roaming the streets when he finds a heaven-sent coin on the sidewalk. He goes to a restaurant where the waiter harasses and scorns him for his ignorance, poverty, and inability to decipher the menu. But just then Charlie meets the girl again. Like him she's alone, and like him she has not been successful. Charlie invites her to sit and offers her lunch. As they are talking, she blows her nose in a black-edged handkerchief and he understands that her mother has died. The coin he'd found on the sidewalk turns out to be fake and Charlie falls into paroxysmal panic, but is saved by an impresario (a movie producer?) who proposes they pose for him. The encounter with the impresario may—perhaps—change their lives, but it doesn't pay for their lunch, and the problem of the unpaid bill is still unresolved. However, Charlie notices that his benefactor has left such a generous tip that he can pay for the girl's lunch. He nonchalantly picks up the tip, finally freeing himself of the aggressive waiter, and leaves with the girl. Happy. In the end the two protagonists get married. It is a sad rainy day.

Diamante got married on a sad rainy day as well, in October of 1919. He, too, had seen *The Immigrant*, a story that moved him and made him laugh. I don't know if he recognized himself in that man— or if that story, which was really autobiographical for Chaplin, seemed his own. Nevertheless, he brought his son Roberto to see it several times in the 1930s—and my father, just as I would have done, never asked him why. Our fathers told lots of stories, but talked very little, or perhaps they didn't talk at all. Mealtime in Diamante's house was so silent his children could hear their teeth grinding and crunching, and to make the time pass they would compete to see who could chew twelve mouthfuls the fastest. Our dinners would have been just as silent if we three hadn't talked for Roberto as well—liberating him of the burden of having to say something to us.

In any case, Diamante didn't miss even one of Charlie Chaplin's shorts, nor did he abandon him when Charlie became famous—a millionaire and as vain as a king. Nor when he became an intellectual and stopped making people laugh, when he was tried for his erotic exuberance and criticized for his attraction to underage girls, when he began to speak—even when he became a communist and fell into disgrace in the United States. Diamante always remained loyal, and his was a decisive loyalty. He followed him as if he were a traveling companion. The mysterious brother he'd never met. He knew by heart Charlie the dentist, Charlie the painter, Charlie at the beach, Charlie the late-night reveler, vagabond, fireman, drunken gentleman, immigrant, fugitive, soldier, glass salesman, gold digger, unemployed man, clown. And his children got to know that clever yet defeated vagabond with black whiskers and clear blue eyes. But Roberto had never understood why, when the rest of the audience shook with laughter, his father sat staring at the screen, immobile and petrified in the darkness. Or why, at the sight of that twirling cane and lopsided walk full of pathetic pomposity and untouchable dignity, Diamante, who was usually so rigid and controlled—no one had ever seen him cry or appear moved— would pull out a handkerchief and furtively blow his nose.

The doctor at the Denver hospital discovered an illness that was difficult to diagnose. Diamante wasn't much help, for he didn't say a word during the exam and refused to answer any questions pertaining to his past or his identity. He remained silent when the doctor asked him how he got the scar on his lip, why he had rheumatism and the early stages of arthritis in his hands, as if he had held a rope or shovel too tightly, why he showed the symptoms of a prolonged exposure to humidity and cold. He stubbornly denied he was Italian and claimed the piece of paper in his pocket was not his. The doctor conjectured a "psychophysical breakdown." Diamante let him talk and did not betray himself. He would have liked to tell him he didn't feel broken down, just empty. Without substance. Suspended between two shores with nothing to hang on to. Light. Like a piece of cork that could end up anywhere, following currents or tides, but never choosing the direction. Light things don't sink to the bottom. But they have a hard time landing. The doctor lanced his back to bleed him and said, "You probably know better than I do what your illness is called." "Yes," Diamante said. He knew.

His illness was to have dreamed a different life, and to have had that life betray him. To have lost that life, and even the dream of it. To be unable to remember. To believe that his years in America never existed. To pretend he'd dreamed them. Because once something's passed, how, in the reality of the present, is it any different from an illusion or a fantasy? Even if it did exist once, but now exists no longer, except in his memory. And if even his memory is unable to hold on to it, then it will be as if it never existed at all. To lose his memories, day after day, in the immobile fixity of the sky framed by the window. To attribute them to someone else's life, not his own. To forget the bad in order to survive, to restrict, cancel out the most atrocious facts, the wounds and the pain. And then to make an even harsher selection, so as not to live on deception and nostalgia. To remove the most intimate gestures, the most beloved faces. Because the pain of a vague memory is less acute. That was the first thing he'd learned in America. When he was unable to avoid imagining his father placing a hand on his shoulder, Diamante would shut his eyes and try to concentrate on the objects around him. He would tear himself forcefully away from the past, crush it by closing his eyes. It worked. With time, without his realizing it, his father, mother, and brothers had become phantoms. Now he had to do it again. Cancel out the majestic and grotesque sound of Geremia's trombone, which accompanied his first shave in the kitchen sink. Moe, fingers covered in red paint, up on the ladder painting the underwater bride over the door, whose evanescent smile would greet him for months. Rocco's smile as he pedals across the Brooklyn Bridge and looks tenderly at the boy clinging to the handlebars, his too-big hat falling over his eyes. Vita's tiny hand clutching his as the crowd jostles them on the quays of New York. Her rough mouth while she waits with eyes closed for him to bend over and kiss her. Cancel everything, down to the point where he finds himself pondering names that no longer correspond to real people but are merely the characters in some forgotten story. To forget he ever met them, had shared with them days, nights, hopes. To forget Vita. Forget who you were—your smile, your energy, your reckless joy—and become someone you don't know. A clinical case balled up under the sheets, a vagabond so deeply estranged and contemplative that everyone thinks you're suffering from shock. An anonymous, forgotten stranger in the Denver hospital who doesn't remember his own name, or the sense of his own destiny. Who doesn't know if his future will be more of this intolerable limbo, and doesn't want to know.

"You will never be cured of your illness," the doctor concluded. "You will heal, you'll feel better, you'll be able to go back to work— but if you live, the illness will return. It will always be in you, and you will learn to live with it. You'll only be able to get rid of it if someone donates to you a healthy kidney and takes your unhealthy one, your inexhaustible mine of poison. But that is not possible. So you'll get used to it, this illness of yours, you'll bear it and learn not to fear it, but it will be the only thing you won't be able to forget—it is the most authentic part of you."

His illness was called America.

In the Denver hospital in 1912, they called it "nephritis." They extracted entire bags of poisoned blood so it wouldn't contaminate his healthy organs. As if the poison could be drained away with the blood, as if the poison weren't his very self. His hospital expenses grew to more than two hundred dollars. The patient ignored his medical report and didn't seem interested in his health. He didn't seem interested in anything at all. Who would pay those expenses? Even though he denied it and persisted in speaking a strange American with inflections like East European Jews, the ill man was Italian. The hospital alerted the consulate that there was a young man with no means of paying who had been there for months. Gravely ill and unable to take care of himself on his own. Could they possibly initiate the procedure for "repatriation of an indigent in a state of poverty"? The young man had refused to provide his name—he was unnaturally taciturn, irritable, and aggressive, and he responded violently to the least provocation. His distrust prevented him from establishing relations with anyone, and his excessive pride prohibited him from accepting help. He had a tendency to consider himself unjustly persecuted, discriminated against, and undervalued. His only actual quality seemed to be his "excellent calligraphy," providing that the untitled poem found in his pocket was written—or copied—by him.

The consulate sent a collaborator who was paid piecemeal (so many identifications, so much money) to verify the patient's situation. It proved impossible to initiate the procedure for state of poverty because there were not sufficient funds to take on the burden of all the vagabonds scattered across the United States. The Denver consulate was responsible for thirty thousand Italians (not counting clandestine immigrants) spread over a territory larger than Europe. It cannot repatriate or maintain all of them. They'll have to manage on their own. Moreover, the consul is no longer Adolfo Rossi, who had been a worker himself and had found himself in a similar situation thirty years earlier; now it is Oreste da Vella, a diplomat from a good family, a member of the bourgeoisie who cannot begin to imagine what possible chain of events could have resulted in a twenty-one-year-old's ending up in a hospital in a state of poverty. He furnished his co-worker with a list of names of individuals wanted by the American and Italian police for crimes committed in Italy or abroad in the first three years of their stay—beyond which they could no longer be expelled. The crimes ranged from clandestine entry to theft, property damage, and abandoning marital bonds.

The young man's description did not fit any of the profiles of the individuals on the list. He was not a wanted man. The co-worker's visit was a waste of time. Diamante hardly glanced at the printed form that the man from the consulate was compiling with his characteristics. His hair was curly, not straight. His eyes were blue, not gray. He did not have a Greek nose, and his mouth was not well formed. It was beautiful, and always had been. The man whom the consulate emissary was registering as being in the Denver hospital was not him. He was nobody. He didn't have a name or place of residence. No one would ever look for—or find—him again.

The emissary had also brought another list of names. Diamante barely glanced at it. "Who are they?" he asked as he handed back the sheet. "Boys born in 1891," he replied. "Their families, the newspapers, and the War Ministry are all desperately looking for them. The Italian military is looking for them. They have to do their military service and still have thirty days to report for duty. After which they'll be consid-

Connotati

Statura m. 1,64 ½
Periferia toracica 0.8
Capelli *neri - lisci*
Fronte *alta*
Sopracciglia *nere*
Occhi *grigi*
Naso *greco*
Bocca *giusta*
Mento *"*
Viso *"*
~~Barba~~
Colorito *roseo*
Segni particolari *cica-*
trice al labbro superiore

ered deserters and won't ever be able to return to Italy." "Ah," Diamante said, turning his head away. The hospital window didn't offer him a view of the highlands or the mountains or the sky. It was merely a gray box streaked with rain. He had spent weeks staring at that square and had learned to distinguish all the shades of gray. Smoke, ash, pearl, steel, anthracite, rain. He didn't want to die, but he wasn't sure he wanted to live, either. He didn't want to stay and didn't want to go back. He wasn't an impostor, as the nurses insinuated, nor was he dying, but he was not a healthy man. He wasn't anything. Or he was too many things, all at odds with each other and impossible to hold together.

"All the Italian consulates in America have been alerted, but we cannot locate these young men," the collaborator explained, resigned to the fact that he would earn nothing for this visit to the Denver hospital. "What can you do, America is immense. They've gotten lost." Of course you can't find them, Diamante would have liked to say. Why in the world should someone born in 1891 go back to Italy for military duty and risk being sent to war? He hated soldiers, the obtuse docility of underlings, the arrogance of the authorities, the rigid idiocy of discipline. And the weapons, which, like women, had the tendency to let themselves be handled by the wrong people. "And yet," the other continued, dejectedly scratching his goatee, "if they're badly off, they have a unique opportunity to repatriate, because the Italian government will pay their return voyage." "Really?" Diamante asked, hypnotized by the stubbornness of a fly banging against the window in a vain attempt to get out. Stunned, it fell onto the windowsill and buzzed faintly. "Yes. The Italian government cares about its boys."

Diamante had never noticed. Except for three years of schooling and a passport issued in exchange for eight lire, the Italian government had never offered him anything. He removed his gaze from the fly's agony. "Our government offers third-class travel back to the city of departure," the man from the consulate explained. "And three years of room and board in a barracks somewhere in our dearly beloved country," he added with a chuckle. Diamante closed his eyes. Halfway down the page of that long list was his name.

What Remains

And so Diamante went back. He looked for her where he thought she was, but Vita had moved and no one knew where she lived now. He went to ask Cousin Geremia in his office on Lenox Avenue. Diamante found him there with his partner, a former miner who was now in a wheelchair. Geremia sat behind a desk, typing out contracts. Diamante envied him. As a boy he had always dreamed of becoming an employee in an office like this. But Vita thought offices were about as inviting as prisons. Now he no longer knew who she was. An eighteen-year-old Italian girl in New York. Geremia wasn't happy to see him again and struggled in vain to hide it. While he tried to think up a good lie to keep him from seeing her again, to keep him far away from her, Diamante stared at the huge poster on the wall.

MALAGA CITY. Extraordinary, special sale: lots for 5 dollars apiece. The ideal city destined to become the most important center for Italians in America.

The poster pictured a locomotive in a spotless station set amid welcoming cottages with cheery window boxes and perfectly manicured lawns. There was something sinister about this hypothetical landscape suspended on the office wall, like the call of a whore.

CHARMING POSITION. Salubrious, pleasant climate. High, level, dry ground. Electric train with station stop at Malaga City, hundreds of trains every day. Farms, shops, schools, church, hotel, telegraph and post offices, telephone. Very close to Philadelphia, Atlantic City, and other commercial and industrial centers. Building & Development Co. 2302.04. Visit to the site strongly advised. Paid excursions. Maps sent on request.

Celestino Coniglio, ignorant of Geremia's torments, asked Diamante if by any chance he wanted to join an excursion to see the lots. "We just opened recently and we're selling at good prices. The Building & Development handles plots of land near and far from the center. In the Bronx, Bay Shore, Rutherford, Sheepshead Bay." Diamante was tempted to point out that he couldn't care less about buying a lot. Land fetters you, property chains you down. If anyone had asked him the definition of the liberty he had sought so eagerly, now he would know how to respond: liberty consists in not being ashamed of yourself. This is the only true and authentic liberty. All the rest enslaves. He was about to explain that he'd only come by this hole in the wall of an office to find out about Vita. Geremia's bruised expression told him to keep still. He stared at the knickknacks on the desk. A lit cigarette rested in the ashtray made from an oyster shell, seductive like a woman's mouth. Indecent thoughts. Internal combustion. Obsession. He'd dreamed of her for years, yet he'd never touched her, not even in his dreams. Radiant, she floats toward him, but every time he tries to hold her, she breaks apart like a reflection on the water. That same girl had run off with another man. Had betrayed all his plans, all his efforts, all his reasons. She had left him alone in the sidereal emptiness of those Denver nights, asking himself what he was doing in that part of the world, and why he hadn't left yet. But he could never leave without seeing her again, and only in seeing her again would he know if she was dead to him as he had tried to make himself believe, or if instead she was still alive, pulsating under the wounds he had tried to inflict on

her. He had not forgiven her. He was incapable of doing so. But the
memory of what happened had distanced itself from him with a prodigious velocity, leaving behind a dull sensation of suffering and rancor,
while the memory of those years of fire and promises had moved
closer, grown larger, bringing an intact inheritance of desire and nostalgia. Without Vita he never would have come to America. None of
this would ever have existed. She was the one who had brought him
here.

Diamante pretended to be interested in the announcements that
lined the walls. *Italians of America! Now is the time to leave the polluted air
of the cities! Purchase your dream under the New Jersey sun.* Plans showed
the division of lots in West Hoboken, Grant's Tomb, and Cortlandt
Crest, nine subway stops from 155th Street. The Building & Development offered terrain of every price and dimension, bare land or lots
dominated by white-columned Georgian villas, windswept stone cottages on the Atlantic, or facing a marsh muffled by coots. He tried to
figure out where the hitch was. He didn't believe in deals anymore.
This was certainly all a big rip-off. Land situated lower than the river,
downwind from a sewer, or in hopeless locations surrounded by intersections and train junctions. Or in impenetrable forests three hours
from the nearest station. These cunning real estate agents were growing rich selling illusions by the lot—illusions may be pruned, uprooted, and destroyed, but they always grow back, like weeds.

Geremia was probably wondering if Diamante had come to slash
her face, which is what he would have done if he were truly a tough
guy, or to pardon her, which is what he would have done if he could
have understood her. At times Diamante thinks it impossible to mend
an unraveled sweater, and at times he thinks there wasn't ever a sweater
between them—that it's all just a metaphor, a convention. Vita belongs
to him just as he had belonged to himself, before he'd lost himself in
the secret room where coffins are made or along the railroad tracks.
"Vita went to Bensonhurst," Geremia finally said. In that instant he
hated Diamante and himself, because he had never been able to lie. He
thought he would never see his cousin again, or the girl for whom
he'd stayed in America, that he'd just thrown his life out the window.

Diamante ran off without even so much as thanking him. Seven years and seven months later, he sent Geremia an invitation to his wedding to Emma Trulli. Then Geremia understood that Diamante wanted to pay back the debt: he gave back the gift he'd received on that long-ago April morning.

The girl was leading her clients along a narrow path. She walked quickly, imperiously pushing aside shrubs and bits of wreckage so that the group of buyers trudging behind her wouldn't have time to protest that the train stop wasn't ten minutes away from the hill as the ad claimed, but more like forty. They passed the abandoned shacks of a foundry and headed single file down a path overgrown with brambles. The nearby soap factory filled the air with a sickly-sweet smell, nauseating at that hour of the morning. It was drizzling and the fog was tangled in the tree branches. The excursions constituted a pleasing diversion in her solitary existence. They sent Vita because the buyers were usually people who had lived in America for thirty years or so now and didn't speak Italian anymore. Or maybe because no one would have bought a dream from the likes of Geremia, his hands blackened with coal. She had once sold kisses and words. Now she was selling America to Italians. Land. Hills. Sand. A sliver of sky.

Last month she had sent money to her mother in Tufo so that she could come join her in America. Even though Dionisia was now completely blind, she could still manage to get here. Geremia knew the right people to get her into Canada. And then Vita would go and get her in Toronto. She implored her to come. If she did, everything would have a reason. The family would be reunited. "I'm serious, Ma, you'll live like a lady here." Dionisia had replied that it was too late. She would never be able to change her ways now. And since Vita had started sending her a sum of money every month, she could live like a lady right there in Tufo. She had lived in her house in front of the Church of San Leonardo for too many years to leave it now. She lacked nothing. "I've always been alone and free, and I don't have any intention of imprisoning myself now that I'm old. *Vita mia*, I love you as much as the day you left, and I think of you every moment, but I'm not coming. Your mother." Vita read Dionisia's letter several times, incredulous. Only her mother's great refusal made her realize that nothing would be put back together, no rupture mended.

She didn't turn around to make sure they were following her; she knew the buyers were wrinkling their noses at the brambles and industrial smoke. "The factories are closing," she explained, modulating her voice to sound more convincing. She had always known how to make her lies sound believable, but now she had to make the truth believable. And believe it or not, the latter is more difficult. "In a few years, the factories will be gone. And just think, it only costs five dollars. Nothing, you think. And yet with those five dollars you'll be buying land suitable for building in an area that will soon become a paradise."

Suddenly Diamante emerged from the path. He was running, hat in hand. His overcoat was splattered with mud and doubt was written on his face. He seemed offended by the ashen sky and the squalor of that industrial landscape, which was no longer countryside but not yet urban, spoiled by the stench of the swamp and the smoke from hundreds of factories. He seemed offended that those two real estate agents had the nerve to try and pull off such a hoax. A lumpy hill, steep dunes overrun with brambles an hour's carriage ride from the nearest station. He wondered who would ever pay money for a fistful of sand.

Lots of people. Everybody. Fathers and mothers who'd been raised on the fire escapes of New York ghettos, in overcrowded basements or noisy rooms, intoxicated by the fetor, in dim pigsties that looked onto cast iron and darkened brick. As they walked down the streets of this neighborhood not yet born, they felt their innermost desire was about to be fulfilled. They don't see brambles and refuse. They see porches, yards, garages, light switches.

Dozens of frozen faces turn toward him, surprised by his sudden appearance. A knot of middle-aged people with big hands and the exhaustion that comes of having worked one's entire life. Laborers, mothers, cigarette girls, and rubicund Madonnas. None of them is Vita. They all have ordinary faces, eager and vague. He wouldn't walk a mile to see any of them again. And yet he has crossed America four times for a girl like Vita. Maybe Vita is just like these other women—

ordinary. If only that were true. A plump girl is calculating out loud: "five dollars a month and a fifty-dollar down payment can buy you a lot that is worth five hundred, just twenty minutes from Coney Island and half an hour by train to City Hall." The ground is littered with paper and empty bottles. The grass smells like detergent. Vita's gaze hits him like a whip. She recognizes him because Diamante has not changed. He has stayed small. Like her.

And yet they don't run to greet each other. She doesn't even smile or beckon him to join them. Maybe he's arrived too late this time, too. She merely looks at him diffidently, as if he weren't real, as if he were just a shadow or a reflection. But it is really she standing behind the wicker trunk containing the picnic baskets the agency offers the buyers. A scarf over her hair, a map in her hand. She's darker than he'd remembered, more shapely—more carnal. God, how many times he had imagined this very moment. She always threw herself at his feet, imploring.

Since Vita gives no sign of moving, he approaches her. He dodges the excursionists who are looking at him hostilely, as if he had come to take away their piece of land. He climbs over nettles and puddles, and around black umbrellas on which the day drums. Everyone notices his arrogant expression, his pretentious striped suit, silk shirt, and patent-leather shoes. He doesn't know it, but he already looks like a real American to these people who will never see America. Where to begin? With recriminations? Accusations? Letting things slide? I just happened to be passing through New York and I stumbled on a memory of you?

"Where's Prince?" he asks her, disappointed that there is neither vendetta nor tragedy in his drama. Vita blushes finally, but only because the clients are staring at her dumbfounded—as if they were asking, *What the heck does this guy want?* "He got tired of waiting for you and died of a broken heart," she responds, her eyes brimming with reproach. Can that dog really be the first thing on his mind? "Aren't you going to ask me when I got back?" Diamante lashes out. "Why should I?" Vita rebuts. "You never left."

"I did so leave!" Diamante explodes. "I carried tons of water, I was off ruining my health while you were chasing after Rocco's money!" A curtain of fog falls over his eyes. He'd like to slap her or throw himself at her feet, maybe both. "Why didn't you take me with you?" Vita screams. "Why? I did it for you!" Diamante shouts back. "Can't you see? How could I respect myself if I made you go through what I have?" Oh Christ, he doesn't know what to do with his hands, his face is burning, a lump rises in his throat. He doesn't mean to fling himself at her, but that's exactly what he does. Or at least that's what Vita thinks. She backs into the trunk and knocks it over, sending picnic baskets rolling across the grass. The oil cruet topples as well. Misfortune follows them everywhere. She stretches out her hands, intending to push him away, to defend herself—she doesn't understand that Diamante is merely groping about, trying not to lose his balance. "What about respect for me?" she shouts. "Doesn't that count?" For a second Diamante fools himself that she meant to pull him toward her, and he lets himself be drawn forward, like a nail to a magnet. But the intense and sudden emotion is followed by a lancing pain. She is biting his nose—hard, as if she were trying to bite it off. Her nails have sunk into his face and something cold pierces his side—something sharp and metallic. Diamante cries out as two men grab him and pull him off the girl. He tumbles among the bushes, falls to his knees, incredulous, stunned, blood gushing onto his American suit. "Get out of here," the most robust of the buyers threatens. "Leave the *signorina* alone or I'll call the police."

Oh Vita, what have you done to me? His jacket is slashed open—sliced clean, as if with scissors. He yanks out his handkerchief because blood from his brow is dripping onto his lips with that sickly-sweet taste of rust. One of his eyes is wounded and his eyelid burns. The insult burns. He sees red. He sees Vita, red, up on the crest of the hill, clutching that sharp, metallic object. A knife or a compass, maybe. Whatever it is, it's one blade Vita's eyes never bent. And yet if she were so indifferent, she would never even have grabbed that weapon. Red, with her scarf tucked behind her ear and a lock of hair falling across her forehead. "Diamà, Diamà. Oh God. Go away," she repeats like a chant. "What have you come here for? Go away." No, he doesn't go. He gets up. To think that he once trusted her, a blind, absolute trust, more solid than the trust he had in himself. She was his certainty. He could bare his world to her, expose himself without being destroyed. Why did she shatter all that? He brushes off his pants. She missed him—the blade caught his jacket and barely scratched his side. The smokestack exhales a fetid, offensive stench. Red. Vita doesn't move. She was my girl. Mine, mine. Oh God, why did you let this happen to me? Why do you let a twenty-one-year-old cry like a baby in front of this red and black creature who doesn't even take a step toward him, who merely curses his lack of punctuality as she wipes her eyes with her coat sleeve?

Vita's cold hand brushes against the scar that puckers his lip. It is such an intimate gesture that Diamante puts his arm around her and rests his melancholy face on her shoulder. The brown nape of her neck, black strands of hair against her skin. They don't know where to begin. So they stay there, rigidly locked in a cautious embrace on that hill stinking of rotten shrimp, under a spiteful rain that stings their skin, staring at the dusty water diffracted by the light of the trees. In this instant even he would buy a lot of sand from Vita.

Hope, Vita says all of a sudden, squeezing his hand. Diamante, his legs shaking, leans against a large rock. Because it is wrong, very wrong, to start again where they had been interrupted by the obtuse vulgarity of the world. But when she repeats the word *hope*, he automatically leans forward and kisses her eyelids. *Light*, and Diamante kisses her forehead, *friend*, her hair, *river*, the mole on her right cheek, *railroads* . . .

The clients are calling her, perhaps she needs help? The *signorina* is their guide and the guardian of their future, even if she's just an eighteen-year-old girl. She cannot allow herself to stay there and fight with her lover in the rain. Her clients are truly interested in the land. They really want to buy, they've been dreaming of this all their lives. We have to make them happy, satisfy them—it's our job, that's what we're here for. "Why don't you come back tomorrow?" Vita suggests. "I have to take these people to choose their lots today. I'm free tomorrow. The next excursion is on Sunday, for the Huntington lots on Long Island." Diamante catches a lock of her hair between his teeth. How familiar she is, beating against his chest—her tiny, impertinent nose, her black eyes with their dark shadows. How different she is and how much the same as the memory he guards like a secret. "I'm here now," he says. "Come away with me."

They walk along what is not yet a road, a path that doesn't seem to lead anywhere. Where is she taking him? They come upon a pond. For a moment the water's surface reflects a boy dressed as if he were going to a party, his face scratched as if he'd fought with a puma, and a girl in muddy boots. He with a hand in his pocket, she resting her head on his shoulder. It's not even a nice day. The fine dusty rain continues to fall and shreds of paper and petulant grains of sand are buffeted by the winds. You can't even see the ocean beyond the foggy haze. But it is near. Diamante can sense it, breathe it in. A piece of paper sticks out of his pocket. The ticket the consulate gave him. His steamer leaves on Tuesday. Today is Thursday. They have five days. Five days to learn what remains.

Vita stops. She raises her arm and twirls around, as if to indicate the border of something he can't perceive. "Do you like it?" she asks. "This is it." "What?" All he can see is sand dunes and the vague line of the ocean. Vita smiles and seems about to reveal a secret, maybe the spot where she has buried her treasure. And in a sense, that is exactly what it is. She's explaining that she didn't come to Bensonhurst to sell a hoax she knew how to resist. The land was divided into one hundred lots: some people buy to build, others to resell once the prices in the area start to rise. Right now they're asking six thousand dollars an acre—but over time, given as how there are plans to build the subway out here, they could go up to ten or even twenty thousand. Vita kneels and sinks her hands into the sand. If it's a hoax, she's fallen for it as well. "Diamante, I bought a lot, too. With my savings. I haven't told anybody because you're the person I want to live with here. And if you hadn't come back to me, then there would never be anything here. But now I tell you that on this hill, one day there will be the Mazzucco house. Our house."

She trickles the sand onto her palm. It is white, dusty, cold. She rips a branch off a bush and draws a line, then another—a whole forest of lines. The furrows are walls, the squares are rooms, the rectangles windows. She had always wondered who children were writing for when they drew on the sand. Now she knows. Inside the four deepest furrows will be a garden, and between the two parallel lines a porch. Three squares for the children's rooms. Diamante runs after her, trampling across the kitchen floor and ruining the attic until he grabs the branch, but Vita hasn't finished and wriggles free, tries to close the door, he catches her by the arm and they both fall onto the rectangle that will be the bedroom one day. As he kisses her, he realizes that nothing else remains. What remains is this girl—loved, hated, loved. He wonders if perhaps only promises made can be broken, only words sworn can be denied—the word is *not* life—and betrayal can exist only where there is trust, loyalty, and abandon. The greater the love, commitment, involvement, and dedication, the greater the betrayal. To live where we cannot be wounded—corroded or clutched by pain and disenchantment—is not to truly live. To give and give of ourselves, asking in exchange a guarantee that we will come out of it intact, perhaps even compensated—that is not giving. We can only betray the people we truly love.

On April 18, 1912, it was still winter in New York. The fog was thick and stagnant, and they waited for hours for a ferry to take them back to Manhattan. Vita and Diamante sat on the railing of the ferry station, cold and wrapped in each other's arms. Vita was asking herself why she had shown him right away her treasure buried in the sand—she was always in such a rush, but the patience of water is what wears down mountains. Diamante was asking himself how, after having lived in the house drawn in the sand, he could tell her that on Tuesday the battered *Louisiana* of the Lloyd Italiano would carry him back to Italy. So little time to steal from the umpteenth separation. With every tick of the minute hand of the giant clock in the Coney Island ferry station, his heart stopped dead.

He told her on the ferry, or *traghetto*, as they still called it. Where else? He was from a place called Traghetto, after all. Minturno used to be called Traetto—or Traghetto—because a barge once ferried between the banks of the Garigliano there. It was the only crossing point for travelers following the Appian Way from Rome and the Papal

States to Naples and the Kingdom of the Two Sicilies. That ferry, suspended between two worlds, a mobile parenthesis between two shores,
rising up out of nothingness after miles of solitude, swamp, and devastation in that no-man's-land without even a name—the feudal owners
called it the Land of Work—was all that remained of an ancient Roman city. Then the Bourbons built an iron bridge and the ferry disappeared along with the name of the town. But the shifting spirit of the
place—the river, the two shores, the water—remained. For the first
time in ten years, Diamante realized that water would carry him home
again.

He told her he was leaving just as she was pointing out a silvery
flock of seagulls in the mist. The smell of metal wet with rain brought
the taste of blood to his mouth. He was expecting her to sink her nails
in his face again, to grab her compass and aim better this time. He
feared she would hate him forever, would interpret this departure as a
calculated revenge. Anything, but not her tears. He had desired them
for years, almost expected them, but now he wouldn't be able to bear
them. Vita didn't cry. She swallowed a sliver of cold and simply asked
him why. America wasn't America without Diamante. "They paid my
way, Vita," he replied. "The Italian government paid for my ticket
to get me back. They bought me. I sold the last thing I had left—my
body.

"I have to do military service," he continued. He tried to anchor
himself in the mist, in the glimmer of her eyes. "Military service?
What do you want to go off and be a soldier for?" Vita hugged him,
rubbing her face against the rough fabric of his striped jacket. If only
she could breathe his smell into her, fix in her eyes the curve of his
neck, feel forever the tingling of his whiskers on her lips. How empty
America is without him, how pointless it all is if he gives up. If she
loses him, she will lose herself as well—if he leaves her, that self will
cease to exist and they will never be together again, not amid the rabbit cages on the roof of an old tenement building or on the benches of
the ferry for Manhattan.

Diamante said he needed to be part of something—to belong to
something. To find his place. He would try to enlist in the Guardia di

Finanza, the financial police. The GDF watches over the sea, the only part of the world that seems inhabitable to him, where he doesn't feel out of place. And then there's the pay. A cadet gets one lira and eighty-five cents a day. If he makes guard, two lire and thirty-five cents. Since his service lasts three years, he'll be able to save up some money and not have to be so anxious about the future, which now looms before him like a closed door. "But you can't stand the guards!" Vita exclaimed, incredulous. "Don't listen to the call, desert." "No, I can't. And I don't want to. I'll be discharged in May 1915," Diamante explained. "At that point I'll have done my duty and I'll be free." "You're free now," Vita told him. "You'll never be as free as you are today, Diamà.

"You can't leave now. You've been in America for ten years—the difference between wishful thinking and possible success." Whoever gives up before ten years' time is usually satisfied with a measly reward—five hundred dollars? Eight hundred? The price of a lifeless body. A cadaver. A respectable take, not too scanty, but not much, either. But booty nevertheless, the fruit of a sort of robbery—stolen from his own self. Or he takes home a failure he'll never be able to explain. "You only begin to understand how things really work in America after ten years. What's necessary, what's dangerous." That's how it was for her. To go away now would be like changing jobs after a long and arduous apprenticeship. A mistake. It took Vita ten years to learn the great lesson of America: trust in a better tomorrow.

But that's exactly the point. Diamante knows his apprenticeship is over. There's nothing more that America can teach or hide from him. America has no more secrets, allure, or attractions for him. In a sense it isn't even America anymore: it is simply what it is. A place like any other. "I'll come back once I finish my military service. It'll all work out next time. Everything'll go smoothly." "No, you won't come back," Vita says. It pierces her heart to see that his blue eyes have grown paler. Turquoise when he was a boy, over the years they have faded to an insipid sky blue tending toward a gray fog. Diamante's eyes have only preserved a hint of blue—like the sky clouding over. Who knows if the process is irreversible. "I'm asking you to wait for me,"

Diamante murmurs. "I'm saying I'll only come back if you'll marry me, Vita," he adds solemnly. "I'll marry you now," she replies.

They hold hands as they disembark, faces turned toward that vacillating line of city built on water. By now even they are part of the millions and millions and millions of people who have given this city something of their soul, ideas, feelings, and dreams—over the centuries the immense sea of stone swallows them, transforms them mysteriously, like a coral reef, carving out of that cancellation the destiny of each. Diamante grips Vita's hand, fearful of losing her in that hysterical crowd milling about the docks—and only in that instant does he realize he hasn't asked her to go with him. He needs these three years to consolidate his memories, to find her again—to desire her. The dream of his childhood has been dented like a tin can. He needs to create her again because he can no longer believe her, and every time his eyes meet hers, he asks himself what else those eyes are seeing. He would like to unscrew her head and rummage around inside, and only when he can be sure that there isn't anything or anyone else—that Diamante is her whole world—will he be able to believe her.

Vita knows he is wrong. Proofs aren't necessary because having faith in something or someone doesn't mean wanting to touch the wound but wanting to heal it. In any case, whether he believes her or not, she loves him. So why wait? What good would it do? Life is now. Not in the future, which may never come, and not in the past, which has already dissolved—we are here now, just as we are, with the feelings we have on this day, April 18, 1912—because later we might not feel the same, we might change or be changed, or lose each other in opposite directions, like drops of rain on a windowpane. Feelings fray, promises are broken. This present will pass, and we won't ever be able to call it back. Why wait? Haven't we waited long enough? What does a band of gold matter, the blessing of the law, the approval of the Church? The reality of a house, an income, and the same key in their pockets? Those things won't marry her to Diamante. What will is the pleasure that lights up his face when he sees her, his desire to find her eyes amid millions of gazes—and so from today forward Vita will be his bride.

They get a room in a little hotel facing the port and say they are just married, on their honeymoon. The clerk doesn't believe them but doesn't really care. With his cantankerous competence he sizes them up merely to figure out whether they'll cause a ruckus—that young man leaning on the counter, his face streaked with blood, and the girl a few steps behind him, a pale smile in the shadows of the hotel lobby. He decides they are two quarrelsome youngsters who will start fighting again soon, and since the police never come down to the port, it's better to avoid certain customers. He asks them right away how many hours they plan on staying. "No, not hours," Vita corrects him courteously, flaunting a fluent American that amazes Diamante. "We'd like to stay until Tuesday. As we said, it's our honeymoon trip." (But our journey will be around our bed, and his arms the sweetest country I'll see.) Diamante will have eleven days on the ship to sleep, thirty-six months to rest. "Listen, boy, this hotel rents by the hour," the clerk growls at Diamante, ignoring Vita's explanation. "For whores and sailors. I won't ask if your girl's underage, and I don't give a damn if you've jumped ship and broken your contract. If you want to stay in your room all week, all month, or all year, that's your business. But here you pay in advance."

As Vita heads for the wooden stairs, Diamante triumphantly drops five dollars on the counter stained with watermarks. He watches her climb. Her pace is quick, causing her bosom to sway lightly but not to bounce—a harmonious gait, solid and invulnerable. On the first-floor landing, she turns and calls to him. "Are you coming? What are you waiting for?" Diamante jingles the keys.

He marries her before God, who hadn't recognized that night on the Coney Island beach now buried in the abyss of time. He takes her as she is, and lets himself be taken as he is, in a hotel room rented by the hour, facing the port while the winches creak and the chains screech and the shouts of the dockworkers echo on the misty wharves, and the ship whistles call out to each other on water wrapped in fog. In the warmth of a skimpy bed that causes him to sweat and her to glow, she embraces him and holds him tight and doesn't promise him anything other than her willing flesh, her soft bosom, her vindictive and compassionate nibbling on his scarred lip, and the scathing echo of her joy as they sway against the rusted headboard—a sort of dirge that sounds like a song.

Evening comes, and then night, and then the dawn, blue as a gas flame, begins to filter through the curtains. The red circle of the sun disperses the mist and daylight floods the room. Diamante relaxes against the pillow and wraps himself in the blanket while Vita, naked and glowing, crosses the light of the room and knots her hair at her nape, revealing her thin, brown neck. She raises the water pitcher and rinses his opaque semen from her skin and then adorns herself with a drop of perfume.

At eleven in the morning the traffic of fleeting, ephemeral, and economic loves starts again in the adjacent rooms—sailors' steps and bored, distracted girls' coughs are followed by moaning and sucking, then by voices, protests, venal discussions, accusations of theft and bitter negotiations. Embarrassed, Diamante puts his hands over her ears and whispers—wanting to drive away the assault of the world beyond these four walls, so precarious, so thin—to prevent her from listening, from growing distracted, from withdrawing again. But Vita laughs. What do we care if this hotel is a whorehouse and our neighbors don't have much imagination? We are not here, we're on the Union Pacific train flying toward California, in a first-class cabin on the steamship *Celtic*, in the lifeboat of the *Republic*—wherever we want, but not here.

On Monday night the doubts return, the bitterness and bile, the rancid taste of a shattered dream. He is tempted to test her again because if Vita abandoned her group of buyers and the company's picnic, if she made up a lie so as not to go back home this week, if she came to this hotel down by the port to spend his last night in America with him as she had his first, she could forget him tomorrow for Cousin Geremia or someone else and follow him to a hotel down by the port, here, in another city, anywhere, simply because she doesn't want him to feel alone, wants him to be happy—it's our job, that's what we're here for. Because Vita is incapable of torturing herself or grieving for too long, and now that he thinks about it, he has never seen her cry except for the day they disembarked so long ago, and at the time she had no idea who she was. "But if I were to decide to not come back to America," he asked loudly so as to be heard above the din of whistles and hammering, "if I decided to stay in Italy, would you cross the Atlantic to be with me?"

Vita throws off the blanket and jumps up. She pulls back the curtains and opens the window. She sticks her head out the guillotine-shaped window and looks at the ships lined up along the quays, their prows taller than their third-floor window—as if she were seeing them for the last time. The cornucopia of crates, goods, baggage, the immense winches and police boats, the coming and going of commissioners, the poles and fences for unloading human herds, the signs, the smiling ads, the beauty of a world in which everyone knows his place, the delicate workings of a mechanism that transcends the individual who doesn't have to do anything more than what is asked of him in order to be accepted. "I like America, I'm happy here. Here I'm appreciated for what I am, and they don't ask me why I'm not married at eighteen. If I went back to Italy I'd have to go back to all those things I escaped from." Diamante leans against the headboard and lights a cigarette; he wants her to think he's arrogant and proud—a tough guy. But he'll always be a loser. He squeezes the butt between his lips as Vita searches for the turquoise in his light blue eyes. No, she doesn't believe the fading is inevitable. But how to reverse the process? Where can she recover the blue? "But yes, Diamante," she responds, touching the scar on his lip. "I would cross the Atlantic for you."

Diamante smiles. He has found the missing Italian girl, and she is his. Vita lets her head fall against his chest—Diamante has grown strong, slim, and muscular. She rubs the spots on his shoulders hardened by all those pails of water, the red blotch on his back from injections—his new body is like a book, covered with signs, codes, stories. "I wish you were ill," she whispers. "Then they'd reject you and you could come back to me sooner. I miss you already." Diamante presses his rough cheek against hers. How much time has passed? How much do they have left? His beard is already growing back. He glances at his watch. Seven hours left. So few, almost nothing—yet time is elastic, they will be long hours, savored and held by the tail. But the minute hand glides too fast. Alarmed by the ticking of his watch, Diamante reaches out and turns it to the wall. For a moment, silence. Time flying, separating them. The word *time* could only be masculine, Vita thinks—*il tempo*, something that burns, runs, consumes.

Diamante gropes for his watch and tries to halt the gears, to silence that damned, hallucinating buzz. But he can't—he would have to swing it on its chain and shatter it against the wall. And so Vita does it again. She still can, after all this time. This day will never end. She stares at the metal hands that run circles of hours, stares at them until they start to move. But not in their usual direction. She pushes them back. Now they have ten hours, eleven, twelve—they turn back to the night spent together, to dawn, earlier still. Diamante smiles. Her eyes. Will—so that's all it takes. Vita has not agreed to be part of banal and guilty reality, of the essential ill of the world. Vita hasn't changed. She hasn't lost her gift, and no one will ever take it from her. She stares until the watch hands go limp on the white face, droop like melted wax. In the silence there is only Vita's quick breathing and the far-off whistle of a ship. The ticking stops. No more buzz. Even time has stopped.

The light fades. Enough with seeing. They have their hands, their bodies, their skin. Touch comes before sight, before taste and speech. It is the only language that knows no lies. Enough with promises. Enough with talk, stories, memories. Everything has already been said. In his suitcase Diamante packs words—they will be his only baggage, the only wealth he takes away with him from America. Perhaps they aren't worth anything, but it doesn't matter. All he has found, and all he has lost, he leaves to Vita. He leaves her the boy he was and the man he'll never be. Even his name. But the words—those he takes with him.

My Desert Places

The story of a family without a history is its legend. A legend that is enriched from generation to generation with details, names, episodes. That legend, passed on during the distracted indifference of childhood, is then rediscovered too late, when no one is left to respond to the simplest, most necessary and nagging, eternal questions: Who are you? Where do you come from? Of what destiny are you the final link? That is exactly what happened to me. Be it by chance or destiny, I was the last one. No one was born after me—and with me the chain breaks, the name will be lost. With me, all of us who came from nothing dissolve into nothing. Thus the legend of one's origins becomes all the more urgent, the desire to remember almost an imperative. Our legend was called Federico. My grandfather's grandfather, an officer who arrived in the South with the Piedmont army during the war of 1860. The officer is wounded in the battle of Volturno, the last clash between the Garibaldini and the Bourbon army as it flees toward Gaeta, where King Francesco II will surrender and witness the birth of Italy. Federico is paralyzed and is cared for in Minturno. And Minturno, which until then was a "not ignoble town of the Kingdom of Naples," will become, like the officer, loyal to the

Kingdom of Italy. The officer will never again leave that town. He will lose himself in the lush Mediterranean landscape parched by the sun. Officer Federico possesses a gift that is perhaps superfluous in the region of the Po, Stura, and Dora Rivers, but precious in a perennially thirsty village in the southern countryside. Federico is a dowser. He intuits the source, feels the magnetic tremor in the vibrations of his body. He wanders about with his divining rod and always stops in the right place. He knows where to dig the well, knows where to find water—and life.

I didn't come to Tufo di Minturno to look for Federico the dowser—that is another story—but for Diamante and Vita. I am searching for news, witnesses, proofs. I want to know if it is true that Antonio used Diamante's American money to buy back a piece of land that the devastating agricultural crisis of the 1880s had taken from him. If Diamante quickly sold it again because he finally realized, after having suffered so for that piece of land, which was the damnation and hope of the family, that what he wanted was another life, not that land. If it is true that Vita wanted to buy it again for Diamante thirty-eight years later, perhaps to live there herself, together with him. Above all, what happened to Vita—where and when did she disappear? After her visit to Italy, I had lost all trace of her. As for the dowser, the mythological founder of the family, I never think of him.

In my research, I come across stories I wasn't looking for. Like that of a man named Froncillo, who died at age one hundred in the year 2000. For more than forty years, he was an obscure civil servant in the town of Minturno. Today the registrar's office faces the courtyard of the old convent adjoining the Church of San Francesco—a courtyard that seems like the well of history, where mysterious fragments of ancient arcades can still be glimpsed in the abyss. It is housed in two bare rooms, where the furniture has aged along with the employees, and the floors with the dust. The records of births, marriages, and deaths are stored on shelves or in small metal filing cabinets. But all this, which I anxiously rummage through in search of Vita, would not even exist if it weren't for the man named Froncillo. In January 1944, when the German army positioned along the Gustav Line clashed so furiously with the Allies attempting to make their way up the peninsula,

Minturno was conquered, stormed, lost, destroyed. Houses, roads, and bridges were blown up. Without asking anyone's permission, Signor Froncillo loaded all the documents on a cart and took them to Latina. A few days later the Minturno town hall was razed to the ground. But its memory was saved. And today those files still contain the story of Vita's father, the first to request a passport for America; of Antonio, who never managed even to disembark; and of the unhappy Angela and their five children born to die of hunger before reaching age twelve. There is no sign, however, of Federico the dowser or of Vita.

And yet, following the fleeting tracks left a century ago by two fugitive children, I once again come across the traces of that legend and discover its falsity and artifice. I finally discover that the divining rod was a product of Diamante's imagination, told to his children and then to me. And in its invention lay his secret, his true identity—as well as my own.

The Mazzuccos did not come from Piedmont. They did not march down the peninsula with the Piedmont army, driven by ambition or the pretext of liberating the South from the Bourbon yoke. Many officers were urged by the desire to see Italy united and all one color on the map, while some, like the dowser, dreamed of liberating it from its millennial misery. The Mazzuccos were no different from the millions of landless peasants and farm workers who flooded southern Italy. When I ask Father Gennaro for permission to consult the San Leonardo parish's baptismal records, I know that I need to look for Vita's birth date in order to find the date of her death. The Church of San Leonardo is one of the few buildings in Tufo that survived the 1944 bombings. Today a rather unusual monument marks the spot—a clump of houses later reduced to rubble—where Vita grew up and Diamante brought his children in the summer, by that point feeling like a visitor to a foreign land, a tourist freed from memories and nostalgia. A recent monument with a bronze woman crowned in laurel (the Nation) remembers those who gave their lives for Italy. On each side are the names of the fallen. The First World War. The African War. The Spanish War. The Second World War. But the longest list is on the fourth side. There the names of the dead are not in uniform. They are not soldiers or officers, but civilians, simple inhabitants of the village killed by their torturers as well as by their liberators. In any case, due to a less ingenious miracle than the registrar Froncillo's rescue, a good part of the parochial records survived the flames and were exhumed intact from the ruins of the village. The history of the Mazzuccos is contained in those files.

The San Leonardo parish hall is a dark little room at the top of a rickety staircase. The gray walls devoid of any decoration, the crooked chairs, and the rusty metal desk exude an almost evangelical poverty or abandonment. An anonymous place, as is the village now—so different from picturesque, dilapidated Minturno, which looks like the villages on Procida and around Naples. Tufo was annihilated, canceled, and rebuilt in a disorderly and hurried fashion, out of anarchy and improvisation. In fact, as I wander about the tiny streets waiting for the clock to strike the hour of my appointment with the parish priest, an elderly woman with a toothless smile who perhaps knew Diamante and almost certainly shares my name stops me and apologizes: for a foreigner like me there is nothing to see here. Even the precious documents are contained in a cheap, beat-up metal cabinet. The books are as bulky as dictionaries or old encyclopedias, with hundreds of pages of parchment, inscribed in hand, in Latin. They are in poor condition; the covers are swollen and moldy, the ink faded, the pages mottled with humidity and stained with the dirty fingers of careless readers.

The first volume—the *Liber Baptesimarum*—contains thousands of names. Everyone baptized in Tufo between 1848 and 1908. In that era, lots of babies insisted on being born. Few lived, but all were baptized. As the responsibility passed from one parish priest to the next, the handwriting that records the baptismal names and the names of the midwives, godfathers, and godmothers varies from precise to sloppy to intricate. The story of a village and the five families that comprise it unfolds before my eyes: the Mazzucco, Tucciarone, Rasile, Ciufo, and Fusco families. Matrimonial tangles, kinships, familiar figures such as Dionisia the letter writer, Petronilla the midwife, Agnello, Nicola. Here and there, between one baptism and another, the glow of tradition and the repressive obsession of morality. Across two centuries, the *Liber* includes only two illegitimate births—two women forced to baptize their children *ex patre ignoto*. It is not hard to imagine the fate of these two women. Their last name is the same as mine. Everyone in these worn pages has my last name. It is like a blurred dream, a city teeming with homonyms, doubles, interchangeable identities, faceless souls. But that is not all there is to find among the pages of the *Liber*. The story of those poor names, attributed to babies now long since dead, reflects or bears witness to larger events, decisive changes. Illusions. One hundred fifty thousand people from Toronto to New York believe, remember, or think they come from here: the phone in the registrar's office rings constantly, and from the other side of the ocean American students ask the registrar to consult the archives in order to discover the name of the relative who left here a hundred years ago. In the *Liber Baptesimarum*, after so many babies named Maria, Lucia, Genoveffa, Judith, Agata, Adalgisa, after so many christened Virgilio, Desiderio, Filippo, Ignazio, and Giovanni, appears a baby girl whose parents—the mother, a Tucciarone, is the village midwife—call her Amerinda. It is 1895. It is the beginning of a collective dream, brief and intense. An ephemeral blaze. In 1897 Americo is born, followed by his homonym in 1898; Almerinda is born in 1900, Amerinda Mazzucco in 1904. And then nothing. Whoever left is already gone, and whoever returned will forget America. It's already finished.

Nell'anno Domini Mill.mo octing.mo nonag.mo primo die sexto novembris ego sub parochus huius ecclesiae S. Leonardi Tufi pagi Minturnarum baptisavi infantem die tertio dicti mensis natum cui impositum fuit nomen Benedictus. Obst. Petronilla Tucciarone.

Joseph Conte Larochas

Benedetto was Diamante's baptismal name. But there is no trace of Vita's baptism. I start to flip through the registry from the back, swimming upstream in that river of names. I find the baptismal record of Antonio, son of Benedetto, born in 1851, when Tufo was still called *pagus Trajecti*, and the record of Angela Larocca, born in 1854. I follow the origin in the older *Liber*, written by a priest with a finer, more studied handwriting. There I find the record of the baptism of Angela's mother, Maria Mazzucco, born in 1818, and of Benedetto, son of Antonio, born on April 28, 1814. Of Antonio born in 1792 and of the child who would become his wife, Rosa Ciufo, born in 1791. And so on up the tree, its trunk and maternal branches, moving back in time until the first pages of the oldest *Liber*, which covers 1696 to 1792. Back to the beginning. Seven generations, nine, ten. I find Ferdinando Mazzucco, born in 1796, Pietro and Maria in 1762, Agnello in 1738, Biagio in 1723, Nicola in 1713, Bartolomeo in 1704. I find an Apollonia born in 1699, a Giovanni Mazzucco born around 1690, and an Agnello of the same year, a Stefano Mazzucco born around 1680, a Giuseppe Mazzucco, father of Apollonia and therefore born between 1660 and 1670. Until the *Liber* ends. I have climbed back to the first page. Then silence.

Older records do not exist. Only after the purchase of the feud of Traetto by Don Antonio Carafa does the parish begin recording the "state of the souls." Before that, Tufo was merely a "hamlet" with ten hearths and fewer than fifty inhabitants. And as I try to get my bearings, tracing the web of ancestors, sons, daughters, fathers, and mothers, mapping the meridians and parallels, I suddenly realize that I have sunk into the swamp of time. We are in the century of the Baroque, of wonder and enchantment, of Marino and Pietro della Valle, of the eruption of Vesuvius and armies that overrun the peninsula, of the Spaniards and the plague—and still no trace of Federico the dowser. The Mazzuccos were here for centuries before his arrival—they appear out of nothing at the end of the 1500s, perhaps Arab pirates, perhaps Spanish, Swabian, or Norman soldiers, stragglers or mestizos. They never moved from here, but lived on this hill far from capitals and close to solitude, swamps, and malaria, the abandoned and impassable Appian Way, a hump of tufo, that hard yet malleable, solid yet friable, radioactive, mortal stone. A steep green hump, coveted only by pirates and Saracens. They lived here since the edge of time, bound to the earth like the serfs they probably were. None of them had ever left that strip of land that wasn't theirs—in the Bourbon land registries covering centuries and centuries, there is not one document of ownership. None of them are inscribed on the voting lists; they were not wealthy enough. Antonio never lost his land in the agrarian crisis because he never had any land. They didn't have anything other than their name, and not even that belonged to them. It had always belonged to someone else first. They inherited their name as their only wealth and passed it down as their only gift. They believed in some sort of immortality. And yet they didn't go far—they didn't go anywhere. Birth relentlessly follows birth, generations disappear, are swallowed up, canceled out, dispersed, but the names remain, return. A mill or a chain that sucks them and me into a thrilling yet painful vertigo. There is something atrocious and inexplicable in the fixity of their destiny.

Only now do I realize that Diamante, squeezing the hand of a little girl, was the first to open a passageway in that net of baptisms and death certificates, that grating as thick as prison bars. It was Diamante, a twelve-year-old boy whose only inheritance was the unlucky name of two dead brothers, one at three months, the other at four years— that boy with blue eyes, a third-grade education, and ten dollars sewn into his underwear was the first who managed to escape, appropriating the unrealized dream of his father. His gesture exalts and damages him, baptizes and breaks him, transforms and destroys him, but it liberates him and liberates us. Federico Mazzucco the dowser is born with his flight—to rearrange the order of the pages of a book already written. To confuse the tracks, ennoble the past, change and redeem it. To declare that he has come from far away, with History—and he is going with History, unconcerned about being late.

It's getting late and Father Gennaro must close the parish hall and say mass. I give him back the precious and anguishing books, thank him, and go out into the piazza flooded with sunlight. Behind the monument to the fallen, there is a railing along the cliff; the view from there is a vision and an enchantment. The medieval village of Minturno, preserved in the distance, rises on the crag, encircled by the vegetation of the Mediterranean—an oleograph of prickly pears, oleander, bougainvillea, wild roses, wisteria, palm, olive, and lemon trees. The ruins of the Roman settlement—a few columns, the skeleton of a theater, fragments of temples and altars—are lost down there in a stretch of pines. The Garigliano River is green as it flows toward its mouth among reeds and tiny boats anchored in the current. The bridge, or bridges, rather—one of iron, one of reinforced concrete, and one for the railroad—score the plain pockmarked with buildings and black asphalt shining in the sun. In the background loom sharp crests, dry and desolate like the mountains in Greece. But the coast is near—I feel I could almost touch the beach with my fingers. In the blue, an island—green, mountainous, and steep. Ischia, so deceptively near, but so elusive. And then the sea, for as far as the eye can see, until the horizon curves away.

"Did you find something?" Father Gennaro asked me as he adjusted his thick glasses—he is nearsighted—and flung open the door to the church. "Yes," I answered. And it is true. Precisely because I found neither Federico nor Vita. Her existence has not been entrapped in those merciless registries. She has escaped the registry of death, the aged pages, the ordered archives of time and memory. One spring day, with a clear blue sky just like today, she gave Diamante her hand and followed him out onto that far and elusive sea, which she must have seen every day from her window, and which she must have looked upon as a promise. They dove headfirst into the only gap in the net, and together these two fugitives invented another story.

Rescue

The bell rings for the third—and last—time. Then the hatches will be closed from the outside, the bolts will slide in place, and darkness will descend over the dormitory. Vita is hiding at the top of the stairs, buried up to her nose in sawdust. When the sea is rough, the crate is emptied and handfuls of sawdust are scattered on the floor, between the cots, even on the pillows, to absorb the vomit and diarrhea. Electrified by her courage, she can barely breathe. She had been told that she would cross a sea of tears, but this voyage has proved to be a thrilling adventure. A halo of light illuminates the sour face of the guard, and she can smell the foul odor of his breath. Vita doesn't move. She waits until the sailors complete their rounds on the bridge, ferreting out possible transgressors. The sailors are young, listless, and annoyed with the dreadful weather reports and the rain that whips across the decks. They are Italian. Shiny faces peer out from under their caps; their waxed cloaks are drenched. One of them waves his torch and picks out a recalcitrant shadow, which he grabs and encourages with his foot toward the hatch. The shadow tumbles down the stairs. The sailors laugh and then disappear, swallowed by the dark. The guard whistles. Everything seems in order.

The hatches bang on their hinges, the locks seal the hold. Now they are prisoners of the night. All of them except for her. She has defied them. She has escaped from that fetid hole. The deck is now a pale, deserted strip. Lamps like moons fray the fog. The dripping parapet forms a metal road—the thin barrier between all and nothing, between herself and the ocean. The ship belongs to her.

She rises from the crate, shakes the sawdust from her hair and skirt, and breathes deeply; the air smells of smoke, salt, and gasoline. This is her first voyage. She has never been on a ship before. She should be terrorized because it's late, she didn't respond to the third bell, and has disobeyed the Company. But that's not how she feels. She is happy. Two thousand people are sleeping prisoners, but she is free. She climbs on the parapet and balances there for a few seconds, immobile, suspended above the darkness that bellows a hundred yards below her. The ocean is not the sea. It is a road, a route, a way. The staircase climbs into the darkness but then halts abruptly. The way is blocked by gates and locks that can only be opened on one side. The other side. She looks around. Officers' white uniforms, rubber boots, muffled footsteps, then nothing. The wind twists an iron chain around a pole. The lock now dangles sadly in the void. Fused, melted. To climb onto the forbidden deck, all she would have to do is push open the gate.

So this is the other people's realm. It looks like a castle rising out of the plains of the deck. High, encircled by steep ramparts, impregnable. It is said that the two hundred passengers up above recline on deck chairs to read or survey the horizon and, occasionally, the two thousand passengers down below. One group is the theater for the other. It is said that they play cards in the saloon and dance in the evenings. You can hear the music down below, but the dances remain a mystery. But all of that is over now. It's been raining for three days and the sailors have taken away the umbrellas and deck chairs. The saloons are dark. When she presses her nose against the glass, all she can make out are the shadows of empty couches, the glimmer of the floor, rows of chairs, and the dark outline of the piano. The side deck is lined with portholes illuminated from within by electric lights. The curtains are closed, and when she tries to peek into a cabin, all she can see is the nubbly surface of the bedspread. Outside in the wind, all she has are the scars of light trapped on the glass.

Vita walks quickly along the deck, hugging herself in her shawl. She has a date. Never make a man wait. Men have no patience. The rain melts the fog. Water rises from the ocean and descends from the skies. It is April 9, but in this nothing surrounded by nothing it could be winter. She couldn't say how many days they've been at sea. She forgot to keep count; there was the day they embarked, and then it was too late—time has taken on a circular rhythm. The dawns repeat themselves, as do the nights. Get up, wash your face in the bathroom, stand in line to get a cup of coffee and a piece of bread, wait for heaven knows what, make time pass, look for the person in charge of our group—the one we have been assigned, or consigned, to—follow his instructions, get in line again for lunch, make the hours pass some-how, eat, sleep, get up. Always the same, as if there were nothing else, as if the only goal were to eat, sleep, get up, fill up, sleep, until it's over. But she would like it never to end. On the other side of the railing is a dark, turbid mass. All around her, everywhere she looks. Suspended who knows where in the middle of nothing. She isn't going anywhere and has come from nowhere. In other words, she has arrived.

She has never owned a watch, so she doesn't know if the time fixed for the meeting has already passed or if she is early, as usual. She has never dared defy the third bell before, has never escaped from the prison of the night. "We'll meet after the third bell," she had said. "Where?" was all Diamante had asked. As if it were all so easy, so pos-sible to take what he had no right to. As if it were easy to stay together. But it wasn't easy. Hers is the worst bunk in the whole dormitory, the top one; it almost touches the ceiling, not even thirty inches between her nose and the stink of new wood. Ten hours being deprived of space, air, and light, while her stomach turns in the stench of piss, vomit, sweat, sour milk, and women's juices. Vita had to hide not just from the guards but also from her travel companions, or else some jeal-ous or meddling or churchy woman would have betrayed her to the brutish sailors or the spying doctor, who would have snatched her and given her a few swift kicks to encourage her to resign herself to the dark awaiting her. Half an hour goes by. Or maybe a minute. But Diamante hasn't come. What will she do now, all night long out in the open, alone in the middle of the ocean, with no place to hide, with all the hatches bolted closed . . . ? All the portholes shimmering in the rain, her teeth chattering as she leans against the parapet sticky with salt, her soaked shawl covering her head. Without knowing what she is doing here, why she has come, where she is going. The lifeboats sway and creak on the iron cables, moving with the inclination of the ship. There'll be real dancing tonight; the weather report is predicting a storm. A black shadow hovers on the deck. Vita shudders, but then realizes it is her own.

The first bell is to separate the married couples. Not even they are allowed to sleep together here. The second bell is to separate the sweethearts. They linger, nestled one against the other, caressing hands, touching lips, or simply gazing into each other's eyes. They always feel there is never enough time to say all there is to say, everything that hasn't yet been said. The guard shines his lamp on them, goading them. He often thinks that if the world were a ship, the disease of loneliness would be eradicated, like the plague. The third bell is for the lovers. Lovers are deaf, blind, and obstinate. They don't hear the sound that forces them to part, don't see the light that approaches, and refuse to submit. Secrecy is already the norm for them; deception, flight, and lies are already a habit. The sailors and the guard search every corner and every recess of the decks. They lift up covers, rummage in every pile of rope, cord, or trash. They thrust their lamps under the stairwells, in pails, even in the stinking toilets and washrooms. The lovers have discovered secret passages, removed planks, hollowed out spaces amid pyramids of tin cans. They hide in the kitchens, in gigantic pots and cauldrons big enough to hold two bodies. Vita doesn't understand what desperate force drags lovers into the most lurid holes on the ship, what they are looking for, whom they are fleeing. All she knows is that whoever rushes to be closed into the fetid corridors of the ship's hold doesn't expect anything from the future.

The lovers are always discovered. Ferreted out, separated, forced to descend into the dormitory. The Company prohibits and severely punishes any sort of promiscuity. The Company guarantees respect and the continuity of values: control and social well-being. The Company guarantees the division of the sexes—and the classes. When they embarked, the twenty-four passengers from Minturno were rudely divided into two lines. Men on the left. Women and children on the right. All Diamante's friends on the left, all headed for the railroad in Ohio, enlisted by Agnello's boss. All destined for the pick and shovel. They all wear the same clothes, have the same first and last names. They're all related, or perhaps not. Who remembers anymore? But they all accept their place. They all obey. But Vita and Diamante held hands and did not want to be separated. "We have to travel together. My father said so," Vita yelled. But the ship's commissioners concluded that Diamante no longer had the right to stay with the women and children. They separated them. Diamante felt he had received a big promotion. Eleven years and five months old, and he was already put with the men. So that no one would molest him during the night, they had him sleep between Pasquale Tucciarone and a priest. Diamante told her that one night, the priest didn't come back after the third bell.

It's raining hard now. The waves crashing against the ship are getting higher and higher. The decks are all slippery with sea salt, and it's hard to keep your balance. The ship creaks, lists to one side. It's long and narrow, like a bean pod. With just one smokestack, so high it looks like a bell tower. The Italian ships are a disgrace. Twenty years ago they were already too old to carry passengers and were only good for hauling cargo. But human beings bring in more money than oxen, and there are more of them. So they repainted the ships and filled them with bunks even though the wood was rotting underneath. But this is an English ship, new and resplendent. Even its name is beautiful, like a promise: *Republic*. It came out of the Belfast shipyard just a few weeks ago. The English built it to carry Italians because it's the Italians, not the English, who want to go to America. The other passengers pray and commend their souls to the saints, but Vita isn't afraid of shipwreck. She trusts this English company, and believes that everything foreign is automatically better. Besides, the ocean reassures her. Her mother had always told her to look at the sea when she felt confused. The horizon helps you to think more clearly: a simple, clean horizontal line dividing sky and water, good and bad, future and past, life and death.

Perhaps she had dozed off because the frog call wakes her with a start. Since there aren't any frogs in the middle of the ocean, Diamante must be nearby. "Vita, where are you?" he whispers, remembering they must keep hidden. "Can't you see me? I'm right here, silly." "Where?" It's all dark now, all the lights are out. The deck is one huge puddle, the sky is black, the ocean black, the smoke billowing black from the chimney. I would like to see you, would like to find you, but I am ashamed to look for you. Ashamed to tell you that I only came up here because you asked me to. And then he sees her. She is here. The third bell has not managed to separate them. They have not been divided. Vita had been entrusted to him. Or he to her—who can say?

Vita is in the lifeboat, the first one, which sways over the void. She is sitting at the prow, scanning the ocean. She turns the silver knife in her hand, sharpening it on the rigger. Engrossed, she peers into the darkness. Who knows how far away America is. Diamante climbs up next to her, straightens his cap, and looks at her. His eyes are an intense turquoise color, gleaming like a diamond in the palm of a hand. Who knows where that horizontal line is tonight. What is right and what is wrong. They are sitting in the lifeboat, with no land and no sky— suspended in water, between rain and ocean.

"And now what?" Diamante asks, worried because the April shower has become a flood and the temperature is plummeting toward freezing. "If we stay close together, we won't feel the cold," Vita says. Diamante hesitates, then slides along the slippery seat. Their legs touch. Vita's barely reach the bottom of the boat. She is still a child. Her teeth chatter. She is soaked, dressed in a flowered cotton dress and a shawl full of holes. A night like tonight calls for an overcoat or a blanket or at least a sailor's raincoat. But what does it matter? There is nothing to see, nothing to hear, the ocean is a distant storm, the air is heavy with fog, not even a star or a constellation to tell them if they have changed skies, if they are headed in the right direction.

We have escaped, but we don't know what to do with this night. It came too soon. At age eleven, he'd been put with the men—but he isn't a man. Now Vita is almost wishing it were already day. Freedom has the smell of salt on Diamante's jacket. The other passengers didn't believe Vita was traveling with him. Such a dangerous voyage, so far from home. There are two thousand people on the ship. And Vita goes around telling all of them that Diamante is all she has left in the world. Orphans. She's a terrible liar, but everyone believes her. In the old country lying is not a crime. Lies are like dollars or gold coins: they dazzle and blind. And they console. The passengers hate and harm each other in every way they can, stealing space, money, and hopes, but they do everything they can to seem nice to her. They rush to bring her an apple, an orange, an extra serving of salted meat or onion soup. The cabin boys steal things from the kitchen for her and offer her the dishes the cooks prepare for the passengers in the castle. A waiter gave her some silverware from the restaurant up there, telling her to hide it because it's silver and she'll make some good money selling it. Diamante advised her not to accept it because she'd be accused of stealing if someone found it, but Vita doesn't give a hoot about his advice and keeps it hidden in her stockings. So even she goes around with a knife. Armed, like everyone else here. We arm ourselves, but we're not sure who the enemy is, and we end up hurting each other. The ship doctor spies for the Company, reports the lovers to the crew and the sick to the American officials so they can be sent back; but when Vita comes down with a fever, a bad cough, and the early stages of pneumonia, that bastard doctor who doesn't hesitate to report anyone with a cloudy cornea or a pustule on his genitals will not write her name on the list. Vita possesses something Diamante doesn't have and doesn't recognize, but cannot do without. Something phosphorescent, almost, like the invisible algae that make the ocean's surface shimmer. The darker the ocean, the lighter it becomes. It sparkles and doesn't sink.

Vita lifts up the waxed tarp covering the lifeboat. She slides along the bottom, wiggling among the planks. "Come on, Diamà, it won't rain on us in here. We'll be warm." They pull the cover over them and tie it down at bow and stern. It's a game, like building a tree house. Only this house is suspended by two iron cables alongside the steamer: a boat that has never sailed, a boat that will sail only if there is a shipwreck. No one will find them now. They can stay here until the rain stops, until daylight comes, until they dock on the other shore, on the other side of this immense water, until the voyage ends—for as long as they want. They can stay together and no one can prevent it.

They stretch out on the seats, resting their heads on the buoys. To keep warm they put on the life jackets and cover themselves with the extras. The jackets are stamped with the words WHITE STAR LINE. But where the white star is, Vita can't say. She has never been able to see it. The ship seems still, going nowhere. It rocks in the dark. Creaks, moans. It dives into the waves, into the abyss, the void. There is no other shore to reach, no space to cross. It is so dark in the belly of the boat she can't even see Diamante. So she takes his hand, to be sure he is there next to her. His body against hers, a boy with a cap. She squeezes his hand. "Why are you looking at me like that, Vita?" Diamante asks. "I told you I would come." "Why didn't you come sooner?" "I'm here now."

Acknowledgments

This book could not have been written without the words of my father, Roberto. "Remember to remember," he once said to me, but it has taken me more than thirty years to understand what. The omissions, deductions, inferences, betrayals, and distortions in this novel are uniquely mine, however. I am grateful to Amedeo Mazzucco, who, despite suffering from a painful form of blindness, nevertheless tried to resuscitate fragments of distant memories and reflect on episodes his father had told him more than seventy years earlier. I would have liked him to read this book, as he would have been its best judge. I took too long to write it. He died in October 2002 as I was correcting the first draft. I hope that he will understand and forgive me, wherever he is. Thanks to Marcella D'Ascenzo, who gave me the only photographs of her mother, and to my mother, Andreina Ciapparoni, who, despite being surrounded by mountains of paper and dust, never threw anything away and has kept letters and postcards from people she never met. Thanks to Brigida Mazzucco, Agnello Mazzucco, Antonio Mazzucco, Antonia Rasile, Genoveffa Mazzucco, Pasquale Mazzucco, and Elisabetta Mazzucco, whose stories and adventures flowed into these pages; to Professor Gemma Mazzucco, who provided me with Mario Rasile's scholarly volume *Cenni storici di Tufo* (Arti Grafiche Kolbe, 1987), and to Father Gennaro of the parish of San Leonardo in Tufo; to Mr. Catenaccio and Mrs. Colacicco at the Minturno Registrar's Office, who allowed me to follow a thread through the labyrinth of relations among the inhabitants of Tufo. Thanks to the curators of the Ellis Island Archives in New York, who allowed me to unmask some of the "lies" that had infiltrated the stories of my family. The archives of one's memory do not have an index; they have a few key words at best. *Vita* was the key word for me, and the rest is probably less important. Thanks to Professor Carlo Vallauri, prodigy of advice; Ms. De Simone of the State Central Archives; Ms. Puglisi, head of the Newspaper Office of the National Library in Rome; and Antonella Fischetti of the State Record Library in Rome, who guided me through the oldest recordings of Enrico Caruso. I am indebted to numerous authors of studies of New York in the early 1900s, immigration, and the building of the railroad in the United States: their research allowed me to frame the far-flung adventures of my characters. In particular I would like to mention Amy A. Bernardy, Betty Boyd Caroli, Luisa Cetti, Miriam Cohen, Nando Fasca, Emilio Franzina, Robert F. Harney, Don Hofsommer, Eric Homberger, Kenneth Jackson, John F. Kasson, Salvatore Legumina, Cecilia Lupi, Augusta Molinari, Louise Odenkranz, Nicoletta Serio, John F. Stover, S. Hartman Strom, Nadia Venturini, Elisabetta Vezzosi, and William Foote Whyte. I used the version of the Circassian fable of the Lady Tree and the god Lhepsch proposed by Asker Hedeghalhe Maikop in *The Narts: Circassian Epos*, vol. 1 (The Circassian Research and Science Institute, 1968). My thanks to the Bellonci Foundation, Annamaria Rimoaldi, the City of Rome, the Casa delle Letterature and its director Maria Ida Gaeta, Professor Francesco Erspamer of New York University, and the Library of Congress in Washington, D.C., whose invitations to New York in 1997 and 2000 helped me begin and continue this book: without them I would never have convinced myself to go to the United States and never would have rewoven the broken thread of my history. I cannot fail to remember here two friends I lost in 2002, Antonella Sangregorio and Sebastiana Papa: I miss their intellect, advice, and understanding. I thank Mafalda S—— for the prayers she had said for my grandfather's soul in the Sacred Heart Monastery of the Holy Trinity Fathers of Pikesville in Baltimore: I didn't arrive in time to tell her. Thanks to Rebecca Ann Wright, Dora Pentimalli-Melacrino and Miriam Levi, Francesca Cersosimo and Corrado Formigli, Benedetta Centovalli, Alexis Schwarzenbach and Silvia for their linguistic advice, hospitality, and friendship, and to

Luigi Guarnieri for everything he knows. Thanks to Malcolm Fergusson and Margaret Taylor of the Royal British Legion, who put me in contact with the associations of British combatants and veterans of the Second World War; to Graham Swain, national secretary of the Italy Star Association of New Milton; to Major Shaw, regimental secretary of the Royal Highland Fusiliers, who sent me the memoirs of Colonel J. C. Kemp, thanks to which I was able to reconstruct the episode of the retaking of Tufo in January 1944; to soldier Jack Hassard of Dungannon, Northern Ireland, of the 2nd Battalion of the Royal Inniskilling Fusiliers, 13th Brigade, who, despite his claim that "my memory is failing," wrote to me what he recalled of those days. He was in the first boat that crossed the Garigliano River on January 17, 1944. A few days later, he was sent with his patrol to the beach to look for fallen companions in order to identify them and certify their death. He recovered sixty bodies. To all those who helped me in memory of their friends who fell on the Gustav Line in 1944 and are buried today in the military cemetery in Minturno, I offer my gratitude.

October 2002